THE SHADOW OF THE SCHOLAR

Kathryn Malcolm

Tea With Coffee
— Media —

Acknowledgements

To my husband, Matt, for supporting me while writing this, bringing me tea and wine (which may have inspired some aspects of the story!), and without whom this wouldn't have been possible.

To my bookworm parents, for filling my childhood with fantastical stories and giving me a lifelong love of reading and writing.

Also a big thank you to Alys and Shaun for reading through the early drafts of this book, for tolerating my questions and giving honest opinions on the characters and story.

Thanks to my editors, Sarah and Grace, for putting up with my mistakes and offering amazing guidance.

And finally, to my brother, Alex, his girlfriend, Ellie, and all of my other friends who helped me pick the perfect title

CONTENTS

*H*ELL IS JUST A *frame of mind. But that place is no fable; it is wherever demons dwell. It has no limits, and wherever Hell is, they and their descendants must ever be. It is inescapable. For those who tasted the joys of heaven then fell, the separation from that place of everlasting bliss is pure torment. As for the children of such beings, there was a life to be carved from their new rugged and cruel landscape. Jewels glinted in the fiery sands, and in dark forests, there was joy in perpetual night. Soon, others joined them in that place—not those who were born demons, but who were rejected from the world. Demonised, yet powerful. They too moulded the hellish landscape and made it their own.*

And what of humanity? There have always been those who sought council with angels and bargains with devils. Blood was mixed; hybrids—Nephilim and monsters—were born, and the Watchers were punished. It was slow at first. In the early days, the monstrous spawn was struck down or banished to Hell. Rules were tightened, worlds more readily separated, but it did not stop the slow trickle of demonic blood into the veins of humanity. Half-demons, appearing very much human aside from their vivid green eyes and subtle demonic features, began to appear on the earthly plane. Feared at first, these children of demons gradually became commonplace, though marginalised.

I

Like Brute Beasts that Pursue Virtue and Knowledge

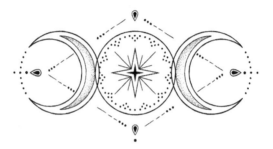

S AIYAH COULDN'T REMEMBER MUCH of her early life in Hell, though she knew she was born there. It was a blur of darkness, still images of violet hues, shadows, and mist. Amongst it all was her mother's face, pale as the moon with burning green eyes and a dark mass of hair. Her features, however, were blurred to Saiyah, twisting and changing as she tried to remember her. She had no photos to look back on, so she clung to that memory.

Saiyah flicked through a copy of Dante's *Inferno* to distract her. It wasn't perhaps the best choice for that day, but it was gripping enough to make her forget what was happening. Legs crossed, she tapped her foot rhythmically with the repetitive clatter of the train.

Daniel, her godfather, sat opposite her on the train to London, his hands laced together and resting on the table. He had tried to dress inconspicuously, but somehow still looked like a geography teacher on holiday. His pale eyes watched her with a frown.

It had all been planned. They would split up on arrival, as there were a great deal more gods in London, and questions might be asked if they were spotted together. She would go straight to the embassy while he waited in Hyde Park. It was near enough to collect her if things took a nasty turn, but far enough not to be suspicious. Though Daniel was certain nothing would happen, and assured her he was just being a concerned godfather.

Saiyah's eyes inadvertently flickered up and she caught his worried gaze. She tucked a loose strand of dark hair behind her ears, fallen from her messy low bun. Daniel reached out and laid a hand over her trembling one, making her lower the book.

"It's going to be fine," he assured her in his usual warm tone.

"What if they realise I'm a missing kid on their most-wanted list?" she asked cynically, laying her book down completely.

She took out a letter from her satchel, its seal already broken, and unfolded it. The thick, expensive paper was stamped with official government ink, and a second seal, which turned her pale.

"They won't." Daniel tapped her hand affectionately before leaning back, though there was a note of worry in his voice. "Whatever your parents did, I doubt they'll be looking for you in this world," he added in a whisper.

Saiyah shivered involuntarily. Daniel never left her with any illusions over what *The Host* was capable of: strict with their laws, little tolerance for demons, and ruthless.

Saiyah spoke in a low voice. "What if I hadn't revealed myself like this?" She gestured to the letter. "What if I'd not registered as a half-demon? I could live a quiet life, never do anything remotely demonic, and no one would be the wiser."

Daniel tried to frown, but the expression didn't match his normally cheerful demeanour. "You wouldn't be able to hide it forever. Besides, if you were discovered as unregistered, the consequences could be worse than anything that might happen if you were wearing an armband."

Saiyah lowered her eyes and made a face of disgust, winning a sympathetic glance from her silver-haired godfather.

It had been about a decade since people had figured out that demons, or more commonly, half-demons, walked among them. Once they began showing themselves more frequently and panic ensued, the gods had no choice but to step in. Normal mortals were aware of gods now, but they were more secretive in their appearances. Their military-like order, *The Host*, worked in the shadows to slay and banish demons from Hell back to whence they came, and keep half-demons in check. Though she'd always hidden her true nature, there was a time when Saiyah had feared for her life—when there had been calls for half-demons to be treated the same. It was only that mortal part of her soul that protected those like her, provided they didn't step out of line. Now half-demons were tightly monitored in a manner Saiyah thought bureaucratic and draconian.

When they neared Waterloo, Saiyah was nauseous. Sweating, her stomach was plummeting. Intense fluttering resounded in her torso. Vertigo threatened to set in. She closed her eyes and exhaled. When she stood, her legs were hollow and shaky. People flooded out of the train with Saiyah. Adrenaline kicked in as soon as she started walking. Never had she wanted to disappear into her own shadow more, and she actively fought not to. Were her eyes showing? Had she remembered to disguise them?

Though she was only on the tube for minutes, it felt like a lifetime. Her tongue was withered, and the summer air was languid and stuffy underground. The fluorescent lighting never seemed bright enough in the sunless tunnels. Sounds of rattling trains echoed along the dark tracks like a roaring beast.

Once she surfaced, the humidity of London was little comfort. Blinking, she shielded her eyes from the glare reflected off the pavement, worn down to smooth stone by decades of footfall. The heat prickled her pale skin pleasantly.

She sipped from her bottle of water. "I can do this," she whispered, clutching her stomach and justling her knees.

A sense of foreboding gripped her. She could be dragged away and banished to Hell, locked up in a demon's prison, or worse–Daniel could be discovered concealing her and be punished in some awful manner.

Her memories of Hell, and her mother, were extremely faint. It was all a blur back then. She remembered a dark world that flickered and glittered, indistinguishable between day and night. She recalled her mother's face as if it were a mirror of her own: pale, lilac skin, dark hair, and bright green eyes. She was sure they were happy, but any such memory was diminished by her final memory of her, though it was more of a feeling... the day they were violently parted.

Beautiful houses with pillars and black railings lined each side of the street. Saiyah paced parallel to the grand architecture of the natural history museum, peering at the plaques of the pretty white offices. Checking the map on her phone, the little arrow showed she was in the right place. Tapping her foot erratically, she stopped outside the French consulate, which was perfectly well-marked with a sign and a flag.

"Lost?" came a voice from behind.

She turned to see a young man swaggering towards her. He was a demon, or half-demon, judging by the orange armband on his arm, a black stripe running down the middle. She regarded him unsurely. It was the second-highest colour issued for danger, and the black stripe indicated he was more likely to cause harm to humans, though that was no reason to suspect he would. He had expertly groomed coiled hair, dark skin, and wore flamboyant clothing. Removing his designer sunglasses, he revealed sea-green eyes with serpentine pupils.

She raised her chin. "I'm looking for the god's embassy."

He grinned dazzlingly and pointed back the way he'd come. Beyond, a handful of hooded figures in the midnight blue uniforms of demon slayers were hidden in the shade.

"Thank you," she said, embarrassed.

"Anytime," he replied genially with a twitch of his eyebrow, then made his way past her.

She collected herself, gripping the strap of her satchel, and walked towards the soldiers. Cloaks draped across their shoulders and chests before falling down their backs. One glanced up at her. Unlike the others, he didn't wear any armour over the uniform, and there was a white sash at his waist. He looked as though he didn't really want to be standing on the streets of London.

Saiyah came to a stop a little way before him, opening her mouth without speaking. He regarded her sternly, his striking eyes luminous and impossibly blue, then issued an exasperated sigh. He gestured towards the steps of a building that she hadn't noticed before.

"I have an appointment," she blurted out.

"I know." Impatience and indifference glimmered on the demon slayer's stony face. "Come along. I've got better things to do than to shepherd young half-demons." He ascended the stairs gracefully and held the dark, lacquered door open.

"Thank you," she whispered.

His eyes followed her studiously as she stepped into the embassy of the gods. Towering stone pillars supporting a vaulted ceiling in the cavernous, temple-esque foyer. There were no windows, but pale light reflected on the marbled floor. It was bustling with gods and demon slayers, some rushing about with swords at their sides, others carrying stacks of folders and scrolls, scurrying between various archways leading down dim passages.

"Wait here." The demon slayer indicated a row of wooden benches by an empty desk.

Saiyah sat on the slippery pew, taking in the hushed business of the embassy. It reminded her of the interiors of cathedrals she'd visited with Daniel.

The slayer threw his hood back as he walked away, revealing a plain face of ambiguous Middle Eastern origin and radiant white hair. It wasn't white with age, just brilliant white, as if he'd been born that way.

After a moment, a female god appeared from the same passage, passing him with a dazzling smile. She walked with a boy, presumably on the cusp of his eighteenth birthday like Saiyah, who was awkwardly attaching a green armband with a white stripe to the sleeve of his hoodie. A white stripe would be best, obviously, but green or yellow could invite taunting. Orange or red might arouse suspicion and fear.

Her shoulders dropped as she reached for a book from her bag to hide behind, but the female god appeared at Saiyah's side. She wore the same shimmering blue cloak of a demon slayer, but her clothes were modern. Champagne-blonde hair cascaded in perfect waves down her back, half clipped back.

"Saiyah Greyson, is it?" she asked in a bubbly American accent, keeping her distance.

Saiyah nodded nervously.

"No need to look so nervous. I don't bite," she said with a dulcet laugh. "I'm Gabrielle Remiel. I'm the captain's secretary, and his ambassadorial assistant."

Saiyah followed her brisk steps and tried to keep up as she walked away, beckoning her to follow.

The area she led her to was reminiscent of a medieval castle fortress. Antique rugs ran the length of the floor, tapestries and paintings decorated the walls, and display cases held scrolls and relics. Saiyah was drawn to examine them. There was a series of scrolls in a display case, adorned with elegant calligraphy. She lingered without releasing.

"Come on, you can't possibly read that anyway," Gabrielle said humorously, standing with hands on her hips in the doorway.

Her office appeared unexceptional and dated in comparison to the area they'd just passed through. There was something remarkably wartime about it. Saiyah sat at one side of the desk while the goddess retrieved something from a metal filing cabinet.

"Please fill this out and let me know if you need any help," she said, passing her a form carelessly before falling gracefully into her chair.

It asked for basic information about herself, enquiring how often she utilised demonic or occult powers. The scratch of graphite against rough paper was the only noise as she wrote. There were two blank pages for details. Saiyah wrote three sentences and handed the forms back diligently.

Gabrielle examined the forms sceptically. Her extremely light eyes were unnerving. When she'd finished, she threw it down on the desk, folded her arms, and leaned back.

"Alright, Saiyah Greyson. What are you hiding?" she asked sweetly.

Saiyah froze and floundered for words. "I-I'm not hiding anything!" An acid taste filled her mouth.

Gabrielle rolled her eyes, but Saiyah's nervous expression made her soften. "Calm down, I'm joking. This seems a little basic to me." She gestured to the form.

"I just want to get registered and go home. That's all," Saiyah said honestly.

Gabrielle rapped her manicured nails on the desk thoughtfully before standing.

"Alright. But seriously, there's nothing else?" She pursed her lips and pointed at the few lines Saiyah wrote.

"That's all."

Gabrielle shrugged. "I'll see if Captain Hezekiah is ready. All set to show us your true form?"

"This is pretty much it," Saiyah told her, artlessly gesturing to her reflective eyes, the typical green colour of demons. Her skin took on a faint lilac hue when the light caught her.

"No tails, horns or hooves?" Gabrielle teased. Confused, Saiyah shook her head and Gabrielle laughed exquisitely. "I'm assuming you've never tried to push the limits of your demonic energy?"

"Um, no," Saiyah stammered.

"Well, be warned, you'll likely push those boundaries in your lifetime. Demons always have something to weaponize. Don't be shocked if your appearance changes or energy rises temporarily. Alright?"

Saiyah nodded dutifully and followed Gabrielle out of her office.

At an unassuming door at the end of a passageway, they stopped. Scorched into it in god script was, 'Captain I. Hezekiah.' Saiyah could hear the faint sound of music coming from within. It sounded distinctly like a hymn, played on a stringed instrument.

Gabrielle knocked and the music stopped abruptly.

"Enter," a distant voice snapped.

The room had an ancient feel. It was airy and minimally decorated. One stone wall was filled with shelves of neatly organised files, and there was a central desk with orderly piles of paper. Saiyah's attention was drawn to an open set of sizable wooden doors at the far end. Beyond was a lush, green lawn with a scattering of apple trees and the faint sound of birds. In the distance, a grand but plane dwelling with white, angular walls and terracotta roof tiles could be seen.

The blue-eyed god from earlier entered and closed the doors behind him, blocking out the daylight. The gloom comforted her.

Gabrielle introduced Saiyah and Captain Hezekiah acknowledged her, statuesque behind the desk as he read her files. Though unremarkable in appearance, his uniform combined with those eyes and a faint celestial glow was spellbinding. A sword was secured at his waist with an olive-branch motif engraved on the hilt.

"Your shadow ability–could you demonstrate it now, please?" Gabrielle asked.

Saiyah took a moment to breathe. Focusing on her shadow, she allowed her body to meld with it and faded into the floor, then moved to the wall and stretched into a perfect silhouette. Stepping out from the wall, she was a blur of darkness, flickering midnight and violet, a shade of herself.

Gabrielle scribbled something on her clipboard.

Captain Hezekiah signed something with meticulous precision in ink."That's enough, thank you."

Saiyah returned to herself and relaxed.

The captain stepped forward and carefully removed his sword from its sheath. Saiyah tensed and took a step back. He pointed it to the ground, non-threateningly, and walked around Saiyah in a circular motion with the tip hovering just off the ground. Sparks of divine energy emitted and fluttered to rest in a perfect circle, glowing magnificently and illuminating the room in a ghostly, electric, cyan.

Saiyah scratched her palms and squared her shoulders back. Daniel warned her this might be uncomfortable.

Saiyah shifted her weight from one foot to the other."What's going to happen?"

"The limits of your energies will be assessed," Captain Hezekiah said in an automatic voice. "Try to stay calm.

If you can." He added the last bit kindly, but it had the opposite effect.

Sheathing his sword, he closed his eyes and held his palms out. Tiny sparks crackled from the circle, becoming brighter. It was rather ritualistic, the sort of practice expected from occultists. Saiyah blinked in the brilliance of it, and a dull, humming noise reverberated around the room. A hint of a frown appeared on Hezekiah's forehead as the noise increased to a high-pitched screech, so cacophonous Saiyah couldn't hear anything. She put her hands over her ears, but the sound wasn't coming from the circle, it was coming from her.

It was unusually familiar at first as she became dizzy with her own power, but quickly her head pounded, and her body became startlingly weak. There was a subtle shift in her brain, and she dropped her disguise, slipping out of control completely. She clutched her head and groaned, muted in the white noise. Blood trickled from her nose. Her heart beat in her ears. Her vision blurred and swayed. She stumbled to her knees in an effort to keep herself together. Saiyah screamed, somehow silent despite the feeling that her throat was tearing apart.

Hezekiah opened his eyes and looked at Saiyah with a hint of surprise. Swiftly he brought his hands down and the glowing ring faded away, as did Saiyah's pain. Her senses rushed back abruptly, and the room was inexplicably, perfectly silent. Abashed, she stood easily, strangely intact, and wiped the blood from her face. There wasn't the least semblance of the torture she'd undergone, as if the previous five minutes had never happened.

S AIYAH WAITED ALONE IN the museum-like corridor. They should've told her which armband she'd receive straight away, but the captain delayed the decision. She tapped her foot nervously and distracted herself with the artefacts on display.

Pacing the corridor casually, she came to what on first appearance seemed to be an alcove, but was actually a short passage to a cavernous room of books. She smiled as the familiar scent of paper, vellum, and centuries-old dust reached her. She stuck her head around the corner and received a wrathful, glowing stare from a librarian god or deity. He was ageless like all gods, but she immediately got the impression he was thousands of years old. She quickly retreated away from the gloomy library, gritting her teeth in alarm, and distanced herself from the passage.

She came upon an ancient painting of earthy, basic colours adorned with gold leaf. It was the kind of art with colours made from crushed beetles and precious stones. It depicted a woman laying on a cloud in a golden sky. Above her was a winged creature, not unlike the traditional picture of an angel, with fiery wings and eyes.

"What do you think it depicts?" came a cool voice, making her start.

The captain stood a little way behind, arms folded and focused on the painting.

"A myth," she told him confidently. "I know the story, but I've never seen this painting before."

He nodded and took a few careful steps closer. One hand remained on the hilt of his sword. He didn't seem as old as the librarian god, or even as old as Daniel. Something in his face hinted at an impression of mature youth.

"You're an appreciator of art?" he asked with a hint of intrigue.

"I have an interest in religious mythologies," she replied amiably, but with a sharp edge.

Hezekiah made a sound of amused annoyance and stared up at the painting, unblinking.

"Were they real?" she asked, unable to hide her curiosity.

He gave an odd twitch of a smile. "I am not allowed to tell you."

Saiyah wanted to question further but was cautious not to aggravate him after what had just transpired.

He removed something from the inside pocket of his uniform and handed it to her without a second glance. Saiyah's heart sank upon seeing the flash of red.

"Know that I do not make this decision lightly," he told her with a note of warning as he handed her the armband.

Her hand came to her head, and when it was waved before her again, she eventually took it.

"I am trusting you with a white stripe," he said sincerely. "Familiarise yourself with your energies and above all, obey the law. I would prefer not to see you here again under negative circumstances."

His words were faint and distant to Saiyah, who was contemplating walking outside with a red armband. It wasn't unheard of for people to try and provoke demons, to catch them out and cause trouble, but she wasn't sure if anyone would try that with a red armband. She steadied herself against the cold stone wall.

"Speak to Remiel before you leave. She can put you in touch with people who may be able to help you." Hezekiah ushered her towards the foyer.

By the archway, he gave a quick but polite bow of the head and disappeared with a gentle rush of air.

Gabrielle returned and walked with her to the grand foyer, picking up on her distress better than the captain had. She produced a packet of tissues and offered one to Saiyah. She had half a mind to refuse, but her eyes threatened to overflow, so she decided it was wise to accept. She then handed Saiyah a leaflet that looked like it had been designed in the twenties. In faded green ink, 'The Albion Circle' was printed on the front. A scrap of paper fell from inside with a couple of phone numbers printed on them, clearly their idea of an update. "Here, take my card." She handed her something else more modern in design. "You can call me if ever you need anything or think you're getting into any trouble."

Saiyah took the crisp, white business card and thanked her, receiving an unexpectedly warm expression.

II

The World was a Secret I Desired to Divine

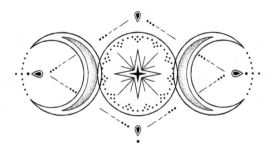

ON THE STREETS OF London, it was midday in the midst of a heatwave. The colours appeared washed out compared to the rich tones inside the embassy. Demons in London were almost normal, and Saiyah deliberated over whether to put on the new armband or not, though she didn't legally need to yet. Glancing back up at the steps of the embassy, flooded in cool, comforting shade, she was met with the steely gaze of the guards. She glared with determined resolve and slipped the red band over her arm. No need to worry about her eyes glowing that telling emerald green now.

Hyde Park was teeming with people. Two horse-mounted police officers eyed her suspiciously as she entered and she tried to look as harmless as possible, inwardly cursing that she should need to. Daniel waved, clearly relieved that she'd emerged unscathed. His eyes shimmered silver with joy, then he noticed the vibrant red, half covered by the sleeve of her blouse, and his expression turned to horror.

"Not what we were expecting." She raised her eyebrows slightly.

"No, indeed not." He smiled thinly, forcing himself to relax. "Let's go home. Back to that quiet, hidden life you wanted." He said it good-naturedly, putting an arm around her.

Saiyah didn't want to recall her experience at the embassy, but shared her glimpse into the library with Daniel. He gave her a wary glance, the kind he'd given her as a child for doing something she shouldn't. He could request access to the library himself, and promised to borrow some books for her. He continuously regarded her red band with thoughtful contemplation on the train home.

Saiyah took a long breath and closed her eyes, tilting her head back to rest on the seat. She smiled faintly.

"Nerves all okay?" Daniel inquired.

She opened her eyes and nodded. "They are *now*. You should have seen me earlier, I was a wreck. I'm shocked

I managed to hold it together. Thankfully there was an awful lot to distract me while I was waiting."

"Do you think anyone noticed?" he asked in a lowered voice. Then, seeing Saiyah's look of alarm, added, "Not to worry you or anything."

Saiyah scratched the palms of her hands, a nervous habit. "I don't think so. The secretary was a little suspicious, but I think she put it down to general nerves–it was awfully embarrassing." She rolled her eyes. "And the captain was more concerned with the high level of this." Saiyah gestured to her armband.

Daniel raised his brows and tilted his head forward. "As am I."

Saiyah pinched the cottony edge of it unsurely. Other passengers were glancing at her as if she might jump up and attack them at any minute. She slipped it off her arm and into her bag. No need to be wearing it just yet anyway.

WHEN THEY ALIGHTED IN their home of Winchester an hour later, the sun was setting alongside Saiyah's apprehensions from the day. She and Daniel began a gradual stroll downhill through the medieval town. It was too late for the old bookshop to be open, or any bookshop for that matter.

Amber rays reflected from the darkened stained glass of the cathedral windows, looming over them like a benevolent titan. Stepping into its shadow, they walked through the grounds. Gravel crunched beneath their feet as they passed quaint Tudor and Stewart-style buildings.

Daniel had long been associated with that cathedral, he was a lesser god and was largely forgotten by the likes of *The Host*. His official station was to protect the cathedral from destruction–a valid and noble position long ago, but somewhat ceremonial now. These days he occupied himself with teaching at a local school.

Though she'd only attended a regular school, Daniel delighted in teaching Saiyah everything that interested him, and to a high standard. Almost humorously, he was a professor of Religious Studies, and Saiyah was the only student taught things he couldn't in good conscience teach normal pupils. Daniel was careful she didn't know too much, to her great disappointment. For his secrecy, he'd been rewarded with a sceptic.

The path became tarmac and gave way to a narrow street with hunched Stewart houses. Their colourful little dwelling was ahead. Saiyah's shoulders relaxed. It was akin to arriving at an oasis after delayed flights, cramped conditions, a humid taxi ride where the driver couldn't understand the archaic Greek dialect Daniel spoke—like stepping into a cool, tidy villa with a basket of treats and a fragrant bottle of local wine on the table.

Inside, Saiyah shed her sandals by the door and made her way up the narrow stairs. Everything in her room was orderly apart from the strategic scattering of books on her desk. Artefacts from their travels were neatly arranged on the windowsill, and a somewhat tacky but treasured model of the pyramids sat pride of place in the centre. The largest wall was covered with shelves full of books of all kinds: poetry and classic literature, history, world religions and mythology, and multiple language-learning guides.

Saiyah flung herself onto the familiarity of her bed and stared at the ceiling as it turned from pink to grey. In this strange time where demons had long been known to live amongst humans, they were tolerated but still not quite accepted. They never would be. Who would trust a demon, even a half one? Daniel had done all he could to shelter her, safe in their quaint, small-town life. But knowing the secrets of other worlds, other paths to take, she yearned for more.

Opening her satchel, she pulled out the leaflet with the faded green ink which Gabrielle had given her. It appeared to be a kind of academic institution, comprised of half-demons in London, though their purpose was vague. It was as if they were holding information back, which considering the general distaste towards demons, was probably wise. The captain had said they might help her though, this *Albion Circle.*

Over the next few days, Saiyah didn't leave the house, taking her vow of solitude seriously. She wrapped herself in words and spoke only to Daniel. She had childhood friends from school, but was never close enough with any of them to make visits to their houses or lounge on the grass at the front of the cathedral. She'd often see them and wave, but preferred the company of Daniel and his perceptive mind. Familiar notes of 'Clair de Lune' sounded from her headphones as she hunted for *Dante's Inferno* to return to its rightful place.

A gentle rush of air made book pages rustle, and Daniel's tall, neat figure appeared at her door, seemingly from nowhere. He'd gained a faint radiance since arriving home, like an intangible aura. She'd only seen what he truly looked like once, but usually, he appeared in his late thirties, tall, with a kind of lanky elegance and thick-framed glasses.

Daniel lifted his hand and muttered a few words in his language to place a ward around the room. No one would hear or disturb them. Saiyah gave an exasperated laugh. Of course, *The Host* could be checking up on her at any time.

"It's not the end of the world," he said, trying to console her.

Saiyah sat up, frowning in concentration. "It is. I'm marked out, no one will want to have anything to do with me. Jobs and universities won't take me seriously, I probably won't even get served in restaurants. People are afraid of half-demons."

Daniel's shoulders dropped. "I met with a she-demon. Azeldya. In Hyde Park, while you were at the embassy." He spoke slowly, without meeting her gaze.

Saiyah paused and changed her tone from serious to teasing. "I thought your lot didn't approve of that sort of thing."

Daniel tilted his head to the side, exasperated, and gave her a begging look to be serious.

"Though, the ancient Greeks would certainly disagree–"

"Saiyah. Please." Daniel said firmly but evenly. "She is the one who brought you to me."

The silence rang about Saiyah's head. Azeldya. That name was familiar. "What did she want?"

"She's head of a demonic establishment in London. *The Host* is aware of the organisation, as is the government, it's all very above board." He fumbled his words as he explained.

"The Albion Circle, by any chance?" Saiyah raised her eyebrows.

Daniel tilted his head curiously. "Yes. How do you know?"

Saiyah flicked the leaflet between her fingers. "*The Host* recommended I get in touch with them." She shrugged. "So, this mysterious woman who knows me wants me to join, too?"

"Yes. I wouldn't recommend the idea if *The Host* weren't so heavily involved..." He paused, then added grimly, "What worries me is it's monitored by my lot. But at the same time, it may be dangerous for you to carry on living with me."

Saiyah bowed her head. "The thought had crossed my mind." The red armband in her bag burnt at the corner of her vision. A wave of anxiety creeped upwards from her stomach, and she gripped the edge of her desk until her knuckles were white. She pressed a hand over her forehead. Inadvertently, her cheeks flushed their unique lilac shade and her eyes brightened to that unearthly colour. "You taught me that gods have strange rules and fears. Perhaps living amongst half-demons like myself would help me after all. It's not as if I'll be able to go to any university now." Her eyes welled at the thought.

Daniel sat at her side and awkwardly took her hand in his. He'd taken a great risk keeping her alive, not knowing what her demon mother and human father had done to anger both gods and demons alike.

"I can't tell you what to do, Saiyah. In this matter, I just don't have the answers. If you want to meet Azeldya, then do so, but be careful."

Saiyah turned her head, examining Daniel with a curious frown. "Careful of what?"

Daniel regarded her with a chilling stare which re-minded her of the gods she'd seen at the embassy.

"Of what might be buried in the past." He gave her hand a little squeeze and looked towards the window. "Sometimes it's better—safer, to know less."

Saiyah was too shocked to speak.She'd never seen him so serious. Suddenly, his soberness melted away and he patted her hand familiarly. "I'll make us some tea. It's been a long day!" Then, as if embarrassed, he left as quickly as he'd arrived.

The idea that this Azeldya was the reason she came to be with Daniel, that she was connected with what happened to her parents, caused a pang of fear and intrigue.

ON THE MORNING OF her birthday, Daniel made her favourite breakfast of pancakes with lemon and sugar.The strong, oily smell of it woke her. Barefoot on the red-brick tiles of the little kitchen floor, she slipped in silently as she often did, light as a shadow with her feet partly translucent. Daniel had his back to her, and she watched him fuss over pans while humming an unrecognisable tune. He straightened up suddenly and fell silent, then turned.

"Happy Birthday, Saiyah! How long have you been standing there?" His smile was characteristically warm, but there was a note of sadness, or pity, in his voice.

"Thanks." She dipped her head as she grinned. "Not long, I promise."

She made her way to the gas hob, where a kettle was boiling, and began to pour them some tea. She set the colourful woollen tea-cosy over the pot when she was done and helped Daniel serve. As they ate, she caught glimpses of sympathetic expressions from him. What could he possibly say, after all? A reminder of what turning eighteen meant for a half-demon was hard to digest.

Gods didn't need to eat, really, but Daniel was completely assimilated with mortal habits.

Saiyah looked up from her plate with poised apprehension. "I am going to do it. Meet Azeldya, that is." She lowered her voice to a mild interest. "Before the end of summer."

There was a flicker of a frown on his face, but he hid it well.

"Well, you'd have to go to London again if you still want to meet her." He stabbed at a rogue piece of pancake. "Do you think you can manage?"

Saiyah took a breath and swallowed, then after a moment's thought began to slowly nod. "Honestly, I felt more comfortable with the armband in London. I saw other demons there, too. People stare less." She shrugged, as if that explained everything.

Daniel nodded forlornly. A crease appeared between his brows. "I'll arrange something. We'll have to get a hotel."

Saiyah sat up straight and carefully laid her cutlery down. "Actually, I was thinking I could go on my own," she said hopefully.

Daniel's eyes became dark, and he laced his hands together on the table. He was quiet for a long while before speaking, and Saiyah tentatively began to clear their plates.

"Very well. I suppose you are legally an adult now. I'll have to get used to that," he told her with a wan smile.

After sitting in their quaint living room resembling a vintage, rural style with pink flower motifs against cream walls, Daniel produced a small parcel wrapped in brown paper. The colourful label indicated it was a birthday present. Despite his dislike of material things, he gifted her a gold necklace with a half-moon pendant, knowing she liked things with a lunar theme. Once she'd finished eating, he announced he had another present for her.

"It's not really a present," he admitted, returning to the kitchen, "but it might be useful."

In his hands, he held something hefty, wrapped in a thick woven cloth with faded gold thread embroidery. It was the sort of thing that should have been buried hundreds of years ago, draped over the body of a saint. Unwrapping the bundle, Saiyah uncovered an ornate book, not unlike those on display in the cathedral. Saiyah carefully lifted the leather-bound cover to reveal fine parchment inside. The spine cracked with age. It was handwritten in heavenly swirls and lines, the language of the gods, with beautiful pictures, and grand graphic letters decorated in gold leaf and lapis lazuli. It was as familiar to her as Italian or French, and she recognised one of the words on the title page: *Demonology*.

"I borrowed it from the embassy library. *The Host* uses it as a point of reference in training. I expect a lot of it may not be relevant, but I'm sure there will be something useful to you."

Saiyah's fingers brushed lightly over the timeworn script. She examined the first few pages carefully; they were dry as papyrus, but soft to the touch. The book went about categorising the demons of 'Sheol', an old word used by gods for Hell. Saiyah noticed some pages were newer and less brittle, as if they'd been inserted more recently.

"Thank you," she breathed, mesmerised to be holding something so ancient and ethereal. The idea of analysing it and the unknown knowledge it contained thrilled her.

S AIYAH'S PERIPHERAL VISION SWAM with glowing ritual circles, swords and shadows, gods and demons. She drifted on a night breeze into a world of darkness, both comforting and stifling. It felt like home. Like the vague memories she had of her infancy, yet she was restricted, as if her hands were bound and her vision poisoned. Shades of liquid night enveloped her in this world of inky blackness. There were voices in the distance, she knew this, yet she couldn't hear them. They would have green eyes.

But there was an intangible force which wanted her to see something else. A force which felt protective and terrifying. Blue eyes. The glowing blue eyes of a god glimmered like tiny diamonds in the distance. She tried to focus on the face, and the force urged her to do so. She tried to move closer, but she could not feel her limbs in this world. The eyes faded into obscurity, and she was alone in the darkness–apart from the distant green eyes, which watched her, invisible in the shadows.

Saiyah woke drenched in sweat. Her eyes glowed brilliant green in the darkness of her room, and she had the distinct feeling that she'd either been conscious the whole time, or had been trying to gain consciousness.

She shook herself. It had been a long day. It was just a dream.

III

Adders and Serpents, Let me Breathe a While

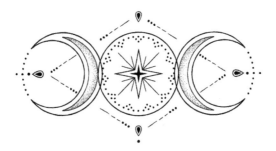

S AIYAH'S JOURNEY INTO LONDON was more relaxed than the last. Although warm, a cool breeze flowed through the city. She searched the pit of her stomach for feelings of anxiety but couldn't locate any despite her nerves over meeting the demon, Azeldya. Azeldya, who'd apparently known her mother and rescued her from whatever hell, quite literally, she'd come from.

With time on her hands before their meeting, Saiyah wandered into the British Museum where they'd arranged to meet. She was quickly confronted by the Egyptian and Assyrian exhibits, with large statues and reliefs expertly preserved from historical exploits. As she perused the nearby displays, passers-by and loitering students veered away from her in a way she'd not encountered before.

She wasn't a naturally social creature by nature, nor was she shy, but she regarded the museum-goers who shot fleeting glares at her with annoyance. She exhaled, smoothing her expression. It wasn't their fault. Most demons in this world were half-demons, but the public were still wary. Destruction, chaos, and violence frequently followed them. Many turned to a life of crime after being shunned by society. It was a vicious cycle, and not one that was new to humankind. Intolerance begets intolerance. Though thankfully, this country was more lenient than others. She shuddered at the memory of televised scenes featuring the devastated mothers of half-demons in more religiously superstitious countries.

There had to be a way to make them understand.

Irritated, she drifted into a room containing a beautiful monument to Nereids, set between decorative pillars housed under a classically Greek temple structure. Though the statues had crumbled, leaving the deities headless and limbless, the fluidity of their forms captivated her.

After a moment, she glanced to her side with a start. Another demon with a red and black armband stood beside her. Her skin looked as though it'd been bathed in midnight, and her irises were startlingly black against the whites of her eyes. Ghostly hair fell in soft ringlets, brushing her shoulders in a vintage movie star fashion. She dressed like one too, and there were two sleek, black horns poking through her hairline and curving backwards.

The demon stared at Saiyah with an unreadable expression. "I am Azeldya." She dipped her head gracefully, like a greeting of old. "I hope you can forgive me for intruding on your musings." Azeldya's voice was so captivating that Saiyah hung on every word. She spoke with a subtle accent that over-pronounced the letter 'o' in the most beautiful manner.

Saiyah raised her eyebrows and cleared her throat. "Not at all."

Azeldya's powerful gaze wavered as she blinked and smiled ever so lightly. She gestured to a bench, and they sat.

"I am glad you want to know more about my organisation, The Albion Circle. We are a group of demons and half-demons dedicated to curating and preserving the knowledge of worlds. Our acolytes study demonology and the occult. Amongst other things."

Saiyah's face lit up. It was the darker side of the coin of what she already knew, things Daniel wouldn't be able to teach her.

"So, is it like a job, or school?" Saiyah adjusted her posture to something more comfortable.

The edge of Azeldya's mouth twitched towards a smile. "It is both, and neither. If you wish to pursue an academic qualification, many institutions offer our members that right, although you would remain within our walls. However, that is not our true purpose. We are the keepers of knowledge too dangerous for mortals or the demons of Hell. We strive for unity amongst half-demons, and aim to represent the skills we can offer this world, rather than the danger."

Saiyah tilted her head. "Aren't you a demon of Hell?"

Azeldya seemed to consider the question, a soft smile blossoming on her lips. "There are those who are considered trusted by the gods."

Saiyah's eyes widened, but she managed to suppress her shock. "They're...not in charge of the Albion Circle, are they?"

"No. But in the last decade, we have forged a tenuous alliance with the Embassy here. We hold all knowledge and artefacts considered too unholy to taint their homeland on their behalf, and the most experienced of us act akin to peacekeepers in the demonic community." Azeldya leaned forward a little. "Saiyah, this is more than just cataloguing and occasional missions to Hell. If you were to join us, you'd have access to thousands of years of occult history, as well as the most reliable guidance on how to use your demonic energies."

Saiyah chewed her lip. It was tempting.

Azeldya tilted her head, curls bouncing enchantingly, and indicated that Saiyah should walk with her. They talked at length, and she was soon hooked on Azeldya's temperate, careful voice. The Albion Circle wasn't a vocation; it was a lifestyle. It was about collecting knowledge and artefacts, mainly from Hell, but also occult artefacts of this world. They even had some things from the gods. Saiyah understood she couldn't reveal everything to an outsider, but got the distinct notion there was much unspoken.

Saiyah scratched her palms and took a breath before speaking again, "If you don't mind me asking, how did you know my mother? How did she die? And why did you bring me to a god to be raised?"

Azeldya looked Saiyah up and down pensively. "Her name was Asramenia Melanthios, and I was her friend and mentor." She said it softly, almost wistfully. "She was a good person, brave and fierce, as I'm sure you will be, too. "

Saiyah relaxed her rigid posture.

Azeldya cast slow and careful glances around them. "I do not know how she died, only that she was killed. I am sorry to be the one to tell you this. I brought you to Daniel Cassiel because she instructed me to."

Saiyah blinked, taking a moment to process it all. Her head swam. A hand landed on her shoulder, steadying her.

"Daniel always said the gods might persecute me for my parentage. Though he could never say why." Saiyah stated dubiously.

Azeldya's dark eyes shined with alertness. "I will not tell anyone you are Asramenia's daughter, even within the Circle. Rest assured."

"I don't understand. Why would it matter whose daughter I am?"

"Her position as a High Priestess in Hell, and her actions, posed a threat to the gods." Azeldya's hand was rigid on her shoulder now. Carefully, she pulled something from an inside coat pocket. Standing close, she pressed something into Saiyah's palm, and her fingers met smooth, dark stone, lightly polished and rectangular. Faded carvings of stylized feathers covered the surface with flecks of emerald and lapis where it'd once been painted. Her palm tingled with energy. "Your mother gave this to me. I do not know what it contains, but if you are able to open it, I would be as interested as you to know the contents," she said in a low, serious voice.

Saiyah held the strange stone container; it was larger than her palm, but slim. There was no opening, but under closer inspection there were some minute markings in an alphabet she didn't recognise.

"It is an important choice, my dear. Don't make the decision lightly," Azeldya said as they came towards the bright, reflective whiteness of the atrium, busy with tourists. "Should you join the Circle, we will talk further of your mother." Azeldya stepped back, her sombre tone lifting. "Now, I must bid you farewell, I have business at the embassy. A half-demon named Bezbiel will meet you outside when the museum closes and take you to our little world."

Saiyah opened her mouth to speak, but with the fluidity of air, Azeldya was gone.

ALONE, SAIYAH PERUSED THE rest of the Greek section, and a familiar sense of worry accompanied her. Vague memories of her mother, which may or may not have formed from her dreams, walked alongside her. She barely remembered what had happened all those years ago, or why the fear echoed.

Saiyah sat atop the wide stone steps of the museum and looked out over the lawn as the sky dimmed, waiting for whoever was supposed to meet her. Tourists stopped to photograph the striking building and groups loitered before closing time.

At the entrance, a man with an orange armband appeared to be making his way directly toward her. Saiyah put the container away, took a reassuring breath, and stood. They met at the foot of the steps, and Saiyah's eyes flashed with recognition. He was the same demon she'd briefly met the morning of her registration. He lifted his designer sunglasses smoothly, revealing the snake-like eyes beneath, and held out his hand.

"Pleasure to see you again. I'm Bezbiel," he said in a low-pitched, honeyed voice.

She hesitated, causing him to grin amiably. As she touched his warm, dry hand, she tried to keep her composure, maintaining a steady but friendly expression.

"Nice to meet you."

Out on the street, passers-by glanced at them suspiciously. The sun was obscured behind the buildings, and some of the lampposts flickered to life.

"Are you one of the leaders of the Albion Circle?" Saiyah asked politely. He appeared to be in his mid-twenties, but demons, even half-demons could be long-lived. He could be any age.

He laughed out loud. "Not at all. Think of me as a perpetual scholar, if you like, but I do tutor the younger initiates." He added the last bit with a wink. He spoke in a profoundly melodious way, completely unlike Azeldya.

Bezbiel sidestepped through wrought-iron gates into an unassuming garden, but stopped before Saiyah could descend the small flight of steps leading into a public garden. Although, there was nothing about it that warranted footfall. The rectangular lawn was worn, and a dirt path ran the perimeter.

Bezbiel smirked and pulled from his pocket a long green object. It was palm-length, marbled with black, sharpened to a point at one end and a serpent head at the base.

"Malachite," he said by way of explanation. "Those of us not blessed with show-stopping abilities like Azeldya have to rely on our craft."

"The occult?" Saiyah asked sceptically.

"If you want to get technical." He shrugged playfully. "We don't normally let outsiders in. They wouldn't even be able to see anything, but Azeldya is making a special exception for you." He gave her a curious look.

With a flurry of complicated hand movements, Bezbiel drew shapes in the air directly below the entrance. There was nothing physical to see, but when he'd finished there was a delicate ripple in the gateway. Saiyah blinked as the view of the street melded with what looked like another garden. Not the shabby lawn behind them, but something darker, richer, and altogether more otherworldly.

"Welcome to the *Old Roads*. Just focus on where you are, or you'll make a rift in the mortal world for any passing occultist to stumble into."

She didn't dare blink again.

The gates they'd entered had stood between stone pillars with decorative spheres atop, but as they stepped through, there was an arch with a gaslight hanging from the centre. Gradually focusing, Saiyah moved forward.

It took great mental effort for her to stay present in this new world, using the part of her brain associated with disguising herself. It was like slipping into her shadow form, but less stable.More concentration and control was needed.

"Shall we?" Bezbiel said theatrically with a tilt of his head.

She walked on a stony path through a walled garden beneath the dusky sky. Statues lined the path. Their visage and poses were more dynamic than other ancient sculptures. Some had horns, others had skeletal wings, or feathered wings, or hooved feet.

"Are these demons?" she asked with a hint of surprise.

Bezbiel took off his glasses. "Some of them. I'll tell you about them when you join."

"What if I decide not to join the Albion Circle?"

He chuckled. "Oh, you will. Trust me."

He ushered her out to a street with centuries-old gas-lit lampposts. Gothic buildings ascended on the horizon, and tall, red-bricked terraces clustered close to the road, blackened with age but well-maintained. Their placement was addled and disordered, making it hard to tell where one house started and finished.

"The initiates live along here," Bezbiel told her offhandedly.

Around another corner, the first of many tall stone buildings with arched windows could be seen. Their lower floors were converted into whimsical shops and cafes, and dim figures and shapes moved inside. Where the British museum would have stood a remarkably similar building. Bezbiel led her toward its entrance.

Inside, footsteps echoed dully, and gas lighting flickered from various wall lamps. The small but empty entranceway gave way to a grand staircase ahead. At the top was a landing area with more unusual statues and additional staircases spiralling up the cuboid tower. Above, the walls changed from lavish wooden panels to timeworn stone, and there was a single, unstable-looking stairway of rough wood. Bezbiel steered her along the main corridor, polished yet laden with age and memory.

"Welcome to the Barbatos Library."

The first room was a communal reading room with a fireplace and a gilded mirror above. Sumptuous armchairs were inhabited by demons and half-demons, noses buried in literature. They glanced up but didn't pay them much attention. There were tables at the far end with books carelessly left open with a promise of return, and a chess table under the window. The polished wood floor made hollow creaking sounds, and bookcases with glass doors lined the room. Bezbiel walked through it all to a tidy set of double doors, arched in a point much like their entranceway. He flung them open theatrically, and Saiyah gasped as she caught sight of the rooms ahead.

As far as the eye could fathom was room after room of books, separated into sections by grand archways. The smell of old parchment was strong in the air. Towering mahogany bookcases stood in rows, each encased with exquisitely carved wooden pillars. Above, galleries of shelves with ladders propped up against them sheltered alcoves with gothic windows. Overhead, a beautiful arched ceiling of carved chestnut sheltered the library.

"The Albion Circle's primary role is to preserve knowledge on demonology, uncanonized or blasphemous religious artefacts or texts, and as much recorded history of Sheol, Tartarus–or Hell as most call it–as possible. It's far safer here than in Hell. We protect it as scholars, regardless of their nature. Curators, if you will." He spoke with a certain sense of reverence as he surveyed the bookscape.

They twisted and turned through shelves and Saiyah struggled to keep up. The press of knowledge surrounding her in endless books and cabinets of curiosity enveloped her. Bezbiel pointed out everything so quickly; she wanted to linger and examine the books for herself. Each section consisted of different topics, and were arranged by language. Latin, Greek, Italian, Arabic, Coptic, New and Old Demonic, and many more. All of them stirred a temptation within her to leaf through the soft, leatherbound pages and uncover their secrets. Here and there were display cases containing illuminated manuscripts, pottery fragments, amulets, and ancient instruments which faintly hummed with demonic energy. When they reached the end, a vast domed window of warped glass framed the eventide.

Bezbiel appeared pleased with the look of awe and intellectual hunger on Saiyah's face. She caught him smirking, and realised her eyes and mouth were both wide open.

A tome caught her eye: *The Modern Hellscape,* written in Italian and looking less-than-contemporary. She took a step towards it, but before she could touch it, Bezbiel calmly laid his hand across the spine and stepped between her and the book.

He shook his head mirthfully. "Sorry. No forbidden knowledge for outsiders."

"Do you keep information on specific demons?" Saiyah asked.

"Historical figures, yes. If they did anything *particularly* noteworthy, or terrible, their name might pop up in *The Host's* records here, too." He smirked at the confused look on her face. "Oh yes, we have their materials too, both freely given copies and those salvaged from a warzone. Not that it's any use to us untranslated, but as the saying goes, knowledge is power."

Bezbiel showed her study rooms, lecture theatres, and a glimpse at the alchemy labs. Some buzzed with a residual demonic energy, which she was beginning to recognise. Others were still, but full of the green eyes of half-demons of varying ages and ageless ancient demons. Some had horns, others tails, hooves, luminous eyes, or inhuman skin colour or texture. Many were dressed in plain, modern clothes, while others seemed to have stepped out of time. Despite the apparently extensive tour, many doors were left unopened.

Back out on the street, Bezbiel directed her into one of the establishments. It resembled a giant greenhouse with tropical plants crawling up pillars and hanging from the glass roof. Tiny electric lights glistened like gold dust, and a bar was nestled amongst the florae. White cast-iron tables housed a handful of people who sat drinking.

Bezbiel ordered them both coffee and sipped his drink, studying her quietly. "So, what do you think?" he asked in a way that hinted he already knew the answer.

"It's magnificent. I don't know what I was expecting, but it really is beautiful," she admitted.

"I told you. You want to join the *coven*."

There was a question on Saiyah's face.

"That's just what we initiates call it," he explained. "Rolls off the tongue better than 'The Albion Circle.' Don't tell Azeldya I told you that," he added with a wink.

Bezbiel retained a faint smile on his face, almost mocking. His oddly mesmerising serpentine eyes never left her face, studying her like a curious artefact.

Saiyah mustered up the courage to speak again. "How much involvement do the gods have with *the coven*? I mean, do they come here and dictate what you do?"

His expression went blank for a moment before giving a short burst of laughter, disturbing the other customers. Saiyah caught a glimpse of his forked tongue and cringed involuntarily.

"It's more complicated than that. Following the gods' laws allows us to operate undisturbed–relatively. They *think* that if demons are here, they're less likely to cause trouble elsewhere," he said musingly, a mischievous grin on his face. "It's an arrangement which benefits both parties. They leave us be, and when they ask us to store dangerous literature or objects, we ask no questions. It's not like they want to put it in their homeland."

Saiyah stroked the rim of her cup pensively.

"Then of course there's the odd research or diplomatic trip to Hell. That's the fun part if you don't mind a little turbulence." Bezbiel was smirking at her, arms folded across his chest. "You'll be back. I guarantee it." He flashed her a wicked grin and finished the rest of his coffee.

As they exited the building, another demon walked up the steps towards them. There was a spark of recognition when he saw them. He was tall, broad-shouldered, with dark curly hair and a widow's peak atop his round face. His skin had a purplish tint to it that was far stronger than Saiyah's, and his wide, yellow eyes resembled an owl.

"Bezbiel," he said enthusiastically, patting his shoulder and shaking his hand. His wide eyes fell on Saiyah. "Who is this? A new initiate?"

"Yes. Saiyah Greyson," Bezbiel said without giving her a chance to protest. "This is Zulphas. Like Azeldya, he runs our little world. The library is his domain."

Zulphas took Saiyah off guard when he bowed with a sweeping motion of his arms, causing his dark robes to spread like wings. "A pleasure," he said in a quiet but eloquent voice. "I look forward to knowing you." With a polite smile, he made his excuses and carried on up the steps.

"He may be odd, but he's one of the good ones," Bezbiel remarked.

On their way back to the gardens, Bezbiel chatted amiably. He was exceedingly knowledgeable about the architecture and history of the place, and he spoke eloquently. Although, he rather liked the sound of his own voice.

As they passed the statues again, she noticed there were strange markings similar to the gods' language at their base.

"What does that say?" Saiyah asked, pointing to one of them.

Bezbiel raised an eyebrow. "It says it's *Mephistopheles*. I take it you were never taught Old Demonic?"

"No. Only the gods' script," she responded.

Bezbiel stopped in his tracks and grabbed her arm. Saiyah pulled away, startled, but he held her lightly.

"What?" he hissed in a hushed tone, looking around them worriedly. Bezbiel stepped closer, then, noting her distress, he let go. "I would advise you to keep that to yourself," he whispered.

Saiyah gulped and nodded. He regarded her curiously, and they walked on again.

"Well, well. It appears you are more than meets the eye. How the hell do you know that language?" he asked in a low voice. "I'll not tell a soul."

Saiyah shook her head. "I can't say."

He tilted his chin upwards. "Very wise. You'll do well here."

IV

Knowledge is Stronger Than Memory

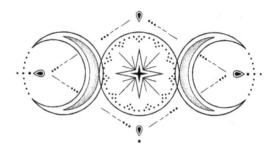

S AIYAH MUSED ENDLESSLY OVER her decision, not least because of the beautiful libraries of the Albion Circle. Laying on her bed in her dressing gown and damp hair, she held aloft the dark stone container, turning it over before her eyes.

Swinging her legs onto the floor, she drifted towards Daniel's room and knocked at the half-open door. Gods didn't need to sleep, so he took the smaller of the two rooms. There was no bed, just soft rugs and low furnishings. Daniel sat in a meditative position before a little altar of candles and incense. She waited until he opened his eyes and put away whatever she wasn't supposed to see. He was still respectful of laws pertaining to what divine information gods were allowed to share with mortals and demons.

"Come in," he told her brightly when he'd finished.

Saiyah sat with him on the circular rug, slanting her knees. The room was lit by a few candles left on the altar and a dusky blue light from below the horizon. Pungent incense smoke was illuminated by the flames.

Daniel noticed the stone container and became alert. She handed it to him casually.

"Where did you get this?" he asked, raising his brows.

"Azeldya gave it to me. She said it was my mother's, but I can't find a way to open it."

Daniel was holding the object close to his face, his irises luminous silver in the gloom.

"That is because it's an *Osiris Coffin Box*," he said. "I've never seen one before. Artefacts of Hell aren't my area. They're notoriously difficult to open."

She leant forward. "Do you know what it says on the side there? The Old Demonic?" Daniel shook his head with a slight laugh. "I've not tried to read Old Demonic since I was in school, but..." He stood spritely and beckoned Saiyah to follow. "We might be able to figure it out."

At the back of the room was a chest with dark iron hinges from the 17th Century. Daniel found a key from somewhere on his person and opened it, rifling through layers of old books and scrolls. They weren't nearly as well looked-after as the tome from the embassy, crumpled and amber from age. He retrieved a scroll, wound onto two fragile pieces of wood, and closed the chest.

"This has some basic translations, mainly for alchemical or ritualistic markings. It may not help, but I can always get a more thorough guide from the embassy. Perhaps we could learn the language together and figure it out?" He offered, though he seemed unsure of his own words.

Saiyah shot him a dubious look. Without either of them knowing where to start, it would be quicker to simply ask Azeldya what it said. Nevertheless, they examined the box thoroughly and copied the text down as best they could, so they didn't need to keep squinting at it to compare it to the scroll.

"I'm surprised Azeldya hasn't been able to open it. Maybe she can't read it either?" Saiyah mused.

"I doubt that's the case," Daniel said, glancing from the scroll to the box. "For a demon as ancient as she is, I wouldn't be surprised if it's her mother tongue."

Saiyah's finger flew to one of the rune-like symbols on the scroll and allowed a faint expression of triumph. "'To open' or 'to unlock,'" she read aloud. "Well, that confirms this at least gives instructions on how to get in, if nothing else."

Daniel nodded. "Let's hope all those others are on here."

Saiyah lowered her eyes and drummed her fingers on the stone. "Did you know my mother's name was Asramenia?"

Daniel became very still. He slowly lowered the scroll to his lap. "No, I didn't," he admitted, a waver in his voice, and shifted the parchment to the next section. "And had I known, I probably would've asked more questions of Azeldya."

"Why?" Saiyah countered quickly, the pitch of her voice rising. "Would you not have taken me in?"

"Of course, I would have." He took off his thick-rimmed glasses and sighed. "It's just...that name carried a certain reputation at one time."

Saiyah closed her eyes and exhaled before speaking. "I thought you didn't know my mother," she said with a sharp edge to her voice.

"I don't. Only by reputation, as I said." He let the scroll drop and he shook his head in annoyance, his hands twitching as if he didn't know whether to don his glasses again or not. "She was the leader of some kind of religious-political coup, or revolt. That's what I heard, anyway. I don't know."

Saiyah picked up the box, a crease appearing on her forehead. Daniel didn't know enough about demons or Hell to give her the information she needed, but joining the coven would break Daniel's heart.

"Aha!" He pointed to another symbol. "This one means 'Inside.'"

She rolled her eyes. "Great. Now we know *for sure* it's a container."

"Don't be like that, Saiyah. I'm trying to help."

Saiyah gestured to the scroll. "Yes, well, we've nearly exhausted that thing, there must only be a few symbols left. I could learn Old Demonic easily if I join the Albion Circle–"

"There's no need–"

She groaned. "Come on, Daniel. I genuinely believe this place could be of help to me. In more ways than one!"

"I understand. I can't stop you. But this is a group of demons–"

"Intelligent, academic demons!"

"Even so. It could be dangerous."

"You said yourself it was all above board. Why are you changing your mind?"

"You'd be between worlds. If you need me, I'll not be able to find you," He responded, a whispered note of warning in his voice.

Saiyah did her best to keep her head as she spoke. "I might not need you, Daniel." Her eyes glowed with emotion, and she tilted her head imploringly. "And even if we get this thing open, it might not answer all my questions. Someone there might know what happened to my parents, they might hold that knowledge."

Daniel's face softened and he touched her lightly on the shoulder. "Just promise me you'll be vigilant if you do choose to do this? It's unlikely you'll uncover the truth, but if you do, just..."

"I'll be alright," she assured him. "I can handle it, whatever it is."

Daniel nodded slightly and bit his lip.

Saiyah glanced between him and the Osiris Coffin Box, noting his pained expression wasn't leaving. "What's wrong? Is there something else you know about my mother?" she added suspiciously.

Daniel leaned back against the wall, statuesque, then rubbed his temples lightly. "She led a good mortal man I once knew down a dark path. She embroiled him in the occult, in demonic affairs, puppeteering him before ultimately taking his soul."

Saiyah was taken aback. She shuffled across the carpet to Daniel. "This man, did you raise him as you did with me?"

Daniel nodded faintly.

Saiyah tapped her fingers on a nearby box. "It's not—that wasn't my father, was it?" she asked tentatively.

Daniel took a breath as if to steady himself, then smiled thinly. "No. This was many hundreds of years ago. But I wouldn't be shocked if the circumstances were similar for your poor father. Whoever he was."

Saiyah nodded, relieved but a little disappointed. "But despite all that, you're fine with Azeldya?"

Daniel wrinkled his nose and tilted his head from side to side. "Azeldya is an ancient demon, making her more closely related to gods. She works within the parameters of the law and, judging by her appearance and that she's not been slain or banished, has chosen to keep her demonic energies in check." He became surer of himself as he spoke. "Ask her about your mother, by all means. And whatever you find of hers in that box, know that whatever her nature, it doesn't affect who you are."

Her stomach fluttered and she grinned. She'd received his seal of approval as far as she was concerned, albeit reluctantly.

"Go on, get some sleep," Daniel prodded, his cheery demeanour reappearing. "I'll work on this and see if I can open it another way."

Saiyah regarded him warily, unfoundedly worried he'd get rid of it somehow while she was sleeping. Daniel promised he'd be careful with it, and she believed him. She went downstairs, feigning retrieving a fresh glass of water, but she slipped her phone from her pocket as she did. She'd already put Azeldya's number in. With a thrill of nervousness that wasn't entirely unpleasant, she made the call, leaving a voicemail to confirm her acceptance. She pressed the phone to her chest and retreated to her room, daydreaming of the notion of studying Old Demonic, and presumably, something called New Demonic?

Then there was Bezbiel. Saiyah blushed. He was arrogant, that was for certain, but he had a certain charm, and was clearly intelligent. She was looking forward to seeing him again, too.

I T WAS BEZBIEL WHO showed Saiyah to her spacious lodgings. The blackened, red-brick terraced house was narrow but went a long way back. A small flight of steps led up to a scarlet door, and from there she could see the floor below with its subterranean frosted windows. There was a sizable entrance hallway with a staircase hugging the perimeter and winding up two more floors. Balconies connected the staircases, which led to the rooms. To one side of the house was an alcove stretching to the top of the roof where a glass ceiling let in natural light. The living area had ample space, a fireplace at each end, and plenty of empty shelves. Each bedroom had a study area attached, like a personal library. Saiyah took the room on the first floor, the only bedroom on that floor. There were two more above. At the very top of the house was a roof space with a neglected greenhouse of deadened and overgrown plants, though it smelt pleasantly of soil and herbs.

Saiyah's two new housemates materialised a few weeks later, though she discovered one had been quietly living in the room above hers for days. She recognised him as the boy with the green armband at the embassy with Gabrielle. He was a small, raven-haired half-demon with a pale complexion named Jack. Oversized hoodies emphasised his skinny legs, making him appear like a robin in winter with its puffed-up feathers. He was pleasant enough, but painfully shy.

When Hex moved in, there was no mistaking her presence. Her box-dye green hair had two slender, needle-like horns poking through, and sometimes she braided her hair around them. She wore handmade gothic-Victorian clothing, and the whir of a sewing machine could often be heard from her bedroom.

The three were the only new initiates, appropriate to the exclusivity of the coven. Together they focused on the basics of demonology and basic knowledge of world religions, a lot of which Saiyah knew already. Trawling through ancient tomes and their translations was a great comfort to Saiyah amongst the lingering uncertainty of becoming part of the coven, and the fact that she could research whatever she wanted for now was ideal.

Saiyah took lessons with Bezbiel every other evening in the magnificent library. The older acolytes kept strange hours, as many of them had forgone the need to sleep. They would sit in one of the gallery alcoves, coral light pouring through an arched window and casting warped patterns over the table. Bezbiel always set a gramophone in the corner, on which a scratchy recording of Für Elise played discreetly.

He was always charming in an old-fashioned way when they first sat down, but as a tutor, it was like a switch flipped and he became serious and dedicated. He was attentive, and knew exactly what she struggled with before she articulated it. Without a doubt he had a natural flair for teaching, that's all he was thinking about, nothing else.

Saiyah wasn't the first person he'd taught to read demonic languages from scratch. It was prevalent amongst half-demons who'd been raised by one mortal parent to forego learning. The language had 28 letters, and the grammar was similar to that of the gods' language, which made it easier for her to pick up and interpret phrases. Most of the books were lengthy, so Bezbiel brought her shorter scrolls. It wasn't an easy task, but soon words started to recur and become familiar. Not all books were unreadable, and many came with translations for newer initiates.

Their lessons would finish before midnight, and she would always turn down Bezbiel's offer to have dinner or go to a party afterward.

There was no sign of Azeldya yet. Bezbiel said she'd been in Hell on business and didn't know when she'd return. She wasn't quite proficient enough in New Demonic, let alone Old Demonic, to know what the inscription on her mother's box said. The symbols were starting to look familiar, but she didn't know if that was simply from staring at them for so long. Azeldya had very simply left her a note on the first day which mysteriously appeared on her nightstand. It instructed her to learn the Demonic languages with Bezbiel, and a suggestion to research Asramenia and the revolutionists of Khabrasos.

What Saiyah knew of the revolutionists was a general history. Their movement started hundreds of years ago but now only echoes remained. Ancient demon lords were overthrown by their descendants or other demons in a bid for power, as was the way of succession in Hell. Many of these newer rulers were revolutionists. Unlike their predecessors, they had their own ideas on what souls should be damned. Hell was overcrowded with souls who did not please the gods. Too many were barred from the gates of paradise. Endless lines of souls guilty of forbidden love, good pagans and those unbaptised awaited for eternal torture. All were minor sins to demons. It was hard to say if the revolutionists really were rare kind-hearted demons who knew not all souls deserved such a fate, or if they instead saw an opportunity to create an afterlife of painless servitude to benefit the demonic elite.

Hell was divided. Not all kingdoms agreed to this idea and they began to fight amongst themselves for dominions. *The Host,* disapproving of these battles, and perhaps fearful the revolutionists overarching goals, grew encampments in Hell. When it became clear the revolutionists were victorious and often the more reasonable side to deal with, *The Host* acknowledged the new order of Hell for the sake of peace. Their rules did not change though, the same souls were damned, but what happened to them was up to the demon lords, revolutionist or not.

That was all over now though. The revolutionist momentum died not long after power was taken. New rulers became comfortable. The heavenly encampments remained, angels of death, lingering to keep watch for any rebellious stirrings which might cause a war between worlds.

"EXCELLENT PRONUNCIATION THAT TIME. You're really getting a grasp on the additional vowels," Bezbiel said earnestly, pacing lazily beside the gramophone. He was never short on praise when deserved, and always patient when it came to correcting.

"You just need to speak a little louder," he added.

Saiyah raised an eyebrow. "Is it part of the pronunciation?"

Bezbiel flashed a grin which usually signified the lesson was over. "No. But it'll help with incantations later on."

Saiyah raised an eyebrow. Why would she want to get involved with practising magic, or the occult? Reading about it was appealing, but actually doing it?

Bezbiel's expression became serious. Standing opposite her at the table he leaned forward, placing his palms down flat. "Being a part of the coven isn't just about researching and looking after all these lovely forbidden books. It's about unlocking the mysteries of the universe and achieving great things. We can bring about all kinds of change." He gestured toward the window wistfully before returning to his usual self with a shrug. "Consider it."

Saiyah eyed him curiously and began to collect her things. "Like the revolutionists in Hell?" she said offhandedly.

Bezbiel raised his eyebrows, but smiled all the same. "Exactly. If that's what you want to do," he said softly.

"Are you a revolutionist?" she asked.

Bezbiel chuckled, scooping up his textbooks. "In a manner of speaking, I suppose. There are very few around these days who are active. Azeldya is one of the last."

"What does she do?" Saiyah pressed him.

"Investigatory work, diplomacy, that kind of thing. Nothing too dangerous. That's left for the likes of Titania and Xaldan." He rubbed the back of his neck, his smile falling. "Everyone wants peace in Hell. It's all gone on too long now."

Saiyah scratched her palms. "I'm not sure about the mysteries of the universe or joining any revolutions, but do you think there's any chance of convincing humans that we're not here to corrupt and destroy? At least not all of us."

He gave her a warm and whimsical smile, collecting the rest of his things. "You should meet my friend, Medea. You'll like her. She's one of Zulphas'."

Everyone got a mentor here eventually, she'd learned. Jack and Hex were too new for either of the four leaders to have decided on them yet. Some initiates took years to prove themselves worthy of mentorship to the leaders, though no one knew precisely what they wanted. Bezbiel had explained that Zulphas took on those who were more studious, book-smart, and often with an interest in Herblore or Medicine. Asmalius was another older demon with a pointed beard and red and gold robes, looking like he stepped right out of a Renaissance painting. He took on initiates with talents of the mind, and psychic abilities. Belthazeer was a beast of a man with hulking shoulders who mentored those with physical abilities. Azeldya's preference was harder to define. By rights, Bezbiel should be with Zulphas or Asmalius, but he was one of Azeldya's. She rarely took on mentees and when she did, they were often talented in multiple categories.

Saiyah stood and they returned their books and scrolls to their rightful places in the library.

"Do you know anything about a revolutionist called Asramenia Melanthios?" she asked cautiously.

Bezbiel gave her an appraising look. "If you mean Asramenia the revolutionist leader? She's hardly a mystery. There are a few documents I can recommend," he offered, "but in exchange, come out for dinner and a few drinks." He held up his hands innocently. "It won't just be me, there'll be other members. You should meet them."

Saiyah smirked and rolled her eyes. "Alright. But I refuse to stay out all night," she added assertively.

Bezbiel laid a hand over his heart. "I promise, it will be a highly civilised affair. Meet me by the gateway tomorrow at 8 o'clock, be prepared to spend a considerable amount of money, and wear something... formal."

With a final charming grin he collected his jacket and bag and strode away, leaving her to the solitude of books.

It didn't take her long to better understand her mother, who was from the land in Hell named Khabrasos, where Azeldya mentioned the revolutionists were from. It was described as a dark land in the South, on the edge of chaos, whatever that meant. She'd led the revolutionists in a coup against the previous Katomet–a word used for 'Duke' or ruler of hellish dominions—and taken his lands. Devouring her way through minor accounts in New Demonic and their rough translations by candlelight, Saiyah gathered that the main differences between the revolutionists and the lords in power were their opinion on human souls—what to do with, and the treatment of them. Saiyah became engrossed in the account of a particular few years during which she would have been born, where her mother liberated an area in Khabrasos, sheltering the lost and tortured souls of those whose crimes she deemed too severely punished.

She wondered if the Occultist Daniel raised centuries ago was among them now.

All of her findings were general, giving accounts of various activities all over Hell, with all sorts of demonic names and places she'd never heard of. Without context, it was difficult to understand. She'd have to start from the beginning, hundreds of years ago, and learn the changing layouts of the maps of Hell. Azeldya wanted her to understand her mother. Though it didn't seem very useful to the coven, Saiyah did as instructed, and relished every scrap of information.

V

When Night Darkens The Streets

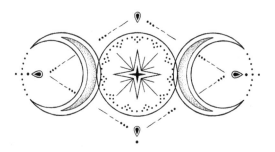

S AIYAH SHIVERED AND PULLED her coat tighter around herself, wishing she'd worn something thicker or brought a scarf. Out in the open countryside, exposed to the rushing wind, it was far colder than central London. The clouded sky threatened to rain at any moment. Still, the neolithic stones and the rolling green hills in the background were a wondrous sight. Saiyah had read about the Avebury stones, and remembered visiting Stonehenge on a warmer day as a child. Now, she was seeing them through new eyes, as if they really could be part of old English magic and folklore.

Hex and Jack stood beside her, huddled together for warmth in equally inadequate clothing, along with a few slightly older initiates. Bezbiel was enjoying playing the part of a country gentleman in his practical, khaki green attire and walking boots. A tweed waistcoat peeked from beneath his waterproofs, and he adjusted his flat cap.

"The oldest of these stones are nearly five thousand years old," he called out over the wind. "Some things have taken place here, though I couldn't say what, which have caused them to resonate energy–energy which you should be able to sense. This could be demonic energy, divine, or occult. Today, just focus on deciphering demonic from celestial frequencies."

The three initiates strolled across the damp grass and muddy pathways, each one finding their own stone. There were many tourists also touching the great stones, and even a man in a wildly decorated fedora who'd been embracing one motionlessly since they'd arrived.

Saiyah stood before one of the smaller ones, though it was still larger than her and thankfully supplied some respite from the continuous wind. She regarded it dubiously before placing a hand on its rough surface, and for a moment was ready to give up completely.

"Any luck?" Bezbiel said, appearing from behind the stone.

He carried a thermos of hot tea and handed it to her.

"I don't feel anything," Saiyah admitted.

He chuckled faintly. "I don't think you're trying hard enough."

Putting his thermos away, he motioned for her to touch the stone again, and she did as she was told. He put his hand close to hers, so the sides of their fingers were touching. Saiyah flushed lilac.

"Close your eyes, it'll help you concentrate," he told her softly.

Self-consciously, she did so, and felt his breath on her cheek as he continued to whisper.

"It's very faint within this one, but it is there. You know what it feels like when you use your own power. Just reach out for it."

Saiyah felt a tingle against the palm of her hand. She was sure there was a mild vibration in the air, like a dragonfly's wing. She opened her eyes and was shocked to see a small but tangible shadow flickering and swirling of its own accord around her fingers.

"I've got something," she gasped, astonished it worked.

"You certainly do," he said, his voice distant and distracted.

She looked back at Bezbiel. His face was very close to hers, but his snake eyes were fixed firmly on her hand, watching, open-mouthed. He let his hand slide away, brushing against hers lightly as he did so. He stood back and shot her an expression of satisfaction.

"I see why you've got a red one." He gestured to her armband. "Be careful with all that energy."

S AIYAH TENTATIVELY EXPLORED DEMONIC powers by learning about different types of demons and what their usual powers were. Precognition, insanity, transfiguration, transmutation of objects, and classes of *cunning* were all prevalent traits. Saiyah hadn't thought of her power as transfiguration, but it did fall into that category.

Jack could transform into a raven. His other abilities were hard to pinpoint. He was sensitive to occult spells and rituals as they happened, and said that he could 'see between worlds.' Though this didn't mean seeing the dead, it was something more complicated and ambiguous altogether.

Occult practices were banned for new initiates, as they were more likely to accidentally manifest things into reality. Hex, as an already practising witch, was disappointed.

The three of them would spend time together in the reading room some afternoons, not because they particularly liked each other, but because there was no one else to be with. Saiyah carefully flicked through the beautiful book Daniel loaned her, keeping the cover and spine hidden in case anyone noticed she was reading the god's script. Every page was adorned with lavish illustrations and detailed information on types of demons, more often focusing on how to kill them. Each depiction referred to a demon as being 'of the line of...' and yet she couldn't place the subsequent words. It wasn't until a few pages in when trying to make out the words phonetically that she realised many sounded like ancient pagan gods and deities. It was strange Daniel had never mentioned this to her, knowing her interest in the subject.

The clock on the mantle chimed and she carefully closed the book, wrapping it in its cloth again.

"Not staying, Saiyah?" Hex said with a wry grin, her legs flung over the arm of the sofa.

She spent most of her time with Hex and Jack, though by now they were all thoroughly unimpressed by each other's mannerisms, personality, and company, but comfortable in that same company, nonetheless.

"I've got plans with Bezbiel," she replied matter-of-factly.

Hex smirked and laughed under her breath. Jack shifted uncomfortably.

"What's so funny?" Saiyah said austerely.

"I'm sure you'll figure it out soon," Hex said sweetly.

Saiyah glanced at Jack, dwarfed in an armchair. "Snake eyes," he mouthed, pointing at his own eyes.

Saiyah paused, swung her bag off her shoulder and perched on the edge of the sofa. "Just tell me quickly what's going on," she demanded impatiently.

Hex just grinned inanely, eyes cast down toward her book, while Jack wore a more pained expression than usual.

Finally, he cleared his throat. "You can't trust anything he says."

Saiyah shrugged impatiently. "What are you talking about?"

"He means that your entrancing tutor is exactly that. He's a *Manip*," Hex explained.

Manipulation was a common enough demonic trait, the most prevalent in fact. Hex was one herself, though she didn't give details. She had a red armband too, so it must've been something strong.

"Look. Not that I care what you get up to in your spare time, but it's something to bear in mind," Hex said casually.

Saiyah stood unhurriedly. "Thanks," she said bluntly, hiding her concern.

S AIYAH WORE A SIMPLE, black, off-the-shoulder dress which made her green eyes with their subtle glow quite striking against her pale skin.

It was sunset, and the glass in the lamp above the entrance to the Old Roads reflected the sun's deep orange rays. Bezbiel waited for her in a dark suit and waistcoat with a button-up shirt and an evening jacket over one shoulder. He grinned as she approached.

Saiyah's heart fluttered, but she didn't break her stride.

"You look enchanting," he said, taking her hand and planting a kiss.

Saiyah blushed subtly. "Thank you. Not too shabby yourself," she responded cheerily.

This pleased him, and he spun smoothly to show off his outfit. Saiyah rolled her eyes but couldn't conceal her amusement. Bezbiel offered an arm, and they stepped out into the noise of London.

When they reached Soho it was already bustling. Different coloured eclectic lights illuminated and reflected on glass fronts. People in all sorts of clothing, from black tie to nightclub attire, to drag, were starting their evenings, and restaurants teemed with people. Bezbiel steered her inside one whose every table was full, and the noise of chatter was unbearable. Pulling Saiyah through the maze of tables, they came to a lobby area between the restaurant and kitchen. He stood before a tall bookcase and gave it a push. Of course, it was a secret door, and not a particularly well-disguised one either.

It led into a cocktail bar, still busy, but the talk was subdued and refined over the clinking of glasses. Demons and non-demons alike mingled together, all dressed in their finery. Bezbiel headed to a table at which three people sat.

A woman in a slinky black dress, her glossy dark hair in a French twist, noticed them approaching first. On her arm was an orange armband. "Bezbiel!" she called out.

Eyes flickered in his direction and fell onto Saiyah curiously.

Beside the woman was a yellow-armband-wearing man with slicked-back dark hair, dark skin, and ram-like curved horns. He stood and greeted Bezbiel with a bear hug and offered a seat. "Who's the newcomer?"

"This..." Bezbiel paused with dramatic flair and a sweeping hand gesture. "Is Saiyah Greyson. She's recently enrolled with us."

The trio responded with sounds of polite intrigue. The horned man introduced himself as Xaldan.

"This is Titania." Bezbiel indicated the girl who'd greeted him. "And this is the lovely Medea." He nodded to a gorgeous woman with a green armband. She was slim and curvaceous in all the right places. Ruby painted lips matched her backless dress, and blonde locks which curled at the ends danced on her ghostly skin. She glittered with gold jewellery

"Stop it, Bezbiel," she chimed in, though clearly enjoying the praise. "Charmed." She shook Saiyah's hand daintily.

Bezbiel poured red wine for himself and Saiyah as she struggled to keep up with the conversation. She already had no idea what they were talking about.

"That's rather lowbrow," Bezbiel commented.

"Uncultured and unrefined," Titania said with a strong Irish accent.

"Do you have any descriptive words that don't begin with the same letter?" Xaldan teased.

"Ignoramus," Titania snapped back, getting mock support from Bezbiel.

"That's a rather big word for you," Medea muttered tauntingly, raising her glass.

Titania arched her brow. "I'm surprised someone who spends so much time with herbs and bones knows what it means in the first place," she snapped.

Bezbiel let out a peal of laughter. Saiyah was absorbed in the banter and laughed along. Bezbiel topped up her wine even though she'd barely drunk half a glass.

Titania's eyes caught Saiyah's. "So new girl, I *loathe* to be so forward..." Her comment was met with smirks and mutterings of, 'oh here we go again' and 'that's not like you *at all* Titania.' She shushed them and leaned forward. "How come you got a red band?"

The room swayed. Saiyah wished she'd eaten something before drinking. "I'm not really sure I have an answer to that if I'm honest," She shrugged.

Bezbiel put on a sly smile that let Saiyah know he was about to turn on the charm. "Come now. Titania, just because yours is one lower, that's no need to feel threatened."

Titania wrinkled her nose at him.

Medea watched Saiyah with her strange, ghostly green eyes, but she smiled kindly when she caught her eye.

"I trust you're settling in well with the coven?" Xaldan questioned politely.

"Yes, Bezbiel's been helping me."

Medea made a sound of amusement, toying with her wine glass. Xaldan was in on the joke, whatever it was.

Titania furrowed her brows before looking at Saiyah with pity. "Oh hell. He isn't giving you private lessons, is he?"

"I'm tutoring Saiyah in the demonic scripts, yes. Azeldya has personally instructed me to do so," Bezbiel retorted evenly.

Titania made a noise of disgust.

"Careful of him, Saiyah. He'll put all sorts of ideas in your head," Xaldan said, flashing a dazzling white grin.

Everyone giggled, apart from Bezbiel, who gulped his wine without reacting.

"Gabrielle, darling!" Medea called out in a plummy voice.

Saiyah turned to see the secretary from her registration. She wore her cloak, but this time her hair was completely loose and shining like liquid starlight. "I might've known it was you I could sense," she greeted with a hint of sarcasm. "I hope you're not going to cause any trouble tonight?"

She was met with a chorus of playful denial. Gabrielle gave the group a knowing look, then turned to Saiyah. "I'm glad you took my advice on joining these reprobates. With any luck, you'll be a good influence on them."

"Why don't you join us, darling?" Medea said, reaching for Gabrielle's hand.

"Thank you, but I'm working tonight. Don't do anything that'll make me have to call in the others, okay?" she warned, already retreating before fading away completely.

"The god-squad," Bezbiel murmured after she'd gone.

"On that note, I think we'd better drink up," Xaldan muttered.

Saiyah struggled with what was left in her glass, swayed as she stood, and a hand slid around her waist. She jumped, expecting it to be Bezbiel, but it was Titania, smiling as if they were old friends.

"A word of advice from a fellow female," she whispered. "Be careful. Bezbiel's an excellent tutor, but you can't trust him in the way you want to."

Saiyah frowned. "What do you mean?"

Titania rolled her eyes. "Have you ever heard of impulsive thoughts? Demons get them all the time, more so than mortals and nearly always act on them. Bezbiel has it bad for a half-demon. Not to mention his unique powers of persuasion."

Saiyah didn't quite understand why that was a reason not to trust him. He'd been nothing but helpful and amiable since she'd met him, if a little arrogant. Nevertheless, she made a mental note on the impulses of demons. Hopefully that wasn't something that would affect her.

At the back of the restaurant was a smoking area decorated with paper lanterns. After the group stepped outside, Bezbiel took a packet of cigarettes from his pocket, and Medea let him light one for her. Seeing them close together, Saiyah felt a twinge of annoyance.

They followed Xaldan through a side gate which couldn't have been there before. It was part of the Old Roads, and the few other smokers around didn't notice their disappearance. They crowded onto a tiny patio. High stone walls surrounded them. Flowerpots with long-dead plants lay scattered and broken, but footprints in the sludge underfoot hinted at previous visitors.

Bezbiel stepped forward and reached inside his blazer to retrieve his malachite wand. Crouching, he scratched a circle into the slippery flagstones around them, muttering under his breath. Saiyah shivered. She recognised the words 'north,' 'east,' 'south,' and 'west' in demonic language, and the four elemental alchemy symbols. Unlike the circle Hezekiah drew, this was un-fastidious and primal. There was a familiar vibration in the air, subtle and foreboding. He raised the Malachite over his head and then brought it rapidly to the ground. It made a surreal clinking noise, profound enough to sober Saiyah despite her otherworldly vertigo.

A fishy smell made Saiyah gag and she did a double take at her surroundings. It was like they'd stepped into a mirror world. For a moment, she wondered if they were in a circle of Hell.

Everyone justled out of the circle, and Bezbiel prompted Saiyah to do the same. As if in a dream, she wandered forward and came out of the stone garden from behind a fountain. She stood at the end of a long, dim street with crooked buildings and old-fashioned electric lighting. Bezbiel leaned over and pressed on a little copper rod sticking up out of an ornamental fish, splashing water in his face.

At the end of the street, voices called out in another language. A river ran alongside them, along which boats with market sellers and their wares were moored up against the stone walkway. Locals perused the wares under strings of lightbulbs, talking, laughing, and drinking. Stringed instruments echoed in the background of the midnight market.

"Are we in Venice?" Saiyah gasped.

Bezbiel grinned mischievously, enjoying her surprise. He responded with a casual nod.

Saiyah could barely contain her excitement, but it paled when the others took their armbands off. Her stomach turned to stone, and she glanced at Bezbiel anxiously. Xaldan's horns were gone, and Bezbiel's snake eyes were a perfectly normal chocolate brown. Of course. There was a curfew for half-demons here.

Noticing her worry, he put both hands on her shoulders and made her stand still. "Breathe, Saiyah," he told her, leaning forward so all she could see was his face. "Listen to me, Saiyah. It'll be alright. Just enjoy yourself."

Saiyah did her best to stay calm as she removed her own armband. They linked arms and began to walk onwards. Abruptly, Bezbiel stopped and glanced back the way they came.

"What is it?" Saiyah whispered.

Bezbiel shook his head, appearing confused. "Nothing," he said, though his eyes darted around uncertainly.

They reached the Grand Canal, which was thronged with people. The festive mood lifted Saiyah's spirits. Looking at Bezbiel, he didn't appear deterred. Xaldan hailed a water taxi whilst Bezbiel procured a bottle of champagne from a waterside restaurant. He leapt aboard, affording cheers from the group. The night air was more humid in Venice, but there was still a chill on the water. They all laughed and joked as they floated along the Grand Canal. Bezbiel popped the cork, and the golden liquid was passed around.

Over dinner, there was more wine to accompany the rich and exquisite food. Saiyah relaxed, enjoying their demonically intellectual conversations. When the conversation turned to Renaissance art in Venice, she found she was able to contribute equally. She was teased for ordering tea at the end of the meal, but there was no malice. Saiyah watched as the air from the lagoon played with the vapours from her cup and wafted it out on a Mediterranean breeze.

After the meal, they followed Medea in a merry daze. The city at night was a whirl of colourful architecture. Flickering lights reflected off the water and back onto the buildings with their grand windows and antique shutters. The smell of rich food mingled with the saltiness of the canal.

Saiyah was so caught up in the atmosphere that the appearance of someone's private boat startled her. She barely remembered stepping aboard. Music blared. She saw Xaldan dancing and drinking with a group of people; his horns were back. Green eyes were everywhere. She heard someone mention 'The Order of Rhea Silvia.' Like them, they were just another coven.

Bezbiel approached her, his hand out. "Dance with me?"

Saiyah shook her head, but he took her hand and pulled her towards the throng of dancers. He held one hand up high and placed the other at her waist. Relaxed, Saiyah laughed as he tried to teach her some basic steps, but it was hard to hear over the music and chatter.

Quickly, the dancing developed into fast-paced steps. Bezbiel twirled her around and spun her away, then pulled her back to close position again. Saiyah was sure they weren't particularly good, but they weren't the only ones dancing like that. She was out of breath, breaking a sweat, but kept going out of sheer enjoyment. The night repeated itself with dancing, drinking, and light-hearted chatter. She danced with demons without names or memory, but always came back to Bezbiel.

She'd no idea what time it was when her head started to ache, and her vision spun uncontrollably. Perhaps she was seasick. She sat at the back, near the engine, with a glass of something unknown. The boat slowed.

Bezbiel appeared and put an arm around her. "Do you want me to take you home?"

Saiyah let her head fall onto his shoulder. "I think that would be sensible." She spoke carefully, trying not to slur her words.

Bezbiel chuckled and helped her up.

Saiyah couldn't remember exactly how they got back to the stone garden. She may have been carried at one point, maybe off the boat? At the fountain, she stopped and got some water for herself. Bezbiel was patient, and uncharacteristically quiet.

Saiyah slumped on the stone bench and fell asleep while Bezbiel performed the ritual again. The cold air of England made Saiyah a fraction more alert. As they walked, Bezbiel lamented more than once that he wasn't usually home so early.

Inside the Old Roads, they stopped at the crossroads at the end of her street where Bezbiel would have continued.

"Do you want me to walk you to your door?" he asked mischievously.

Saiyah giggled sluggishly. "I'm sure I can manage," she said softly, untangling herself from his arm. "Thank you for convincing me to come out. I had a good time."

Bezbiel tilted his head. "I knew you would." He was standing a little too close, staring at her, unmoving. "Good night, Saiyah." He drew away from her with a roguish grin.

Catching her breath, Saiyah watched him go. She placed a cool palm on her head and then smoothed it over her stomach before quickly heading home.

VI

Good Men and Monsters

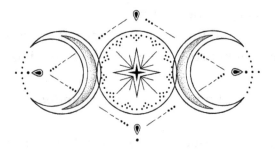

SAIYAH SOON SURPASSED NOVICE levels of Old Demonic, and Bezbiel subsequently reminded her she'd promised to teach him the gods' script. Their roles were reversed. Bezbiel took it exceedingly seriously, practising every letter and writing them out with reverence. Her lessons with him decreased as he focused more on his own studies. The evenings out increased in frequency. They were often lavish, expensive, and fantastical. Hex started to join them, but there was no persuading Jack. The housemates often walked home together from the porthole in Soho, but often Saiyah went alone or took a taxi after mastering the art of drinking less around the older demons.

Beneath the streetlamps, Saiyah walked home after one such night. Sirens echoed in the distance; the noise of traffic was ever-present. She adjusted her coat as a bitter wind blew. Saiyah had little fear of being out at night in London alone. Even if she wasn't entirely sober, she was a demon. One with a red armband at that.

Just then she stumbled, catching herself on a railing. Bewildered, she looked through the fence into Hyde Park. This wasn't quite where she'd intended to walk. She often came this way in daylight hours—her feet must have walked by memory.

She entered the park and trudged down an empty path beneath the clear night sky. As the light faded, her powers grew, and her body felt stronger. She allowed it to surge through her, not using it, but becoming familiar with how it felt. Grand rooftops from a myriad of time periods bordered the edge of the park before giving way to the rising treetops as she progressed.

A flash of white overhead startled her. She turned, expecting to see a bike with a headlight or teenagers with phones, but the path was eerily empty and suddenly very far away from the busy roads. She hunched her shoulders and continued, but as she approached a sheltered grove of trees, she hesitated uncharacteristically before the darkness. She wanted to use her ability and become a shadow, but it would be highly illegal if she were caught. Her hair stood on end, and there was an unnatural prickle at the back of her neck. It reminded her of a feeling she'd had at the embassy, albeit faint.

The prickling sensation elevated when she heard a noise behind her, a footstep on the gravel. She spun sharply, but there was no one there. The path behind was darker and hollower than ever.

"Hello?" she called, her voice thinner than usual. She froze, clutching the strap of her bag. "It's not funny!" she added, cringing at how pathetic it sounded. When no one replied, she mumbled under her breath, "By the pricking of my thumbs..."

"I didn't mean to startle you."

Saiyah jumped and stumbled back, kicking loose gravel, dropping her bag and spilling half the contents. The voice, soft but deep, came from close by, and she turned to see Captain Hezekiah standing placidly before her. He had a faint silvery glow about him, and his arctic eyes appeared more intense than she remembered.

"Judas," Saiyah swore under her breath, winning a disappointed look from the god. "What on earth do you think you're doing?" she scolded, gaining her voice again.

He folded his arms over the dark armour on his chest. "You should check your tone, demon. Confrontation could earn you a night in the cells." His tone was even, but authoritative enough to leave Saiyah with no doubt that she should hold her tongue.

She clenched her fists and gritted her teeth, staying perfectly still.

"It is my duty to keep track of demons, particularly at night as their power grows," he said automatically, as if he was reciting practised lines. "And you have a very unusual demonic energy about you. What are you doing out alone?" He stepped sideways to examine her scattered things.

She crouched and started to retrieve her fallen things back into her bag. Saiyah pushed strands of hair behind her ears where it'd come loose from her bun in the night breeze.

"I wasn't doing anything, just walking home," she said as calmly as she could manage.

Hezekiah shook his head slightly and glanced discretely down the dark path from which they'd both come. "I was not accusing you of anything," he said flatly, but there was a flinty edge to his voice. He knelt, seemingly to help her, but his hand lay absently on the hilt of his sword while he passed her things with the other.

There was an array of silver daggers at his waist of varying sizes, one even large enough to use as a sword. Others were strapped to his shins, but they seemed too small to be practical. Saiyah's eyes were fixed on the needle-point sharpness of one with an exposed blade, and in a wave of repulsion she looked away and continued scooping up her things.

"Where did you get this?" Hezekiah's voice was wispy, and his face vigilant.

He held the Osiris Coffin box in his hand. Saiyah reached to grab it, but his hand retreated at an inhuman speed as he stood.

"That's very personal to me. Please give it back," Saiyah said evenly, getting to her feet and holding her hand out for it.

Hezekiah looked from her to the box and regarded the dark stone casually. "Do you know what it is?"

Saiyah nodded.

"What do you keep in it?" The captain took a step towards her, gravel crunching beneath his feet.

Saiyah wasn't sure if she was obliged to answer or not. She certainly didn't want to get in any trouble over this if she didn't. She opened her mouth, then closed it again, keeping her composure as best as possible.

"You don't know what's inside," he said, an edge of relief to his voice. "They're near impossible to open." He turned it over by tossing it in the air, then handed it to her.

Saiyah drew it towards her protectively and stowed it in her bag again. "No," she admitted. "I can't read the inscription."

Captain Hezekiah gave no reaction. Indeed, he appeared to be looking everywhere but at her. "I will escort you home now."

Saiyah raised her eyebrows. "Oh, no. That won't be necessary, thank you." She floundered, already retreating.

Hezekiah was unphased. He glanced back down the path again before giving her a decisive nod. "You misunderstand. I will accompany you out of the park, at the very least."

Saiyah shivered. Perhaps it wasn't *his* energy she'd sensed. Perhaps there was something else in the dark. Hezekiah appeared at her side, and they walked silently.

Fearful yet resigned, she nodded with a shrug. "Why are you helping me?" she asked, irked despite the knot in her stomach.

He tilted his head to one side with a confused expression. "I have a duty of care to your mortal soul," he said forcefully.

"*My mortal soul,*" Saiyah blurted out, her voice dripping in amusement. The alcohol refused to quiet her tongue. "If gods had any regard for that, we wouldn't be systematically forced to wear these ridiculous, segregating, armbands." She folded her arms stubbornly.

Hezekiah frowned. "Nevertheless, I do."

"And what if I decided to defend my own soul?"

"You'd be arrested, naturally," he said in an exasperated tone, though there was something close to humour in his voice.

Saiyah smiled falsely. "Well then, I will do my utmost not to anger the gods," she said with a sarcastic flourish.

"Good. Prove to me the word of a demon can be trusted," he said with a nod.

Saiyah scowled and gritted her teeth, but kept her mouth shut in favour of not provoking him. They were almost at the edge of the park when Saiyah tripped again. The Captain caught her deftly by the arm and set her upright in a quick motion. She flinched from him and the jolt of unexpected divine energy at his fingertips. It was alien, yet familiar.

They stood at one of the many entranceways and she looked to him, waiting for permission to part, though she felt idiotic doing so.

He paused before leaving. "I do not care much for the 'ridiculous armbands' your government prescribes either." He paused, grimacing. "I have seen a similar practice in this world before. It did not end well." He inclined his head slightly before swiftly turning to leave. "Good day, Miss Greyson."

Saiyah caught her breath as she watched him go. He started to draw his main sword before turning back to her. His sudden glance left her flustered.

"*'It can only be opened from within, by one of my own line,'* that's what it says," he called back without raising his voice.

Saiyah's brow creased, and she opened her mouth to ask something, but he disappeared as if a sudden storm had spirited him away.

Shaking her head in disbelief, she continued, and emerged into the bright streets of London with shaky limbs and a scowling countenance. She'd never been spoken to quite like that by anyone, even as a child being scolded. What could she rightly have said back to a member of *The Host*? A demon slayer no less. Her brow furrowed, and she scrunched her eyes shut for a moment before nearly running the rest of the way home.

I T WAS LATE WHEN Saiyah lit the candles in the little library alcove of her room. She wasn't trusting of the gas lamps in the house, especially this late at night, and there was no electricity on the Old Roads. A fire crackled near her bed, lit more for light than for warmth.

Sitting down, she stared at the Osiris box placed carefully on a mound of books. *'One of my line,'* she mouthed.

Just like in the book from Daniel. How could she prove to the box that she was her mother's daughter? Blood? Saiyah considered for a moment the possibility of cutting her hand and letting the blood flow over the container. No, it couldn't be that.

Her heart hammered in her chest as she lay a hand over the stone. Saiyah closed her eyes and relaxed, reaching out for the energy of the box, the energy of her mother. Shadowy energy expanded from her hand as it'd done before. It was tangible, visible, and physical. Not a part of her, yet controlled by her. It enveloped the box.

There was a sharp crack. It shook the air in the room and drummed in her ears. The stone had split cleanly across the top, creating a lid. Saiyah lifted it, and for a moment, warm, fragrant air with an odd heaviness to it reached her nostrils. There was a single piece of paper within, rolled up like a scroll and secured with string. Saiyah carefully lifted the brittle paper and untied the string, letting the scroll unfold on its own. It was a letter, written in simple New Demonic, in delicate, dignified dark ink. Her eyes welled to see her mother's cursive.

She leaned back and wiped her eyes on the sleeve of her dressing gown, then grabbed her dictionary and laboriously began to translate through the night.

To my darling daughter,

If you are reading this, then I am presumably dead, and it is my great regret that I did not get to watch you grow. Wherever you are, know that you are very much loved and wanted. Parting with you is unbearable, but it must be done for your safety.

I have given instructions to deliver you to the guardian Daniel Akrasiel, who I know to be a good man. Be vigilant in revealing to him that you are the daughter of Asramenia after reading this.

I'll tell you plainly, I fully expected my death and hopefully, I fought to the end. Do not mistake my words for a heroic death in battle, for as I write I am completely alone, and with Azeldya bearing you to calmer shores, I am without a single trustworthy friend.

I do not wish you to seek revenge, but Azeldya, if you are reading this also: I know now that the individual or parties who conspired with the gods to bring about my murder were aware I had left Xalvas Tis Nyx, and that their lies began not here in Tartarus, but elsewhere. Continue my work, if you are able, and aid the lost souls of Khabrasos, for I am certain they will suffer greatly when I am gone.

I received a letter from your father, warning me of the betrayal he had overheard in the encampments of the gods. Mercifully, he has tried to petition my case while I stay in hiding, though from his correspondence I sense an impending doom in his hurried hand. He has not written to me in some time, and I fear he has been discovered to be in league with me. Hell knows what they will do to him.

I have little time to explain. I flee to Dualjahit in hope of gaining sanctuary amongst allies. It is here I shall hide his letters in trusted hands, I hope, or at least with those who will be careful enough to keep an Osiris Box safe without suspicion. They are common enough here. There are stolen documents amongst them in the language of the gods, which I am sure will uncover the truth.

The traitor may yet be amongst my supposed allies, and I speak not of simple spies or demons with their selfish motives, but a Judas of the purest kind. Be wary of who you trust, and remember you will always be able to retreat to shadow for aid.

Your loving mother.

VII

What in Me is Dark, Illumine

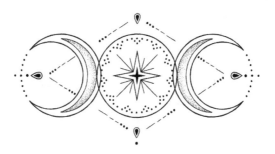

S AIYAH READ THE LETTER a dozen times before standing. Her fingers trembled. Her mother's death
wasn't a surprise, but the idea of being betrayed and
murdered by a friend sickened her. Still, no one knew
when Azeldya would be back, and there was no one
else she could speak to. She stared at her phone, where
Daniel's name flickered on the screen. But would he
understand?

Too alert to sleep, Saiyah stepped out into the darkness and made towards the library. No one would be
there now, except perhaps Zulphas, and the others
wouldn't wake for hours even if they were home al-

ready. She was approaching the crossroads when she recognised the familiar hum of demonic energy nearby. Demons were forbidden to use their powers in public, but this was the Old Roads. Saiyah walked faster, not wanting to get involved. Something about the tone of this energy was malignant. It was familiar. She'd felt it last night, too.

Something made her turn and look towards the gateway through the gardens and at the end of the path. The air swirled defensively, and at its barrier stood a figure with darkened, deep-set green eyes, watching her. Their face was concealed with a hood and bandana, but she got the impression of dark, greyish skin beneath. Blackened fingertips with long, grotty, claw-like nails protruded from its sleeves. It lifted a hand and slowly raked on the barrier. As nails pierced through, so did the rasping voice. It was painful to hear, and she was too frightened to understand, but one name stood out powerfully clear:

"*Asramenia.*"

Panicked, Saiyah took on her shadow form. The demon moved inhumanly towards her, his shadow independent of his body, closing in on her. In desperation, she willed herself to disappear further and melded with her own shadow.

The sounds of the night vanished with the kind of falling sensation experienced when waking from a dream. Saiyah was surrounded by inky darkness, knowing instinctively that this was Hell. Blurred shapes with green eyes hovered, and fragments of dappled light moved between them. Terrified and helpless, Saiyah thrashed around, unable to feel her limbs, not unlike sleep paralysis. She feared she wouldn't be able to get back to a solid form, that she would be trapped in this dark world. The figures whispered, comforting voices which could've been deceivingly inviting. They washed over Saiyah, calming her, oddly familiar. One voice stood out amongst them, warm and soft. It lifted her, and her flimsy shadow solidified.

London materialised around her.

She was still a shadow, and the demon was searching for her. Keeping close to the buildings, she started to run.

Gabrielle. She had Gabrielle's number. Reaching for her phone out of the ally she'd materialised in, she was stopped when grotesque fingers gripped her arm. Blood dripped from her skin as she tore it away and dissolved into shadow again, marking the pavement red. She took a turn down a residential street which would take her back to the gateway. There in the archway was the demon. No, another demon. There were two.

Vertigo hit, and she stumbled as a devastating demonic force came over her. A demon crashed through a sudden rift in reality behind her, like stepping through a dark pane of glass. Two more followed, looking straight at her, her shadow form ineffective in the open. Saiyah froze in the middle of the road.

A glimmer of white twinkled above the houses. A cloaked demon slayer whirled from out of nowhere, landing between her and the demons. The god exuded light, making the demons hiss and squint, blindly raking ghastly claws across the air. The god lodged the sword between the nails of one and gave a sharp twist. There was a loud snap. The demon shrieked with an ear-splitting sound as its nails split at the nerve endings. It wailed inhumanely.

Another demon leapt forward holding a jagged knife. Air rippled through her hair. A cracking sound halted the second demon. Saiyah winced to see the god's sword in its spine. He glanced up and she recognised the ice-blue eyes of Captain Hezekiah. Saiyah jumped back as its body skidded across the tarmac, coming to a halt close beside her.

Another slayer with blonde hair appeared and swiftly cut through the third and fourth demon. Black blood splattered the tarmac. Saiyah scrambled backwards as the killing blows were delivered, cradling her injured arm.

The first demon with the bleeding claws turned back to the slayer. Hezekiah's sword was out of reach, still lodged in the spine. A swift blow knocked the captain to the other side of the street, but landed expertly on his feet.

More slayers gradually appeared, joining together in closing the unbearable rift in reality.

Injured but determined, the demon at her feet shook its monstrous head and glowered at Saiyah. Adrenaline coursed through her and in the chaos of gods and demons, her fingers locked around the hilt of the sword still lodged in its back. It tingled pleasantly in her grip. It was weighty, but comfortable.

The other gods were agape to see the sword apparently moving of its own accord.

Her heartbeat was audible. She raised the sword as the demon bore down on her. It rebounded in shock, sending both of them stumbling back. The blade barely touched it, but a faintly glowing barrier encircled Saiyah like a thin line of silver.

The demon growled and stepped forward. Suddenly, the demon staggered backwards as if compelled.

Hezekiah stood near the dark pane of glass that blended with reality, making strange hand motions and muttering with his fellow demon slayers. The demon glanced from him to Saiyah and ran at the god. It came so close that the sleeve of his uniform caught in the claws. But some force compelled it to be pulled back into whatever realm it came from, spewing demonic profanities. Hezekiah sealed the Hellgate.

The demonic buzz of energy disappeared, and Hezekiah turned, his hood down and his face full of wrath. A few light cheers came from a small audience in the inhabitants of the flats above. The Captain of *The Host* didn't acknowledge them. "Show yourself!" he boomed, looking in her general direction without seeing her properly.

The slayers stood with their blades drawn, waiting to attack when ordered.

Tentatively, Saiyah let her shadowy form dissipate and she lowered the sword, profoundly aware that her movements were being watched not only by gods, but humans as well. Bleeding and wide-eyed, she was hardly the image of a harmless half-demon.

Hezekiah's face softened with surprise, but was no less angry. He spoke a few words to the blonde god, who nodded, regarded Saiyah curiously, and went to attend to the arrival of police cars. The remaining slayers relaxed. Only a few kept their blades fixed on her while the rest began to hide the evidence of any disturbance.

"Drop the sword and stand over there with your back against the wall," Hezekiah commanded harshly, pointing to the side of a building with bricked-up windows. Saiyah's momentary relief turned to anxious fear. She lay his sword carefully on the tarmac, making a faint chiming sound. She limped to the wall under his watchful eyes. Only when she reached it and slumped against it did he move to claim his weapon.

The captain appeared pitying but no less steely as he regarded her bloody arm. It was glossier than a normal human's, but not as dark as the demon's blood dripping from his blade. He stood indecisively with his arms folded.

"I'm sorry, Captain Hezekiah. I was just trying to get away!" Saiyah gestured to the carnage.

Her eyes were wide, unable to look away from the torn bodies of the demons.

Turning his head slightly, he spoke evenly and calmly. "You have broken two agreements of your registration that I have witnessed. I am obliged to place you under arrest and take you in for questioning regarding what transpired here."

Saiyah hung her head in despair. Tear tracks ran down her face from before, which she rubbed away as her eyes welled again. Above, people looked at her disapprovingly. A few people shouted unkind remarks.

"However," he continued in a hushed voice, though no less harsh. "Considering the circumstances in which you were under, and your recent admission to The Albion Circle, I will only be issuing you with a warning."

Saiyah's head shot up in surprise.

He paused, taking a breath as he carefully stepped forward. "These good people will be expecting an arrest, and I have to be seen doing my duty. Humans must be made to feel safe. If you would come quietly with me, it would be appreciated."

Saiyah was staring at him open-mouthed. Hezekiah stood motionless, expecting an answer.

"Miss Greyson?" he snapped roughly when she didn't reply.

Saiyah replied with a weak nod. Head lowered, she pushed her body away from the wall as he approached. The sound of cuffs clanked from beneath his cloak, and their nullifying energy resounded. Saiyah held her hands forward, but to her surprise the god paused, slowly replaced the cuffs, and carefully took her wounded arm by the wrist. He tore his sleeve where it'd already ripped and bound the cuts gently. It quickly stained the material dark red, too light to be demon blood, but too dark for a human.

He held her good arm behind her back, placing his hand on her shoulder to walk her away. "We will see what we can do about your arm once we reach the embassy."

Saiyah hung her head, humiliated.

When they reached the embassy Saiyah exhaled. The foyer was dark apart from the faint glow from Hezekiah. With a clap of his hands, little orbs of pale light faded in from somewhere in the vaulted ceiling. She trailed behind him like a delinquent child.

A pair of soldiers appeared in the corridor, wearing dark armour over their uniforms. They eyed Saiyah curiously and saluted Hezekiah, speaking in hushed voices. Saiyah heard the name 'Remiel' mentioned. They bowed their heads and saluted before continuing on. In the embassy, the foyer was alive with more activity than the last time she'd been there. Demon-slaying soldiers moved briskly around in groups, and other lesser gods like Gabrielle darted around with messages. There was a curious wail from one of the darkened archways which made Saiyah shiver. A couple of gods quietly led another demon with hoofed feet, head hanging in shame, in chains in the same direction.

Hezekiah hadn't said a word to her since he'd 'arrested' her, even when they entered his office. There was no electricity, so he quickly but carefully lit the candles mounted on the walls. The smell of burnt-out matches filled the room. There was only one chair at the desk, and he indicated that she should take it. Behind her, he opened the large doors so that moonlight spilt into the dim room. It made a considerable difference, though Saiyah didn't normally have an issue seeing in shadowy places.

Hezekiah placed a bowl of water with a cloth draped over it onto the table and stood to one side, keeping his distance. "May I?" He gestured to her arm.

Saiyah painfully lifted her forearm and Hezekiah took its weight at her wrist. He attentively unwrapped the wound, and Saiyah winced as the dried blood peeled away with it.

"These are rather deep. I'd wager you lost a lot of blood," He said matter-of-factly. "You do look pale." Hezekiah eyed her uncertainly before a knock at the door diverted his attention.

Gabrielle stood at the threshold, surprised to see Saiyah. "You asked for me, Captain?"

"Yes. Could you bring me some tea, and something for Miss Greyson, preferably with sugar? Contact The Albion Circle to inform them the stability of the Old Roads has been compromised. Help with repairs, et cetera. Oh and, er..." He looked distrustfully at Saiyah as he cleaned her wounds. "Have a room prepared for Miss Greyson, please."

Gabrielle raised her eyebrows and Saiyah's mouth fell open. She made some stuttering noises of protest.

"In the cells, Captain?" Gabrielle asked hesitantly.

Hezekiah shook his head. "No, Remiel. In the embassy residency if you please."

"What?" Saiyah said, loud enough to make the Captain turn towards her alertly.

A stern glance made Gabrielle remember herself, and she disappeared out of the room as Saiyah stared at Hezekiah in shock.

"For your safety," he said simply.

Saiyah was about to protest again when he set the cloth in the now-turbid water and laid his palm across her forearm. He closed his eyes, a look of concentration on his face, and the underside of his hand glowed with a silvery light. Saiyah felt a mild irritation, as if antiseptic had been sprayed in the wound. She recoiled, but Hezekiah held her firmly. The procedure took no longer than a minute, and he let go as soon as it was done. Saiyah expected a scar, but the wound was completely healed. Nothing was left except a streak of blood on the skin.

"Thank you," she said, astounded, examining her arm.

Hezekiah stood silently and took a moment to clean his sword before finally sheathing it again. He stood frowning with his arms folded, contemplating deeply.

"I'll question you in full tomorrow, but there is something I'd like to ask you now."

Too tired to care, Saiyah shrugged.

Hezekiah stared down at his feet. "What did you do, exactly, when you wielded my sword?" He watched as he waited for an answer, a look of wary concern on his usually-stoic face.

Saiyah shook her head. "I don't know. The sword did it on its own."

Taken aback, Hezekiah frowned more deeply.

Gabrielle arrived with a tray of tea and set it down on the table. "I'll have your room ready by the time you've finished."

Once Gabrielle left, Hezekiah poured them both some tea. "The sword doesn't do anything on its own. It's just a tool."

"Well, perhaps it's part of my abilities that I haven't discovered working through it," Saiyah offered, shaking her head.

"You have no idea what you've done, do you?" He sounded frustrated, alarming Saiyah.

Saiyah leaned forward in her chair. "Did I do something wrong?"

He sighed. "What you did was something unheard of for a demon. That shield you made is one of the first things young gods are taught. If there is a way you've discovered to channel our power, you'd be wise to admit it now," he warned her.Saiyah was petrified, but did her best not to show it. She sipped her tea and considered her words wisely. It must be something to do with Daniel, she thought–perhaps because he raised her? Or the gods' language. Maybe knowing it caused this? Regardless, Saiyah's desperation was sincere.

"Whatever I did, I did completely by accident. I really did think it was the sword. I don't know–"

"I believe you," He said, cutting her off. He lifted his tea to sip, then set it down. "I don't have your file to hand, but your mother was a demon, correct? Was she one of the original fallen, do you know? Or perhaps a Watcher? Or even descended from one?"

Saiyah knew what he meant by 'Watcher.' It was a term used for angels who'd taught mortals things they shouldn't have known yet, and also had children with them. The progenitors of such a union were usually monstrous creations. It was a taboo subject according to Daniel, and she was surprised Hezekiah dared to mention them at all.

"No. I don't think so," she said assuredly.

Hezekiah regarded her seriously. "There are some that might regard you as something called a Nephilim."

"I know what a Nephilim is," Saiyah said irritably, straightening up. "They're described as monsters or giants, and were hunted to extinction by the gods."

Hezekiah smiled ironically. "Yes. Although I suppose you don't look like either of those things. Leave it with me, I'm sure it's nothing of concern."

When their cups were empty, Hezekiah walked with her out of the large doors and across the lawn to the house she'd seen before. Strangely, this didn't seem like London anymore. It was more like a large walled garden in the countryside. The midnight sky was still and clear, full of stars, unlike the polluted sky of London.

"You live here?" Saiyah questioned.

"Of course," he said, opening the door.

"I thought you all, you know, went back." She pointed upwards, unsure what to call the place she was talking about.

The gods were excessively secretive about where they came from. Daniel always referred to it as the 'upper world,' which he made clear wasn't the actual name.

Hezekiah shook his head. "My post is here on earth," he told her with a hint of melancholy.

Inside, the space was large and undecorated apart from the mosaic floor and hand-painted ceramic tiles on the walls. A large atrium with a spiral staircase opened up before her. She was so tired that the prospect of a bed, any bed, pulled her forward without stopping to admire the scene.

Hezekiah directed her to a room and they both hovered awkwardly by the doorway. Saiyah wasn't sure if she should be thanking him, or saying anything at all. Hezekiah stood stiffly.

He cleared his throat. "I will commence questioning in the morning. Rest well, I'm sure you need it."

Saiyah dipped her head in thanks, smiling discreetly to see a god behave so artlessly.

Her sleep was broken, and her heart raced anxiously. Strange sounds from deep within the house drifted up to her like sweet, muffled music. It didn't stop her from falling back into that dark world. It was involuntary. The same force from before pulled her in, familiar this time. It was so clearly her mother. Green-eyed voices surrounded her, but they weren't here to hurt her. She couldn't understand them, though she caught words of both Old and New Demonic.

VIII

Within Dark Woods, the Way is Lost

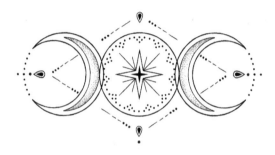

I NTRICATELY CARVED WOODEN ARCHES covered the wall behind the bed and framed the windows opposite. The mattress was soft and deep, like no one had ever slept on it. Surrounded in crisp white sheets, it was as if Saiyah was in paradise.

Unnerved, Saiyah examined her perfectly healed arm, running her fingertips over it. What Captain Hezekiah said about tapping into god powers and the Nephilim was worrying. It couldn't be true, but if the gods decided it was, she was in serious trouble.

She sat up in bed. The room was flooded in daylight which seemed to pour through the gauzy curtains like ambrosia. The floor was beige stone slabs, and every-thing was made from exquisitely carved wood and mar-ble surfaces. On the bedside table was a note addressed to her:

Good morning!

I've taken your clothes to be washed. Capt. Hezekiah is in his study. There are clothes in the wardrobe, and help yourself to anything in the kitchen.

-G.

In the wardrobe hung loose, colourful robes and dresses with a classical appearance. She picked out a mauve one with a shrug and slipped it over her head.

Cautiously, she made her way down the wide stairs. The marble was chilling on her bare feet. The house felt large and echoey, so she employed her shadow abilities so as not to make any noise.

The small kitchen was all wood and marble, with beautiful hand-painted teal tiles in floral mosaic pat-terns. She helped herself to some tea and fresh bread that was left out. There was hardly any food in the cupboards, but an abundance of tea and archaic teapots that resembled something Oriental.

There were three closed doors in the hallway, all with iron hinges, more beautiful than menacing. Trying the latch of the nearest door, it was locked. In a surge of curiosity, she became shadow and slipped through with the draft. It was dark inside. Meshed panels of the same carved wood gave way to an inner chamber, from which glimmers of light emerged. Finding the entrance, she stepped into what looked like a war room. There was one tiny skylight which lit the mahogany table. Upon it lay maps upon maps. She recognised some as modern, overlaid with more dated ones which seemed warped in comparison.

Above a mantle was what she assumed at first was a world map, but when she looked again it was nothing like what she knew. It was a map of the underworld: Hell, Sheol, Tartarus, and many other names she was less familiar with labelled the page. It appeared vast in comparison to Earth.

She stepped back into the hallway, worrying she'd overstayed her welcome.

The second door opened when she pulled the latch, though it was stiff and unwieldy. It gave way to a dining room which would've been grand once, but there was dust on the floor and sheets were thrown haphazardly over the furniture. Saiyah drifted over to something covered in the corner. Lifting the sheet at the edge, dust fell away in waves. It was a piano. She touched a few keys and instantly regretted it. It hadn't been tuned in years, and the sharp notes shattered the silence.

A faint sound made her jump and she swept back through the dust. Stepping into the corridor, she came face to face with the captain. An involuntary gasp escaped her. He didn't have his cloak, but wore the uniform trousers and a loose white shirt that revealed his collarbones. He took his hand away from his sword and glanced into the dining room.

"Do you play?" he asked placidly.

"I used to. It's been a long time, though."

He gave a grunt of acknowledgement, lost in thought. He turned and made a gesture which indicated she should follow. She trailed him to the third door, which now stood ajar.

His study was unlike the rest of the house. It was a mess of papers, more maps, and various artefacts. Bookcases covered one side of the room, and the far wall consisted of long windows and flowing sky-blue curtains.

Hezekiah removed his cloak from a chair at his desk and put it on, inviting Saiyah to sit in an armchair by the fireplace. He lifted a notebook and a ball-point pen from the little table in front and proceeded to ask her questions about what transpired. How she'd been attacked, the details of the demon's appearance, and how she'd used her powers. If he was shocked at her strange transgression to Hell, he didn't show it.

"Thank you, Miss Greyson. Azeldya will come to escort you home" Hezekiah closed the notebook.

"Who were those demons?" she asked. "I saw them step right into our world, as if the gates of Hell had opened right in front of me."

Hezekiah placed the notebook in a desk drawer, carefully locking it. He sat down in the chair before he responded.

"Scavengers. They are unable to take mortal souls, and so feast on human flesh to satisfy themselves," he explained matter-of-factly.

"Why were they chasing *me* then?"

Hezekiah looked up at her for the first time and his hard, bright eyes made her shrink back in the armchair a little.

"You are half-mortal, are you not?" he said accusingly, getting to his feet.

Saiyah blinked in astonishment. "You haven't mentioned anything about what I did."

He considered his words meticulously. "I will be conducting a thorough investigation. Should the results be favourable, I will inform you."

Saiyah stood, close to anger. "And if not? I'm not an idiot, I've heard what the gods are like when they disapprove of something." Saiyah's voice caught in her throat.

Hezekiah remained unnervingly calm. "I will make a fair decision based on my findings."

Saiyah scowled and hugged herself, too shocked to know how to react to this glacial god. Mercifully,

Gabrille showed up a moment later, saving her from having to respond.

Gabrielle escorted Saiyah back through the embassy. When they reached the foyer, Saiyah's face brightened to see Azeldya.

Once back on the Old Roads, Azeldya took Saiyah through a passage in the Barbatos Library to a door she'd not been to before. It wasn't unlike other rooms in the building, Georgian in style with hand-painted botanical wallpaper. There was a desk at one end of the room, but Azeldya sat with Saiyah on a sofa in the centre and poured her a cup of coffee. She touched Saiyah on the arm where she'd been injured. Though perfectly healed, her eyes saw through it.

"Something has changed within you," she said simply, examining Saiyah's face attentively.

"The scavenger spoke my mother's name," Saiyah said faintly. "Everyone keeps telling me it is dangerous to be my mother's daughter. I did something. I fell through worlds, didn't I?" Her words poured out of her, relief filling her as she spoke from being in the presence of someone she could trust.

"You did not," Azeldya said. "You never left this world, just moved through its astral plane. Your mother could do the same. There are some who are afraid you will share in all her powers and would continue her cause. I expect you know by now; the revolution was never fully realised. To some, it is an ongoing, yet hidden, battle of tenuous alliances with gods and demon lords."

Saiyah reached down to her satchel and removed the Osiris box. It clicked open under her touch, and she removed the letter, holding it out to Azeldya.

Azeldya's expression was one of surprised curiosity, until she noticed the anguished expression on Saiyah's face and frowned. Wordlessly, Azeldya read over the letter, her frown deepening with every line.

"Do you know who she could be talking about? The traitor?" Saiyah asked breathlessly, placing her satchel heavily at her feet.

Azeldya shook her head. "It could be anyone. Your mother valued loyalty above all else. In the months before her death, she trusted few of those she once called friends."

"Surely someone must know," Saiyah pressed.

Azeldya was pensive. "I have no doubt someone does, but demons keep secrets." Her eyes flickered a baleful look before she folded her arms and took on a business-like tone. "Your mother allied herself with high-ranking demons, sometimes gods, but also had many enemies even amongst them. Your exposure during your registration has caused your existence to be whispered about in Hell. I've already been contacted by old allies asking to meet with you."

Saiyah nearly choked on her coffee. "Why would they want to meet me?"

"Because they hope you'll rally her old followers and support them in turn," Azeldya explained calmly.

Saiyah felt dizzy at the thought of the responsibility, and shook her head in disbelief.

"You needn't worry, I can deal with them," Azeldya assured her. "You are far too young to be grappling with the powers and politics of demons. We have more pressing matters right now, and we must keep your nature hidden. Tell me everything that happened."

Saiyah explained the events of the previous night. Azeldya remained silent. Eventually, she stood and went to retrieve something from her desk, returning with a book bound in black, tanned hide. There was faded gold leaf at the corners, and the pages were stiff with age. She placed it on the table before Saiyah with reverence, keeping her hand over it as if the pages might fly open.

"I fear it is no coincidence you have gained some divine ability. Indeed, it makes me question many things I thought were buried." She stared at the book, unblinking before coming back to herself. "This was one of your mother's first journals. I found it after she died. It is incomplete, but it may provide you with some sort of explanation of her life, and an occultist she associated herself with." Her lips curled in disgust.

Saiyah blanched and reached for it, but Azeldya was reluctant to let go.

"Be warned, the contents are not for a faint heart. You should be fully prepared before reading it." Her words trembled with a demonic energy, and her dark eyes were more alive than ever before.

Saiyah shivered inadvertently.

"Now, we must do something to shield you, lest the gods become suspicious. Let me see that necklace of yours?"

Confused, Saiyah took off the crescent moon pendant Daniel had given her and handed it to Azeldya's outstretched hand. She took it to her desk and with the help of some candles, herbs, and a seamless incantation, placed a protection charm on it. Saiyah was dubious, but a faint demonic energy rang from the necklace. It would diminish her slight celestial energy and protect her from harm while Azeldya was away.

"In the meantime, I need you to keep taking your language lessons with Bezbiel and researching your mother."

Saiyah nodded. "I have no objections to either, but...I don't see how it's useful to the coven. In fact, I'd probably be doing the latter in my spare time if not instructed."

"It is for that very reason, my dear. It is good practice for your reading, and it keeps you interested. Besides, the knowledge you gain from her history will be invaluable to you in the future."

Saiyah nodded and stood, but lingered at the door. "Is that why you wanted me here? To have me take the place of my mother?"

"No. I brought you here to protect you." Azeldya wore a forlorn smile with a slow blink of her long lashes. "Besides, you are half-mortal and therefore could never be what she was, not fully. Now, go. And if you discover anything about this traitor your mother spoke of, let me be the first to know."

I T WASN'T LONG BEFORE Zulphas approached Saiyah and informed her rigidly that she'd be taking lessons with him in astral projection. It was unusual for new initiates to be allowed to undertake occult practices, or even have a mentor. Zulphas wasn't overly pleased with the prospect, and in the ensuing days demons gossiped and made all sorts of assumptions. Saiyah did her best to ignore them.

Zulphas wasn't a natural teacher in the way Bezbiel was. He expected her to learn right away, forgetting to explain the finer points of things which were so obvious to a demon of his age. It was easy to forget how the young learn. The other thing contrasting him with

Bezbiel was his subdued personality. He was so quiet in his movements, like a feather drifting on the breeze as his dark robes trailed around the room.

With a wink, Bezbiel pulled her aside one day after her lesson with Zulphas, slipping his warm hand into hers. "You'll get nowhere fast being taught like that."

Bezbiel led her up the old wooden staircase to the observatory, an impish grin on his face. Saiyah faltered, dubious of his intentions, but his demeanour was light-hearted. When he opened the door she saw a room full of telescopes, astrological charts, and brass contraptions of unascertained use. Medea was there, sitting at a desk in one corner which she'd evidently made her own. Shelves full of plant life trailed vines and flowers onto the workspace, which was a mess of soil-stained books, implements which would have been more at home in a kitchen, and a copper pot atop a bunsen burner. Medea herself was pristine aside from a sappy green substance coating her gloves.

"This fine lady is a master of the occult," Bezbiel praised dramatically, making Medea roll her eyes. "Astral projecting can be used for many things–slipping into other realms, yes, but also travelling on *this* astral plane safely, even speaking with spirits of the dead."

Medea rolled her eyes again, peeling off her gloves. "It's a little more complicated than that. Although I understand that for you, it's an ability that comes naturally."

Saiyah blushed. "Yes, but I can't control it."

Medea gave her a dazzling smile. "I'm sure we can change that," she said, surveying her wares. "The coven doesn't want to be plunged suddenly into another realm, after all."

They spent many days together perfecting the art. Saiyah would begrudgingly complete her lessons with Zulphas, biding her time through the mind-numbing lessons, and afterward head straight to Medea for what she soon began to think of as her real lessons. Often, Bezbiel would join them. In each lesson, Medea would induce Saiyah to sleep with various ritual circles and herbal concoctions. Saiyah would enter a shadowy mirror world that was both dark and beautiful, and with a little practice, was able to walk her consciousness down the stairs, meet Bezbiel in his fleshy form at the bottom, and converse with him.

She could step through doors and walls if there was a gap or a crack. She'd always been able to do so, but Bezbiel suggested isolating parts of her body, such as her hand. After some practice, she was able to put her arm through a screen and then make her hand solid in order to grasp an object. Then, she would turn the object to shadow as she did with her clothes, pulling it back to the other side. It was easier to do so while on the astral plane; otherwise, greater wells of energy were needed.

Only once did she feel herself slipping into the hellscape, where whispers and green eyes pursued her.

It was the end of a long day, and Saiyah and Bezbiel were packing up after a lesson. The heat had risen in the tower, making it fragrant with sawdust in the red light. Medea had already left; she was embroiled with outreach projects and meetings with low-ranking officials on the treatment of demons. She was so captivating to look at, and so intelligent, that she was the ideal candidate for such a task.

Bezbiel smiled at Saiyah tenderly and her face became warm. He was ever so attractive and charismatic, but she turned her face away. It could have been his eyes with their slit pupils or the snake-like tongue. Discriminating based on someone's demonic looks was beneath her. No, it was something else that cautioned her.

With careful movements she reached out for his hand, causing him to wear a look of surprise. Carefully she leaned forward, but Bezbiel moved back, floorboards creaking.

"You barely know me," He said.

Saiyah closed the distance between them. "Then let me know you." Standing on tiptoes, she placed her hands on his shoulders.

But Bezbiel pushed her gently backwards. His eyebrows furrowed in reluctant restraint. "I can't," he said simply, and stepped away from her.

S TILL SEETHING FROM REJECTION, Saiyah skipped Bezbiel's lessons over the next few days. Inside the
vast library, satchel over her shoulder, Saiyah navigated
to the recent history section where she usually found
accounts of her mother. There were few texts on her
specifically, but several others regarding the revolutionists made mention of her. They were infuriatingly im-
personal, but despite that, she couldn't help but glance
at them with a kind of wistfulness. They were full of
truths she should've known and learnt as she grew up,
raised by her mother in her homeland. Yet, she still
couldn't be sure of the life she could've had, that had
slipped away from them both so cruelly. The journal
weighed her bag down agonisingly, but she couldn't
bring herself to read it until she was completely alone
and calm.

Scholars from the coven traipsed quietly through the
library or sat studying at tables, green eyes all. Some
were young like her, all skinny jeans and white tees,
while others wore unusual garments and striking, fantastical coats. She was slowly learning that those who
had been to Hell or were born there, adopted the local
attire freely. The librarians had an unofficial uniform of
dark robes with musty embroidery, much like Zulphas.

Just then, Zulphas wheeled a cart full of recently curated and catalogued books through the central walkway. Most were covered in dust, yellowed with age, or smelt strongly of some kind of preservative. As he swept past in his brocaded robes, he nodded to her. She grinned and approached him at a quicker pace. He halted his trolly with a squeak.

"Do you know if I can find anything on the revolutionists or Asramenia that isn't in this section?" she asked, gesturing to the shelves behind her.

The sheepish smile he wore as she approached disappeared, replaced with a frown that wrinkled his forehead, and he narrowed his eyes. Pressing his lips together, he made a hum of acknowledgement.

"You may find them referred to as 'rebels' depending on who the account is from. We keep reports from *The Host's* envoy in Hell, which might mention them as such. But have a care, I doubt the gods would be too happy to know we have them." He gave her a shy but mischievous look, pressing a finger to his lips.

"I won't dream of mentioning it," Saiyah said, smiling back at him.

"Well, I can take you there, but I don't know how much good it will do you, as it's all written in the gods' script."

"That's alright," Saiyah said, remembering to keep her secret. "I'd still like to look. Just out of curiosity."

Saiyah thanked him after he'd walked her to the section in question, and he and his trolly disappeared with a squeak.

The sections of The Host's reports were divided by the century they'd been obtained rather than precisely chronologically. No demon could read their language in order to decipher the exact date.

Saiyah felt an old divine energy in the area. These were their backups, where *The Host* stored their infinite records. Saiyah didn't know where to start. However, in the corner was a single shelf of loose scrolls and odd papers, all burnt at the edges or pierced carefully back together under glass after their attempted destruction. These were the ones *The Host* knew nothing of. The taste of the original apple was in her mouth.

She only spotted the word for 'rebel' in one. It was heavily smoke damaged, and even had what might've been smears of blood, and was browned with age. In a pang of paranoia, Saiyah slipped some of the papers into her satchel to decipher at home. Better not to have them checked out on record. She slipped out of the library, thanking Zulphas as he wrote with his violet-inked quill in the library ledger. Her satchel was weighty with secrets that she itched to discover.

IX

Curious Volumes of Forgotten Lore

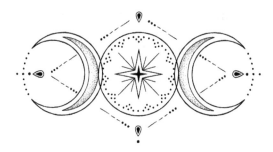

I N THE ALCOVE OF her bedroom where the desk was, Saiyah placed the book Azeldya had given her on the desk and contemplated it for a moment. It was thin, and the inner pages looked like dried leaves. Remembering Azeldya's warning, something about the strange black cover unnerved her. She flicked through the pages of the journal. It was written in New Demonic, and there were only a few pages filled before it ended abruptly with an abundance of blank pages.

The now-open Osiris box lay beside it. One item from the start of her mother's life, and one item from its end.

She'd removed the stolen fragments from her bag and tried to examine them, but the smoke damage was extensive, the writing faded and scratchy despite the language appearing more familiar. Her eyes squinted in the dimming light.

Saiyah lit a few candles and started the fire. The nights were starting to bring frost with them, so she wrapped a blanket around her for good measure and poured a glass of wine.

There was no avoiding it. She'd have to read her mother's journal.

Hemera Selenes, 24. Thargelion, 1585

I begin this account in retrospect, for merely days ago I would never have dared to confess such thoughts or actions for fear they would be discovered.

I walked on the edge of night in the Xalvas tis Nyx, carrying out my daily duties as a sylph maiden, a priestess of Nyx, hunting for lost souls. Their soft, helpless cries were familiar to me as I soothed them to enchantment though darkness and gathered them to the High Priestess at the temple of our lady of night. My father, the overseer, would assess our catch, putting some to work and others to eternal torment.

It was a loathsome job, which I feared on account of my proximity to the gods. Their patrols on the edge of the cosmos were known, and assaults were regular.

As I came close to our borders, I glimpsed the lands to the North, visible only for a few moments in our twilight. It was at that moment that I saw a shining figure walk from the incandescent rays and I took up my bow. He stumbled forth from the grey sand, and I hid, lying in wait to cast a cloud of blinding, soothing shadow over him. Despite his light eyes and golden hair, he did not shine in the way a god did.

Though I be young, I can sense the quality of souls. Some are purer than others, and oft I would see plainly that though all mortal souls that enter our realm are marked to be damned, not all were wretched. His light was akin to a flickering candle, and his soul was the purest I had ever witnessed, and I confess I was afraid. His face was not pale and drawn, but rosy with blood, and his heartbeat was deafening while somehow still light as the wing of an insect. I revealed myself, and he looked at me not with the terror of a mortal soul, but with wonder. He was mortal, and I sensed his goodness. It was powerful enough to bring me to tears.

He swayed and fell before me, and I did so before him, for my knees were weak to see a living human. I knew then two things. I understood what it was to crave souls for power and pleasure, or to yearn for mortal flesh. Most importantly, I realised my own wickedness against his goodness. I had none it seemed, and I pined the loss.

He spoke a language I did not understand, though it was clear he was beseeching me for help. If I took him back to the town, his body would be torn and mutilated for entertainment. He would be kept alive for as long as possible before his soul was ripped from his living form and offered as a sacrifice. My father would always select the purest to offer to the Katomet.

I helped him stand and carried him to a sheltered glade. I gave him our dark waters which restored his speech, and he spoke in my own tongue. He told me his name was John, and he was indeed a mortal. I knew nothing of healing, so I drew my night upon him in the hope he would sleep.

On the edge of the night forest lived Old Moon Face and his child, shunned by the Katomet and therefore by all of this dominion. He often attended to the most severe injuries of the soldiers, and I had once seen him talking with the High Priestess and a group of souls in the temple when he should not have been there. The next day, the souls were gone.

When he saw the mortal he assured me he would tell no one of what I did. He would take the mortal, John, back to the land of the living once he was strong enough. He taught me to attend to him and treat the ails of his fragile body.

As John grew stronger we exchanged tales of our homelands. I was enthralled with the world of the living. He was not afraid of gods or demons as other humans were, he said.

I came home later than usual, and my father was enraged. He told me he could smell a strong, pure soul upon me, and accused me of all sorts of things. I pleaded with him that I had not broken my sacred vows, and my mother entreated him also. He and my brothers dragged me into the square, tied me to the statue of our Katomet, our despot, and had his soldiers take turns flogging me with a whip of scorpions. I was black with blood when Old Moon Face took me to the High Priestess and healed me. I was weakened for days, and the High Priestess warned me I may never heal completely. We confided in her the discovery of John the mortal.

I wanted to see him one last time, to feel his unblemished soul, so despite my weakness, I went to him. He held his rosy hand in mine and promised he would return. I believed he would try, but not that he would succeed.

I was too young to leave the family home, but the High Priestess appealed to the Katomet, and he bestowed his permission for me to live with my sisterhood at the temple. The town watch did not make it easy for me to fulfil my duties. They spat at my feet as I passed, and worse. Knowing my father's dislike of me, they would take the souls I caught and make them suffer before me to see my reaction, but they got none.

On the day of the year that gods were able to peacefully enter for a census of souls, they refused to let me back into the safety of the town. I felt the power of the gods approaching, and I fled to the glade, preparing to spend the night in the hollow of the tree John had slept in.

I awoke to the sound of rippling water and felt the presence of a god. I took up my bow and hid in shadow. I heard my name being called. When I saw a man standing in the water, I knew it was John. He was stronger than the last I saw him, and was able to stand tall without aid, his face rosier than ever. There was something changed within him, and he told me he had stolen fire from the gods, which is why I mistook him for one. He said he wanted to end the war between the realms, and there were many demons who wanted peace, not by way of victory over the gods. What he proposed was revolution.

He asked me to walk with him to the edge of night to prove himself. I was fearful when his celestial essence grew in a way which unsettled me, but he swore he would not harm me. He showed me to an encampment in the dusty plain. Hundreds of demons of all kinds stretched out before me, clustered around red-flame fires. John asked me what other demons within the town they could trust. I told him about the Priestesses of our lady of night, and John instructed me to warn them of their attack. I beseeched him not to harm my mother, father, and brothers. For despite everything, they were still of my line.

I did not sleep that night. After the gods left and were far from sight, bells and screams and the sounds of war carried to us. In the morning, the streets were awash with blood, and I wept freely with the sisters of night as we buried the dead. I crossed the square to the house of my parents. Within I found my mother, lifeless, a bottle of poison in her hands. John told me my father and brothers had been captured. I went to see them, and my father cursed me to death and oblivion. The rebels prompted me to have them killed, but I refused.

I returned to the temple to free myself of the curse before it took hold, and Old Moon Face warned us that the Katomet of Khabrasos marched his army here. The priestesses of night placed wards over the town and sheltered both demons and souls in the temple.

On the steps, I saw a great being in the sky, which paralysed me with fear. I could have screamed, but I was frozen. Below *on the battlefront, John flickered with light hanging on his shoulders like the moon, and I had hope. Though this light only served to discover sights of woe, floating carcasses and brown chariot wheels. Then came legions of yellow-eyed demons of the abyss who battled the rebels and the living mortal.*

The High Priestess gathered us, and we evoked our lady of the night through her, and soon she appeared, stretched over the sky with her body of night and stars, and fought her sibling of darkness.

I saw my father close to the temple steps, and when he spied me his rage was terrifying. He advanced, cutting down my sisters as he cursed my name. My hands trembled as I shot my arrows, but he was not deterred by his injuries. I made to flee but I was caught, and he dragged me by my ankles through the battlefield and rivers of blood. I could not break free. The sounds of war quelled, and he stood before the Katomet, throwing me to his feet. He offered me as a sacrifice to Molek, for though I had no soul, I was still chaste. The Katomet picked me up in his great talons and I felt his ancient power. It was visibly evaporating from his putrid skin as he exerted energy. I was so overpowered that my limbs slacked, and I could barely hold my head. I was gripped tighter and soon blindness fell over me, as I had done so many times to souls. All I could do was weep.

Then I felt John's happy soul nearby, and I was falling. I heard the clash of swords and my father crying out. The power over me released though I was still blind, and I cried out as I felt John's arms around me and the searing pain that came with it. It was as if my shadow was being burned away and my skin withered. I heard his feet drumming swiftly over the bloody ground and he apologised for the pain he caused me. He set me down in a safe place and promised he would return for me, pressing a dagger into my palm. When he left, the pain his bright soul caused me diminished, and though I was blind, I felt my skin was still smooth and unharmed. I shrouded myself in the comfort of my night, but I had never been so fearful of this pure darkness which was now over me, waiting for John's return.

Shuddering, Saiyah closed the journal. She needed a break, and some sleep. It wasn't long before her eyes closed as well, and she drifted off to sleep.

X

The Devil Assumes a Pleasing Shape

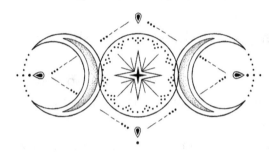

MUCH AS SHE'D LIKE to, Saiyah couldn't avoid Bez-biel forever. In any case, surely his rejection proved he wasn't what everyone had warned him to be? Ahead, there was a crowd of demons conversing much louder than usual in the library. Zulphas stood with a trio of librarians, seemingly trying to pacify the frantic whispers.

She spotted Medea towards the back; her ghostly green eyes were wide as she clutched a book to her chest. Saiyah approached her.

"What's going on?" She tried to peer over the crowd.

"There's been a fire," Medea said, her voice empty. "Just in one section."

Saiyah craned her neck for a better look, frowning. Her chest jolted when she realised she was looking in the section she'd been in yesterday with the gods' records. It was mainly undamaged, but the small area she'd been in with the tattered fragments was black and reduced to dust.

"Do they know who started it?" she said, her voice breathy.

Medea shook her head. "Maybe someone with an aversion to the gods, but everyone is saying it *was* a god. A breach of our contracts."

Saiyah absently put a hand on her satchel where the fragments she'd taken remained and made swiftly for the exit. The reading room was almost empty as she passed back through; everyone was investigating the commotion.

"Weren't you in the library yesterday, Saiyah?" a lightly accented voice sounded behind her. It was Titania, dressed all in black as usual. Today she wore a tunic-like dress which hugged her figure and exaggerated the curve of her shoulders. "I'm sure I saw you in that exact section that's been damaged."

Saiyah couldn't hide the alarm in her face, nor could Titania suppress a twinge of triumph in her gaze.

She tilted her head and stepped forward. "For someone so new to the coven it would be extremely unwise to be causing this sort of chaos. You should admit it if it was an accident. Azeldya and Bezbiel will understand if you couldn't keep your special powers in check." Titania didn't bother to lower her voice, continuing brazenly and conversationally while Saiyah's eyes darted about in panic. Did she know? She couldn't possibly.

There was no one around, but she could see Medea approaching swiftly from within the library.

Titania smiled thinly. "I feel it would only be fair to warn you that other members of the coven might not take the news of a hidden Nephilim amongst us so well." She spoke softly, placing a hand on Saiyah's shoulder. Her mannerism was one of helpful guidance, but her grip was uncomfortably tight.

"That's what you think I am?" Saiyah scoffed.

Her disgust was quite convincing, and Titania's expression wavered. Saiyah tried to shake Titania off, but her grip was firm.

"You're one to talk," came the fierce whisper of Medea over Titania's shoulder. "As a demon with energy associated with fire, surely you must be worried you'll be considered a suspect?" She raised an eyebrow slightly.

Titania's hand dropped from Saiyah's shoulder as she turned to square with Medea. Her expression was one of a naughty child that found their telling off amusing. It was a gleeful grin. Likewise, Medea had a perfectly tailored expression fixed on her face. Serene, yet stern. Saiyah wasn't sure what she was witnessing. If the pair had some kind of rivalry, this was the first she'd heard of it. Titania and Medea were often found arm in arm, gossiping and giggling together, with Xaldan and Bezbiel too. However, Medea always seemed on the fringes of the trio. Saiyah put it down to the age difference.

Titania was the first to crack, her gaze wavering for a moment and her bravado receding.

"I'm just looking out for Saiyah. It would do her no good to be getting into trouble on top of everything else," she said convincingly.

"I can look after myself," Saiyah piped up. Her hands gripped the strap of her bag, and she raised her chin.

Medea's eyes glittered in approval. Titania flashed them an innocent grin before making her excuses and leaving. Medea linked arms with Saiyah and gently pulled her in the direction of the exit.

"Come on. Let's go to the palm house. I have some excellent tea which will calm your nerves." Medea's voice was feather light in contrast to the way she'd spoken before.

Saiyah thanked her but declined. Her hands shook as she left the library. She needed air. Real air. Fresh air. Unstifled by heavy demonic energy. She needed a friend.

D ANIEL ANSWERED THE DOOR with an ecstatic grin, ready to sweep her into a hug, but his face dropped at the sight of her. Saiyah's shoulders sagged, and her lips were trembling before he'd appeared. He drew her inside and held her as she suppressed a sob.

"I'll put the kettle on, and you can tell me all about it," he said kindly.

Saiyah managed a slight laugh through her tight throat.

While Daniel disappeared into the kitchen, she placed the open Osiris box and the letter on the coffee table. Upon his return, he noted it with grim realisation. He read it through carefully, pacing as he did so. When finished, he sat and laced his hands together.

"Before we get started on that," Saiyah said, unable to look him in the eye, "something strange happened."

Daniel was instantly alert with apprehension.

"I was attacked by a scavenger demon from Hell."

Daniel set down his tea fiercely. "What?" he gasped, enraged.

Saiyah retold the events, including her strange night at the embassy. Daniel's jaw was slack. "*Idris* Hezekiah?" he questioned.

"You know him?"

Daniel frowned. "Only by reputation. He's young for a god, and fairly new to the post of captain. His family is powerful."

Saiyah folded her arms to hide her shaking hands. "He talked about Nephilim," she began, to which Daniel scoffed in annoyance. "If I were one, you would tell me, wouldn't you?" she added apprehensively.

"Saiyah, you are anything but monstrous. Besides, a god and a demon, together like that, is unheard of. Taboo." he said darkly.

Saiyah scratched her palms. "Azeldya told me my mother asked for me to be brought to you." She caught Daniel's frantic look. "It was because of the boy you raised before, isn't it? His name was John, right?"

"How can you know so much?" Daniel lowered his head and placed it in his hands, seemingly holding his breath. "It is not an easy memory to recall," he said with a shaky voice. "John Greyson was an orphan taken in by the monks of the cathedral. He soon became one himself, and I took him under my wing. Of course, I didn't teach him in the way I taught you. He was incredibly bright, a scholar, and soon suspected I wasn't mortal. He began to practise the occult after an ill-advised trip to London. After that, he quit the church. Men of science and medicine called themselves 'Wizards' in those days, and he immersed himself in everything from astronomy to alchemy, apprenticing himself under John Dee. He sometimes came to me with his discoveries, hoping I would validate them, and his ambitions grew wilder.

"He said he'd been to hell alive. I believed him; I could sense his soul had morphed somewhat. He talked of the knowledge of 'angels;' he meant gods of course, and was angry with me for not sharing it. He declared he would return to Hell, for he knew he could find 'angels of death.' He showed me his workings, and though crude and baseless I feared his actions, so I took them from him.

"I saw him twice before he died, and in both meetings he was far from the god-fearing child or inquisitive scholar I'd once known. He came seemingly to boast that he'd stolen the knowledge of life. His soul had shifted further to something... *superhuman*, we might say now, as strong as that of a lesser god like myself. He called himself *Prometheus*.

"John said he'd met a demoness called Asramenia, and he was in love with her. I thought nothing of it at the time, as her name was not known to me then. The last time I saw John, his soul was tainted beyond repair, marked for damnation. There was something innately demonic about him." Daniel shuddered."I named you Greyson because I wanted to teach you everything I could to equip you for the realities of the dark world of which you now touch the surface of. I should have done so with John, but I didn't, and that was his downfall." Daniel finished with a shaky breath, and he wiped a hand over his face.

The room was silent aside from the ticking clock in the kitchen.

"That's why the gods had him executed," he whispered.

Saiyah closed her eyes and furrowed her brows. Her heart ached for her godfather. She went to sit on the arm of his chair, draping one arm around him. They held each other for a moment until Daniel was able to right himself.

"Do you think it's possible that I may also have 'stolen from the gods' as he did?" Saiyah asked softly.

Daniel looked up at her warily for a moment before giving a hesitant smile. "No," he said, touching her face. "I don't see that in you."

Saiyah bit her lip and moved away from him. He watched with concern as she removed the moon pendant he'd given her. No sooner had she set it down on the table, Daniel shot up with divine speed, a hand clasped over his mouth.

"What do I do?" she asked in a strained voice. "Is it the same as John Greyson's soul? How do I get rid of it?"

Daniel shook his head in disbelief, angered and distraught all at once, beside himself with woe. Saiyah paced, readying her arsenal of words, screwing her fists.

"Tell me!" Saiyah snapped through clenched teeth. "You're the only person who can help me! I don't want to be executed." She trailed off weakly, her voice breaking.

Daniel slumped back into the chair while Saiyah replaced the pendant.

"I don't know," He admitted. "And yes, it is the same as John's. You're not damned, but there is something changed about your soul."

Saiyah scratched her head patiently, but Daniel was not forthcoming with further answers. "What do you think they'll do to me?" Saiyah hissed. "Hezekiah said he wouldn't tell anyone until he uncovers the truth. Whether he does or not, I wager the outcome will not be favourable."

Daniel took her hand and held it, wordlessly pressing it to his head. Saiyah softened, and slumped down beside him, catching her breath.

"Do you still have the notes you took from John Greyson?" she asked, and Daniel responded with a serious nod. "I'd like to have a look. Perhaps there's some way we can reverse this."

Saiyah and Daniel spent much of the day in the attic of the little house, in which there were a myriad of ancient chests, some crumbling with age and filled with parchment dust and brass objects. Daniel knew which century he was looking for as he dived into one with a Tudor rose carved on the surface. She noted he kept what he was looking for in a sealed box wrapped in what would have been anointed cloth. No sooner had he unlocked it did he set it down on the floorboards.

"I don't wish to look at it," he whispered, his eyes showing the same bewildered fear that Azeldya's had.

Saiyah exhaled as Daniel stood back. The joints were stiff, and she could feel the grit between them as she opened it. Inside were a few loose pieces of parchment, torn on one side where they'd been removed from a book. It was written in early modern English, and was quite decipherable, though it reminded her of studying Shakespeare at school. There were also rough diagrams with flecks of red to emphasise.

Most of the notes were John Greyson's ideas of the 'angel's' hidden power and where it was kept. He was decided that although God was the source of their divinity, the angels themselves carried the secrets of the universe within them. There were theories involving rituals, circle casting, and the use of celestial blood to obtain the knowledge he sought. One note pondered the notion of using alchemy to turn celestial blood to water and drinking it as a sacrament to obtain forbidden knowledge.

It was like the ravings of a madman.

The last page was more concise. It seemed that John Greyson had settled on his method. He spoke of using his master, John Dee's, obsidian mirror in a ritual circle along with celestial blood to transmute the power into him. There were a handful of incantations, all of which were written in what he called 'Enochian,' but Saiyah recognised it as the gods' script. It was remarkably similar to what she knew to be the correct practice of calling the corners, though there were at least two dozen calls here rather than four or five. It wasn't the same as Dee and *Kelly's* usual workings; he'd changed much to suit his purposes, simplifying greatly. If it had worked, Saiyah would be impressed.

The incantations after the calls read:

I call upon thee, Mother Eve, who first tasted the apple of knowledge,
I call upon thee, Watchers, who first taught humanity secrets knowledge,
I call upon thee, Prometheus, who stole fire from the gods,
I call upon thee, Enoch, who walked equal to the divine.
Open the way for me, imbue me with your learning,
Fill my chalice for consummation of enlightenment,
Strengthen my body to hold the divine power,
Lucifer, light bringer, I beseech you.

"You were right, this is highly irrational," Saiyah said once she was done. "I can't see how this could've possibly worked but, may I take these with me in case they provide some clue?"

Daniel waved a hand, happy to be rid of them. "Of course, but promise me you'll show them to no one. Even Azeldya. The consequences of knowledge of this kind amongst demons would certainly find their way back to me, even though it is null."

Saiyah inclined her chin firmly. "I promise."

S AIYAH ADVANCED INTO THE reading room like a storm, causing bewildered looks from other initiates, and dashed up the stairs to the alcove in the gallery. The gramophone was on, as usual, playing Beethoven's Moonlight Sonata. Curiously, there was a Bunsen burner on the table and an odd smell in the air. The room was illuminated by gas lighting and a small reading lamp on the desk lit half of Bezbiel's face.

Bezbiel looked up and his brief look of delight turned to confusion at the sight of her wide eyes and distressed countenance. His hair was tousled from deep thinking, his fingers inky, and his jumper was abandoned on the back of his chair. He swiftly stood, scraping the chair, and walked around the table.

"What's the matter?" he asked, seemingly wary of her.

Saiyah ran a hand over her face. How could she possibly begin to explain? There were things she couldn't tell him, and the whole business with her mother was still baffling. She took a deep breath and surged straight into Bezbiel, knocking him back a few steps as she wrapped her arms around his neck and pressed her body against his. Bezbiel was momentarily surprised but gained his balance and put an arm awkwardly around her. After a moment he pried her away, and she hid her reddened eyes under her lashes.

"Is this about the other day?" he asked gently.

Saiyah scrutinised him.

"The attack, I mean," he clarified.

Saiyah furrowed her dark brows and nodded. Bezbiel led her to a chair so she could sit.

"If you want to talk about it, I'll listen. Or if it's something else bothering you, you can tell me anything."

"Can I trust you?" she asked in a thin voice.

Bezbiel adjusted his footing, leaning slightly over her. He gave her a look of serious amusement. "That depends, can I trust *you?*" he countered.

Saiyah was taken aback.

"It's not that easy, is it?" he said with a smirk. "It depends on what your definition of 'trust' is, I suppose."

Annoyed, Saiyah pushed him lightly. "I don't want to have philosophical discussions in the middle of the night. I just need to know."

Bezbiel moved away, a thoughtful look on his face. He struck a match with a crackle, lighting a set of candles on the table. Then he turned the volume of the gramophone down slightly and walked to one of the bookshelves. He pulled aside a book, revealing a bottle of something golden and two whisky tumblers. He liberated them from their hiding place and sat down.

Saiyah accepted the drink.

"You can never fully trust a demon," he said solemnly. "It's a hard-learned truth. It's in our nature to be deceitful and the like, so I suppose you'll have to make that decision about me on your own."

Saiyah frowned. It was undeniably true that she was deceiving him also. She was unsure if it was because of her demon nature, or self-preservation. She rubbed her head and sipped her drink.

"I can see you are distressed," Bezbiel said. "If you think it would make you feel better to tell someone what's on your mind, you should. I'll be there to listen if you need me to." He caressed her face and brushed loose strands of hair behind her ears. "Now, shall we get back to our books or shall I get us something stronger and do something to take your mind off things?" He smirked.

Saiyah gave a quiet laugh, unable to look him in the eyes. Putting her glass down, she shifted in her seat. "My mother was Asramenia."

Bezbiel lifted his head slowly. "I did wonder."

She proceeded to tell him about her mother's letter, Azeldya's tasks, and her suspicions of future political grooming. She vaguely referred to the journal, but admitted it was unlikely to provide answers on her abilities. And finally, her meeting with Hezekiah and his intended investigations.

As she came to the end of her tale, Saiyah finished the warming alcohol in her glass quickly.

"I wouldn't worry about Hezekiah if I were you," Bezbiel assured her with a grin. "You are protected by the coven, he knows that. And it's very clear to anyone that you're not a Nephilim. How could you be? You're as mortal as any one of us. As for Azeldya, you're likely right. She's been preparing me for political influence in Hell for years. In fact, it's already begun. It's hardly surprising she'd be doing the same for the daughter of Asramenia. You may feel your hand is being forced, but maintaining an alliance between the gods, Hell, and this world is a key part of the coven. Everyone wants peace in Hell."

"I don't even remember living there, but I know I want that too. I yearn for a place I don't remember. Is that not strange?" She half smiled bashfully. "And stranger still that part of me wants to follow in my mother's footsteps. Even after what happened to her."

Bezbiel blinked in surprise, something like fear crossed his face for a moment, but it was quickly subdued. "I'm sure you'd be perfect for it."

A moment of silence hung between them, and Bezbiel reached out and held Saiyah's hand, peering at her with darkened eyes.

Saiyah leaned toward him. Daring him.

He hesitated only for a moment. His lips were soft and warm. Saiyah stood to be closer to him, and Bezbiel slowed her down, but soon he held her as if he couldn't pull her close enough. The feeling of his forked tongue startled, but didn't deter her.

He lifted her jacket off her shoulders. She gently pulled away to stare into his eyes, lips still parted as she took off her turtleneck. Surprised, his hands fell to her hips as she gradually unbuttoned his shirt.

XI

Deceiving One's Self, Deceiving Others

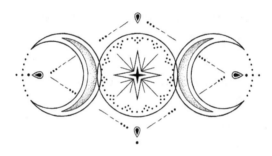

S URREPTITIOUSLY FLICKING THROUGH DANIEL'S tome by
candlelight, Saiyah smiled to herself as she recalled
the previous evening with Bezbiel. He wasn't what people said about him, she'd decided. He could be trusted.
Why else would he wait so long to be with her if he
weren't a gentleman?

She sat with Jack in their living room as they studied.
She stroked the vellum pages carefully as she came to
the end of the catalogue of demons to a section titled
'Demonic Deals and Bargains.' It was largely a caution-
ary tale, and recommended gods not to engage in such
activities where possible, though she raised her eye-

brows at advice on how to go about such matters where necessary. All deals were binding, either through contracts or gestures–anything from handshakes to sacrifices. Only the demon had the power to make and break deals, and they had to be of considerable power to fulfil them. Even gods couldn't back out of a deal once made. It seemed to be their one weakness.

She shook her head and blinked back tiredness, pulling the dripping candle closer and casting flickering light over the pages, she scribbled a few notes.

"Hey," Jack whispered. "Do you want to go with me to Medea's Solstice party?" He paused, adding quickly, "Just as friends."

Saiyah gave him a sceptical look, disbelieving there would be any kind of Christmas celebration in a place like this. "Sorry, no. I'll probably go with Bez anyway."

She reached to pull out her mother's journal, but not before catching Jack's disappointed expression.

"Why don't you ask Hex?" she offered encouragingly.

He made a face of distaste. "I'm not sure. Everyone expects me to go with another new initiate, which doesn't give me much choice."

"How flattering. What's wrong with Hex exactly?" she asked with a hint of amusement.

He grumbled, shrugging his shoulders. "She's... boisterous."

"Oh hell, Jack. Just ask someone else then. It doesn't *have* to be a new member." Saiyah opened the book to where she'd earmarked it to indicate she was busy. "Look, I'll help you with asking her, it'll be fine."

He gave another grumble before returning to his own book.

Saiyah fixed her attention on her mother's journal and began to read:

In the darkness I waited until I heard my name being called. It was John, and I shrank back from his burning soul. He struggled to control it but eventually helped me stand. He carried me back to the Temple where the High Priestess lifted my blindness. Our starry night had never been so bright.

John had been true to his word and had not killed my father. He'd been detained again with my brothers. I went to see them, and gave them the choice between joining us or death. All of my brothers chose death, calling me a traitor and a whore, readying curses on their lips. The rebels swept in and cut the tongue from my oldest brother before he could speak. They were taken to the place where souls were tortured to meet the same fate before death, a taste of their own medicine. I pleaded with my youngest brother to reconsider, he was only a boy. But even he cursed my name, believing the only way to live was on the subjugation of souls. I allowed him a swift death, free of pain.

As for my father, I would not permit him such an easy escape. I had him dragged over the corpses of the town in the same way he'd done to me, and the people threw stones at him. I had no tears for him. He was thrown atop the temple steps for all to see. I had him held down, and I watched as his hands and feet were nailed into the stone. I do not think I cared for his cries, and as I stood over him with an obsidian blade I balefully began the soul ripping ritual which he would have inflicted upon me—a humiliating end.

I dedicated his sacrifice to our mother of night who aided us, a symbolic gesture. As his body was broken and torn, writhing before me, John watched. His eyes were bright and observant, and I felt he was willing me on. Coated in dried blood and slick with it to my elbows, I tore my father's heart from his body and held it aloft for the crowd to witness. His body hung inverted at the gates of our city, entrails falling, and his head was mounted on a spike at the temple.

I was free.

Saiyah paused, placing a hand on her stomach. Saliva filled her mouth and she swallowed, trying to keep the nausea at bay.. Jack glanced at her with mild concern as she stood to get water, blood rushing to her head. Shadow swirled around her comfortingly, and faint whispers reached her ears.

She shook the sensation, forcing herself to stay in her solid form, though she grabbed her coat using nothing but her shadow. It moved as if it were an independent person, placing the coat around her shoulders dutifully.

The lights were on at Bezbiel's house, casting vertical illuminations through the slatted blinds. As she reached the top of the steps, she heard the gramophone playing. Laughter and raised voices sounded from inside. Saiyah wondered if he was having some kind of party–but he couldn't be, he would have invited her. There was something strange going on. She became shadow and slipped through the letterbox with ease.

The large hallway was dimly lit from rooms upstairs. Quietly she ascended the staircase. The voices mixed with deep, leisurely laughter and the odd scream of delight filling her with dread. Glinting charms hung from the above his bedroom door and window frames, and entwined around the bed frame. This room was well protected. It was strewn with exotic artefacts which could have been from Hell or antiquity. Books lay haphazardly about the place with little order. The room was empty, but it smelt of him.

To the right hung a tapestry which had been pinned aside to reveal a hidden doorway.

The door was already half open. Fuelled with jittery malice, she approached it.

People were strewn across the floor, tangled bodies inside a ritual circle. It vibrated faintly with demonic energy, Bezbiel's mingling with the others. The air was salty with sweat. A few participants glanced at her; she noticed Xaldan amongst them. Then there was Bezbiel, kneeling in the centre, malachite in hand like a demonic conductor.

She gritted her teeth at the sight, too angry to say anything. Her throat caught as she gasped.

Bezbiel turned and looked straight at her, an apologetic smile on his face. Saiyah made a disgusted noise and briskly left.

Bezbiel called out for her soothingly. He wouldn't be able to leave the circle quickly. Her head floated as though astral projecting, and she wafted away visions of green eyes and demonic whispers. At the top of the stairs, she stepped headlong into Titania, wearing only her underwear.

She flashed a malicious grin. "I did warn you," she said sweetly.

Saiyah gaped at her for a moment, then pushed her aside and ran from the house, balling her fists and wiping her eyes. She headed to the gateway instead of home, and ambled out onto the cold streets of London. The air was cool and clear despite the tang of pollution, and she breathed deeply as she walked, briskly and aimlessly.

Clutching her moon pendant for reassurance, she faltered. A flash of white above indicated the presence of a god. She groaned with vexation, startling passers-by. They clearly noticed she was a demon from their expressions, but something was wrong. She wasn't wearing her armband. Cursing, she ran back the way she came, rummaging through her bag for the band.

A figure appeared by the entrance of the gardens in a demon slayer cloak. Saiyah's breath caught and she slowed. The hood was thrown back, and Saiyah sighed in relief to see it was Gabrielle. Her arm was outstretched, Saiyah's red armband in hand. Saiyah ran to her and took the armband, hastily putting it on.

"What's wrong?" she asked softly, taking in Saiyah's red eyes and distressed demeanour.

Saiyah couldn't speak. There were so many things wrong. Before she realised, Gabrielle's arms were around her and the goddess was whispering comforting words. She offered to take her home–gods were allowed on the Old Roads only when invited. Saiyah permitted her.

When they reached her house, Bezbiel was lounging at the top of the steps. He sat with his head in his hands and looked up at them like a naughty child. Without a word she marched up the steps, keys in hand, leaving Gabrielle standing dubiously behind.

"Screw you," she said austerely, stepping around him and giving him the finger.

Bezbiel sprung to his feet and tried to turn her about. "Saiyah, please. I just want to talk to you. It's important." His tone made her falter–it was far more serious than she'd ever heard.

"Go on then," she snapped impatiently. "Better make it quick."

He was apparently rattled by her harshness, or perhaps unnerved by Gabrielle watching, fingertips laying lightly on her ceremonial sword as if ready to spring to action. He cleared his throat.

"You have to understand, demons–a lot of us demons are just like this." He gave an apologetic shrug.

"*What?*" Gobsmacked, Saiyah almost laughed. "I can't believe I actually thought you–ugh, just leave me alone." Saiyah turned, opening the door.

She beckoned to Gabrielle, who flitted up the steps and inside the house.

Bezbiel pushed through the door after them and slammed it behind him. Astonished at his unusual intensity, Saiyah stepped back. Gabrielle drew her sword in a flash, an instant reflex, startling both the demons. Bezbiel held up his hands.

"I did–I do like you, Saiyah, more than you know. Please just listen to me." He spoke evenly, no anger in his voice. "Let me defend myself."

Saiyah scoffed. "I don't think there's much to defend. I got an awfully good eyeful of what was going on, thanks."

Gabrielle lowered her sword a little. "What exactly is going on here?" she muttered.

Bezbiel continued. "I was going to tell you. I hoped you might understand after being with the coven for a while. It doesn't mean I like you or respect you any less. It's just a spell, just a bit of experimentation." He spoke passionately now, with sweeping hand gestures.

"I beg to differ," Saiyah responded with a trembling voice, narrowing her eyes. "I see it awfully clear now. Thank you, lesson learned."

The silence rang out around them. Bezbiel was quiet, averting his gaze.

"You should have told me, especially if you think this kind of behaviour is normal," Saiyah added, sadness lacing her voice.

Bezbiel grimaced apologetically. "I'm a demon," he said with a shrug.

"*Half*-demon. Hiding behind that is no excuse, it's childish."

Bezbiel closed his eyes briefly, defeated. He put his hands in his pockets. "I *am* sorry, Saiyah. I hope that you will forgive me one day."

Saiyah gritted her teeth, unable to find words angry enough. He stepped forward, as if he were about to console her. She held her hand up authoritatively, producing a blunt dart of shadow that pushed him backwards to the doorway. He staggered, doubling over and grabbing the bannister to stop himself falling down the steps.

"Just get out," she commanded.

Bezbiel lowered his head, glancing back at her as he contemplated the door.

"You heard her," Gabrielle added smugly.

He scowled and left quietly, closing the door behind him.

The dark hallway rang with silence, broken only by the sound of Gabrielle sheathing her sword.

"Is it always so dramatic amongst demons?" Gabrielle asked, a sense of exhilaration in her voice.

Saiyah shot her a sad smile and shrugged. "Seems so. Have a drink with me."

Gabrielle couldn't stay long as she was on patrol—though she loosely considered this as part of her job—nor would she drink. Sitting on the edge of her bed, Saiyah explained what happened with Bezbiel, to which Gabrielle made all the right sarcastic comments, cheering her up somewhat.

Gabrielle peered at Saiyah. "Is there anything else bothering you?"

Saiyah bit her lip, careful on how to proceed. "There was a fire in the library," she admitted tentatively, gaining Gabrielle's cautious attention. "No one was hurt. Many acolytes think it was the gods, trying to hide things from us. Do you know anything about that?"

Gabrielle parted her lips, shaking her head with disbelief. "No, I don't. And I assure you that if we were going to do anything like that, we wouldn't hide it."

She put a cool, reassuring hand on Saiyah's shoulder, and she felt a tingle of divine energy. It did not burn her in the way Captain Hezekiah did; it was gentle and comforting like Daniel's.

"I think Captain Hezekiah is a little spooked by you," Gabrielle said in her beautiful American accent.

Saiyah began to laugh lightly. "What makes you think that?"

"I've known him since he was a child and I've only seen him treat demons and half-demons in their own respective ways–as a threat, or a professional responsibility. He's confused by you."

Saiyah pressed her lips together, looked quickly to the ground, and made a noise of acknowledgement.

So, he'd been true to his word and kept quiet about her.

Saiyah changed the subject. "How old are you then?"

"Almost one-hundred," Gabrielle admitted, taking in Saiyah's raised brows. "That's not old for a god!" she defended, holding up her arms. "Time runs differently for us–and you, too. Look, I know what you must think about us gods, and yes, the older ones are stuffy and strict, but we're not all like that. Give us a chance."

Young gods, Saiyah thought. The idea of living for hundreds of years, even as a demon, was baffling to her. The concept of childhood for gods, and how they must view things like time and age stretched the edges of her mind. She shook her head and blinked. Best not to dwell on it too much, or she might start to sympathise with the position of a young god like Hezekiah with such responsibility.

XII

That Holy Shape Becomes a Devil Best

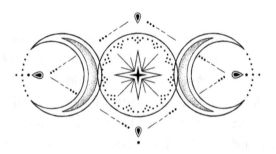

H EX WALKED OUT OF the dressing room in a long black dress with ruffles at the hem and a strapless, sweetheart neckline.

"What do you think? It's certainly sexy, but I'm worried it's too girly for me."

Saiyah poked her head out of the curtain of her cubicle. She looked Hex up and down approvingly.

"I don't think it's that girly. I mean, it's black and gothic with a lace-up back. Seems your style. You look great."

Hex frowned, scrutinising the dress. Saiyah tilted her head.

"Look, it's a formal event," Saiyah said. "Medea's invited all sorts of important people, demon or otherwise apparently. It'll be awfully hard to avoid looking a little feminine. Besides, your boobs look fantastic."

Hex glanced down, concealing a grin. "Come on then, let's have a look at yours," she said to Saiyah.

Saiyah grimaced and disappeared for a moment before opening the curtain, a dubious look on her face.

Hex scoffed. "Judas, that looks like something someone's mum would wear," she said bluntly.

Embarrassed, Saiyah frowned.

Hex sighed. "Let me get out of this, and I'll find you something, alright?"

Reluctantly, Saiyah agreed.

Whilst she'd envisioned ancient pagan rituals, the Winter Solstice Party was actually a rather atheist affair. It was being held at Hampton Court Palace, a little way out of London, so Saiyah arranged to stay in a hotel with Jack and Hex.

It was all part of Medea's grand plan to integrate half-demons into polite society and dispel prejudice by proving their worth. Though dreading a formal event, the idea appealed to Saiyah, and the money provided by the coven was more than enough to cover the costs of Oxford Street.

The outfit Hex picked out for Saiyah was a little more daring than she was comfortable with. It was deep purple, almost black, and strapless with a low-cut neckline.

At the waist it faded gradually into shades of rose, lilac, and misty blue, giving the impression of a dusky sky.

She didn't want to admit out loud that she liked the way she looked, that the beautiful dress contrasted well with her dark hair. Instead she simply gave Hex a nod of approval.

Though she was to be going alone, she started to feel a glimmer of excitement for the party again.

ON THE NIGHT OF the event, her hair was loose but swept back with little braids. She made her way down to the foyer. Jack was already there, wearing a dark suit that was ever so slightly too big, but no less flattering.

"You look rather dashing," Saiyah admitted, greeting him with a friendly kiss on the cheek.

Jack put his hands in his pockets, bashful. "Thanks. You look good too. It suits you. With the whole...shadowy thing," he fumbled.

Saiyah laughed and gave him a nudge. His attention was diverted when Hex came down the stairs.

"Remember what I told you," Saiyah whispered.

He nodded rapidly, taking his hands out of his pockets, which didn't make him look any more relaxed.

Hex had dyed her hair forest green for the occasion, contrasting the glint of red in her eyes. Her hair was curled, and the shaved half of her head had decorative patterns shaved into it. She wore studded boots and fingerless gloves with her black lace dress. Saiyah had to admit, she looked rather striking.

Jack walked toward her, his spine straight and his feet not draggin for once. He offered Hex an arm as she reached the bottom of the stairs. She accepted with a little eye roll.

Saiyah had been to Hampton Court as a child. She remembered enjoying the history, but she'd forgotten how enchanting it was. They gathered in the great hall, a large room with high ceilings adorned with carved arches, stags' heads, and a beautiful stained-glass window. Tapestries lined the walls and decorative flowers cascaded over dining tables. The room was lit with fantastical yellow-gold lighting, and wreaths of holly and ivy encircled decorative candelabras. The hall was full of people chattering, laughing, and clinking champagne flutes. Hex and Jack made their way to the bar. As Saiyah lingered on the threshold, a server walked past with a tray of mulled wine. She accepted one of the glasses, thankful to have something to do with her hands.

"Good evening, Saiyah," a thick and precise accent came from behind.

Azeldya looked striking in a long dark dress covered in gems. It was completely sheer aside from where a few precious stones clustered strategically together. Saiyah didn't know where to look.

"Wow. Well, you look fantastic."

Azeldya thanked her with an effortless dip of her head. "I thought it best to warn you that a handful of gods from the embassy are here tonight. Don't worry," she put in quickly, seeing Saiyah's reaction. "It is not because of you. Rather, it is because of all of us. Here, amongst mortals. Also, if you don't mind, there is someone I'd like to introduce you to later. Would that be alright?"

Saiyah was dubious. She had her suspicions Azeldya's motives had something to do with her mother's influence amongst demons.. But her ancient eyes were black as coal and unwavering as she waited for a response. All Saiyah could do was nod politely. Seemingly satisfied, Azeldya sauntered away.

Saiyah took a breath and absently touched her moon pendant.

Bezbiel caught her eye as he walked into the room, easily recognisable despite his mask. Saiyah ignored him and headed for a seat at the bar. Better to sit drinking alone than to fall into an argument here.

Hex and Jack were standing at one end of the bar, discussing the drink menu. She hopped up on one of the high stools at the end of the bar next to a white-haired demon in a dark suit who was studying his drink closely. He glanced at her as she tried to catch the eye of the bartender, and his vivid eyes struck her. Saiyah made a noise of surprise. She'd not recognised him out of his uniform. His usually windswept hair was neat, yet it still retained a slight wave.

Captain Hezekiah was placid as always. "Miss Greyson" He greeted her cordially, looking from her to his drink. "You look... well."

Saiyah let out a nervous laugh. "Thank you, Captain, that's good of you to say. What are you doing here?" She tried to keep her voice calm and detached as the bar man took her order.

"I am off duty. Technically." He glanced absently down to the sword still at his side. "As an ambassador I am required to attend such events." He spoke grimly, tentatively taking a sip of his drink and recoiling. He abandoned it on the bar counter.

It was apparently the end of their conversation, despite the captain's penetrating gaze. Saiyah glanced around desperately for an available friendly face. There were so many coven members she didn't know, or now classed as Bezbiel's friends, it was hard to know where to go. Bezbiel glanced in her direction again and she swiftly turned her attention back to Hezekiah.

"I can't imagine this sort of thing is your strong point," she said darkly, gesturing to the party.

He agreed with a reluctant grunt.

"I would've thought your lack of emotion and conversation might hinder ambassadorial obligations," She said with a smirk as a drink landed in front of her. She took a sip.

There was a flicker of a response behind his icy gaze. "No worse than your own high words and wanted pride," he countered.Saiyah raised her eyebrows and tilted her head in surprise. The corners of his mouth twitched to something close to a smile.

"How come you're like this while Gabrielle is so... normal?" she asked, goading.He glanced to the far end of the room where Gabrielle was laughing at something Medea had said. In her stunning gold dress, she was the very flower of heaven. "Gabrielle has always been on earth. I've been away for decades. Much has changed."

Saiyah lowered her drink. "When did you first come here?"

"In the twenties," He told her, his eyes surveying the room.

Saiyah noticed Hezekiah's clothes were rather old fashioned, possibly even from that time. Hezekiah glanced at her dubiously. She'd been leaning in to hear his soft voice better, but straightened under his gaze and distanced herself, raising her glass to her lips.

"But what a great time to be here," she continued wistfully, crossing her legs. "So many great artists, poets, *revolutionary* thinkers. I suppose it wasn't the same for you, though. I expect I'm seeing things through rose-tinted glasses."

Hezekiah was quiet for a moment, pensive. "I found it all rather fascinating," he eventually said. He smiled properly for the first time, but it was fleeting. "I should get back to work now. However, I do have something I wish to discuss with you tonight. Off the record. It's regarding your... incident the other night."

Saiyah's body became ten times heavier. "You've made a decision about me then?" she said falteringly.

Hezekiah nodded. "We will speak again soon." Stepping down from the bar, he walked in the direction of a moonlit-haired god dressed in the robes of a healer.

Saiyah managed to find Gabrielle, who was still chatting with Medea, and inserted herself in their conversation. She thought about how Medea had been kind to her after the fire, and she certainly wasn't there that night with Bezbiel. Perhaps she could be an ally in all this.

The two of them introduced her to Sapphira Adriel, a Sergeant in Gabrielle's division of *The Host*. She wasn't as easygoing as Gabrielle, but was more cheerful than Hezekiah. Strangely, Saiyah was happiest with Gabrielle's company over anyone else, though it was unusual to be familiar with a god.

Saiyah's attention wandered to a man whom every-one seemed interested in. He had tanned skin, golden hair, and Atlantean shoulders. His eyes were incredibly pale, and when he smiled, Saiyah noticed his canine teeth were especially pointed.

"That's Malik," Medea whispered to her when she asked. "Not his real name, though. He goes by *Wepwawet* in Hell. He's Katomet of Dualjahit, and somewhat of an international demon in this world." She bit her lip and eyed him up and down.

Azeldya, who was speaking with Malik at the time, beckoned Saiyah over. Medea gave her an encourag-ing nudge and her feet managed to move forward in a somewhat graceful manner. Her billowing gown hid any awkwardness.

"My name is Malik Abnawah," Malik said as she ap-proached. "It's a pleasure to finally meet you, Saiyah. You resemble your mother very much, you know."

Saiyah shook hands but felt like a child being paraded in front of distant relatives. He was easily the tallest person in the room.

"You knew her?" she asked, her interest piqued.

"Indeed. We were close allies. I hope when the time comes, we can count on each other for a similar arrangement." He bowed deeply.

Saiyah smiled politely but kept her distance. He was more elegant and charming than Bezbiel, but must have been hundreds of years old. Perhaps thousands.

Azeldya deterred him from speaking about her mother any further with a wave of her hand, flashing a guilty grin in Saiyah's direction as she did.

When the time comes, what did that even mean? Did Azeldya really expect her to follow in her mother's footsteps? The notion both intrigued and terrified her.

Malik took a card from his breast pocket and offered it to her. "I'll not detain you ladies any longer. If ever you should need me, I have an address in this world." When he raised his glass, she noticed brassy claws at his fingertips.

Saiyah escaped to the toilets after Malik excused himself. As she was blotting her face with cold water, Titania emerged from a cubical and began checking her appearance in the mirror, smirking at her reflection. "Who are you here with? I didn't see your date?" she asked sweetly, diluting the poison in her voice.

Saiyah didn't know how to react. She had to react like a half-demon. She feigned a laugh. "I was going to ask you the same. There are so many people you seem to have come with."

Titania only grinned further, giving Saiyah a pitying look. "Aw, you're so naive. It's normal behaviour for demons. You should try it."

Saiyah clenched her jaw and tried to calm herself, grinning in defiance.

"Have a nice evening," Titania said silkily before swishing out of the bathroom.

Not wanting to encounter her again, Saiyah dawdled through the gallery and paused at the bottom of a staircase, reading display boards. The party sounded in the distance. She wished she was having a better time.

"Saiyah?" came the voice of Bezbiel from behind.

Saiyah glanced at him with eternal temper.

He held up his hands innocently. "Can we just be civil please?" he said briskly.

"I don't think there is anything you can say that'll make this right," she said tightly. "I trusted you."

"Look, I'm sorry for what I did. I really am. It was never my intention to get involved with you in the first place. I had hoped we could move past this. What you saw was just a bit of spell experimentation. It meant nothing."

Saiyah gave him a hard stare. She folded her arms and took a few confident steps towards him. "Did I also mean nothing? I thought you liked me. Judas, what am I saying? I was a fool, wasn't I?" she said, her voice breaking on the last words.

Bezbiel blanched, uncharacteristically sheepish. He opened his mouth, but closed it again quickly, his anguish transforming to his usual suave demeanour in a moment as he leaned on the archway, drumming his fingers on the wall.. "You look enchanting," he said softly before backing away.

Saiyah shook her head and made a noise of disgust.

She continued up the gallery slowly. The walls were covered with red brocade and Tudor paintings. There was a large portrait of Henry VIII beside a fireplace, looking both overweight and majestic. She mentally tipped her hat to the artist. There was a sign overhead stating this was 'The Haunted Gallery.' She knew all about how the teenage Queen had come running through to beg for her life. She'd almost made it to the chapel when she was caught.

Saiyah followed the same route. Patches of moonlight lit her way; the walls became green and the wood furnishings sinisterly dark. She jumped at something at the end of the gallery, ghostly in appearance. Saiyah scolded herself. She was a half demon, or some kind of being with stolen energies anyhow, and she needn't be scared of a ghost. Stepping into the airy night, she continued until she came to the open chapel door. Shadow-like, she stepped into the dark entrance, adjusting her eyes to the gloom. The ceiling was royal blue with gold fixtures, sculptures of cherubs, and painted stars. Flames sparked sapphire for a moment as candles were lit. Saiyah recognised Hezekiah this time, glowing gently with a celestial light–the graceful offspring of heaven. He sat at one of the pews at the far end of the chapel. She walked towards him, her heels echoing. He jumped to his feet and held out a hand.

"Stay back! This is still holy ground!" he warned.

With an amused look Saiyah continued towards him and gave a shrug. "It's alright, Captain. I'm not affected. Why are you hiding in here?"

He relaxed and sat down again. "The small talk tires me. And yourself?" he said evenly.

Saiyah sat with him on the pew, as close as she dared. "A disagreement with another half-demon," she admitted.

"I hope you've not caused a scene," he said, the soft, gravelly edge to his voice returning.

"It's a private dispute," she replied coldly.

The captain folded his arms. They sat in silence. Saiyah scratched her palms, taking in the beauty of the chapel. The captain seemed to be doing the same. He was perfectly still, head tilted back with a serene expression. Saiyah surveyed him; his vivid eyes were captivating. He turned his attention back to her and placed a hand on the pew in front of them. Saiyah saw that he laid his other hand on the hilt of his sword. He drummed his fingers distractedly. "I have decided to overlook what happened the other night. No one saw but I."

"Why?" Saiyah held her breath.

Hezekiah shifted uncomfortably. "You are aware, no doubt, of the relationships we have been building across the realms. Our agreement with the Albion Circle is one example. In exchange for disregarding your...arbitrary surge of power, I ask that you allow me to help you control it."

Saiyah furrowed her brows and leaned back. "That's all?"

"Not all. Much like Azeldya or Medea, I would eventually ask you to act as a representative, aiding relations between gods and demons. Reporting to *The Host* rather than the Circle."

Saiyah lightly touched her forehead. "You're just like her," she muttered with a nervous laugh.

Taking a deep breath, she looked at him head on.

"I don't want to be your spy. I don't want to be a part of any political agendas. Yours or anyone else's. All I want is to know what caused this to happen," She waved her fingers in the air, "and go back to a peaceful, uneventful life where I can read old books and drink wine." She folded her arms, deflated. "What will happen if I don't agree to this?"

"Then I will submit my report of the event. It will be the Elders' decision what happens next."

Certain death.

Saiyah shivered. "If I were to accept, and later decide I don't want to be involved in your political games at any time, what then?"

"Then you would be treated as a threat." He paused to let Saiyah contemplate. "However, since this agreement would be off the record, you have my word that I'll not ask you to do anything that's not agreeable to you." He gave a slight bow of the head and leaned back again. "I do not know exactly what occurred when you exhibited that spark of divine energy. Perhaps it was the sword, as you say. Perhaps it was pure chance, or maybe it was all you. Either way, I can offer you an opportunity for answers."

"I would like to accept," she said haltingly.

"You don't seem too certain."

Saiyah raised her brows. "I have no choice, you know that. The gods being what they are."

He nodded knowingly but reluctantly.

"I have conditions, though."

"Name them," he said, mildly irritated.

Saiyah stole herself. If this was to work, truly work, she'd have to summon both enough demonic energy to create a demonic deal, and little enough for Hezekiah not to notice something was amiss. This would have to be perfect.

"If you want to use me for political gain, I want to be like Medea, not Azeldya. People need to know we are not all monsters," she said earnestly, unable to keep emotion out of her voice. "And I won't do anything I don't want to, as you said. No strict laws imposed or forced hallelujahs."

The captain bowed his head soberly, ignoring her hints. "Very well."

"Just one more thing. I also want access to your library."

He blinked in surprise and almost smiled.

"If you really are going to help me, I want to look for answers amongst your texts. Those are my conditions," she said firmly, holding out her hand. "Do we have a deal, Captain Idris Hezekiah?"

He regarded her distrustfully, and she sensed a tingle in the air around her. It was a test. A challenge.

"You ask a lot. I will agree to your terms and seek permission for access to our library. No promises. I ask in return that you obey the laws of *The Host* while within the walls of the embassy." He held out his faintly glowing hand and smiled thinly. "That is all. You have my word. It is against my nature to lie."

Saiyah faltered as she reached out to him, but set her jaw as they shook hands. She prayed it had worked.

XIII

Wisdom is Earned

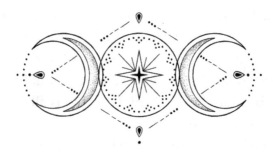

I N A FAR-FLUNG CORRIDOR of the Barbatos building, Saiyah spotted the elusive Azeldya and called out to her. Azeldya turned her head with a flick of her curls. As Saiyah approached, she noticed her odd clothing. It was armour-like, covering her from the neck down, ornate with carved swirling patterns. A mythical crusader of Hell. Beneath, she wore what would have been loose, flowing clothing, and her feet and shins were covered in dust and something viscous that'd dried.

"Hezekiah confronted me about my energies at the Solstice party, and I think I've agreed to something really stupid. I need your help," she said without taking a breath.

Azeldya barely moved. Leisurely, she glanced around to make sure no one was listening. "Come and wait in my office while I refresh myself," she said briskly, then lowered her tone. "You'll not understand yet, Saiyah, but we elder demons have been dying slowly for many thousands of years. I've not ravaged my body with abuse of power like most, but I must be sure not to over-exert myself."

Saiyah frowned in concern, her lips parting slightly. Azeldya placed a hand lightly on her shoulder, leaving a dusty print. "Never mind me. You are young, and I am just an old woman."

Once Azeldya was back in her usual attire, she listened to Saiyah's account of the offer from Hezekiah. She pursed her lips and poured her a dainty, intricately decorated glass of absinthe.

"What he offers may not be so bad," Azeldya said coolly, sipping her drink and crossing her long legs. "It could help you find the answers you seek, about your mother and yourself."

"That's what I thought. That's why I agreed. But I think I'm way out of my depth." Saiyah tested the green liquid cautiously.

"Strictly speaking, the gods are not our enemies," Azeldya said. "Have your wits about you and you may be able to get what you want. You're a demon. Half-demon. Fooling him will be second nature."

"Fooling him?"

"Deny the existence of that energy." Azeldya pointed to her necklace.

"I think it's too late for that. He's quite certain of what he saw. I'm not sure I can do all this." Saiyah sighed, hugging herself. "Is there no way I can get rid of this 'godly' energy? I mean, I'm half mortal. I shouldn't even be able to wield it!"

Azeldya appeared to be pondering something. "You've come across the occultist, John Greyson, in your mother's writings I take it?"

Saiyah nodded, unexpectedly sickened by the thought that she wasn't the only one who had read such a personal account. "Yes. Daniel told me about him, too. He raised him."

There was a flicker of alarm from Azeldya, but she contained it quickly. "I did suspect," she whispered. Azeldya shifted closer and brushed a loose strand of hair out of Saiyah's face. "Take what knowledge you can from the gods about your mother. They will have records; they will know who ordered her death and why. If her betrayer had anything to do with them, there will be a paper trail. My dear, you will be able to do this. You are your mother's daughter. I see that."

Saiyah blushed.

"Be cautious. And show no fear. If you need anything at all, you know I will help you."

*F*OR MANY DAYS WE *were under siege. The rest of Khabrasos cut off our water supply, poisoning it where they could. My hands were full tending to the sick, and Old Moon Face's supplies ran low. What little we had was reserved for our warriors and the rebels, who needed strength.*

John said he would travel North where the muses haunt once again for help, taking groups of rebels with him. The people accused him of abandonment. I had to believe he would return, though our prospects were bleak. I went to him before they departed and told him of my doubts. He said to me, "I returned to you once before, did I not? I will do the same again. We will make a Hell of Heaven and a Heaven of Hell." I said he should return for all our sakes, not just mine. He bestowed his rosy smile and said that I had saved his life, and so he was in my debt. He would return if I commanded it, and I did.

For many days my people suffered at the hands of the Khabrasos legions and their ethereal king of ancient night. Bordering our refuge, they encamped, intent on inflicting their dire revenge. Many souls fled under safe passage of the retreating rebels, and I did not blame them. Every day the priestesses performed rituals to shield the temple and what re-mained of the town, keeping us hidden from our enemies. Our strength waned, as our powers tired and our bodies weakened from lack of water. We made offerings to our lady of night, but she demanded souls, and soon we were asking for volunteers.

One by one we succumbed to weariness, and it was all I could do to stay standing. Only our high priestess, who chan-nelled the night mother through her, remained strong. On the tenth day, the legions broke through. I took the last of my water and drew my arrows with the sisterhood to make a stand.

The heads of our dead were launched back at us, and the sky rained with blood. Great boulders of the void were launched at the temple. The people fled to the underground sanctums and catacombs beneath the city. It was then that many souls begged to expire rather than face the eternal torture that awaited them at the hands of the enemy. I partitioned them not to lose hope, but all promise of aid coming now was lost to them. I consumed two souls as gently as I was able, and watched mournfully as many did the same, unable to refrain from weeping.

The topmost towers of the temple crashed down around me, as it collapsed halfway. My sisters cried out in the patches of void and dust, and I saw the High Priestess fall.

Then a light unlike any I'd seen emerged on swift wings from the abyssal darkness and parted the sky. I squinted as divine beings descended upon us, thick as stars, and I confess I lost all hope, imagining we would all die today at the hands of the gods and their afflicting thunder. But they did not attack the people of Xalvas tis Nyx or the rebels. Instead, they defended us. War waged in the troubled skies, and I wrapped myself in darkness in order to see better, and descended the temple steps. Coming as close as I dared. I joined the battle. They wore dark armour and brightly coloured cloaks, and amongst them I saw fresh rebels with green or gold skin. John's bright essence was there too, standing in a ring of ritual light, unapproached light, commanding a power that was unfamiliar to me but strong enough to stir fear in his enemies.

The battle was won, and to my relief, the shining band of light from the gods diminished somewhat, and most quit the town to an encampment on the borders, leaving us to our own affairs.

I found the High Priestess half crushed at the temple fore-court, holding on to life as Old Moon Face eased her pain, but it was too late to save her. I knelt at her side, and she took my hand, speaking my name. I felt her press something into me and was startled to see the seal of our lady of night. Old Moon Face and the remaining priestesses gasped. She had named me as the high priestess, and I was to be imbued with the power of our lady. It was unheard of for someone so young to take up the position. I was barely fourteen, and there were many other older, equally capable priestesses remaining. I questioned her, but she repeated my name again before slipping away to oblivion.

I undertook the ritual in what remained of our temple, before all who wished to see. A chalice was filled with the clear water of mortality and as the ritual progressed, The waters grew dark with night and glittered with the promise of starlight. The transformation was painful, and when I was ready my nose ran with blood. I took the liquid night into me, and I felt a surge of power like I'd never felt before. I could see everything with exquisite sharpness, and the auras of gods, demons, and souls present were remarkably tangible. I understood now how the high priestess was able to judge souls.

We started to rebuild Xalvas tis Nyx and strengthen our battlements. Rebels came and went with supplies and weapons, and I began to work with John as he and the rebel leaders guided me. They taught me of the lands to the North, which I had been shielded from, and where I would find allies with real armies amongst gods and demons. I was taught the politics of the lands, and perhaps it was the new power within me, but I remembered everything startlingly easily.

John left for the land of the living; he could not explain why, but something in his face denoted urgency.

It is now that I finally feel free to divulge the events of the last few months. I seem to have found myself as the figurehead of this town, and although I still fear we will fall and be punished by the Katomet, it is too late to deny my involvement now.

Saiyah looked up from the page for the first time, allowing herself a sigh of relief. She'd been too afraid to go into the library again since the fire, as the circumstances filled her with unease, but from the reading room she could see the rows of books through the glass pane in the door. From her satchel she pulled out John Greyson's stolen notes and compared them to the ritual her mother had undertaken. He had been present that day; surely there was no coincidence in the similarity.

If her mother was able to gain heightened powers from Nyx, and John Greyson was able to acquire divine energies, there was no reason why she wouldn't be able to rid herself of them. After all, he'd only been mortal, and half of her was of demon blood.

When Saiyah reached home, she made sure the latch on the door clicked quietly. Shedding her coat and scarf, she took a knife and a wine glass from the kitchen and headed upstairs. She passed her room and continued to the top of the house. Jack's bedroom door was open, but there was no light from within. Tell-tale noises of passion drifted toward her from Hex's room.

She continued upwards to a door that emerged directly onto the roof. The space was taken up with an overgrown greenhouse with thin layers of grime across the fragile glass. As she stepped inside, the smell of warm, damp air and an earthy bite enveloped her. Setting her bag down, she took one of the rods leaning on the shattered panes and reached up to open the windows, letting the cool night air flow through. She cleared a space and took her materials from her satchel. She didn't have anything like a malachite wand or obsidian athame, but she hoped a piece of chalk would do the job of drawing her circle.

She called the corners as she had seen Bezbiel and Zulphas do many times, and felt a pleasant buzz of demonic energy envelop the space. She knelt with her effects scattered around her and checked John Greyson's notes again for direction.

Saiyah steadied her breath and held the kitchen knife against the tip of her thumb, whispering a count to three. She counted multiple times, too anxious to make the cut.

"Oh, for goodness sake," she muttered, finally bringing herself to pierce the skin as she scrunched her eyes.

Wine dark droplets fell into the glass and splattered around it. She shuffled back and drew a spherical, alchemical symbol into the dusty concrete. John Greyson had favoured the symbol for the sun, and fire, so she did the same. He'd used a symbol which she recognised as 'to take.' She tried to recall her historical alchemical symbols, unsure if there was such a thing as 'to give.' Saiyah settled on 'to distil,' and flipped the page. There were markings for a symbol of the moon and night, but knowing her true nature, she decided against it.

Saiyah brought the wine glass closer and balanced it between her knees, starting her version of the incantation.

"I call upon thee, Mother Eve, who first tasted the apple of knowledge,

I call upon thee, Watchers, who first taught humanity secret knowledge,
I call upon the, Prometheus, who stole fire from the gods,
I call upon thee, Enoch, who walked equal to the divine.
Shut the way for me, drain me of your learning,
Empty my chalice of enlightenment,
Abate my body to abandon divine power,
Lucifer, light bringer, I beseech you."

A surge of energy swelled within her, and the chalk markings she'd made flared purple—not like fire, but an aurora. Her insides crawled, as if there were a creature struggling to get out, clawing against her stomach and up her throat. She clasped her neck as a metallic taste filled her mouth and swiftly pulled the wine glass to her lips. The thick pearly blood of a god slipped out, mingled with a few swirling droplets of her own. She gasped with delight, grinning as she wiped her chin. She took a breath as the shock from within quelled.

The energy in the circle was vibrating at a higher frequency now, and she grabbed the chalk again, ready to end the ritual. Her hand flew to her stomach, and she grumbled painfully. Lifting her torso straight, her mouth filled with saliva in preparation for another purge of celestial blood and energy. The eruption was more violent this time, and far more of her own blood came up with it, overreaching the glass and splattering the concrete.

Her fingers trembled and throbbed unnaturally. Looking down in shock, she saw dark red blood seeping out from under her nails. The energy frequency climbed, and she reached for the chalk, slipping on the loose sheets of paper as her body convulsed, doubling over onto her hands as she retched more blood. It was all she could do to collect the journal and notes, marking them with bloody fingertips as she stashed them atop her bag.

Saiyah held the chalk with unsteady hands. The tip of it had snapped off, but she carried on with the closing of the circle. As she spoke the words, barely able to hold herself on her elbows, her throat burnt hot, and her organs boiled with tortures profound. More convulsions, more vital fluid and bile. Her eyes welled and she fell on her side. Her head prickled with pressure and blood spots marked her vision.

Darkness engulfed her. Green, ghostly eyes appeared with frantic whispers. Saiyah let them take her, easing her pain. The darkness grew clearer, and rays of something like moonlight pierced though, glinting with disastrous twilight. Impressions of shadowy trees and a reflection of water appeared. Shades of death in human form showed vaguely through the distant trees, and a figure stood before her, motionless as a painting but flickering at the edges. Long blue-black hair, seeming impossible in nature, cascaded around her like a dark veil. Her skin was a stronger hue of purple than her own.

She knew it was her mother. Saiyah felt a mingled sense of terror and sadness at her dead eyes, shining like tiny stars in her face.

Asramenia opened her mouth to speak, a chilling form of demonic spilling from her lips, cold as clay. Saiyah barely had time to make any sense of it before something alerted her to a movement in her physical form.

Through the haze of violet energy, two faces peered at her, frantic and aghast with fear.

"I'll get help!" Jack called as loud as he cared over the din. His clothes fell from around him as he seemingly melted into the floor, a great-beaked raven emerging.

"Wait!" Hex shouted, holding a hand out to stop him. "Get Bezbiel. Azeldya will skin us all alive!"

Jack gave a bob of his dark feathered head before taking off from the rooftop.

Saiyah was barely conscious as Hex reached through the circle with a cry to grasp her hand. Visible energy erupted from the break like a heatwave. Eyes clenched, Hex heaved Saiyah from the circle, getting to her feet and pulling with both hands when she was far enough out. Hex fell back, Saiyah's arms flopping over her legs.

There was a thundering of footsteps on the stairs, and Bezbiel clattered through the door onto the roof. Jack followed, naked and covering himself with a pair of unwieldy wings which trailed across the ground.

Bezbiel assessed the situation with panicked eyes, darting from Saiyah to the well of energy. Impulsively, he stepped forward into the circle, malachite in hand, and uttered the usual incantation of closing the circle.

Three blurred figures hovered over Saiyah before her consciousness faded.

XIV

Tis Magic That Hath Ravish Me

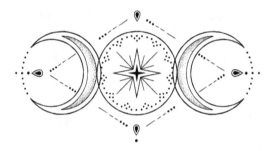

S AIYAH WOKE, HER ROOM overcast with soft pinkish
light. The smell of smouldering wood filled the air
and white-hot ash crumbled in the fireplace. Her body
was uncomfortably dry and stiff as she rolled over. She
groaned inwardly when she saw Bezbiel in her library
alcove. He sat at her desk, his head propped on his
arm, dozing. Beside him was a corked bottle filled with
silvery liquid. Her open satchel was at his feet.

Gritting her teeth, she grappled to her feet as if escap-
ing sleep paralysis. Hobbling over in her nightgown, she
gave a gasp close to a sob at John Greyson's notes and

the fragments sprawled out before him. She steadied herself on the edge of the desk.

"Saiyah?" he asked, making her flinch as the ringing silence broke. He stood and guided her to the chair. Disappearing for a moment, he came back with a glass of water. "Here, you've been sleeping for days."

Saiyah clutched her mother's journal to her chest, scowling, but gulped the water all the same.

"I didn't look," he said softly. "This, however..." He indicated the notes. As his fingers brushed over them, the gold glint of her moon pendant surfaced.

As if possessed, Saiyah grabbed it.

Bezbiel leaned on the desk and rubbed his hand over his face, then looked up at her with his mouth covered. "What on earth do you think you're playing at? You've no idea how to handle the occult yet, especially on that level! Look what you've done to yourself! I'll have to tell Azeldya and Zulphas, you realise? You'll probably be kicked from the coven, but at least you'll be... normal again!" He made wild gestures as he spoke.

Saiyah looked down at herself, touching her arms lightly. "Normal? What's wrong with me?" she said with alarm.

Bezbiel waved his hand up and down at her. "You've got a weird energy about you." His voice softened and he looked back to the blood-stained notes. "What were you actually trying to do?"

Saiyah closed her eyes with a rushed exhale. "It didn't bloody work," she muttered under her breath. "I was like this before. Azeldya already knows. I was just trying to get rid of it." She set down the book and placed the moon pendant around her neck, masking the 'weird energy'. Looking up at him, she bit her lip.

Cognizance lit in his eyes. "Sweet Judas," he breathed. "Why didn't you ever say?"

"I don't see why I should tell you anything if you'll not have the same courtesy to me," she said maliciously.

Bezbiel scowled. "I've heard you're spending a lot of time at the embassy lately. Has that got something to do with this big secret you couldn't tell me?"

"Yes," she said fiercely, collecting her things and walking into her room.

Bezbiel's footsteps echoed behind, and she sighed with frustration. Bezbiel paused, considering his next words carefully. He pointed his chin to Daniel's tome.

"As long as you're not going to be killing demons for them."

It was a poorly concealed joke, and Saiyah knew him well enough to tell there was a seriousness to it.

"Of course not," she said dismissively, blocking the doubt from her voice.

"*Can* you tell me what's going on then?" he said, holding his hands out, shaking slightly. "Azeldya said to keep an eye on you while she's gone and I'm doing a poor job, so just forget about any ill feelings you have for a moment and assure me you're alright?"

Saiyah rubbed her temples. "Honestly, I don't know myself. I can't begin to wrap my head around it all." She sank onto the bed. "My mother was murdered, I've had this strange thing–energy–since I was attacked. I performed god-like abilities, on one occasion anyway, and as it turns out I'm not the first person my godfather knew who was able to do so." She waved John Greyson's notes in front of his face bitterly.

Bezbiel knelt, his hands trembling, sweat forming on his brow. "Alright, alright," he said as if assuring himself, taking her hand. "We need to speak to Azeldya. Once she returns, I'll organise a meeting, okay?"

Saiyah agreed weekly as he stumbled to his feet.

"I take it the fire in the library had nothing to do with you?" he asked dubiously, nodding towards the encased fragments.

"No!" Saiyah defended; her face flushed with irritation as she pulled her hand away.

He held his palms up defensively as he stood. His eyes flickered erratically, and he rubbed his brow. "What do they say? The pieces you took?"

"I don't know. They're so damaged I can only pick out odd words."

Bezbiel hummed. "I have to go now," he said abruptly. "I'll send Hex up." There was a tremor in his voice, and he was unstable on his feet, grasping the door frame as he left.

S AIYAH CLUTCHED HER STOMACH as discreetly as possible, making it seem as if she were just clasping her hands together. She felt toxic. The headiness of the ritual still lingered on her as she entered the Embassy of the Gods for a third time. She began to wonder if the half-moon pendant would conceal any lingering energy or not, but Hezekiah's intense stare nearly made her stop in her tracks.

Her presence in the foyer with its marble interior and towering pillars caused a few glances from passing elegant beings, but it was nothing like his accusatory look. As if he'd been waiting for her, the captain unfolded his arms and made his way straight towards her. Saiyah wasn't particularly tall, and neither was Hezekiah for a man, but he was still a head above her. Keeping his distance, he peered down at her imperiously.

"Follow me," he said, turning on his heel.

They walked down the passage he'd taken her before, the same way she'd followed on her registration day. For a moment she thought they were heading to his office, but there was another discrete door which looked as though it shouldn't be leading to the outdoors, but it did.

She squinted in the unnaturally strong sunlight. The trellis of vines above did little to shade her, and lilac flooded to her exposed cheeks. Stepping off the veranda, she was met with a path that led more or less directly to the Ambassador's residence, winding under abundant apple trees. Saiyah half-ran to keep up with his brisk strides.

"If I have to come here often, won't your men start thinking that strange?" Saiyah asked, already wondering if she shouldn't be accompanied by Azeldya or another coven member.

"I have a system devised for that," he retorted without looking over his shoulder.

Once inside, Captain Hezekiah seated her in his study, not at the chair adjacent to his desk as before, but in one of a pair of grand armchairs of teal velvet and gold embroidery. Between them was a small table with a tray containing two ornate cast iron teapots and two cups. Judging from the steam, it was piping hot, as if someone had left it for her exact arrival.

Without asking, the captain began to pour her a cup.

"Why do you have a different one?" she said, unable to stop her voice revealing a sliver of fear.

He looked up at her for the first time since she'd arrived. His expression was one of astonishment, almost as if he were offended.

"What do you suspect me of?" he asked calmly.

Saiyah clenched her teeth, searching for an answer.

"I meant what I said. And I assure you, I mean you no harm," he told her pragmatically. He poured from his own teapot, which produced a watery lime green liquid smelling aromatically of mint. "Now, to business. I'm sure you are wondering what will happen here, exactly."

Saiyah nodded, carefully lifting her cup. The hot liquid burnt her tongue, so she swallowed quickly and winced as it hit her tender stomach. Either the captain didn't notice, or pretended not to.

"First and foremost, I want to encourage your unusual power to emerge again," he said tactfully. "I have also spoken to Azeldya, your mentor. She refrained from informing me how she is currently mentoring you. I understand she is not encouraging your familial power directly. Correct?"

She nodded again.

"In that case, we will be partly working on this also. You will need to know how to protect yourself."

"What will I need to protect myself from exactly?" Saiyah asked, tilting her head to one side. "If you're planning on sending me into conflict zones in Hell, I've already told you I'll not be your spy."

"That is not what I'm speaking of, Miss Greyson. You know that very well. I have also asked for you to have access to our Library, as requested. That request is being processed."

Saiyah refrained from rolling her eyes. Ruthless bureaucrats.

He finished his tea and turned his heavy armchair effortlessly, so he was facing her squarely. "Let's begin. It may help if you close your eyes."

Startled, Saiyah put down her cup and did as he said.

"Try to picture your power in your mind, and then find it physically within you." His formless words drifted to her ears, seeming calmer without his intense stare and frowning brows.

He'd be much improved if he just smiled.

"Concentrate," he whispered, as if sensing her distraction.

Saiyah swallowed and tried to do as he said, but grunted in frustration as she flickered into shadow form. She opened her eyes to gauge his reaction, but there was none. He was statuesque.

"Can you remember how you did it before?" he asked.

"I would have done it by now if I did," she said patronisingly, earning a weary look from him.

Wordlessly, she tried again. And again. Each time, she only touched upon her familiar shadow ability. To her relief, she wasn't chided for it, though she became increasingly worried she'd slip into that shadowy realm once again. How would Hezekiah react to that? She was feeling increasingly nauseous, but the captain didn't seem to tire, and only patiently urged her on. Only when she couldn't take it anymore and was about to protest did he speak.

"I think that's enough for the day," he said simply.

The door to the study flew abruptly open and Gabrielle entered, carrying a pile of documents and folders, speaking rapidly in the gods language about reports that needed filling in. Hezekiah stood quickly, turning to her.

"Saiyah!" Gabrielle exclaimed with a smile. "What are you doing here?" She glanced uncertainly at the captain.

"Miss Greyson is here on business on behalf of the Albion Circle," he swept in quickly, strolling over to take the pile of papers from his assistant. He set them on his desk. "That will be all, Remiel."

Gabrielle nodded respectfully and made to leave. She cast one more uncertain glance at Saiyah before closing the door.

"Don't mind her," he said, leafing through the files. "I'll speak to her directly if she raises any questions."

"It sounds to me as if you're bending the rules quite a lot to help me," she remarked.

With his back still to her, the captain hesitated for a moment as he handled the papers, but continued without comment. He strolled to the other side of the desk and sat in his seat, almost as if forgetting her presence.

"When can I use the library?" she said bluntly.

He glanced at her briefly while scribbling notes in god's script. "Once you have permission, and whenever I or Gabrielle have time to escort you." He said it flatly, but there was unspoken thunder in his voice.

Saiyah huffed. "I'm happy to go alone."

He chuckled scornfully. "You will need one of us to translate." Her eyes darted around irritably. She stood and walked closer to the desk. "Well, can't I just take a look?"

"Absolutely not, you are restricted from going any-where outside of the residency without an escort," he said harshly, thrusting a piece of paper at her. "This is your record for the day. I will need you to sign it."

Saiyah examined the piece of paper and the fountain pen before her. It was a simple but factual account of their meeting for the day. "A bit risky, isn't it? Leaving a paper trail?" she said with a smirk.

He ignored her. "Wait by the door, I'll have Gabrielle or one of the men collect you. Don't forget to sign yourself out." He got up from his seat and turned his back on her, filing something in the cabinet behind.

She put on her coat with defiant, hurried movements. "What about outside the embassy? Is it still necessary for you or your men to follow me? Because I find it *very*–"

"That is quite enough. I've better things to do than an-swer your childish questions," he said, raising his voice.

There was something delightfully demonic in rattling someone so pious. Saiyah glared at him, but lost her nerve as she glanced at her satchel. Grabbing it from where she'd left it, she gritted her teeth and made for the door.

"Miss Greyson," he called to her, his tone calmer.

She swore under her breath and rolled her eyes, turning around with a daring swagger.

He was statuesque as he spoke, but at least he was looking at her properly. "You are a liability until proven otherwise. So, yes, it is necessary. You may go."

R ETURNING HOME, SAIYAH DROPPED her things at the foot of her bed and lay on the soft sheets. Something incongruous caught her eye: a small cardboard box on her nightstand. There was a note on top.

This should help with your translating, I've done the workings already, but it'll fade in a few hours, so move fast.

Bez

Saiyah opened the box to find a perfectly ordinary-looking whiskey tumbler inside. Turning it over, freshly carved sigils had been scratched around the sides. There was a flash of green as she looked through the base, and realisation dawned on her.

Rushing to her desk, she frantically searched for the stolen fragmented texts. Seemingly of its own accord, her shadow gently lifted loose scraps of paper written in subtly-improving New Demonic. Then she located what she was looking for. Her heart raced as she placed the glass over the fragment from the library. The charm on the glass made the age and smoke damage lift away as she gazed through it. It wasn't perfect, as the missing paper from where it'd torn didn't rematerialise, but it was vastly improved.

They were all dated at least ten years ago, most a little longer. Some documents detailed events where gods posted in Hell had behaved less than admirably. The notion caused a smug smile. There was mention of rebels, and collaborative efforts with gods on some campaigns, as well as records of plans to abandon some of them. Clearly, the relationship was more tenuous than the gods let on. She came to a text that was torn to ribbons, but lovingly reassembled by a dedicated acolyte, though not in a coherent order. Fragments of it were pierced together, forming odd words, but there was very little clear.

Then she spotted it: *'The Katomei of Khabrasos,'* which surely was her mother. *'Secrets,' 'stronghold,' 'relations,' 'portress of the Hellgate,' 'dubious battles,' 'execution,'* a string of words in consecutive sentences that made her heated, but not nearly as much as the final corner of the text.

'Life form... dying since they fell... attaching themselves to humans... further their line.... Parasites... tolerable. Womb of uncreated night... child of chaos, eternal night and the divine...'

With the rhythm of her pulse sounding in her ears, Saiyah froze, petrified. She glanced at her mother's journal and swore. Despite the four-hundred-year separation, she'd begun to suspect John Greyson might somehow be her father, but this confirmed it. It had to.

Flicking through the tattered, water-stained book, she searched for something helpful her father may have written.

Father.

How strange that word sounded even in her mind. The idea was unsettling.

Most of the rituals were basic, and the book was primarily notation rather than full instructions, as if this was from earlier in his life while he was still discovering alchemy and the occult. However, his ambitions and experimental methods shone through.

Saiyah laid a hand on her mother's journal and slid it towards her, accepting the heavy sensation within her. She found where she left off, and skimmed the details on the prosperity of Asramenia's tenuous rule over the city. It was cold, factual, business-like. There were intermittent battles and raids where the number of casualties and prisoners were listed. Was this the life Azeldya hoped for her also?

She stopped as the body text suddenly cascaded continuously over pages, and caught the name 'John' in the first line.

Hemera Areos, 19. Hekatombaion 1585

John and his men returned to us. He needed to stay for longer than usual for replenishing rituals. A living soul in this land tires easily, and his strength was sapped. When I asked John about his curious power, he would not tell me in full. He said it was something of the divine, infused with 'magic' found in the land of Albion, where he was from.

He asked me to aid him with a ritual of his own devising, and asked for a place where he would not be disturbed. Something of the desperation in his voice afeared me, but I was curious. I took him to the depths of the temple, where he insisted on bringing a torch to light the way. I found I did not mind the darkness so much, though the fire dazzled me.

He asked for my aid in the incantation, and I had no reason to refuse. I did not expect, however, that his power would be so great, and I felt its true force swell through me. The incantation was potent, and it was all I could do to stand before him. When John closed his fist around his blade and sliced his skin, it felt intoxicating. Ruby droplets fell on the dark stone, and his strength grew evermore.

Afterwards, I was not weakened, but I was breathless, nonetheless. We sat together in the lonely, darkened corner of the temple. John drew close to thank me, and took my hands in his. His eyes were blue as twilight, muted in the flickering flames. He told me he had also felt my power, and although strong, it was as gentle as the wing of a night moth.

He became humble, and asked me if I would aid him in another ritual. This one was not to replenish his strength, but to allow it to grow stronger than that of a god. I recoiled, not at his tone but because of the way he looked at me and played with my hair in his hands. He showed me his workings, and I drew closer again, fascinated by the capability of his mind. What was depicted shook me to my core. I couldn't imagine a man with this goodness in him contemplating something so excessive and unusual. The methods were harsh, and reminded me of the ways of the Katomet. It would surely damage his soul. I saw what he required of me, and I trembled.

He told me he would need the help of any demon for what he desired, but he wanted it to be my aid he received. I told him no. I had made an oath as a Priestess of our lady of night, and I could not make this unhallowed union with him.

He softened, and my John came back to me. He helped me to my feet and whispered sweet things about when he first laid eyes on me. I couldn't deny my equal adoration, but I was sure his strange energy was affecting me again. He bowed low, apologising for his forwardness.

Hemera Aphrodites, 22. Hekatombaion 1585

I had contemplated John's words for a long while. I spoke lit-tle to him apart from when we held meetings with the warriors and made our plans. I cursed myself for the way he made me feel. I was the High Priestess, and yet I craved another tender look from him.

On the eve of his leaving, I went to him in the courtyard and pulled him aside. I agreed to what he asked, if indeed I was the only one he trusted to help, although I implored him to wait a while, for I would not be of age for over a year. He kissed my hands and my forehead, promising to come back to me once more.

Saiyah slapped down the book with a face of disgust. Her hands trembled, and her eyes filled with tears. She'd had a growing dislike of John Greyson for a while. Now it was confirmed. She hated him. Surely this couldn't be her father. Tears threatened to fall. She took a swig of wine to quell her rising discomfort.

XV

Monsters, Cut Off From All the World

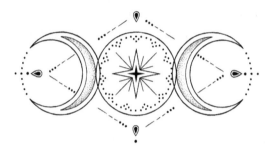

S ESSIONS WITH HEZEKIAH CONTINUED much as they had done the first day. No progress was made in uncovering her god-like power, and still no library permission. Saiyah even wondered if her disastrous blood ritual had worked, and that part of her was completely gone. She still suffered the effects of that night. Her stomach hardened after eating or drinking too much. She ate less and less, but continued to drink. Demons didn't need to eat in the same way mortals did, Bezbiel had told her once. It was the same with sleep. Perhaps it was a natural change rather than just lingering symptoms of a botched ritual.

It had been weeks now, and January slowly wound by uneventfully. She kept to herself, acting as more of a hermit than Jack. She craved to speak to Azeldya, who was once again conveniently absent. Surely, she'd read her mother's journal already though, and therefore knew of John Greyson's despicable act. She didn't know about his notebook, though.

One morning, Gabrielle left her safely inside the residency with a delicate squeeze of her hand. Saiyah had mentioned a stomach complaint when Gabrielle had shown concern over her fragile half-mortal countenance.

The door closed, and she collapsed on an armchair in the hallway below a rack of spare cloaks. Nursing her stomach, she heard the faint sound of voices. One was undoubtedly the captain's. She slipped into her shadow form, walking as a bluish spectre with swirling violet. The door to Hezekiah's study was open, and she drew back when she saw Sergeant Adriel, the one whom Gabrielle had introduced her to at the Solstice Party, standing on the other side of his desk.

"What about her?" Hezekiah's placid voice carried through.

"She unnerves the men. Some have complained that her energy troubles them," Adriel replied.

There was a pause. "Tell the men if they are afraid of young half-demons, then perhaps they should consider a more suitable profession. Is that all?"

Adriel hesitated. "Sir, I request to know why she is here so often. Is she here in Azeldya's stead?"

"Miss Greyson visits here on behalf of the Albion Circle. Our business is confidential. Is that clear?"

"Yes, sir," Adriel said briskly, leaving the room with swords rattling as she marched.

Saiyah pressed herself against the wall and Adriel slowed nearby her, glancing around suspiciously. She shook her head with a shudder and moved on.

Once she was sure the Sergeant had gone, Saiyah materialised again and appeared sheepishly in the doorway of the study. She clutched her satchel protectively.

Hezekiah had his eyes closed but opened them instantly when she took the first step inside. Saiyah scratched at her palms. He gave her a slight nod in greeting, the closest she'd ever gotten to a 'hello' from him. The conversation she'd clearly overheard was not mentioned. Without a word, she unburdened herself from her bag and left it on the armchair by the windows. She'd gotten used to the captain's odd pauses and silences by reminding herself that time passed differently for gods. She'd first encountered him about six months ago, but did half a year feel like the same length of time to him? Probably not, if what Daniel said was anything to go by.

"The energy I sensed within you that night has diminished. I'm going to perform the test from your registration to coax it out again," he explained calmly.

Saiyah hopped back as he stepped out from behind his desk. "I do *not* want to do that again," she said firmly.

"It wouldn't be as invasive. The fact remains that after all this time, you still haven't mastered something a child can do with ease." Hezekiah began to draw his sword.

"Hold on, hold on! You promised me I wouldn't have to do anything I didn't want to," she reminded him. "Does the word of a god mean nothing now?" She forced herself to wear a triumphant smirk.

He stopped, regarded her flustered face dubiously, then let his sword slide back into its sheath. With poorly concealed irritation, he beckoned her to sit. Tentatively, she did so, watching him carefully as he resumed his position opposite her.

"What's changed then?" he said frustratedly.

What had Azeldya said? Something about fooling him into thinking she had no godly energy within her, but that was getting her nowhere. Besides, she wanted to know the truth.

Saiyah unsurely tapped her moon pendant, and he offered a quizzical frown. She took it off. Hezekiah's perpetual frown softened, and his shoulders relaxed.

"Very good," he said, clearing his throat and closing the distance between them. "Run through the exercise again."

Hesitantly, she closed her eyes. It took her a moment to relax as she tried to forget Hezekiah's impossibly blue eyes watching her. In a flash, there it was—a tiny white spark in her mind. Shocked, she recoiled and opened her eyes. He was right in front of her, much closer than usual.

Hezekiah withdrew a hand he'd been holding close to her face, opening his eyes at the same moment. His shock mirrored hers, but he swiftly nodded in satisfaction.

"One more time." He tentatively held his hand up again.

Closing her eyes, she saw it in her mind's eye. It was brighter as Hezekiah's own energy brushed against hers. It didn't make her flinch this time. There was no static or friction, just synergy.

"Now, let it come to your fingertips."

Her hand was gripping the edge of the table. She let her fingertips loosen, and soon they felt warm. She opened one eye. Hezekiah was no longer leaning close to her, but there was a faint silvery light emitting from two of her fingers.

"Well done," he said sincerely. Then he leaned back in his chair and folded his arms. "Do you know why you have the power of a god within you?"

Saiyah blinked rapidly. "No. Do you?" She countered as smoothly as she could manage, worried her heart might burst from her chest. Surely, he would hear her heart pounding in her chest. Gods knew that sort of thing, especially if he was as powerful as Daniel had let on.

With other-worldly grace, Hezekiah shook his head dismissively and unfolded his arms. "You've been granted clearance to our library," he said simply.

"Really?"

He gave her a baffled look. "Of course. Collect your things."

In a moment he was standing by the door and waiting for her, whilst she could only stare in dumb shock. After a second, she grabbed her bag and remembered to place her pendant around her neck again.

How very convenient that she'd be granted access on the very same day she displayed some divine energy, she thought. Or perhaps it was the removal of her pendant that'd won his trust. Either way, this was the start of her search for the truth, the real truth.

The library space was somewhat monastic, comprised of pale stone with squat columns at the perimeter which held vaulted domes of ceiling. In the centre, the pillars rose, not quite to the grandeur of the foyer, but high enough to be simplistically impressive. Diagonal sunlight seeped through, warming the room despite the dim January weather.

Between the pillars, Saiyah could see shelves of wood and stone. They were widely spaced out in the centre where gods walked reverently past the slots of scrolls and shelves of weighty tomes. At the edges they were more densely packed, but the shelves appeared to be almost empty.

Hezekiah spoke to the librarian who'd given Saiyah a start on her first day, explaining he would translate for her. The idea of reading gave Saiyah a headache. She felt like a cocktail of energy. The irony that she was finally in the library but wanted to be anywhere else was not lost on her.

Glancing at the colourful spines of aged books within sight, she translated blurrily, taking a few steps towards them and squinting. They all had dull titles compared to the delights of the coven's collection. She drifted back to Captain Hezekiah as gods in scholarly robes frowned at her and clutched their scrolls close, as if she might steal something.

She waited near the door, idly glancing at an impressively sized book with recent ink inside. It was an inventory of books borrowed and returned, and her spirits dropped at the thought that Daniel's name would be in there somewhere if she turned the pages back. The name 'Captain Idris Hezekiah' jumped out at her in bold cartridge ink, and she looked over it surreptitiously. He'd taken something out some months ago, on the same November date she'd been attacked. It'd been late at night, after she'd entered the embassy. She pulled out her phone and pretended she was looking at something else as she opened her camera setting, and quickly snapped a shot of the name of what he'd checked out: *Account of John Greyson, Warlock.*

"Captain?" she whispered softly, interrupting his tense conversation with the librarian. "I'm not feeling well at all. I think after the energy..." She touched her head. It wasn't a complete lie.

"You wish to leave?" He raised his brows, carefully enunciating each syllable, as if the statement couldn't possibly be true.

She nodded apologetically.

He peered at her, frowning, but it was a frown of concern. "Of course. I'll see you out."

S AIYAH HEADED INTO THE cold. The icy air bit her face. She hugged herself for warmth as she waited for Bezbiel to answer his door, holding the box with the deciphering glass carefully. She waited for a long time with no answer. There was light coming from the living room, so she slipped through the letterbox as she'd done before.

Inside, the gramophone was on, the needle caught playing the same bar on repeat. She tentatively entered the dim room. She'd always gotten the impression Bezbiel was ready to entertain at the drop of a hat, but this was something else. Bottles and glasses covered every surface, stained with wine and coffee. On the table were papers with miniature ritual circles, as if he'd been practising something. They all suggested something to do with health and protection.

As she lifted the needle on the gramophone, a groan sounded from nearby, and she peered over the sofa to see Bezbiel laying flat on his back. His eyes glazed, he was attempting to speak but his voice was breathy, and he groped for the arm of the sofa.

He wasn't drunk (his tolerance level was near-supernatural), but he struggled to stand, and Saiyah moved to help. His skin was clammy to the touch. He cast her an apologetic look as he slipped and she caught him, scrunching her forehead and taking his weight.

"Water," he rasped.

She left him on the sofa, breathless whilst she darted to the kitchen. When she returned, he was gone. There was an odd, caustic scent in the air.

"Bezbiel?" she called into the empty house, taking a few steps up the stairs. "Bez?"

Startling her, he appeared from his little study. He'd changed his shirt, and seemed steadier on his feet.

Saiyah exhaled in annoyance. "I came to return your glass. Thanks." She said it rigidly, glancing from the door to Bezbiel.

He dipped his head. "Not a problem," he said in a low voice.

There was a long silence, both of them waiting for the other to speak.

"This doesn't mean I've forgiven you," she said severely.

Bezbiel smiled ironically. "I wouldn't dare to presume. Now if that's all?" He gestured to the door.

Saiyah lingered in the hallway. "What's going on with you? If you're sick, someone here could do a healing ritual. The gods might even, if you ask."

"They don't go around healing anyone, let alone demons," he scoffed. "You can go if you want, but if you insist on staying you can at least tell me what you're doing with the god squad. I might be able to help, in place of Azeldya," he said sincerely.

She sighed, looking over the mess in the living room and pressing her lips together. She needed to tell someone. Bezbiel wasn't the best choice, given what he'd done, but he had helped her with the glass, and after the ritual. She needed his knowledge, but nothing else. Saiyah agreed in exchange for coffee, and helped him clear the rubbish away. When the room felt more comfortable, she explained the fundamentals of what she was doing at the embassy, and why. He seemed reluctant to believe a lot of what she said until she held her hand out and allowed a flicker of a spark to emit.

Bezbiel stared at where the light had been. Rooted to the sofa, there was genuine shock in his eyes, perhaps even fear.

"What about the rest of it—their intentions for you? Working as some kind of hellish ambassador, is that really something you want to get involved in? It sounds to me like they're kingmaking. I'm as much a fan of Asramenia as the next demon, but it didn't end well for her."

"They don't know she's my mother," she said dismissively. "My father, however..."

Bezbiel raised his eyebrows. "This *John Greyson* character?" He said it in a way that suggested he didn't believe her.

"Yes. Wait, I thought you said you didn't read–"

"I read the first few paragraphs before I realised," he said apologetically. "You have the same damn powers as her, hardly discreet. If someone *up there* realises you could rally rebels, they could control them through you."

Saiyah took a dismissive breath and sipped her coffee.

"You know, I'm not sure you're suited for politics," he said with a shake of his head.

Saiyah raised an eyebrow. "Are you implying it should be you? Are you jealous I've ended up haphazardly in your field of study?"

"No. I'm concerned you'll become a pawn," he said irritably.

"I already suspect that. If the time comes, I'll resist."

Bezbiel leaned back and laced his fingers together. "That's a risky game you're playing."

"And yet, Azeldya would seemingly have me play it out," she said with a hint of bitterness. "For the good of the rebellion, of course."

Bezbiel gave her a hard stare, unimpressed by the lightheartedness of her tone. "And what about Greyson? That book is dated hundreds of years ago. What makes you think he's your father?"

Saiyah gave him an outline of what she'd read, and admitted what Daniel had told her. Bezbiel had already seen the stolen notes, after all. He frowned sceptically, beginning to explain that there was no reason why Saiyah couldn't've accidentally 'stolen fire from the gods' herself, or some other demon had done it on her behalf.

Saiyah dismissed everything. "I found this in the entries of the embassy library," she explained, showing him the photo on her phone. "This was Hezekiah's first thought on me, and from the way he spoke to me yesterday, I think he knows more than he's letting on."

Bezbiel stared at the snapshot on the screen, a hand clamped over his mouth. "Perhaps," he mused, then looked her dead in the eyes. "I think you'll need more than just mine or Azeldya's help. And *you* need to find that scroll."

XVI

Hell is Just a Frame of Mind

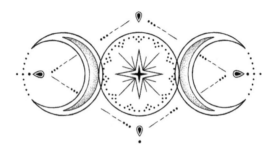

F RESH OUT OF HELL, Azeldya poised elegantly on the
sofa in her office. Saiyah could dimly sense the otherworldly energy emanating from her. It was something
of a tangible, arid sensation, and yet full of the nostalgic
freshness of a world she'd once known.

One corner of the room was cleared, and Zulphas
was setting up a blackboard. Medea was there too, as-
sisting him and looking as perfect as ever in her tweed
skirt suit. Anyone else would've looked frumpy and li-
brarianesqe in that attire, but Medea was infuriatingly
enchanting. The inseparable Titania and Xaldan also
joined them, making Saiyah uncomfortable about what

she may need to admit in front of them. Xaldan, either oblivious to the situation or perfectly used to a certain amount of discretion and peril from Azeldya, greeted Saiyah cordially. Though almost as charming as Bezbiel, she never could quite tell if he was humouring her, a facade to them all. Beneath his sharpened ram-horns and tranquil green eyes, there was a kind of calculated thought, she surmised.

Titania flashed her teeth in a sort of perfunctory grin at Saiyah, then proceeded to lurk in the corner of the room. With arms folded across her strapless, figure-hugging top, Saiyah couldn't help but notice the whiff of Hell on her also. After a few discrete glances, she realised her gauzy, embroidered attire must originate from somewhere in the lower world.

"Shall we begin?" Azeldya said with startling clarity.

Zulphas gave a brief nod and started to cast a circle, stirring vibrations in the air. Unusually, he spoke in English, his tone rather conversational. After a moment, a ghost of a figure flickered in the circle.

"Saiyah? Is everything alright?" came the faint, echoey voice of Daniel as he surveyed the room.

It was a shade of Daniel he'd summoned; his body was safe in Winchester.

Saiyah beamed with delight before her face turned guilty. "Yes. Everything's alright," she said in a thin voice.

Azeldya stood. "Let us begin. We are here to offer Saiyah guidance and protection, but the reasons why must be kept hidden from the rest of the coven for their safety. If any of you wish to remain ignorant, please leave now." She glanced at Medea, who sat bolt upright with a delicate frown and jaw clenched. "Saiyah?" Azeldya invited her to stand.

Daniel became increasingly distressed as Saiyah related the events of her attack, and the god-like ability she'd performed. She explained her mother's position, and her consideration of continuing her work, to which Daniel held a hand over his face in despair. She also told them of her intentions to use her position at the embassy to dispel the restrictions on half-demons, the way Medea did. Daniel had a look of resigned anguish, knowing what was coming.

"I'm half-demon, but I also have reason to believe I'm half god," she admitted apprehensively.

"Nephilim?" Medea said, her jaw wide with shock.

Zulphas closed his eyes in pained concentration. Titania's eyes lit with intrigue for a moment, but any shock was quelled as she clenched her jaw and remained unmoved. Xaldan put a hand to his head as if someone had just given him some mildly inconvenient news.

"Your influences on behalf of the revolutionists can wait. For now, you should gain the god's trust to ease their suspicions," Azeldya said.

Saiyah scratched her palms. "I think Hezekiah already suspects a great deal."

Zulphas interrupted the silence with the scratching of chalk as he wrote 'Hezekiah' on the board. "Your main threat," he stated.

Saiyah continued. "The elders also suspect, to some extent."

Bezbiel turned to Daniel. "What do you know about the Captain?" he said, pacing casually across the room, greenish light reflecting in his eye.

Daniel became serious. "Idris Hezekiah is one of the youngest captains of *The Host*. A second sphere god of the lower class, he's reportedly an excellent warrior, demon hunter, tactician–everything, really."

"Does he have any weaknesses?" Bezbiel asked encouragingly, directed at both Saiyah and Daniel.

"I made a deal with him to ensure he wouldn't order me to do anything I don't want," Saiyah put in.

Bezbiel tilted his head, impressed.

Daniel made a hesitant noise, and all eyes went to him.

Azeldya put her hands on her hips and turned to him gravely. "Any information could make all the difference to Saiyah."

Daniel glanced down and muttered something about the secrecy of gods. "In Hell, he was involved in an incident of defected gods. Some elected to 'switch sides' during the campaign. Though, not of their own volition." Daniel gestured to Bezbiel. "Some of *his* kind saw to that. Hezekiah was in charge of apprehending them, but he avoided killing, and there were rumours he went against the Seraphim's orders by trying to lift their enchantment."

"He bent the rules?" Zulphas asked, alert with intrigue as he wrote on the blackboard.

Saiyah gasped and clicked her fingers. "When he reported the attack, he said he'd decided not to focus heavily on my involvement. He played it down and took it into his own hands."

"So, he's got a soft spot," Xaldan mused.

"That doesn't mean he wouldn't turn on her," Medea added in a raspy whisper.

They discussed how to keep Hezekiah from discovering the truth, or at least distract him from it. Medea elected to speak with Gabrielle to see if he was doing anything out of the ordinary. Saiyah was naturally doing well befriending Gabrielle, but felt guilty about using them both.

"*The Host* are using *you*, aren't they?" Bezbiel said. "Besides, you could win a sympathy vote from the good Captain. Get him to open up." He winked.

"The demon Bezbiel, a *true* master of manipulation," Titania muttered.

Bezbiel shot her an irritated smirk and opened his mouth to retort, but Saiyah interrupted.

"I'm not sure I'm comfortable maintaining this persona for years to come," she grumbled, re-establishing her position on the sofa.

Seeing Saiyah's trepidation, Azeldya levelled a tender, but firm stare at her.. "My dear, you must understand that however unfair, this is politics between *The Host* and the revolutionists, and therefore The Circle. It will always contain a degree of falsehood."

Bezbiel smiled smugly and pulled a chess piece from his pocket. "Think of it this way," he began, ignoring the daggers in Azeldya's eyes. "You're the king. Indulge me, you're the black king. Hezekiah is the white queen, your main threat. He can move everywhere. He's got more pawns at his disposal, and other key pieces: Adriel, Remiel, etc. What have we got? Azeldya, you're queen I suppose, but not much else. He's got nothing to protect and you've everything to defend. How do we put him on the back foot?" He tapped his foot impatiently.

Saiyah creased her brow at his strange analogy.

"Find his king?" Zulphas asked.

"He won't have one," Daniel piped up. "The obvious choice would be too great a power for us to take on." He looked upwards.

Saiyah raised her chin. "We make Captain Hezekiah the king. Level the playing field."

"Exactly." Bezbiel snapped his fingers. "Azeldya, can you put some pressure on him? Discourage him from questioning Saiyah further?"

Azeldya nodded. "I suggest you do the same, in your own *unique* way."

"It would be a pleasure." Bezbiel winked.

Zulphas shifted uncomfortably, adjusting his bulky cloak.

"We should make our 'move' as soon as possible," Saiyah said. "You said yourself, we have no pawns, Bezbiel. As the knight, it should be your move first."

Bezbiel grinned cockily, throwing the chess piece in the air and catching it.

H EZEKIAH'S FOUNTAIN PEN SCRATCHED against cartridge paper as he wrote Saiyah's daily review.

"You're taking to your training quite easily, it would appear," he said, glancing at her with hidden intrigue.

Saiyah finished her mouthful of tea. "Thanks," she said, unsure what the appropriate response should be.

He looked like he wanted to say something as he contemplated silently to himself, but instead continued writing. There was a gentle pensiveness in his irritatingly flawless face which left Saiyah at an impasse. Something about the way he concentrated on his writing was uncommonly admirable to her.

Saiyah opened and closed her mouth as she drummed up the courage to speak. "Do you ever get a break from all this?"

He looked up, surprised. His brows softened. It wasn't a smile, but she'd learnt anything less than a frown from him was a positive. "Usually, yes. However, it's you that is taking up my free time these days, Miss Greyson."

Saiyah blushed, wondering if that meant just their meetings, or any research he was doing on her or her father. She paled again at the thought. "Perhaps we needn't meet here all the time, then. There are other places in London to go."

"It would be suspicious if we were seen frequently together in public," he retorted, as if he'd already given it some thought.

"Why should it be?" Saiyah challenged. "Don't you think people should be able to see their local Ambassador of the gods having good relations with half-demons? Besides, apart from corporate functions and elite social events, do you ever really 'go amongst the people'?"

He stared blankly at her.

Saiyah bit her lip. "Forget I said anything."

"Where would I need to go?" he asked in a hushed tone.

Saiyah raised her brows. Tearing a page from his notebook, Hezekiah suggested she write an address. He examined it carefully before unlocking his deskside drawer and placing it inside. Saiyah craned her neck at the contents before he closed and locked it sharply.

"Can I ask when I'll be taught to use divine energy in combat?" she asked tentatively.

He took the last sip of his tea and gave her a wry smile. "When I think you can be trusted, Miss Greyson. And with your demon blood, that could be quite some time." He offered a polite bow of the head, standing to escort her out.

Saiyah clicked her tongue. "You're quick to judge, though I suppose that's unsurprising. Don't you know, even the souls of the damned don't lose all their virtue?"

Hezekiah shifted uncomfortably as he walked, choosing to ignore her.

When they approached the foyer there was a din of commotion. Raised voices, orders barked, the chiming of swords and unearthly sounds. Saiyah felt the pressure of demonic energy press against her.

"Stay here," Hezekiah told her, striding briskly onwards.

He drew his sword before disappearing into the foyer. His voice echoed, issuing commands in his own dialect. Cautiously, she advanced towards the archway, placing a steady hand on the carved stone.

Her body tensed. Slayers in full armour, already battle-weary, surrounded a larger-than-life creature with raw sinewy limbs, muscles exposed. Its chest was falling apart and leaking some sort of gas, its eyes obscured with a crude armoured head-covering. From its mouth, long tendrils of sentient organs poured forth as if it were vomiting. It thrashed and squealed as slayers bore down upon it.

Saiyah jerked when Gabrielle pulled her back into the corridor and shielded her from the sight. With one arm around Saiyah and the other on her sword, she ushered her out onto the street. There were more slayers at the door than usual, startled by Saiyah's sudden appearance. Gabrielle whispered a quick apology and rushed back inside.

I N THE CALM OF the reading room, diffused light permeated the windows. Saiyah's hand rested limply over her forehead. Hex analysed her tarot spread, and Bezbiel unsuccessfully coached Jack at chess.

"I was so false; I was sure he could hear my heart racing," Saiyah said wearily. "Sometimes he's so placid and others I don't doubt he'd slay me without a second thought."

Bezbiel took his eyes off the game. "Relax. It's not as if he's some kind of teen vampire, and it's not like you're doing anything *seriously* wrong. So long as he doesn't discover your secret, the only thing you've got to lose is the trust of the good captain."

"I don't want to lose it, though," Saiyah grumbled.

Bezbiel narrowed his eyes at her as he moved his knight to a position that left Jack compromised. "I'll meet you next time you're together and use a bit of the old demonic charm," he said with a wicked grin.

Saiyah wrinkled her nose and rolled her eyes.

"Do you have any other book recommendations on revolutionists?" she asked. "I need more factual sources to understand what I'm dealing with."

Bezbiel wiggled his eyebrows. "If you're serious, it would be best to study the political framework of Hell."

"And you know all about that" she said dryly.

"As a matter of fact, I do," he boasted. "I spent months in Hell researching the very subject."

Jack sighed as Bezbiel left him in check.

Saiyah's brows drew together. "How *did* you manage to go to Hell?" she queried, trying not to sound too interested.

"I was invited, and had permission from the gods for my mortal soul to pass through."

A movement in the doorway caught her attention. Azeldya strolled elegantly into the room, heading towards Bezbiel. Saiyah jumped up as she approached the chess table.

"Azeldya, could I visit Hell like Bez did?" she asked.

Azeldya only blinked slowly in response, then cast an accusing look at Bezbiel, who smiled innocently.

"It would be a dangerous undertaking, and the gods would not permit you due to the mortal part of your soul. Bezbiel was invited and protected by a relative with access to a Hellgate," she explained evenly.

Saiyah didn't put much faith in the likes of *Dante's Inferno* as a factual source, but there was no smoke without fire.

"If I'm to continue my mother's crusade one day, I should visit," Saiyah put in tactfully.

Azeldya pressed her lips together thoughtfully. "I advise you to study the cultures and customs of Hell first. I'm sure Bezbiel could furnish you with some appropriate resources, as he's already been so forthcoming with information."

It was more than her practical reasons of wanting to visit Hell that drove her. The curiosity of exploring Hell, something which few mortals experienced, thrilled her. The notion evoked how Howard Carter and Lord Carnarvon must have felt as they planned their final attempt to find the tomb of Tutankhamun.

That evening, in the depths of their library, *Fur Elise* played discreetly on the gramophone as Saiyah browsed archaic scripts on Hell, laboriously translated. Bezbiel was little help as he became busier with his own work, but pointed her in the right direction, occasionally clarifying certain terms and phrases. His first-hand research from Hell was invaluable. Although it mainly consisted of political matters, there were parallels between Hell's culture and contemporary Abrahamic and pagan religions. It was highly captivating, and gave her a small window into society.

"Forget all the fire and brimstone stories," he'd said to her one day, writing an essay on a typewriter brought from home. "Well, not completely, demons have an infernal job to do. But the hellscape varies greatly."

She'd once imagined Hell as a typical fiery inferno, or a frozen wasteland like in Norse mythology, and recently contemplated ideas of Tartarus and the Greco-Roman underworld from her mother's journal. Bezbiel's journal was something else. The way he depicted the dominions of Hell he'd visited wasn't dissimilar to the illustration of an exotic land unfrequented by foreigners, or stepping back in time. It was rich with descriptions and crisply explained details that made her yearn to know what her own homeland was like in the present day. He related wastelands of hollow, blistering winds, and desert soil with gems of gold leading to humid cities. One particular passage piqued her interest: he'd chronicled his ancestral home, residing in a desert oasis of a sunken city, governed by a Jackal Lord, with greenery tumbling from red stone like the hanging gardens of Babylon.

It was wonderful to be immersed in books of a less foreboding nature again, and Saiyah's translating skills improved rapidly.

It was the two of them and Hex one evening, and Bezbiel was acting strangely. She could see he wasn't really reading. His eyes darted from the page to her and back again. She was about to chide him for distracting her when he slithered over and took a seat beside her. Hex had her nose in a book, frowning in concentration.

"Can I ask you a favour?" he whispered.

"If it has something to do with my big problem you're aiding me with, yes. If not, I think I'm still within my rights to say no."

He proceeded to dangle a book in front of her. It was extremely fragile, without a spine or back cover, written by hand in new-modern English, which indicated it may not be accurately academic. Saiyah furrowed her brows as she recognised the handwriting and style of drawings.

"Where did you get that?" Saiyah gasped angrily, lowering her voice and glancing at the other demons in the reading room.

"Swiped it from Zulphas's private collection," Bezbiel told her mischievously. Still with a tight grip, he lay the book in front of her and pointed to a passage. It described a summoning spell, similar to what Zulphas did when he summoned Daniel, and it was surprisingly accurate. But that wasn't the part Bezbiel was interested in. The incantation he pointed to suggested something much darker.

"I just need a *little* bit of that divine blood of yours. Just a drop."

"No!" Saiyah declared, startling a few acolytes. "This probably wouldn't work anyway. Moreover, I'd feel really uncomfortable providing that. Give me the book," she hissed.

"Oh, come on, Saiyah. We could do amazing, impossible things!" he begged softly.

"I don't care. I know you're going to use it to muck around with Xaldan and Titania, so thank you, no," she replied sweetly, snatching for the book again.

He withheld it like a childish bully, then smiled roguishly and placed it into her hands. Saiyah scowled and left the Baraquel building, heading for home.

XVII

When Shadows Fall

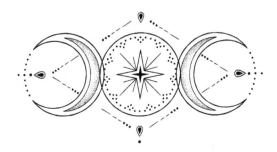

H EZEKIAH WAS UNRECOGNISABLE WHEN he arrived. His sword and moonlight hair marked him out, but his clothes were casual. Saiyah stifled a laugh.

He either didn't notice her reaction or chose not to.

Saiyah was standing outside a café-bookshop. She'd been there a few times on occasions when she'd leave the Old Roads. It was Hex that'd introduced her to it. She'd said it was 'just hipster enough not to be pretentious, but just enough to be relaxed about half-demons. Hezekiah wasn't a half-demon, though.

It was markedly incongruous to see a god without their uniform, or at least without the regal garb which marked them as hailing from a different place in time entirely. People noticed as he passed on the street, and stared.

He stood facing her awkwardly, hands clasped before him as he appraised the establishment.

"You may call me Idris, when I am off duty, if you like," he told her stiffly, stretching his shoulders.

Saiyah beamed in spite of herself. This was progress. Excellent progress. Though she knew in her heart she was using him, and part of her felt good that she was able to fool this god so easily, the thought flashed through her mind that she wasn't using him, not really. She did want to help him, and she was glad he'd decided to trust her. Perhaps if she could just help him see what half-demons were really like, he could help ease the public's general hatred and persecution of them.

"Idris," she repeated, with humorous uncertainty. She liked the way the name sounded on her lips. "Shall we go in?"

He nodded cautiously.

Inside the café and away from the cold, Saiyah directed them to a secluded table, housed in an enclave of books. There was a strong smell of freshly printed paper mingled with pages which once might have been damp, but were now dried. Over it all lingered the scent of ground coffee beans.

Idris ordered mint tea, though he wasn't impressed by the flavour, or the fact that it came in a bag.

"I wish they wouldn't stare," he said, leaning into his collar.

Saiyah laughed. "Gods should *'go amongst the people'* more often."

He straightened and looked down his nose into his cup. "We have no time for that."

Saiyah repressed a groan. "Hence your ever-increasing popularity. Don't you think it's odd that demons are so commonplace that Londoners barely bat an eye, but *this* is their reaction to you? The appearance of gods has *everyone* questioning their beliefs."

Idris' expression betrayed stubbornness. "I would argue, that in order to have faith, it is necessary to ques–"

"Oh please, I don't want to hear it! Though I hold an interest in theology and religious mythology, I don't want a holier-than-thou sermon right now, thanks." She tempered her irritated tone with a grin.

Hezekiah leaned back gradually and folded his arms. "So, in your opinion as a theologist, how should we *'win the people over'?*"

"Firstly, I am not a theologist or qualified to officially advise a Captain of *The Host*," she said, getting a slight laugh from him. "Secondly, I think it would've been less confusing not to reveal yourselves in the first place, regardless of demon problems. Thirdly, does your question apply to collectively, or just yourself? Because collectively, I honestly have no idea."

He frowned, considering what she said. "You're quite thoughtful for your age. I am sure you can give me an answer one day. But for now, perhaps you could advise on how to communicate with mortals, for my ambassadorial duties." It'd been a while since he'd given her one of his intense stares, as he did now, glowing eyes notwithstanding. He sipped the tea he'd previously declared undrinkable. "I have been practising," he admitted. "Yet I still don't understand. I don't know what people want of me; I don't even know what you want of me presently."

He looked away quickly. Saiyah scratched her palms and forced a casual countenance.

She spoke gently. "Well, as with learning a language, I believe the best way is to immerse yourself in it. I could help you, if you like? After all, I'm half mortal."

He examined her face studiously. Cautiously, he gave a slight nod in agreement.

WHILE AT THE EMBASSY, Hezekiah expected to be addressed formally. Saiyah was sternly reminded not to use his first name in front of other slayers.

Often, he didn't notice when they were alone, and was soft-spoken as always.

He was methodical in his itinerary, and liked to stick to an orderly schedule, making sure there was time for Saiyah to coach his social skills. He grasped practical parts of modern life quickly. It didn't take much convincing for him to get a phone, which Gabrielle helped with. He learnt everything as a new set of rules. The subtle, nuanced conversation and banter of this world was what he struggled with, and the fencing club became his practising ground. It was the way he didn't comprehend that Saiyah hadn't expected; he knew *how* to speak and act. He just couldn't understand why. He commented several times, among humans, how mortals spoke so openly. He couldn't comprehend exposing oneself in such a way. It was unnecessary, leaving oneself open to attack.

"People can't all behave like emotionless robots," Saiyah explained after a few weeks as they sat in a busy coffee shop. "You come off particularly cold and unfeeling, otherwise."

"Are you referring to me personally?" He asked.

"As a matter of fact, yes. Is there anything behind that stony, 'above-this-world' exterior of yours, or is that all there is to Idris Hezekiah?"

Idris looked at his mint tea thoughtfully. He did this often, choosing not to answer rather than change the subject or speak. Saiyah drummed her fingers on the glass table.

"It's not professional," he stated eventually.

Saiyah rolled her eyes. "I'm sure when you're obliged to go to your fancy parties with politicians and such, they'd appreciate you showing a little care and compassion for this world."

He shot her an accusing look. "I do."

"That's more like it." she responded brightly, raising her teacup as if toasting him.

"I may not completely understand the people of this world, but I am fond of them," he admitted slowly, his long lashes cast down.

Saiyah softened and leaned in with an expectant expression.

When he spoke, his voice was almost a whisper. "My care for mortals is more than just my station. I've seen the resilience and bravery of mortal souls during dark times. That is why I accepted the call to work within this branch of *The Host* again."

"The *demon slayers*," Saiyah muttered.

He responded with a firm nod.

Idris was dubious when Saiyah suggested they turn to fiction to ease him into the mannerisms of modern life, and ultimately, he was right. In second-hand book shops, they ended up drifting to more fantastical genres. Although his analysis of such things portrayed a warped view of life, they would discuss the themes as if it were Shakespeare. He found plenty to pick apart, reflecting a deeper human nature.

They'd sit in Hyde Park or cafes for hours, discussing theology and morality where gods and demons were concerned, lightly touching on ideas of change and revolution in Hell. She delighted in pointing out flaws in his practices and contradicting his convictions. Idris always had compelling defences, but occasionally a spark of retreat would show in his eyes, and Saiyah knew she was the victor.

S AIYAH ENTERED THE CAPTAIN'S study one January afternoon, months after they'd begun their meetings. Snow fell lazily in large but sparse flakes outside, not quite cold enough to settle. Gabrielle had left tea for them, and the fire was lit. Idris was hunched over his desk with a frown of concentration, but it eased as she entered, and he smiled temperately. The mechanical sound of his typewriter ceased, and the captain set his attention on her.

Before he could say anything, there was a knock at the door, and he stood. A soldier with an expressive face handed him a message. As Idris read, he glanced at Saiyah, instructing her to stay in the study for a moment, and he'd escort her to the exit shortly.

It was as if she'd swallowed a stone. Even after all these months, he still didn't quite trust her. She was left staring at his retreating cloak, swirling around his back.

Saiyah let out a sound of frustration as the door closed behind him and the clink of the lock sounded. She slapped her hand on the fireside in frustration. After a few moments of tapping her feet patiently, it became clear he wasn't returning anytime soon.

She stood abruptly and walked to the desk, crouching by the drawer Hezekiah kept locked. Unlike the Osiris box, there was no way to unlock it from the inside, but she rifled through the papers with her shadow form, feeling for a scroll of some kind. Grasping a few items that fit the description, she pulled them out with a shadowy hand. Each was tied with a string and label, and she swiftly found what she was looking for: 'Accounts of John Greyson, the Warlock.' Saiyah beamed, placing everything else away.

Saiyah glanced around the room for a place to obscure her reading, but there was none. She bit her lip and tapped her foot. She might only get one chance.

Turning to shadow, scroll in hand, she pushed herself through the crack in the door and into the hallway. Hezekiah was conversing in the atrium with a handful of soldiers and Sergeant Adriel, their voices impassioned. Quickly, Saiyah made for the locked door of the war room and passed through, relishing the shadowy visage. Walking around the table, she went straight to the mantle and lifted the Osiris box. He probably wouldn't miss that, and she could always put it back later. She took a seat, placing the box on the table, and hastily untied the string of the scroll. It was written in the gorgeous swirling script of the gods in what looked like ink made of gold.

03. Maimakterion, 1587

For the attentions of the Seraphim,

The mortal known as John Greyson is known to have employed knowledge of earthly occultism and demon practices in order to evoke the divine power of gods. It is believed the rebel demoness and sorceress Asramenia has aided him in this insight, as well as the instruments and workings of the Astrologer John Dee.

This theft alone is cause for concern; however, witnesses have reported that the warlock has found a way to not only sustain the borrowed power, but to grow it. Captain Josiah of the Southern encampment has so far refrained from questioning on the grounds that it is unlikely that the priestess Asramenia was privy to this knowledge, nor any other demon, as well as fear of disrupting the recent alliance.

We can only assume he has discovered a method to access our energies alone for the time being, which begs a greater question of the powers of mortals. The rare few who can access 'earthly magic' in recent centuries do not obtain a power of this level.

Though Greyson possesses little threat currently, his method must be discovered at all costs, lest the demons he associated himself with also draw on his power. It is my recommendation that he is at the very least relieved of his effects and they are destroyed. I would also humbly suggest that his life is ended before he poses a threat, if not immediately, then when his usefulness has run its course. And finally, the rebel leader, Asramenia, her priestesses and known rebels close to Greyson should be interrogated on the matter. I believe it would be prudent to see them all hang regardless.

Your humble servant,
Lord Akrasiel Silas

Saiyah read the letter again, focusing on the part about her father and how he'd come to access divine power. She shook her head, confused and dismayed. The room became marginally brighter, and there was a tickle of energy at the back of Saiyah's neck.

A firm hand landed on her shoulder and Saiyah sat bold upright, twisting to see Idris staring at her wide eyed and faintly glowing.

"What are you doing?" he said, detached.

Saiyah dropped the scroll, open-mouthed, and stood. The captain's otherwise calm demeanour held a hint of wariness. Something reflected at his side. His sword was drawn, pointing downwards, but he gripped the hilt readily.

"Are you *reading* that?" he asked accusingly.

Saiyah glanced at the gods' script then shook her head, "N-no, I–"

"Don't lie," he said balefully. "If indeed you can read our language somehow, it could raise several dangerous questions regarding your nature."

Saiyah stared in horror. When she didn't answer, he shook her ,and she clutched the table to steady herself. His sword wavered as if ready for an attack. Saiyah made a sound of fright, turned to shadow, and slipped from his grasp and halfway through the table. She reached for the Osiris box with her shadow, sliding it towards her just before he could reach, and rushed towards the door.

A ripple of divine energy passed over her and as she reached the edge of the inner chamber. She felt strangely muffled and sluggish, as if walking through water. Still a shadow, she turned to face him.

His head swayed with disappointment. "You realise the demonic deal you tried to impose on me, weak as it was, is now broken."

Saiyah hugged the Osiris box to her chest, motionless.

Idris took a vigilant sidestep and pulled out one of the chairs. "Come out of that shadow. Sit down. Give me the box, and I'll put my sword away. Then we'll talk."

Saiyah took a cautious step forward and he distanced himself from her intended path. She resumed solid form, breathing deeply. Slowly, she sat and held the box outstretched to him. No sooner had his fingertips touched it than his sword clicked back into the sheath.

She let out a steady sigh. His serious eyes locked on her again and he folded his arms, standing before her. Saiyah scrutinised his every movement, gripping the chair at the sides of her legs.

"I'm not going to harm you Saiyah, but you need to answer my questions truthfully. Do you understand?" he said a little more gently.

She nodded rapidly.

"Good." His posture relaxed. "Now, cards on the table, as you mortals say. I find it particularly disturbing that you have the same name as this man." He pointed to the scroll where it'd fallen on the table. "What is your connection with him?"

When Saiyah spoke, it was in a small voice, and came out as a croak at first. "I think he's... my father."

Idris frowned deeply in puzzlement, tilting his chin up as if he'd not expected that answer. "This man would've died centuries ago. It's not possible."

It was Saiyah's turn to be taken aback. "I know that. But John Greyson stole fire from the gods, that's why I'm like this!" She produced a little white glimmer by clicking her fingers.

Idris leant vaguely towards her. "No," he said decidedly, reaching behind her to the scroll. He tapped it in his hand before her face. "You are a Nephilim who has used this corrupt method to acquire a human soul. Or perhaps your parents did so on your behalf."

Saiyah half laughed but nervousness made her waver. "What? That's not–come on, Hezekiah. How the hell did you come to that conclusion?"

He tucked the scroll into his belt, straightening up. "Because I have seen what your blood looks like," he said darkly. Pulling out one of his little knives, he grasped one of Saiyah's hands at inhuman speed and held it firmly, palm up. He lay the blade across the centre and Saiyah pulled away, unable to escape his hold, half standing. Idris hesitated, looking at her calmly. Saiyah held still, readying for the slight pain.

"Well. I'm sure you know what I mean," he said slowly, taking the blade away.

Saiyah scowled and took a few paces back, her face flushed lilac with fury. "I'm sure I don't," she said venomously. "I've not been soul stealing and I'm not a Nephilim!" She thrust a finger at the scroll in his belt. "The Priestess in that letter, Asramenia. That's my mother!"

Idris' eyes became round in shock and a hand fluttered to his brow as he slowly closed them, beginning to pace. The muffled feeling of the room dropped, and Saiyah felt as if she could breathe again.

"So, you see, somehow, he *is* my father. I can't explain how, but he is. He must be."

He shot her an apologetic look. "You have no idea, do you?" he whispered.

Footsteps came from beyond the door and Gabrielle entered. She assessed the situation with her usual straightforwardness and took a step towards Idris.

"Just a moment," he commanded.

Gabrielle shook her head. "They need to know now."

He took a breath and nodded. "Take Miss Greyson off site," he said with a note of finality as he walked past Saiyah and out of the room.

As Saiyah was escorted to the exit by Gabrielle, the embassy appeared busier than ever. There was no eldritch terror in sight, but the soldiers seemed to be readying for something.

ON THE WAY HOME, Saiyah searched for news on her phone regarding gods and demons to see what all the fuss was about. There was nothing. They were good at keeping their perilous work from the mortal world. What she found instead was Bezbiel's face. Panicked, she clicked quickly on a reputable link, taking her to a video clip of him being followed by camera men and microphones in Soho. He'd done nothing illegal, but from what she could grasp, he'd managed to get one of his early essays into the public domain. *Religion in Hell: How does modern day worship affect the governance in Hell?* It was causing interest and unrest amongst the academic and religious communities. Saiyah ran her fingers over her scalp.

She ascended the steps of the Baraquel library in the hope that if one of the others were there, she could stop worrying about the incident with Hezekiah. On her way up, Bezbiel headed towards her with a confident grin.

"Perfect timing!" he said as they met at the top. He fell into step with her.

"What the actual hell, Bez?" she groaned, struggling to be solemn while he was grinning so much. "I take it you weren't trying to rub *The Host* up the wrong way?"

He winked at her. "Not specifically. It was a risk. Everyone will know of The Demon Bezbiel by the time I'm a professor."

"Can you be sure they'll award it to you after all this?"

He waved a hand dismissively. "Some other university will, then. Look, you're going to make your name one day as a saintly ambassador–forgive the irony–or perhaps some kind of Joan of Arc of Hell. And I'll be a respected, pioneering, yet controversial professor. And a damn good looking one at that."

"So, it's about fame then, is it?" she asked cynically.

It made sense, he so clearly loved himself.

"Naturally. Anyway, it's not important right now. I've just smoothed things over with Azeldya, this isn't an attack on anyone, it's freedom of information. Nevertheless, I am throwing a party tonight at the Palm House. Tell your little housemates, they're invited too." He whooped as he retreated towards the high street.

Saiyah shook her head in disbelief.

XVIII

Fearless, and Therefore Powerful

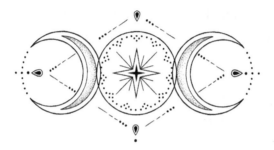

S AIYAH MADE HER WAY home from the library earlier
than planned now that she had a party to attend.
The sky was already veiled in dreary darkness, and a
horizontal mist lurked in the streets. A sudden voice
from behind startled her, and she let out an embarrassingly girlish gasp.

"Have you–you or any member of the Albion Circle
opened a Hellgate?"

It was Idris, breathing deeply with an expression of
intently focused yet business-like worry. He wore full
demon-slaying armour, the midnight uniform only
peeking out at the edges. His hair was windswept.

"Not that I know of," she answered somewhat haughtily, catching her breath. "What's going on?"

Idris glanced around. "Somebody has. Whatever came out was here not long ago. Have you somewhere to go?" he said, practically herding her in the opposite direction.

"My house is over there. I'm supposed to be going to a party," she tried to explain, dumbfounded.

"All the Albion Circle will be there, including Azeldya?" he asked.

Saiyah nodded.

"Very well. Go to the party, but let me escort you. And do not be afraid to use your demonic powers here if you need to."

Idris paused on the threshold of her house, but insisted he enter to make sure nothing unwanted lurked within. Afraid, Saiyah permitted him. He investigated upstairs, silent as a ghost while Saiyah opened a bottle of red wine and poured herself a glass. Turning back to the hallway, she flinched at seeing Idris at the foot of the stairs.

"All clear. I'll be in the area. Let me know when you are ready."

Saiyah lifted the glass in response, and he gave it a disapproving look before he disappeared.

Saiyah turned on every light as she cautiously went upstairs, wary of stepping into a scene from a horror film. She left the wine on her nightstand and showered, shaved, cutting herself on her knee and ankle in haste, and returned to her room. Saiyah hastily slipped into a striking black dress, applied a few coats of mascara, and opted for a classic red lip, leaving her hair loose but neat. By the time she got to the hallway, she could see him shining through the coloured glass in the door. Grabbing her bag and coat, she opened it.

He looked her up and down but said nothing, stepping aside to let her pass.

"You really don't need to do this," she lied as they walked down the street. "It's only around the corner. I'm capable of looking after myself these days," she added, hoping he wouldn't abandon her immediately.

He grinned slightly, but his watchful eyes glanced in all directions.

"I've no doubt you are," he said.

They neared the Palm House. Its grand ironwork and glass exterior glittered with candlelight. Saiyah spotted other coven members flocking at the entrance, staring at Idris. Bezbiel was talking with Xaldan, and running his fingers through his lover's hair. She rolled her eyes. He beamed impishly and came briskly towards them.

"I see you've brought a date!" he called out.

Idris scowled and turned to say something to Saiyah.

"Bez," she greeted firmly. "Be nice. This is Captain Hezekiah, Captain, this is my *friend*, Bezbiel."

Idris said nothing, but Bezbiel grinned cunningly, putting his arm around Saiyah.

"Ah, Saiyah has told us all about you." He held out his hand.

Idris regarded it warily but took it all the same. "Indeed. I've also read your work," he said sternly.

Bezbiel raised an eyebrow. "My *recent* work?" Saiyah could tell he was enjoying this as she tactfully dislodged herself.

"No. But I'm sure I will soon. I'll not intrude," he said to Bezbiel, then turned to Saiyah. "Enjoy your evening."

"Just a moment!" Bezbiel called out, trotting over to the scowling god. "A word if I may, regarding Saiyah. I don't know what you two *get up to* at the embassy, but I'd like some assurance that you'll not do anything to cause her harm."

There was a weight of demonic energy behind his words, and Idris was momentarily surprised–offended, even.

"I give you my word," Idris said solemnly, before flickering out of existence.

"What an odd fellow," Bezbiel said, offering her an arm.

"Did it work?" she asked.

"Absolutely. That's *check* as far as I'm concerned. Now we wait and see if he blocks."

Saiyah glanced anxiously at where Idris had been, but he was already gone. Taking Bezbiel's arm and swallowing her misgivings, she relayed what he'd said about a Hellgate. Bezbiel shrugged cavalierly and told her not to worry, grabbing them both a drink off a table full of potent alcohol.

"I'm sure the good Captain can handle whatever it is. Forget about it, for tonight we celebrate like kings and queens! And we shall dance!" he said, lazily turning her about so as not to spill their drinks.

Saiyah finally gave in and shared his mood of cheerfulness, which pleased him. He winked and stroked her chin playfully before sweeping himself away to another group. She scowled sportively.

The tables in the palm house had been cleared to resemble a ball room. There were more fairy-lights mingling with the tropical plants and glass roof. Strings of paper lanterns hung between the pillars and red, purple, and green lighting illuminated everything from below.

Saiyah made her way towards Hex and Jack, and spent most of her time chatting and dancing with both at first. It might've been the alcohol, but she found herself swept easily into conversations with other demons, some of which hadn't taken an interest in her previously. Often Bezbiel, Zulphas, or Medea were leading the conversation. She laughed and danced with Bezbiel as easily as she'd done before, and found herself in the arms of other members of the circle that night.

Cautious of drinking too much and doing something regretful, she slowed down and drank some water, but continued to dance. It was around 3am when the first partygoers began to peel off. Chilly blasts of air hit her intermittently as the main door opened and closed. Saiyah was shattered when Bezbiel announced he was turning in. A couple of others remained, but shawls and jackets were being put on, and high heels were painfully being worn for one last time. Xaldan and some other initiates were singing a song about *'the sons of Belial, drunk with insolence and wine.'* She rolled her eyes.

Bezbiel regarded her apprehensive expression and sidled up to her, his elbow brushing hers. "Do you want to come back to mine?" he asked quietly. "No funny business, I promise. I'll put you up in the other room." Saiyah bit her lip with a concealed grin, but with a bittersweet expression, declined. A flash of disappointment crossed his face before the usual bravado returned.

They walked in a group at first, heads down and hands in pockets, complaining about the cold even at this time of year. They waved boisterous goodbyes with clumsy hugs when it was time for Saiyah to peel off.

The darkness stretched before her despite the lamplight. She became pure shadow amongst the towering stone buildings. Cautiously, she made her way towards her house. A glowing figure stood close to the steps of her home, looking in her general direction.

"Idris?" she called out as loudly as she dared.

He became alert at the sound of her voice, and she allowed her guard to drop, materialising the closer she got to him. She recoiled at the noticeable splatters on his face and white undershirt. Ash and dirt had settled in his snowy hair. It struck her how handsome he looked, despite his dishevelled visage.

"I need you to come to the embassy. You can't be protected here. The situation is more dire than we imagined." His tone was both stern and urgent.

Saiyah narrowed her eyes and held her ground. "How do I know I can trust you? After earlier."

His composure wavered, but he spoke no less urgently. "Someone is opening Hellgates. Perhaps Malik. Not the scavengers, they're just riding other demons' rifts. Nevertheless, they are very much present in this world." He held out his hand in an unusual manner. "No more questions, I'll explain everything in the morning."

Saiyah hesitated. Was this strange behaviour something to do with Bezbiel's enchantment? Carefully, she took his hand at the strange angle he held it at. He stepped towards her as if they were going to dance, and put his free arm around her, standing so close the warmth of his body permeated her clothes.

"Close your eyes."

Suddenly it was as if he'd slammed into her, and a rush of white light and an unbelievable force pressed her into him. She shut her eyes tight and managed to control her arm, which was flailing numbly, and grabbed onto Idris. It ended after a few moments. She felt soft ground under her feet, and stumbled with vertigo. She held rather tightly to Idris, clutching the back of his filthy armour. He held her gently by the elbow as she pulled away and steadied herself.

They were in the embassy grounds, outside the residency. Idris glanced around cautiously as he led her inside. His slight luminosity was gone, all except his eyes.

"I still have matters to address," he said softly and briskly as he opened the door.

There was something unusual in his mannerisms, as if he had more to say. He bid her goodnight before disappearing with a rush of air again. She gazed at the empty space where he'd stood a moment before, a flutter of nerves in her stomach.

Inside, the house was dimly lit. Saiyah started up the stairs and went to the same room as before. In bed, she tossed and turned for a while, listening for the return of Idris, but eventually fell into a heavy sleep, dreaming of the dark place in Hell she'd accidentally travelled before. The fog lifted, and sounds became clearer. There were dark shapes moving around her once more, green-eyed demons, but also glints of gold and silver amongst the inky blue tones. The faint ripple of water echoed through her mind. They whispered the same phrase as the demon who attacked her: '*Katomei Asramenia, amortiah ix inus'krepuzcalius xalvas. Xalvas tis Nyx.*' She understood what some of it meant now. 'Xalvas' was the word for forest or woodland, and 'Nyx' was night like the primordial deity. The rest was indecipherable.

Another voice cut through clearer than the rest. It was familiarly light and sweet, and spoke in a simple demonic tongue. She felt it was trying to warn her of something.

Saiyah's eyes snapped open. She still saw green eyes floating around her, and sensed the presence she was certain was her mother. It all faded away with the dream. In a cold sweat, she turned on the bedside light. Groggy, her pores were clogged and her skin dry after the night of merriment. She gulped some water but paused at a sound from the landing.

She quietly opened the door, peering into the landing. Moonlight cascaded angularly through the windows. She turned her head and saw Idris entering from another doorway. Illuminated by a glowing hand held to his shoulder, he was healing himself. The dark shade of demon blood was splattered over him again, as well as a few pearly streaks of his own.

"It's alright, go back to bed," he said softly.

"Tell me what's going on," she said, unable to suppress the alarm from her voice.

He took his hand away from his shoulder and held the spark of light in his palm like a candle, walking towards her. He breathed deeply, with an odd look of reverence on his face.

A sudden crashing sound came from behind him. Dropping the spark, he reached for his sword and half turned. Idris grunted as a blade from the darkness ran through his side. Everything went dark. Saiyah screamed, clasping her hands to her mouth.

Instinctively, she became shadow and pressed herself against the wall, holding her breath. Only the glimmer of Idris's eyes indicated where he was, reflected in pearly blood as he doubled over. Sword unsheathed, he was already healing himself fast. Dim red eyes appeared behind him. She tried to call out, but her words were hellish and indecipherable. Red eyes snapped to attention, finding her hiding place. With considerable force, Idris was flung aside. He hit the bannister, splintering it, and crashed down the stairs. Saiyah retreated backward into her room.

A second pair of icy hands gripped around her neck from behind. She slipped between forms but couldn't get free. The first assassin entered the room ahead of her. Struggling for breath, she pushed backwards towards the window and rammed hard against it.

An inhuman rush of air pulsed around her. Tiny shards of glass shattered the midnight sky. Everything slowed until her body landed heavily, her fall broken by the demon. She rolled away, numb with vertigo. Gasping for breath, she knelt, but the other demon jumped from the window and landed ferociously over her, forcing her body backwards at an uncomfortable angle. He held his blade aloft. Saiyah screamed and emitted a shield, knocking the demon back.

Idris appeared on the lawn, hurling a ball of torrid, blueish light at the remaining demon. He charged determinedly towards Saiyah at lightning speed. She felt his arms around her and instantly they were in the air. His speed reduced as he landed unsteadily in the walled garden, his torso wet with blood. Stumbling together, they took cover under a long trellis, breathing hard.

"Are you hurt?" He checked her over but continued to heal himself.

Breathless, Saiyah shook her head. "Where are your men?" she asked, wincing at the sight of his wound.

"Not necessary," he said, his body relaxing by the moment.

One of the assassins appeared at the far end of the trellis. Idris leapt to attention, barely hindered as he rushed towards them. Blades clashed. The assassin was pushed back and pinned against a stone wall. He flung Idris away, jagged blade locking Idris's sleek sword, ringing like a bell.

The other demon appeared suddenly, lashing viciously at Saiyah. She dodged and became shadow simultaneously. Her attacker's blade became translucent and smoke-like; one blow struck like a blunt object, sending her crashing through the vines.

This blade could touch her in shadow form.

Saiyah tumbled across a flowerbed, wheezing. With effort, she rolled onto her side and saw the demon approaching. Holding her hand out, she tried to emit another shield of divine light.

Idris called out to her.

The demon loomed over, wicked blade inches from her face. It stalled abruptly, lodged against something. The demon scowled. From her hands was a shadow, an extension of herself, blocking the blade. Obscure darkness. Saiyah felt it. Fragile, it began to fracture.

With vehement impact, Idris knocked his own opponent off his feet. He shot a dart of crackling energy in Saiyah's direction. Saiyah lay still as it scorched over her, inches from her face, and forced the demon to recoil. A nearby wall ruptured from the blast as she stumbled to her feet.

Saiyah had only a moment to gaze at her hands in wonder as purplish shadows, tangible not with light, but darkness, swarmed. Shaken, she held her ground as the demon slammed into her. She pushed back with the shadows, willing them to grow. Locked in struggle, more shadows writhed onto the ground around her feet. She was dimly aware of Idris speaking to her, warning her of something. Eyes flaming green, she gripped the demon's arms in darkness and heaved him of her into the embers of Hezekiah's blast.

Running towards Idris and the demon he was still locked in combat with, she readied another attack. A ball of shadow readied at her fingertips. The demon snarled as she approached.

"Wait!" Idris shouted.

Darkness erupted from her like black fire, thrusting the scavenger into the wall. Brick dust scattered. The scavenger was no more.

"You should have left one alive," Idris said with a sigh, straightening his uniform and brushing brick dust off himself.

Saiyah tilted her head, dimly aware of the sound of voices and footsteps outside the garden.

Idris froze. "Put the shadows away," he snapped, regaining his footing.

She halted in her tracks and dropped her powers automatically.

Gabrielle, Adriel and a dozen others arrived on the scene, some appearing out of thin air, others pouring through the demolished wall. They made quick work of the battered assassins, then pointed their swords in the direction of Saiyah. Only Gabrielle kept hers lowered, though she peered at her curiously.

Idris stepped in front of Saiyah.

"Stand down. This one is with the Albion Circle. I will deal with her," he said authoritatively.

Saiyah glanced at the body of the nearest demon. Other than exhaustion, she felt nothing.

S CRATCHED AND BRUISED, SAIYAH had multiple cuts all over, deep enough for stitches. In the study, Idris coached her in healing herself. They weren't difficult wounds to mend. He handed her a spare cloak that was a little too big. She took it and wore it like a dressing gown over her blood-splattered pyjamas.

Idris apologised that there was no milk for tea. Saiyah didn't mind, drinking hers black, just happy for the comfort of a warm drink in her hands. The curtains were open, looking out over the destroyed garden.

"Are you alright?" he asked, taking a seat opposite her.

She nodded and forced a smile. "I'm sure it'll only haunt me later," she said breathlessly.

They drank their tea in comfortable silence, only broken when Idris finished, and the cup clattered on the saucer.

"Thank you. For helping me. I didn't expect that." he said softly, averting his eyes.

"Nor I you," she said in a low voice.

The sky started to shift to a lighter shade.

Saiyah bit her lip. "You said before that they were tracking me. Do you know why?" she asked shakily, despite knowing perfectly well what the reasons were.

He glanced down into his lap and took a breath before speaking. "They called you 'Katomei.' My Demonic is not well practised, but it's good enough to know what it means: It's a title given to nobility who earn it rather than are born to it. A ruler. It certainly confirms your notion that Asramenia is your mother."

Saiyah's eyebrows twitched smugly.

"It would explain why there were so many of them all over London. You are their target. We were not able to kill them all, but I'd wager that they'll not return quickly, unless their employer offers a greater reward." He paused, his expression grim. "I'm sorry. I thought you would be safer here."

Saiyah shook her head. "It's alright. Who knows what might have happened had you not been there." She gave him a sincere look, then furrowed her brow with worry as she remembered the shadowy blade. "They had a weapon that could touch me in my shadow form."

"I know. And I doubt they acquired it on their own. Whoever is creating these Hell gates must be powerful, and they know how to attack your demon form. I suspect you are being targeted because of your...condition," he said with a grimace, but then smiled softly. "Saiyah, I want you to know that you can trust me. I will not betray you."

Something in his sympathetic tone made her suspicious. "You mean you'll keep my secret? Not that I understand fully yet what it is."

He locked eyes with her, and a pained expression appeared on his face. He nodded with conviction. "Whatever the truth, perhaps we could help each other discover it."

Abashed, Saiyah smiled thinly, focusing on her teacup. At her fingertips, a tiny, controlled amount of shadow swirled. After a moment she switched her attention back to him with a look of undetermined amusement. "Really?"

"Really." Idris gave an awkward smile and cast his lashes down. "Alright. Begone now, demon," he said in a weary but playful voice.

Saiyah pulled the cloak around her. She hovered near Idris as he tidied his desk. He gave her a questioning expression, but his brows gradually softened. There was a tingle of gentle energy between them, though she wasn't sure if it was his or hers. Both were as startled as the other.

Without a word, Saiyah left.

XIX

How Awful Goodness Is

S AIYAH'S EMOTIONS REMAINED TURBULENT for days after the emotional encounter with Hezekiah. Surely, she was imagining things. Gods gave off a celestial energy which caused a certain reaction in demons. Daniel told her it could hurt them, or simply make them uneasy. It wouldn't be the first time she felt that static from Idris after all.

Saiyah passed Idris in the library the next time she was at the embassy, and he glanced up with a flat expression. She barely saw him during her next few scheduled sessions. He was always busy with official business of *The Host*, but no explanation was given. The lack of communication from him caused Saiyah to fret. Perhaps he would go back on his word after all.

One afternoon, Saiyah walked down the street by the natural history museum on the way to the embassy and spotted Idris from afar, descending the steps. He turned as if sensing her, pausing awkwardly. She flashed him a smile and a wave on approach. Idris looked pained and guilty.

"Have you been busy with something lately?" she asked, catching him at the gates of the museum grounds.

He stepped to the side and out of sight. "Gathering information on your... problem," he mumbled.

"In there?" Saiyah raised her chin in an upward nod.

"No. It seems you need less training with your demonic energy than I imagined," he said in a brighter tone, though still unable to look her in the face. "I take it someone other than Azeldya has been teaching you?"

"Yes. Zulphas and Bezbiel," Saiyah said.

Idris's mouth pulled slightly into a frown. His glare was icy, but it wasn't aimed at her. "Follow after me and keep yourself hidden. Now isn't the time for you to be seen in the embassy. I'll meet you in the library later, wait for me there. I have something which might be useful to you."

With a tilt of his head, he beckoned her inside.

Before the door closed, she turned to shadow and let herself slip through. Flattened on the floor, she watched

Adriel shuffle papers at the entrance desk. It was a difficult task to get across a foyer flooded with celestial light and full of moving beings.

Saiyah spotted one of the healers in their flowing white robes walking at a leisurely pace. He looked as if he was heading toward the passage which led to the library. As he passed, Saiyah latched onto his shadow. She'd hoped she would be able to slip away, but unexpectedly, he went to Idris's office. It was empty, but the great doors were open. The healer continued onwards, out the doors and across the lawn, humming a cheerful tune as he did so. He was looking for Idris.

He reached the door of the embassy residency and paused. Raised voices came from within, speaking frantically in the god's speech. A slower voice cut through which she knew to be Idris's, fading towards a more civilised tone. The silence didn't last for long.

"Oh dear," the healer mumbled in his own language, with a note of sincere sadness. "You can come out now," he said in a kind, husky voice, seemingly looking directly at Saiyah. "I saw you in the foyer. If anyone asks, you can tell them I agreed to be your escort."

Still in his shadow, Saiyah morphed into her human-shaped form and solidified. The healer had an indistinguishable sense of age to him, similar to Azeldya, though his face showed none of it aside from a neat philosopher's beard.

"Thank you," she whispered, "And sorry for following you."

He smiled warmly. "Not at all. I've seen you here many times with my son, I know you are no threat."S aiyah simultaneously blushed and raised her eyebrows. "Your son?" she stuttered.

He chuckled. "Yes. I am Yarid Hezekiah, head of the healers." He held his hand out to shake hers. It struck her then how similar their faces would be without the beard.

Mouth agape, she took it wordlessly. "Do you know what's going on in there?"

He dropped his smile. "There are demons from your establishment speaking with him, as well as the new Director."

Saiyah's stomach churned. There were gods of a higher calibre in there. Perhaps they would know what she was on sight, even if she wasn't sure herself. Yarid noted her apprehension and put a hand on her shoulder.

"Not to worry, my dear. We're not all that harsh." He moved slowly, as if he had aching joints, though as a god and a healer it was impossible. "Come along, then."

Puzzled, Saiyah followed him through the doors as if she were entering as a guest for the first time. He held out a hand to signify she should stay back. Azeldya's smooth, precise voice came from the war room. Yarid paused, then looked to the right instead, straight into the open door of the study. His face broke into a grin.

"Grandfather!" came a tiny voice, followed by a bouncing ball of light with long, fair hair.

Saiyah swayed on the spot in shock. Fingers lightly brushing the side table, she steadied herself.

Yarid scooped the delicate girl up and spun her around. She couldn't have been more than five, and she giggled with delight. He entered the study with her.

Saiyah followed as if in a dream. They both knelt together on the floor. The child had a book open in her lap, pointing to the pictures. Saiyah recognised it as the one with the disturbing fairy-tale which resembled her mother's fate.

Yarid said something to her, an introduction perhaps? Saiyah barely registered, her eyes locked on the child. She was the very flower of heaven, rose-cheeked and radiant.

"This is–" Saiyah stammered, pointing at the angelic child. They both looked up with pure, blue eyes. "This is the captain's daughter?"

Yarid took in her astounded expression and broke into a grin, then a chuckle. "Heavens, no. Zillah is the daughter of my eldest son, Ezra."

The girl watched her with the unashamed stare of a child who wasn't yet self-conscious. The same large eyes as her uncle's.

The door to the war room rattled open, and the sounds from within gained clarity. Saiyah spun about and came face to face with Gabrielle, who'd come to a halt before her. There was a crease between her brows that didn't suit her face, but her expression brightened upon seeing Saiyah. Beyond, Saiyah could see Azeldya's profile through the wood-carved screens, and she caught a wary glance from Idris beyond that. He faltered in whatever he was saying when he saw her, and a smooth golden voice continued. She glimpsed the speaker for a moment. It was Malik, the Katomet she'd met at the solstice party.

Gabrielle closed the doors behind her and ushered Saiyah further into the study. "What are you doing here, Saiyah?" She glanced, bewildered, between her and Yarid. "Healer Hezekiah." Gabrielle greeted him formally with a slight bow of the head.

Yarid reciprocated warmly as he played with his granddaughter.

"Azeldya is here. Don't I also have a right to know what's going on in Hell? It's something to do with the Hellgate, isn't it?"

Yarid's cheerful expression faded, and he glanced at the two women curiously, then at his granddaughter in a protective way.

Gabrielle tried to hide a smirk as she muttered something about presumptuous young half-demons. Voices rose from the adjacent room, this time much louder.

There was a low peel of laughter under it all which was distantly familiar as Malik.

Yarid got to his feet, suddenly appearing tall and opposing though he was similar in stature to Idris. He strode leisurely across the room. Gabrielle opened her mouth as if she was going to say something to stop him, but he placed a hand on her arm and smiled kindly. "Not to worry, my dear." There was a twinkle in his eyes as he passed her. The doors to the war room opened for him, and once closed, everything fell silent.

Gabrielle, Saiyah and little Zillah who sat cradling her book, were equally stunned to silence. The crease between Gabrielle's brows returned. She heaved a sigh and looked down at Zillah. "I need to go. Will you be alright to watch her for a moment?"

Saiyah's jaw opened and closed. "What? Me? Why not you? Where do you have to be that's so pressing?"

Gabrielle offered a feeble shrug of apology, already leaving. She closed the door behind her. Saiyah turned to Zillah, sitting quiet as a church mouse in the middle of the room. Saiyah wasn't sure if she was going to cry or not.

"Hello." She spoke a few notes higher than she usually would. "Are you Zillah? Captain Hezekiah's niece?"

The girl nodded and took a gasp of a breath.

Saiyah couldn't help but smile as she crouched down and moved towards the girl. "I like your book."

Zillah automatically looked at it. One tiny finger was shut between the pages, and she opened it there.

"Is it a good book?" Saiyah asked.

Zillah shook her head. "Well, I do usually like it," she began to explain, lifting her long lashes to Saiyah, "but this one doesn't have an ending."

Saiyah frowned and smiled at the same time.

"What do you mean?"

Zillah turned the page. "The page is gone. It doesn't have the ending."

There wasn't even a tear, just a few feathery threads. Deliberately thorough.

"How does it normally end?"

Zillah looked at her as if it were obvious. "The princess sleeps for a hundred years, and when spring comes again the one she really loves comes to wake her," she said plainly, not dwelling on the matter. "Are you a human or a demon?"

Before she could answer, the door clattered open. Yet another man who looked remarkably like Idris, but with a longer face and a thin mouth, marched into the study. He wore a finely woven cloak laced with gold. The colours of this clothing were blinding in comparison to the slayer's uniform. His expression was already full of rage, but as he took in the sight of Saiyah kneeling on the floor with Zillah, his lips curled back in disdain. He placed one hand on the jewelled hilt of his sword.

"Step away from my daughter, you beast!" he yelled.

Oblivious, Zillah gasped and shot to her feet. "Uncle Iggy!" she cried, running past her father to Idris.

Saiyah clenched her jaw as she readied for confrontation.

Instantly, Idris pushed past him and another unknown, blank-faced god, Zillah still attached to his leg. "Ezra, this is Saiyah Greyson, she is also a member of the–"

"Zillah, come away from it." His voice lowered but was no less cruel.

The little girl bolted towards her father and buried her head in his robes, arms wrapped around his legs, so he was pinned. Azeldya was hovering in the hallway with Zulphas at her side, warily watching Ezra. Zulphas seemed particularly shocked about the remark. Malik's tall, lean form leaned in the doorway of the war room with his arm above his head, a ridiculous grin on his face.

"You're always getting yourself mixed up with the wrong sort, aren't you, little brother?" Ezra glared at Idris, and his intense look was reciprocated. "Still, at least the rumours of you bedding her aren't true."

Saiyah raised her eyebrows higher than she thought was possible and stepped forward. "How dare–"

"Silence. Both of you." Idris barely looked at her.

A chuckle from Malik echoed, and Yarid stepped between his sons.

"I don't think Zillah needs to witness this, Ezra. Why don't we convene in my quarters?" Yarid spoke more genially and calmly than the situation warranted. "I'll see the demons out and meet you there. Let your brother deal with Miss Greyson."

Ezra broke eye contact with Idris for the first time and took Zillah by the hand. "Very well," he said bluntly, before marching away with his daughter.

Idris gave a slight nod to his father in thanks, who only smiled. Azeldya walked over to Saiyah and touched her tenderly on the head with a faint smile.

"Come and see me later," she said softly.

"Of course," Saiyah replied with a hint of puzzlement.

Once they'd all left, Idris closed the doors to the study with a notion of finality and stood with his back to her, fingers lingering on the handles. The echo of footsteps faded, and he let out a deep sigh.

The study was constant as ever, all blues and purples with hints of red on the lampshades and rugs. Warm, polished woods, in a style that was apparently favoured by the gods, caressed the ornate furniture. One of the panes in the long windows was ajar, letting sweet smells through from the walled garden.

"Charming man, your brother," Saiyah said, falling into one of the armchairs.

Idris gave her a warning look. "Ezra is the new director of ambassadors for Earth. After what happened here the other night, he's visiting for a while. We'd better be careful. His assistant, Lord Silas, may be staying longer. But let's pray not." He busied himself at his desk, glancing at the window. "Why did you not wait in the library as I told you?"

Saiyah floundered for words and shrugged. "I sort of just ended up here. I got curious."

"That's not good enough. You know you could have gotten yourself killed?" There was a divine energy to his voice, making it sound unearthly as it resonated about the room.

Idris took a deep breath. In an instant, his vivid aqua eyes were closer to her than a moment ago, and they stood across from each other. There was something icy in his expression which made her recoil. Even his motions were unusually erratic.

"For hell's sake, what's going on here, really?" Saiyah tried to sound authoritative, but her voice trembled as she spoke.

His harsh face softened, and something close to remorse surfaced as he let his hand linger on the back of an armchair absently. "You must be more demon than you are anything else," he said under his breath, shaking his head.

Saiyah closed her eyes in a moment of exasperation. As she was about to speak, he stepped close to her, checking the door as if someone might be watching.

"I know about you," he said. "I suspected it before, but now I know."

Saiyah faltered and looked at him cautiously, fear leaping in her chest.

He looked away with a sigh. "You *are* the daughter of both god and demon. A Nephilim. I have found proof."

She shook her head and took a few vigilant steps back, glancing at the door. "You're wrong."

He held up a hand in a peaceful gesture. "Come with me," he said, and led her though the residence, a hand still on the hilt of his sword.

When they stepped into the war room, he produced a little ball of light in his palm and sent it lighting all the candles in the room. From within the beautiful carved mesh walls of the inner chamber, Saiyah noticed for the first time the dark spines of ancient books in glass-fronted cases. Instead of the maps on the table, there was an array of documents and files. Saiyah moved to stand across from Idris, peering at the yellowed parchment. It contained general notes in the gods' script, minutes for meetings, with a section that'd more recently been circled in biro and other reports. Familiar words caught her attention: *'child of the divine and eternal night.'* Reading as quick as her brain would translate, and not knowing where to start, she realised everything was related to a god named Tobias Malkiel, and his suspiciously close working relationship with Asramenia. Saiyah ran her fingers over his signature on one document.

"The matter was concealed at the time, and most evidence of his divergence was destroyed. I remember it well. The dates added up. There were always rumours there was a child." Idris hovered over her, looking at the parchment warily.

"If you knew this before, why did you not tell me?" she said in a small voice.

"Because it was out of the question, or so I thought. You are young, but surely you must know by now that it is impossible for the offspring of the divine and the demonic to survive. They destroy the mother from within before coming to term."

Saiyah flinched and made no attempt to compose herself.

"Those that do survive outside the womb are monstrous, animalistic demons. But so-called demi-gods are not a new phenomenon. Therefore, I had to assume it was possible that your mother found a way. After all, Asramenia wasn't without skill in the realm of demonic rituals." He took a breath and added tentatively, "Perhaps Nyx, her dark lady, aided her. I don't know."

Saiyah released her breath and wiped her eyes before they became too glassy. Relief that John Greyson and his questionable character was not her father was quickly overtaken with shock. She half sat on the table, eyeing Idris apprehensively. "Are you going to tell the Elders? Your brother?" she asked with a tremble in her voice.

He let out a sigh. "If I were, I would have done so already."

She folded her arms and walked to his side of the desk, facing him. "Why haven't you? Why are you keeping my secret?"

Idris looked to his feet, palms flat on the table, statuesque but hesitant. "It didn't feel like the right thing to do."

Saiyah raised her eyebrows, her mouth twitching from a laugh to a snarl. "You're breaking the laws of your ridiculous order because *this time* it just doesn't *feel right*?" She tested him, her voice filled with disdain. "How many times, I wonder, have you followed orders to the letter and stood by whilst people like my father have been wrongly punished?" she scoffed.

Abruptly he slammed a clenched fist on the table. A faint crackle of energy sparked from the blow, startling and interrupting her before she could continue a well-prepared argument.

"Do not test me!" he erupted. Something of his usual tidiness slipped, and divine energy resonated. "I *abhor* how you—the contention with which you speak! I detest that you can dispute so brazenly our ways and question everything I do, everything *my people* do and what we stand for!" He exhaled strongly, visibly forcing himself to a calmer state as he lowered his voice, "You are a paradox that causes nothing but turmoil to my mind.

Yet, had it been anyone else, it's true, I would have acted... responsibly." He deflated, dropping into a chair.

Saiyah stared at him with her mouth half-open.

Idris rubbed his temples. Defeated, he pointed a finger accusingly at Saiyah. "Do not mistake that I now think you are accurate in what you say, but the fact that you make me question myself is... unnerving."

Weariness showed in his ageless face. She knew he'd calmed when his long lashes finally moved again and flitted up to her.

Saiyah spoke cautiously. "I *am* thankful you've decided to keep my secret. And I know I'm not the best judge of character, but I think you're a good person. That's something you don't need to question yourself on."

He gave a relieved dip of the head. "And I you. Notwithstanding your influence on me."

Her smile faltered. Did he know about Bezbiel's enchantment?

She tilted her head sweetly. "And what is that influence exactly?"

"I wouldn't dare to presume." He paused, with a tortured expression. "It must be a form of demonic temptation."

She cast her eyes down. His words, originally humorous enough, rang into silence as Idris waited for her response. Her heart beat in her ears as he watched her, his mouth agape as if breathless. He turned his head as a pained look crossed him.

"I am not an evil person. If I truly am half what you are, how can I be?" she said, gesturing to the records. "I am not trying to make you do or feel anything, I swear." She implored him, placing her hand down on the table slightly closer to his than intended.

Idris surveyed her hand and where his fingertips strayed close to hers. Saiyah's heart fluttered, and her balance wavered. A familiar, anxious knot was growing in her gut–a warning. Looking into Idris's celestial eyes, she could see the same seed of doubt.

"There is some truth in what you say. As always," he admitted in a strained voice.

The door opened and Gabrielle's frantic voice flooded in, but ended suddenly as she took them both in. Idris stood quickly. Gabrielle halted, blinking as if her vision was blurred. A frown formed.

"What is going on here?" the goddess said softly, though there was a sense of wrath in her words.

Idris stepped purposely away from Saiyah. "I think you should leave," he said, unable to look at her.

Saiyah swallowed her shock. She grabbed her things and walked past Gabrielle, who was still staring at Idris wrathfully.

XX

Souls and Memories in a Trance

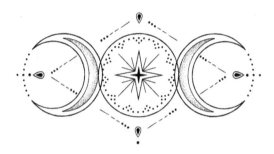

S AIYAH'S HEART WOULDN'T STOP racing as she tossed
and turned in bed, unable to put Idris from her
mind. She didn't know too much about gods and their
relationships with each other. From what Daniel had
told her, they took that kind of thing very seriously.
Of course, gods had children with each other and all
that, but their love was meant to be pure, nothing more.
Their emotions weren't the same as humans.

Vexed, she lumbered out of bed and strolled down
to the kitchen. She uncorked a bottle of red wine and
strolled to the darkened living area. The radio was on
low volume, churning out a static sounding *Classic FM*.

Jack sat silently and rigidly in the armchair, reading a book. His beady green eyes glanced at her.

"You're getting it too now?" he whispered.

"Getting what?" she groaned, rubbing her forehead and flopping into a dining chair.

"Demons don't need to sleep as much as mortals," he said.

"Yes." She shrugged. "Come and help me with this, I'll not drink it all on my own."

Jack fetched a glass and Saiyah poured for him. They clinked glasses cynically.

"Something bothering you? Is everything okay, you know, after your... you know. Incident with the gods?"

She rolled her eyes and dropped her shoulders, fiddling with the stem of her glass. "It's nothing to do with that," she said. "Well, maybe it is, in a roundabout way."

Saiyah turned her head calmly at a movement in the doorway. It was Hex in a long, black, brocade dressing gown.

"What's going on?" Hex asked with a ghost of a smile.

Saiyah gestured for her to sit and shared her wine. "I think I might have fallen for a god," she said, taking a large gulp.

"As in... love?" Jack looked away, embarrassed.

Saiyah nodded grimly. "Well, yes, or something like that."

"Well, shit," Hex said simply. "That's unexpected." Jack shook his head wordlessly, unable to comprehend.

"Captain Idris Hezekiah himself, no less." Saiyah chuckled morbidly.

Hex straightened up. "Judas."

Hex swore, then said, "I'll get another bottle."

The three of them talked late into the night, musing on the nature of gods, demons, and their ways of life. It was the early hours of the morning before they retreated to their rooms.

Saiyah locked her bedroom door behind her and went straight to her mother's journal. She skimmed through the pages, looking for mentions of John Greyson again. She had to confirm that he wasn't her father. Her stomach was filled with both dread and determination. There was little mention of him over the next few years, aside from comments of receiving letters and the occasional battle plan. It was as if she was indifferent to him. Or scared. Perhaps he had died just as Azeldya said.

Hemera Kronou, 01, Pyanepsion 1587

I'd been wondering if John had remembered our conversation about his ritual and my coming of age. He'd said nothing to me of it since he arrived, and I wondered if I should be the one to speak up.

He knocked on my chamber, his book in hand, and I let him in. We talked at length, where he explained to me exactly what would happen, leaving me under no illusions about what we were about to undertake. I told him I was certain I wanted to do it still, and he kissed me ever so sweetly, easing my apprehensions.

We drew the circle and began the ritual in the usual way. His incantation was in a language I did not understand, but I felt power in them akin to demonic. I joined as best I could, raising the energy. John removed his shirt. I looked away, but soon I saw blood on the stone. A symbol was carved in the centre of his chest. He took my hand and pulled me close. It was easier for me to do than I'd imagined. His blood tasted so sweet and pure, and he held me close as I took it.

He was pale when he stepped away and held the knife to my chest. I readied myself, but he did nothing. Evenly, he took the knife away and cupped my chin, I felt the sting of the blade at the base of my neck. He held me fast and I endured it. John lifted me to sit on the altar so he could reach. I held him tight as he took my blood, continuing the incantation. I was weakened and breathless when it was done.

John's face looked so strange to me with my inky blood on his chin. I should have taken his blood not twice more, but he insisted as he was mortal it should only be once. He drank from me not twice, but three times. He said that because I was a demon I was stronger. I was dizzy when it was done. I had no doubt that he was a more powerful being than I now.

I was glad when he kissed me on the mouth and not my neck. I was too weak to stand, so he lay me down. There, I broke my vows as a Priestess.

Saiyah shivered and cursed John Greyson under her breath.

Taking a swig of wine, a pensive expression stuck on her face. After a moment of unblinking, glazed eyes, she pushed piles of books and scrolls aside and cleared a space. She rolled the rug back, exposing the rough floorboards for a flatter surface. Laying candles around her in a ring, she lit them one by one then took a gulp of wine from the bottle to relax her mind. Saiyah sat cross-legged as if she were meditating. She didn't need Zulphas or Medea to induce sleep for her now, and she slipped into a state of half-consciousness.

Opening her eyes slightly, her room was out of focus and monochrome. Shapes were illuminated strangely as she turned her head, seeing double. She shut her eyes again and released her shadow from her body, pouring her consciousness into it. The falling sensation wasn't unusual for her now. She'd tried to visit Hell many times, but always ended up in the same place. Luckily, it was the place she now wanted to go to.

There it was: the familiar setting. Violet-leafed trees emerging through the darkness, moonlight dancing off rippling lavender waters and motes of mauve dust in the air. There were shadowy figures with pastel coloured skin reclining by the waters. Some seemed to move within it, and laughter like the ringing of bells echoed amongst the splashes.

"Mother?" Saiyah said tentatively, her voice reverberating unsettlingly. "Mother, are you here?"

The nymph-like figures in their dark robes turned towards her, abruptly silent and still. Their faces were beautiful and terrifying all at once, but their glowing green eyes assured Saiyah of their trust.

One nymph stood and stepped forward. She wore nothing but a dark cloth draped over her, barely resembling clothes. She appeared much younger than Saiyah, barely adolescent.

"Asramenia is not here," the girl said. "Though her memory lingers, this is not her final resting place."

"Where can I find her?" Saiyah asked.

Another nymph with a deeper, sultry voice of authority spoke next. "She does not know where she slumbers, daughter of Asramenia. Ever since she last sought you out, she has been bound to that place."

Saiyah clenched her jaw and lowered her chin. "I will find her," she told them resolutely, already fading from their world.

Saiyah's vision returned. Swaying, she steadied herself as she blinked away the darkness. She knocked one of the candles over, but the shadow of her hand managed to grab it before it tumbled. One by one she blew the candles out.

There were only two people who might know where Asramenia's final resting place was. In fact, one of them should know for certain. Azeldya was one of them, but she'd be gone by now. That left her with one option, but she'd have to act fast.

XXI

Suspicious. Reasonless.

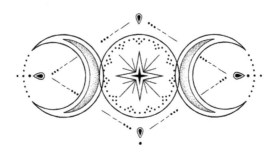

WHEN SAIYAH REACHED AZELDYA'S office, she was almost in tears. Azeldya looked up from her desk with only mild concern and came to her instantly, hushing away her fears. The ancient demoness mixed a concision of herbs and unknown substances for Saiyah, serving it to her in a painted glass goblet. It was lemon-yellow and sugary sweet, tasting like vanilla and cinnamon. It calmed her nerves.

"Did you finish the journal?"

Saiyah shook her head. "Not quite. I came to a part where they performed a... dark ritual. Idris said Greyson was not my father, that it was another god he knew, and that my mother betrayed the gods. I was checking if it was true. About John Greyson, that is. Then I contacted some shades that knew my mother and they said her body isn't where it should be–"

"What?" Azeldya became very still.

"That's what they said," Saiyah elaborated weakly.

Azeldya was silent for a while, then she stood and paced towards the window. "What of this... other god?"

"Id–Captain Hezekiah called him Tobias Malkiel. He also said it was impossible for a god and a demon to have children. I want to know how I came to be."

"That is something I'd also like to know." Azeldya sighed. "The first time I met Asramenia, there was a child inside her, a Nephilim. It was destroying her from within. I helped her be rid of it." A hint of horror flashed in her eyes. "It was neither demon nor god. She came to me many times over the years while she knew Tobias, wishing to find a way to let her unborn children live, but I couldn't see a way which didn't involve her death. When she handed you to me centuries later, I truly thought you were the result of a miracle."

Saiyah caught her breath. "Do you think John Greyson participated in this *miracle* somehow?"

"I simply don't know," Azeldya said in the weakest voice Saiyah had ever heard from her.

"Captain Hezekiah said that demi-gods had existed before. But I don't feel like I could be one of them," Saiyah said.

Azeldya raised an eyebrow. "I won't pretend I don't know something strange is transpiring between yourself and Hezekiah," she said, making Saiyah sit up straight, starting to deny, but she cut her off. "Whatever the arrangement, be careful. Especially whilst the likes of Ezra Hezekiah and Akrasiel Silas are around. We may be able to protect you and help you escape to Hell, but while you are with the gods, there is nothing I can do. Remember you set out to find out who killed your mother, not who your father is. Have you made any progress there?"

Saiyah hid her distaste behind a gulp of her drink. Something in Azeldya's tone betrayed impatience, and though Saiyah was well aware she was being used for unfulfilled revenge, it still irked.

"My mother was going to Lord Malik shortly before she died. I'd like to meet him again and see what he knows," Saiyah said earnestly.

Azeldya regarded her seriously. "If you are to associate yourself with the likes of Katomet Malik, friends and enemies alike may assume you wish to be the new Katomei of Khabrasos and see you as fair game."

Saiyah took a breath and nodded resolutely. "My association with the embassy is already causing me to be close to danger."

Azeldya turned and performed a half-smile. "I suggest you speak to Medea. She is experienced in dealing with demonic aristocracy. She and Bezbiel will be seeing Malik soon for one of his parties. You should go."

Saiyah promised she would. Azeldya blinked slowly and gave Saiyah a look which bore through her. "The captain and yourself. I can't oppose what you are doing, but a word of warning, my dear: though he is an ally now, it does not mean he will not become your enemy in future." Azeldya took her hand and squeezed. "Despite appearances, gods are fickle and callous. They are loyal only to themselves, and abandon alliances as readily as the wind changes direction."

"Much like demons then?" Saiyah countered, but bit her tongue under the glare of her coal-black eyes.

Azeldya moved closer to Saiyah, her face constant as stone. "We are all of the same feather. It is true they are not like they once were—bridled with all these rules and laws—but at their core they are unchanged. Don't forget that."

"I'll be alright," Saiyah responded soberly.

Azeldya gave her a hard stare which was impossible to decipher, but eventually released a breath. "You should know, there is trouble brewing in Hell. There appears to have been a quarrel amongst a company of *The Host* and some possible revolutionists in Kuruh. Either Zulphas or I may have to be absent for a time to diffuse the situation if possible."

"Is that why you were at the embassy yesterday? What was Malik doing there?"

Azeldya smiled. "Several of his people were seen amongst the revolutionists in question. Due to his reputation as a former revolutionist, the embassy wanted to be sure he was not involved. Dualjahit may operate differently from other regions of Hell, but Malik's ambition for peace in Hell died with your mother." Her expression grew forlorn. "Besides, he is far too self-serving these days, as you will soon discover."

Saiyah stood to leave but paused as she lifted her bag. "There was one more thing I wanted to ask. In my mother's journal, she mentioned someone called 'Old Moon Face' frequently. Do you know who that is?"

A delicate smile crossed Azeldya's face. "I remember him well, he was an original demon like myself. He once tried to become the Katomet of Khabrasos, thousands of years ago, but was a healer in later life. Zulphas is his son, you should speak to him if you want to know more."

Saiyah's eyes widened, causing a quizzical expression from Azeldya, who stood as her suspicion grew. Saiyah half-ran down the corridor, passing the reading room leading to the library and risked a glance through. Zulphas was whispering with Xaldan and Titania; she inadvertently caught his eye. He shot her one of his nervous half-smiles and Saiyah walked briskly on.

Medea would have to wait. Saiyah was eager to get back to the embassy. Her stomach fluttered just thinking of Idris. She pushed it from her mind, convincing herself it was the thrill of finding out about her mother that drew her there.

ARRIVING FOR HER WEEKLY session of energy mapping with Idris, she was surprised to find him on the corner of the street on her way to the embassy. He'd been waiting purposely for her.

Saiyah took a deep breath as she approached.

"Should we get some tea?" he asked cautiously.

"I don't know. Should we?" Saiyah responded, narrowing her eyes comically.

Idris sighed wearily and walked on. They fell into step together.

With hot drinks in takeaway cups, they walked through Hyde Park. Their warm breath was visible in the air. Idris's smelt powerfully of mint. Thoughtlessly, they wandered off the path and under the trees where early spring flowers reared their heads. It was quiet there, away from the curious public.

"I am sorry for my behaviour yesterday." Idris's voice was husky with concern. "It was... out of character. Please forgive me."

Saiyah took a breath, irked at the direction he'd started the discussion on. "You didn't *do* anything. There is nothing to forgive," she said resolutely and gave him an imploring look.

Idris turned to her. "This is dangerous, Saiyah."

Saiyah bit her lip. "It shouldn't have to be."

He regarded her with a strange wistfulness she'd not seen on his face before. "You know our laws. You know what would happen if anyone even suspected that..." he hesitated and slowed his speech. "Suspected what you are," he finished in a hushed tone, looking ahead.

Saiyah walked quietly with him for a moment. Her heart had been all aflutter and her head felt light. Now, it was as if she was plummeting.

"You're right, I know you're right." Saiyah rubbed her temples. "What should we do now then?"

Idris stared down at his feet. "Stay out of trouble. Especially whilst my brother and Akrasiel Silas are visiting." There was a finality in his words.

"Who is this Akrasiel Silas anyway?"

"A god who likes to know the business of other gods. He is Ezra's assistant, but is essentially his spy."

The only sound was their footfalls on the half-frozen earth.

Saiyah turned to him cautiously. "I would like it if we could be friends."

Idris appeared bewildered. "Friends?" he tilted his head dubiously.

"We *are* supposed to be on the same side. I endorse my mother's ideas, the revolution. Not just because I'm part of the coven. I can't stand what the original demons are doing. It's barbaric."

Idris adopted his usual seriousness. "The revolution," he said in a cynical tone. "How can you be so sure the gods truly want that? It is little more than a dream amongst young demons. Almost nothing has changed in four centuries. Besides, your mother betrayed us, how can I be sure you won't?"

Saiyah was wide-eyed, and stopped in her tracks.

Idris slowed, turned to face her, and unfolded his arms. "You didn't know."

Saiyah shook her head, distraught. "It's not true. Azeldya would have said. The books say nothing of it, her rebellion and independence of her people was everything to her." Her eyes welled as she continued to protest. "Her journal..."

Idris looked at her pityingly, stepping awkwardly towards her. He reached out to place a comforting hand on her shoulder but dropped it quickly when Saiyah shrugged him off. She backed away, scowling at him and deliberating moving.

"I am sorry," he said softly as she turned to walk away. He lowered his head and drummed his fingers on the hilt of his sword. "My offer still stands to help you find out for certain what you are, or how you came to be this way."

Saiyah glanced back. "Why?" she said, wiping her eyes discreetly. "You know enough now, and care little for my mother, I'm sure."

His eyes flickered heavenwards. "Because, much like Akrasiel Silas, I dislike not knowing the truth. And because regardless of what you are, for allowing you to live, it is my duty to make sure no one is born this way again."

Saiyah furrowed her brows, watching him in quiet contemplation.

"Perhaps if we compare evidence?" he suggested.

"You mean you'll let me read anything you've got on my parents? Restricted files?" she said with hopeful curiosity.

Idris closed his eyes, clenching and unclenching his fist on the hilt. "Yes," he breathed reluctantly, then raised a finger to point at her. "But, if we're to work together in such a transgressional way, we would have to be extremely careful. You must also let me see whatever materials you've come to your own conclusions with."

Saiyah pressed her lips together, then gave him a hard stare. She raised her chin. "I accept," she said evenly, reaching out for a formal handshake. "No demonic deals this time."

Idris nodded promptly and shook her hand.

I N THE GREAT LIBRARY, Saiyah retraced her steps over the months past, perusing the recent history section for everything she'd read on the revolution regarding her mother. She couldn't have betrayed her alliance with the gods. From all the research Saiyah had done, she didn't recognise her mother in that act.

Zulphas gave her a curious look as she checked out a dozen or so books, as many as she was allowed.

"Is there something in particular you're looking for?" he asked.

Saiyah shook her head and smiled sweetly, glimpsing Bezbiel descending the staircase to the gallery through the shelves. "Oh no, I'm just reading over them again."

Zulphas shrugged and logged her books as Bezbiel approached. He sauntered towards them with his usual charming grin and commented on her books in his own way. Saiyah rolled her eyes. He helped with her mountain of books, walking with her out of the building and onto the streets.

"John Greyson isn't my father, as it turns out," she explained in a low voice. "It was some god my mother was seeing."

Bezbiel's serpentine eyes widened. "What?" he whispered fiercely, creating a slight hissing sound. "Saiyah, are you sure?"

She nodded firmly, ascending the steps to her house while struggling with the keys. They placed the books on the hallway table with a groan.

Bezbiel looked at her with concern. "Saiyah, if that's the case you should be careful who you tell. But..." He leaned in close to her with an odd expression. "You do have a mortal soul. I can smell it."

"I know, I know," she protested, waving her hand then putting it on her hip. "You can smell it? That's... kind of unsettling. Anyway, the fragments from the burnt section of the library make more sense now. The ones I took before then talked about a child of the divine and eternal night, or something like that. I'd presumed, correctly, that eternal night represented my mother, or her edge of hell at least. I'd thought the 'divine' was something to do with John Greyson's stolen celestial energy, but it was in fact more literal."

"That doesn't explain your mortal half," Bezbiel said, rubbing his chin.

"I'm convinced John Greyson still has a hand in all this," she said. "Naive as my mother seems to have been when writing that journal, I get the distinct impression he was up to something. Maybe she even knew herself. Would you be able to make me another of those scrying glasses? I'd be taking it to the embassy, if that's alright?"

Bezbiel frowned. "Of course, but what business have you at the embassy?"

Saiyah was unable to meet his gaze, "Id–Captain Hezekiah has allowed me access to their library, as well as other records."

Bezbiel raised his brows. "He knows you can read the god's script?"

Saiyah gave him a hard look, taking a breath as she opened her mouth to reply, but his face became dark, and he spoke before her.

"How much more does he know?" he said accusingly, raising his voice.

"He's always known there was something," Saiyah said defensively.

Bezbiel's expression softened to a wary surprise. "You should tell Azeldya. Tell everyone, you need to get out of here–he'll turn you over in no time." He clicked his fingers for effect.

"He won't."

"He will!" He grabbed both her shoulders and shook her. "Gods do not piss about with stuff like this! How can you be sure he's not using you in the same way you've been using him?"

Saiyah wriggled free through shadow form and tucked her hair away. "Don't worry, Bez. I know I can trust him. Besides, your enchantment still holds sway over him."

Bezbiel's brows were furrowed so deep that his slit pupils had dilated. "Tested it, have you?"

"None of your business. Can you get me a scrying glass or not?"

Bezbiel huffed and nodded in agreement. Leaving, he slammed the door behind him.

XXII

Knowledge Forbidden

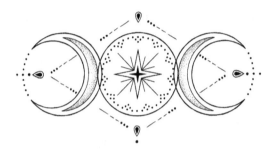

I N THE CAPTAIN'S STUDY, all cards were laid on the table. Idris went first, quite literally laying out all the documents he'd uncovered on Saiyah's mother, John Greyson, and even studies on Nephilim births. Ancient parchments, letters, and scrolls overflowed from the desk and across the carpets, stopping before they reached the fireside. He'd left no stone unturned.

When it was Saiyah's turn, she spoke of her mother, and she spoke the truth. She told him of her memories, her troubling dreams, and her astral projections. Idris listened attentively as she poured out her fears and knowledge all wrapped in one. She was more comfortable telling him this than Azeldya, who she was supposed to trust the most. They talked through the night over candlelight lit by a celestial blue spark, whispering to each other their theories and conundrums. When morning came, Saiyah slipped away, a silent shadow through the little world of the gods and back into the realm of London.

It'd been a challenge, getting her in and out of the residency unnoticed. They would meet under the cover of trees in Hyde Park. Idris would whisk her off to his gardens, and they'd sneak in through the back door. She came and went like this now. Secretively.

Akrasiel Silas, the blank-faced, dead-eyed assistant of Idris's brother, had not left as Ezra had. She'd often notice him with Idris in his office as she slipped past. They would have heated debates on how the embassy was run, standards and duties to be conducted, or dull conversations on administration. The most recent topic was the frequency of which Hell gates were being opened.

The early evenings and the small hours of the morning were the best to catch Idris alone and conduct their research in the seclusion of his study. They would read for hours, comparing their findings and writing out old texts more clearly. They'd often go until two o'clock in the morning when Idris led his second patrol, battling rogue demons and troublesome half-demons of the land.

She pushed those thoughts from her mind.

One evening, Saiyah sat a little way from his desk in one of the armchairs. She held one of the many reports on her mother in the years prior to her death, and disappointingly, they all pointed towards her suspected betrayal. From the gods point of view, anyway. There was no reason she could fathom from the Albion Circle's records and books as to why her mother would break ties like that. There had to be a plausible reason.

They'd been sifting through each other's material for days. Saiyah still had a long way to go with the dull scrolls, but Idris was almost finished.

As the wind rattled around the house, she couldn't stop glancing at him apprehensively. His ageless face was lit by soft candlelight, and her books lay on his desk, along with the new scrying glass and its greenish shimmer. In his hands he held Asramenia's journal, reading the part's she'd carefully earmarked. It was taking him longer to read, as his New Demonic was out of practice, but Saiyah saw that his expression had gone from placid and studious, to mild alarm.

Silently, she rose, taking her scrolls with her, and sat wordlessly opposite him. Idris glanced up at her and back to the book with a flustered expression. He closed the journal carefully and cleared his throat, blinking a lot.

"Their ritual. What were they doing, do you think?" she asked in a whisper. "It seems... dark, even for demons."

Idris swigged the dregs of his cold mint tea as if it were whiskey and stood, running a hand through his already tousled hair. "It's not all that uncommon," he said hoarsely. The moon was rising, casting a soft light through the window. Obscure shapes and leafy debris rattled and danced across the glass. He closed the curtains. "Blood bonds, oaths, and other ritual blood-letting are frequent in Hell, as well as–" He stuttered, unable to look at her, "*carnal* rituals. What bothers me here is the method and frequency of which it is described by the young Asramenia. It was unbalanced."

Saiyah shut her eyes and exhaled angrily. "I knew he was a charlatan," she muttered disdainfully, then spoke up. "Do you think it is at all relevant?"

"I wouldn't discredit it," Idris said more brightly, taking a seat again. "But without knowing the details, we are at an impasse. My guess would be some kind of power-sharing objective. Although that wouldn't affect any offspring either of them had. This, however," He pointed to the delicate burnt fragments, "seems to me altogether more promising. Whoever wrote this knew about you, and either the author or someone known to them wanted it destroyed."

Saiyah chewed her lip and sifted through layers of papers to pull out the reports he'd shown her the other day. "Which is odd, because even though Tobias Malkiel's defection was, as you say, kept quiet, there were no destroyed papers or anything like that."

"Exactly. That we know of."

"That we know of," she agreed. "And other than the fact it says here," She held up one meeting memo, "according to *Michael*, he was consorting with Asramenia, it doesn't allude to a relationship of any kind, or a child."

"It would be a worse crime than defection," Idris explained with a harsh edge to his voice, though it wasn't aimed at Saiyah. "I'm not surprised the event was downplayed, but from the lack of evidence, bar this burnt fragment, it makes me think someone knew an awful lot about it all. While others, myself included, have been left completely in the dark."

"Then how can we even be sure Tobias is my father?"

"Because I was there. I remember it being spoken of by my brother," he said faintly.

Saiyah sat back in her seat, feeling embarrassingly young. "We need to consult a source that was there during that time."

Idris shook his head dismissively. "I can't very well do that without raising quest–"

Saiyah went to her satchel and produced her mother's letter from the Osiris box. She thrust it at Idris. It didn't take him quite as long to read. There was a glimmer of pity beneath his snowy brow, and a look of bewilderment on his face.

"I want to try opening the one you have, just in case it is hers," she said, making swiftly for the door.

Idris appeared suddenly before her, blocking her exit. Saiyah was aghast, but he held up a hand, giving him a chance to speak.

Saiyah wore a look of open-mouthed accusation. "Is there something you're not telling me, Hezekiah?" she said sharply.

Idris tilted his head back and placed a hand absently on his sword. He sighed. "I was on the side of the gods in your mother's situation. Whatever is inside may change your view of me."

Saiyah rolled her eyes. "I hardly care about that."

In the war room, Idris lifted the Osiris box from the mantlepiece, handling it with reverence. Lit properly, the room was rich with golden woody colours. The fire blazed, reflecting with sharp contrast in Idris's blue eyes. Saiyah reached out to the box, turned her hand to shadow, and put her fingers inside.

Idris made a sound of displeasure. "That's not how it's meant to be opened," he said. "You should use your inherited power."

Dubious, Saiyah retracted her hand and held it over the box solidly. Shadow crept from her fingers and engulfed it in nightfall. Nothing happened. Saiyah was downcast, and Idris exhaled as if he'd been holding in a breath.

"Do you want me to open it anyway? Pick the lock?" she said, shrugging off her disappointment.

Idris was still glaring at the box. "Try your celestial energy," he ventured.

An involuntary shiver ran through Saiyah. She produced a soft white light from her palm. Instantly, the box made a clicking sound, and a seal appeared where there hadn't been one before. Saiyah looked up at Idris with a vague smile, but all his attention was on the box. He came to her side gracefully as she lifted the lid. There was a rustle of tightly rolled papers loosening after decades. Saiyah managed them carefully, unravelling them to reveal a handful of letters, each one titled 'To Asramenia,' and signed off, 'Tobias Malkiel' in New Demonic. A hand flew to Saiyah's mouth. She had to place the other hand on the table as her knees weakened. There was more. Her mother's letters to Tobias were intermingled with his. She arranged them in order.

Idris fetched chairs for them. "You read them first," he said in the faintest of voices, settling down with his chair facing her. He watched her unnervingly as she began to read the first letter.

To Asramenia,

Troubling rumours spread through the encampment. There are reports that you plan to turn on us during the next raid.

Josiah asks me to confirm your allegiance. Whatever the answer, I will not put you in danger, but please tell me the truth.

Yours faithfully,
Tobias

Saiyah read every word very carefully, trying to gauge what kind of man had written the letter, what kind of man her father was. His words were urgent and sincere, and his handwriting hurried. She hoped her father was a better man than John Greyson, though it wouldn't take much to achieve. She passed the first letter to Idris, who took it carefully.

Dear Tobias,

That is ridiculous. I do not intend to betray the gods. You may confirm my continued allegiance in the name of the revolution.

Asramenia.

To Asramenia,

I have tried to trace the source of these unfounded rumours, but I can find none. I am doing all I can to plead your case, though Captain Josiah is dubious. I've no doubt that someone outside of The Host has an agenda against you. I am being sent to meet with you again before any action is taken.

I am sorry for what I spoke of when we last met, but that is not important now. I think I have found a way for us to safely have a child. There will be no more monstrous creations, I swear to you. Meet me on the borders of your realm in two days.

Forever yours,
Tobias

Saiyah raised her eyebrows with smug satisfaction as she passed the letters to Idris. It was proof enough to her that her mother was no traitor.

Dear Tobias,

I'll have my spies smoke out traitors if I have any, though I believe all my allies to be loyal at present. I will meet you at the usual place.

I find your notion ambitious, and I wish you wouldn't speak so openly in our correspondence. You only put yourself at risk.

Asramenia

To Asramenia,

I have returned to news of your planned arrest and probable execution. They suspect our relationship. You must flee my love, forget your pride and keep our child safe. Send word to me of your location, I will meet you there.

Do not trust any gods you meet, least of all the lordships. Silas has been dispatched for you, and there are others who seek you as well.

Forever yours,
Tobias

My dear Tobias,

I cannot leave my people. I am well protected, and I know those loyal will guard me at all costs. I have retreated within my dominion to an ancient place I once called home.

Our child grows strong, and I am in no pain. I think it is a girl.

Yours always,
Asramenia.

The final letter was on crisper paper, as if it'd been placed fresh in the box, though there were dirtied marks all over it. It was dated a few years later.

Dear Tobias,

You were right about Moon Face; I find myself increasingly alone and in deeper danger. I cannot trust anyone. I travel to Dualjahit to seek refuge with Katomet Malik.

Come to me on the shores of dark Acheron, if you are able. Come and meet your child.

All my love,
Asramenia.

Saiyah's teeth were clenched to stop her lip trembling when she finished the last letter. She passed it reluctantly to Idris. Though it wasn't about her as such, it was like laying her soul bare.

He finished the letters and let his eyelids rest for a moment in appeasement, then he lay them neatly back in the box. He watched her warily before speaking. "I'm sorry, Saiyah. Are you alright?"

She shook her head and sighed, passing a hand over her face to disguise wiping away tears. "I need a drink," she said with a wan smile.

He regarded her disappointingly. "We've none of that here. We can continue tomorrow."

XXIII

Brighter than Flaming Jupiter When He
Appeared to Hapless Semele

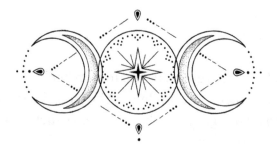

S AIYAH ARRIVED EARLIER THAN usual at the embassy.
The sky still held a hint of indigo as she crept
into the house. She expected Idris to appear, surprised,
perhaps angry, but there was no sign of him. Instead, a
delicate, sublime sound floated through the residency.
Saiyah followed the pleasant melody, a familiar hymn
from her childhood: *Jerusalem.* The door to the room
with the piano was ajar and cascading light illuminated
dust particles from within.

Idris had his back to her, leaning against the table as
he played a violin. He was rather good. With flourishes
and vibrato, it was as if the instrument were singing.

Saiyah stood motionless. It wasn't difficult to believe he was some kind of angel in his resplendent, midnight cloak and shining countenance. As she crossed the threshold, he stopped the sirenic music, turning to her unhurriedly.

"I always rather liked that one," she stated, her voice echoing. "That was beautiful."

He appeared somewhat bashful. "I used to play the lyre—before. Cliche, I understand. When I first came here, this piece was the first music I heard." He spoke in a much gentler tone than she was used to hearing, as if he didn't want to upset the lingering music in the ambiance.

Saiyah settled herself on the piano stool by Idris and raised her eyebrows humorously, "Is it coincidence I wonder, that it's still the tune you favour?"

Idris dismissed her comment, beginning to put the instrument away. She caught a whiff of rosin. Saiyah crossed her legs and gazed up at him admirably. "What else can you play?"

He regarded her unsurely. "Nothing that you would approve of."

"Oh, go on." She tilted her head expectantly.

With a thoughtful look, he played a few experimental notes. "I attended a performance of *The Planets* suite just after the war. I never learnt any in full, but one has a pleasing bridge section." He looked uncomfortable and averted his gaze.

Saiyah nodded knowingly with a bashful smile. He was a lifetime older, and the thought was disquieting.

Idris played, falteringly at first, but as he found the tune and moved to the second refrain Saiyah practically felt her heart melting. It was hauntingly beautiful. When he finished, he was watching her serenely. Saiyah suddenly came back to herself, as if she'd been under a spell.

Idris looked to his feet and put the violin away properly. "Let's go where we can speak freely," he said, his tone once again business-like.

He meant away from where Gabrielle or any of the other gods would stumble in on them. Saiyah's increased presence at the embassy hadn't gone completely unnoticed.

The study was a mess of papers from the previous day, and yet more paperwork had arrived for Idris to undertake in his role of Captain or Ambassador. Their shadows grew long, and Idris's face displayed a determined concentration as he sat to work which Saiyah found admirable.

Idris set down his pen and she looked away quickly, but not before he motioned her to join him. Together, they arranged their collated evidence in chronological order. She told him about the mention of 'Moon Face,' and what Azeldya had told her about Zulphas, as well as him pointing her to the section of the library where the fire had occurred.

"You think he is your mother's traitor?" Idris ventured.

"Impossible to say." She sighed, looking at the burnt, blood-stained fragment again and running her fingers through her hair. "She could've meant anything."

"I'll have him watched. Just to be sure."

Saiyah laid one of the reports she'd just read on the desk and pushed it across to him. They mentioned Tobias being sent away to meet with Asramenia, returning to assure her loyalty, though the author, *Captain Josiah*, wrote as if they were unconvinced. Later it was mentioned that Tobias was promoted under orders of *Michael*, and was moved to work serving the Seraphim.

"A cover up," he said morosely. "He was never seen again after that."

"Daniel Cassiel told me things about you," she said, chewing her bottom lip. Idris became confused and she grinned. "Don't worry, he'd no idea who I was when he agreed to raise me."

This time Saiyah had come prepared with wine, drinking it from the disempowered scrying glass. She divulged what she knew, about him and his task of hunting his own kind. Idris's face grew increasingly troubled, eyeing the tumbler of wine as if he might drink some himself.

"It is true," he admitted slowly. "I was tasked with tracking a group of lesser gods—defected soldiers. However, I felt it was my duty to try and save them from the gallows rather than...what I was ordered to do. There were some who accused me of being complicit, but nothing came of it." His expression darkened as he spoke, and he drummed his fingers restlessly.

"Why did you bend the rules?" she asked, leaning forward.

Idris heaved his chest. "They were under manipulation from 'the snakes,' a criminal gang. I thought I could find the culprits and slay them instead."

Her heart pounded. She knew 'the snakes' were like Bezbiel, with powers of manipulation. Bezbiel, whose enchantment not to harm her was still on Idris.

"I was notified that Asramenia was in the area, and to keep a lookout," he said, tapping his fingers on the desk. "Later I was charged with looking for Sergeant Malkiel also. Your father. I was told he'd defected, complicit with Asramenia, and headed north, where I was based. I never put much faith in the accusation at the time. I tracked his movements for months."

Saiyah's whole body was tense. "Did you find him?" He shook his head solemnly. "That achievement was gained by Akrasiel Silas. When Tobias was apprehended, I helped with examining his belongings for evidence. That's how I came by the box."

Saiyah went quiet and lifted one of her father's letters with his careful but urgent handwriting. "Then what?"

"I know he killed a number of gods before he was apprehended. He was taken to be executed, but was difficult to eradicate. Gods heal themselves quickly, but there comes a time when they tire." Idris made a resigned sound of displeasure. "Tobias Malkiel required a second execution date."

Grimacing, Saiyah clenched her teeth and willed herself not to cry. She poured more wine, contemplating it rather than drinking.

"I was told not to share information, and soon after I was transferred back here," Idris murmured.

She took a swig of wine and drew her knees up. It was completely dark now; only the flickering candles and embers from the fire lit the room. Absently, she smoothed the letters from the Osiris box. The backs were smeared with greyish marks, like ash or faded ink. There was even a fingerprint.

"What's this grey stuff?" she asked, looking at the smears on the back of the paper.

She'd not thought much of it before, but the fingerprint gave her pause.

"God's blood," Idris said casually.

It made sense that it would dry that colour. She picked up the fragment hurriedly and held it close to her face. Idris caught her bewildered expression and stood, moving to look over her shoulder.

"What the hell is this then?" she said.

She held a glowing hand behind the thin parchment to show blood stains dried brown. Mortal blood. Something glinted on its surface. Handing it to Idris, she fumbled for her mother's journal, flicking through pages madly. Horrified wonder dawned. She pointed to where Asramenia described the silvery sheen in John Greyson's blood.

Idris's eyes widened. "It couldn't be," he said, his voice detached.

When Saiyah spoke, her voice was shaky. "John Greyson was here, still alive. He was involved somehow."

Idris held the edge of the book, his thumb tracing along the same line over and over. Saiyah's face tingled knowing he was close, but he was fixated on the book.

Idris turned to her. They locked eyes in breathless shock. Idris straightened and paced towards the fire at the other end of the room, placing an outstretched hand on the mantle, head lowered.

Saiyah felt giddy for multiple reasons. "That proves it, doesn't it? John Greyson was involved somehow." She drew her hand close to her, rising to follow him.

Idris took a moment to speak. "I pray it is not," he said slowly, surprised to see her over his shoulder as he turned around. "This is far more hazardous than I ever imagined."

Saiyah's eyes were animated. "He could be the reason I was born, the reason I have mortal blood. Perhaps he helped my parents. Do you think the Seraphim knows about all this?"

"It's hard to say. The First Sphere certainly doesn't like anyone knowing this much. You should forget all this while you can. Forget about Tobias and Greyson. Keep yourself safe." Idris gave her a hard look, glancing from the mess of papers on his desk to the fire. He made to move past her.

"First Sphere?" Saiyah questioned.

Idris waved his hand in a vague gesture. "The Seraphim - the highest level of god. Third Sphere are those like myself, operating in this world. The Second are go betweens, or sometimes in Hell."

Saiyah glared at him and took a daring step closer, blocking his path. She caught the upper sleeve of his uniform to detain him. "So that's it then? They move in their mysterious ways, and I simply do nothing? I suppose your supreme God didn't like the rest of you asking questions, did they? Well, that won't be me."

Idris clenched his fists and adopted his usual authority. "Be careful of what you say," he warned. "This is a tremendous risk for both of us."

"I'm already at risk just by existing," she said, her voice catching.

He gave a resigned bow of his head and looked as if he was about to argue again, but instead his face softened.

"You've done nothing wrong, Saiyah," he said in a hushed tone. "But if our findings are ever discovered and they decide you know too much, neither of us is safe." He took an unconscious step forward.

Saiyah's heart rate quickened. He examined her face tenderly, but abruptly looked away, as if ashamed. He inched back, a hand to his head as if he were dizzy.

Saiyah closed the distance between them, moving clumsily and too quickly towards him. Idris blinked down at her in surprise. Their bodies were close enough to touch, and she could feel his energy flickering erratically on the surface of his chest. What did she think she would do?

"Please stop. Whatever you are doing, stop," he said quietly.

"I care for you. Maybe more than that. And I think you feel the same way about me."

His body was rigid. "Do you love me?" he said flatly.

"I do. I think. It's not as simple as that. All I know is I trust you more than anyone I know, and I'd rather be here with you than anywhere else."

He placed his hands lightly on her shoulders, as if afraid to touch her, his shock fading to something more tender. Saiyah lifted her chin slightly and inched her face close to his.

"No," he said simply, but not unkindly. Their lips brushed against each other as he spoke, and he held her more firmly. "I am a god, and you are not. I can never love you in the way you want me to."

Her brows furrowed slightly. "It's alright," she whispered. "I know how the emotions of gods work. I still feel the same."

Idris peeled himself away from her. "Saiyah, don't be a fool. I cannot ever love you. It is not in my nature. Your mortal life is a flicker of a candle to me, not bright enough to last, to truly make an impression. I'll admit that I do care for you, for reasons I cannot fathom, but as a mortal creature. That is all."

Saiyah backed away, slipping from his grasp. She'd been so sure.

"Perhaps we should distance ourselves for a while," he said, giving her a look of anguish. "Spend time with your own kind. Speak to Zulphas, and Malik. Go to Prague. Remember why you are doing this, and only return when you are done with this childish infatuation."

Saiyah's jaw slacked, and her eyes welled up. How could he? How could he suddenly be so cold? Although, perhaps he always had been. She'd been so blind.

Without a word or need for prompting, she collected her things and stole away into the night.

B EZBIEL'S HEAD WAS DOWN as he sat in one of the back rooms in the library, dating and cataloguing 'new' books. So intent was his concentration, that he didn't notice Saiyah had drifted into the room until she closed the door behind her. He looked up with a hint of a smile, but it faded as soon as he saw the serious expression on her face.

"How can I help you?" He still retained a hint of good humour.

"I want to ask you about the enchantment–the manipulation you put on the captain," she said, standing rigidly in front of him.

Bezbiel put down his pen and leaned back nonchalantly. "What about it?"

"Is it still on him? Can we be certain?"

He shrugged. "As far as I can tell. Though it was nothing potent, so it might've eased by now."

"I want you to lift it."

Bezbiel leaned forward, narrowing his eyes. "Why?"

Saiyah scratched her palms, pausing with her mouth open. "It's not fair," she said simply.

Bezbiel raised his brows and looked like he was going to laugh, but a sliver of annoyance crept in. "Not fair?" he repeated, his voice slightly raised. "Is it fair that we are quite literally demonised because our distant ancestors dared to question the supreme God?" He said with a malicious chuckle.

Saiyah rolled her eyes impatiently. "Bez, will you just do it please?"

His brows drew together. "I only inferred that he wouldn't cause you any harm, nothing more."

"I don't care. Whatever hold you still have over the Captain, I want it gone," she insisted.

"Consider it done," Bezbiel told her, baffled.

Saiyah searched his face before relaxing. "Thank you," she said with a nod, reaching for the door handle.

"Are you sleeping with him?" Bezbiel said in a lower tone, surprise mingled with malignance.

Saiyah shot him a warning glance, brightening her eyes. "I am not," she said resolutely, but he paid no record as he gradually stood.

He glowered back at her for a moment before she made an irritated sound and left.

XXIV

A Malignant Devil

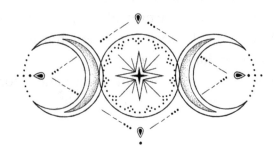

IN AN EMERALD GREEN dress, the brightest colour Medea could convince her to wear, Saiyah sipped champagne on Malik's sizable panoramic rooftop terrace. A delicate springtime heat that still could've burnt her pale skin if she stood still for long warmed her shoulders. Even as the sun was setting, it was far warmer than England. On one side, Prague was dotted with colourful buildings which faded to a smudge of pastel on the horizon. Saiyah could see the castle high up on a hill, like something out of a storybook, and in the distance, glints of white from the Vltava on either side of the Charles bridge were gradually turning a dusky blue. Behind, everything was flat with practical greyish buildings, but the vast, densely packed landscape was no less stunning in the sunset.

The rooftop was crowded with fashionable demons like Medea and wealthy middle-class socialites who Malik had charmed into his flamboyant lifestyle. They all wanted the excitement of mingling with demons and half-demons. Bezbiel revelled in the attention. Medea, barely appearing a day over thirty, chatted with the partygoers and Malik in perfect ease. Despite her ghostly skin, with her captivating eyes and endlessly long legs, she was like an ethereal siren. She uncurled her fingers from her pale hair in a flirtatious motion and made towards Saiyah with a dazzling smile.

"Straighten up, smile, he's coming over. Remember what I taught you."

Saiyah eyed her in annoyance, but her face was placid when Malik appeared and greeted her formally.

"I am so glad you were able to come," he said with a pointed grin. He took Saiyah's hand and raised it to his lips, and if he'd not bowed slightly, Saiyah would've almost needed to stretch. "How are you enjoying Prague?"

Saiyah found it hard not to return his amiable grin. "I've not had much of a chance to explore yet, but it is beautiful," she said, glancing out at the view as she took a drink. "Though it is strange, I don't think I've ever been in a landlocked country before. I keep expecting to see the sea."

Malik grinned again. "You'd find it stranger still in Hell. It's so vast it may as well be Pangea."

Saiyah responded with a polite laugh, and they fell into amicable conversation about Prague and the Czech Republic. Malik recommended sights for her to see with animated movements and delved into the history of Alchemists in the city, of which he'd been heavily involved. Saiyah listened agreeably and they went on to discuss Florence, Ithaca, St Petersburg, Tallinn, and all sorts of places they'd both been in fond retrospect. Malik's travels far outweighed her own, and he spoke of history as if he'd been there for it all. She was just a child to him.

Saiyah stroked the rim of her glass and took a quick breath for courage. "Could I ask you a little about Hell?"

Malik's face lit up and he leaned on the railing casually. "Of course. You want to know about your mother, no doubt?"

Saiyah looked to the horizon momentarily with a shy smile. "I can't deny that's my intention."

"You're nothing like her, you know. You're far better travelled than she was in four hundred years, and knowing her when she was your age, more intelligent I'd wager."

Saiyah flushed lilac, which seemed to please him. Gripping the railing, she adopted a serious expression. "I wanted to ask you about the end of her life. I've reason to believe she was travelling to you in Dualjahit when she died."

Malik's face dropped, but a forced pleasantness remained. "I guessed she was," he said simply. "But as I'm sure you've fathomed, she never arrived."

Saiyah pressed her lips together. "Do you know what happened to her?"

Malik swung himself around, facing away from the other partygoers, drumming his fingers on the railing. "When she didn't arrive, I had scouts sent out. There were signs of her and the gods pursuing her, but it was days before we found the body."

Saiyah took a moment to process it all. "Where–" She halted, and Malik glanced back at her. "So, in the days she was missing, the gods were still looking for her?"

Malik nodded, a crease appearing on his golden brow.

"Where did you find the body? What happened to her?" she asked briskly. The two questions had gnawed at her for a while, but she bit her tongue at her eagerness once they were out.

Malik showed his teeth then chuckled. "This is a rather morbid subject, don't you think? Perhaps another glass, and we can discuss this under the comfort of nightfall?"

He was ushering her away, strolling towards a group of light-hearted banter when someone tapped Saiyah on the shoulder. She turned, startled, to see Gabrielle. She was without her cloak, her goddess-like luminosity toned down. She looked almost human. Gorgeous, but human.

"Can we talk?" she asked, agitated.

Saiyah glanced at Bezbiel to indicate he should be watchful. They moved to a quieter area, away from the bulk of the partygoers.

"I don't know what's going on between you and the captain, and I don't want to know," Gabrielle said frantically. "But I care about him, and you. I don't want to see either of you with your head on the chopping block!" Gabrielle ran a hand through her hair, increasingly distressed.

Saiyah placed her drink on a side table. "What are you talking about?"

"He thinks I've reported him. I called him out, yes, but only to his face," she said in a strained voice.

A rush of gooseflesh ran up Saiyah's arms, and her heart began its familiar anxious rhythm. "What's happened?"

Gabrielle shook her head, narrowing her eyes. "Akrasiel Silas." Gabrielle took Saiyah's drink from the table and took a gulp. "He's taken control of the running of the Embassy and sent the captain away. He wants to meet you."

Saiyah swore, pushing back sickness in her throat.

Idris was gone. Her world spun. She was still furiously embarrassed by what happened, but that didn't matter now. She didn't even have an opportunity to say good-bye.

"I'll speak with the coven," Saiyah told her eventually. "Thank you for the warning."

Gabrielle looked at her sharply. "You'd better do all you can to make this right. I'd be gone too, if they knew I was here." Then she disappeared in a rush of air.

After weighing her options and calming herself, Saiyah sauntered back to the throng of people, placing herself strategically near Malik. She had to do something; time was evidently running out. Catching Malik's eye, he politely bowed his head.

"What exactly entices a demon Lord to surface and partake in this sort of thing?" she asked playfully, getting a murmur of a laugh from other guests.

Malik showed his teeth in his friendly manner. "Like any demanding job, it's healthy to get away. Also, the company is rather diverting."

They laughed more committedly this time. Saiyah mirrored his cheerfulness and reciprocated, raising her glass. She tilted her head and batted her lashes. "You know, I'd awfully like to visit your dominion one day." She turned sideways to lean on the railings. "It would be beneficial to better understand you revolutionists."

Malik smirked impishly. "You want to follow in Asramenia's footsteps?"

"Yes. And I'm sure I would be open to an alliance with Dualjahit."

Malik raised his eyebrows, glancing around to be certain no one was listening. He chuckled lightly. "You're hardly in a position to be making such offers when you don't have any dominion to rule over," he said with a note of intrigue. "You are still very young. Even my youngest children are hundreds of years older than you. Are you sure you want to be involved in all this?" He clicked his fingers and his admirers dispersed, leaving them standing alone together.

Saiyah hesitated before nodding. "I fear it's already too late not to be involved. Assassins from Hell have already been sent after me, and now it seems I have adversaries amongst the gods." Malik gave her an understanding look. "Perhaps in return for safe passage to Hell, an invitation from you perhaps, we could come to an arrangement?"

Subtly, his dazzling grin grew hard and menacing. "Have you ever made a deal with a demon before?" His genial manner fell away, and in the encroaching evening tide his eyes reflected like a nocturnal predator.

Suddenly apprehensive, Saiyah shook her head.

He leaned in, revealing pointed teeth, the whites of his eyes turning sickly yellow. "A word of advice: you may not want to go in so willingly when bargaining. Softly, softly."

Saiyah recoiled instinctively, catching a glimpse of concern from Medea across the rooftop.

Saiyah collected herself. "I've not actually requested a deal or bargain of any kind," she said playfully, taking a drink to disguise her shaking hands.

Malik appraised her, unblinking, before laughing abruptly.

"Very well little Katomei, no deals today. However, if visiting Sheol is what you desire, perhaps that is something we can discuss elsewhen. You have my card." His face had returned to its normal charming grin.

Saiyah kept quiet for a moment, casting her eyes down. Without warning, Malik slipped an arm around her and walked her around behind the bar to a seating area with little booths. It was difficult for her to walk with poise, as he was so much taller. The light had faded. Strings of lights above illuminated them, and citronella candles flickered on tables, casting butterfly shadows on their faces. He leaned her against a wall, and although he simply stood adjacent to her with arms folded, his tremendous height and demonic presence made Saiyah freeze to the spot.

Malik was quiet, looking at her intently before speaking. "Before we begin, what exactly are you accusing me of?"

Saiyah opened her mouth to protest, floundering. "I'm not accusing. I just want to know what happened to my mother."

Malik leaned back, his face serious. "She was found in the North of my land, floating in the Black Lake.

It's hard to say where she was killed exactly; her body could've been disposed of there. There was a single wound through her heart. It would've been a quick death." He spoke quickly, as if wanting to move away from the topic as fast as possible. Seriousness didn't suit him.

"The Black Lake, is that the Acheron?" Saiyah asked, her voice barely a whisper.

Malik nodded.

"And it was definitely the gods who killed her?"

Malik gave her a wrathful look, baring his teeth. "Yes," he snarled. "The scent of their energy was still on her."

Saiyah held out a hand quickly. "I didn't mean to infer–I wasn't implying–"

Malik chuckled darkly. "Worry not, little Katomei." He took her hand in a gentlemanly fashion. "It's not you I'm resentful of." He raised her hand to his lips again and regarded her for a long moment. "I hope we meet again."

When he'd gone, Medea and Bezbiel appeared from around the bar.

"What was that?" Medea asked sharply, a note of panic in her voice.

"Nothing, nothing," she protested, waving her hand. "I have bigger problems than Malik anyway. Gabrielle was just here."

THE PARTY WAS CLOSE to ending, and after the strange exchange with Malik and lurking threat of divine danger, the three of them departed. They stopped at an outdoor bar near the Staromák, or old town square, for a nightcap. The town was still lively with tourists and partygoers, and they watched them glumly from under their decorated canvas canopy. Medea went back to the hotel, still alarmed by Gabrielle's warning. Saiyah and Bezbiel strolled across the medieval paving, worn down with time, heat, and endless footfall until they became smooth and slippery. They passed the throng of tourists waiting for the astrological clock to chime for midnight and paused to watch the little display for a moment.

In the square, surrounding buildings were lit with coloured lights, and a turreted building overlooked it all, lit up pink and purple like a fairy-tale castle. Despite the late hour, many young people, perhaps students, were still loitering in the square with picnic blankets, screw-top bottles of wine, and canned beer. Street performers did their best to procure a few more Koruna before they turned in.

They sat on the burnished cobbles, still radiating warmth from the heat of the day, listening to one of the buskers.

"Did I mention you look lovely in that dress?" Bezbiel complimented mischievously.

"I fought Medea tooth and nail over it," she said.

He chuckled and tapped his fingers on the stone. "What's going on, Saiyah? All this business with Hezekiah?"

Saiyah looked into his familiar snake eyes, and there was no sign of the malice she'd seen before. She sighed. Despite everything, no one in the coven knew her better.

"You were wrong about what you said before," she said. "But not completely. There is something there, his behaviour has been quite... tender. And he admitted he cared for me."

"My, my, Saiyah," he said, with a hint of forced humour, running his hands through his hair. "You really are in the thick of it."

Saiyah rolled her eyes and nudged him playfully. "Yes well, that's all over with now. He wants to distance himself from me, I think."

Bezbiel frowned then grimaced forlornly. He took off his jacket and put it around Saiyah. "Well, that's his loss."

BEFORE THEY WERE DUE to teleport to their next destination, Bezbiel and Medea were keen to explore some of the Alchemical history of the city. Saiyah wanted to do anything but that. There were several touristy museums in the old town and nearby, all claiming to be the best or most accurate, and they ended up in one of the smaller ones. It was tucked away from the usual footfall, in a colourful little building. As soon as Saiyah stepped inside the dim room, she was enchanted with a sense of nostalgia. The entrance room was dark and decorated with apothecary tables and glass implements, all for show, but it gave the effect, nonetheless.

Bezbiel rang a little bell on the desk, and while waiting they perused the 'love' and 'elixir of life' potions for sale with a smirk. Soon a young lady appeared, speaking heavily accented English, and sold them a ticket into the museum. She barely batted an eye at the fact that they were demons. The bustling cities of central Europe seemed to care less about that kind of thing.

Once a few other people arrived, the tour began. They were ushered through secret doors and bookcases that opened to reveal hidden rooms; it was all a bit theatrical, really. The guide was young, probably a student or volunteer. Saiyah's mouth twitched into a smile upon seeing markings of each element at each corner of one room.

"And this is the only surviving building in Prague where alchemists actually lived," said the tour guide.

Saiyah expected all the museums claimed this. "The reason it survives is because there was a secret passage where they would practise in secret." She then proceeded to open a wall, much to Saiyah's astonishment.

The passageway led down some treacherous spiral stone steps to small domed rooms filled with dusty glass bottles and primitive fire pits. Maybe there was something in this. The tunnels went on and on apparently, but they couldn't continue due to flood damage and cave-ins.

Saiyah became dimly aware of a man standing close behind her as everyone was allowed to explore. Saiyah regarded him curiously, somewhat offended as he stared at her with a passive smile. Though mortal, he had the faint whiff of the occult about him.

"You know, these tunnels led out of the city to the forest where they would collect their ingredients," he told her amiably, in better English than the guide.

Saiyah gave an upwards nod, unsure how to respond.

"Forgive me. I'm somewhat of a demon-fan," he said, beaming. He had the first signs of fine lines around his eyes when he smiled, and his hair, pulled back in a low ponytail, had a few strands of silver. "Since your existence was discovered, people say these tunnels actually lead to the gates of Hell." He tilted his head forward conspiratorially.

Saiyah drew her brows together and looked again down the darkened archway, a rope barrier drawn across it.

"If that were true, I expect it'd be heavily guarded," she said with assurance. She didn't want this man to get any strange notions.

The man broke into a grin again. "Of course," he said simply, backing away with his hands in his pockets.

At the end of the short tour, Saiyah stood with Bezbiel outside the museum. He lit a cigarette while they waited for Medea to finish buying things from the gift shop. She saw the friendly occultist again as he left, raising a hand to her in farewell. She nodded and gave a polite smile.

XXV

Friends in Desolation

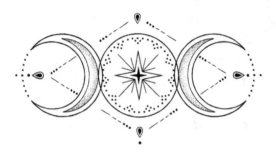

ONCE BACK IN ENGLAND, Saiyah hastily changed out of her sticky clothing and took a welcome shower before heading straight for the embassy, Bezbiel trailing just behind her. There was an acid taste at the back of her throat, and her stomach trembled anxiously. There was something different in the air, or rather in the people she saw. She heard it in snipits of radio broadcasts, and saw it on the covers of newspapers. No doubt it was plastered all over social media. There was trouble brewing in Hell. Perhaps the recent Hellgates were something to do with them? Desperate refugees or half-demons unpracticed in the occult tearing doggedly through worlds to fight for their homeland.

But the conflict in Kuruh was of little consequence to the mortal world. It was how it made demons and half-demons behave which worried people here. By now Saiyah was well used to the glances at her armband and tell-tale green eyes. But now it was like every mortal was staring intently, and with malice. She quickened her pace, and as she approached the street the embassy was on, a young man narrowed his eyes at her and opened his mouth to hurl an insult. Saiyah glowered at him defiantly, exercising a tiny amount of demonic energy. He closed his mouth and stepped back.

On reflection, it wasn't perhaps the wisest thing to do at a time like this.

Jack was somewhere nearby in the form of a raven. Azeldya suggested he stay close in case he needed to fly for help, but Saiyah was confident it wouldn't come to that. Bezbiel squeezed Saiyah's shoulder encouragingly, giving her an upside-down smile. He'd been against her coming here most of all, but she decided meeting with Silas would be her best option. Especially if she was going to get Idris back somehow.

Gabrielle met her in the grand foyer. There was an abnormal stillness about her, and none of her usual smiles. Indeed, the whole place seemed curiously hushed, but no less busy. Soldiers marched in a much more regimented way, and the administration kept to themselves. There was no sign of the healers at all.

They walked to Idris's office in the main building and Gabrielle knocked. When a voice called to enter, she gave Saiyah a nod and hovered in the doorway.

Saiyah stepped into the familiar room where she'd first had her registration. There was a different energy to it now. The doors at the far end were open, and she could see Idris's house beyond. A man sat in what was usually Idris's chair. Stern faced and of imposing stature, his robes were blinding white, edged with glyph-like patterns and motifs of shields and spears intertwined. He had uncommonly dark hair for a god, nearly slicked back from his face and tumbling down from his back. The most startling thing was his eyes. The irises were so pale they were almost completely white, only showing because of the grey flecks within.

Silas stood and beckoned her towards him in an almost perfunctory way. She approached the desk slowly. It was so wrong to see him in Idris's chair. He held out a hand expectantly. It wasn't for shaking though; she'd seen this sort of kingly, archaic behaviour in religious settings before. She grimaced as she took his hand and lowered her face to it.

"Saiyah Greyson. The half-demon who has been sighted so many times within these walls," Silas said in a clipped, conceited voice. "Tell me, why is that?"

Saiyah backed away, a lingering expression of re-vulsion on her face. "I've been working with Captain Hezekiah on behalf of the Albion Circle."

"And what is it exactly you're working on?" he said, barely looking at her.

"Networking," she said without missing a beat. "We were devising ways in which to assure the public that not all half-demons are a threat, and how to have gods perceived as more approachable."He forced a smile. "I am Captain Hezekiah's replacement for the time being. Your services will no longer be required." His smile dropped. "If it were my decision, you'd not be tolerated at all, but as it stands, you've likely already learnt too much from Captain Hezekiah and therefore you make yourself a necessary evil."

Saiyah gritted her teeth. Idris's sword with the olive-branch hilt was leaning against the desk. "Where is Captain Hezekiah?"

Silas's brows came together cruelly. "He has been granted temporary leave as a reward for his efforts here. Never fear, child. Despite your demonic nature, we will soon have you on the path of righteousness. There is still time for you to atone for your desire, greed, and pride." He spoke with a benevolence which she found spurious. His flat expression changed for the first time, though it was slight, and he reached out suddenly, grip-ping the half-moon pendant at her neck. Saiyah held her breath as he examined it, turning it over, looking down his nose at her. After an agonisingly long moment, he let it drop back in place. "We will watch over you," he said profoundly. Swiftly, he turned his back. "You may go."

Saiyah took slow, uncertain steps out of the room, but once in the corridor, she hurried to the exit.

By the time she reached the Old Roads, anger seethed from her. Once safely in the gardens by the gateway, she let her fury ebb over her. She took a breath before continuing resolutely to the library. She walked past Bezbiel's communal office, and his head raised as she stormed past, stopping abruptly at Zulphas's desk.

"I need you to call a meeting with Azeldya immediately," she told Zulphas commandingly, placing her hands on the desk and leaning towards him. "And then I need to speak to you. Privately." The passion in her eyes made him hesitate, but he nodded wordlessly and scampered away.

Saiyah smiled with narrow eyes as she watched him go, glad she'd rattled him.

SAIYAH PACED AZELDYA'S OFFICE animatedly, accepting a sugary glass of her near-toxic absinthe. Hex and

Jack sat stiffly together on the sofa, much to the speculation of the others. They already knew more than anyone, apart from Bezbiel, and she certainly trusted them more than Zulphas.

"Hezekiah isn't the *queen* anymore," she said darkly, using Bezbiel's chess analogy. "He's the king, just as we wanted. Silas is the new queen, and far more dangerous. I don't know his reasons for being at the embassy exactly, but he's made it clear he detests and suspects me." She turned to Azeldya and Bezbiel with a pleading look. "He noticed the enchantment on my necklace. And I don't know if Hezekiah managed to hide our findings before he left."

Azeldya's delicate brow wrinkled, and she stood. Walking to Saiyah to retrieve the pendant and strengthen the charms, she stroked her face lightly.

Saiyah rested her eyes and rubbed her temples. Her worry was mirrored on everyone else, apart from Bezbiel, who was scowling.

"Would you like me to summon your godfather?" Zulphas offered.

"No." She spoke harshly, making him blanche. "It would only distress him. I need to distance myself from the embassy before my cover is blown."

"And the evidence you've been gathering," Azeldya said, ignoring Saiyah's groan. "Can you retrieve it?"

Saiyah took a breath and clenched her jaw. She nodded resolutely and Azeldya put a hand on her shoulder.

Bezbiel leant forward, hands on knees. "Let me speak to Malik. He's a border-crosser, I'll arrange to get Saiyah away from here."

Azeldya shot him a dubious look.

"Are you sure he will be so easily accommodating?" Zulphas put in.

"Positive. He knows me," he said with a wicked grin.

Azeldya returned Saiyah's pendant and stepped into the centre of the room. "Medea, find out what you can from Gabrielle. Bezbiel and Hex, if you get the opportunity, influence any of the gods against Silas."

Hex appeared uneasy, but agreed.

"Zulphas, find out what you can about this *Silas*. And be prepared to inform all our members of the situation. The Circle may have to decide whether to disperse or defend."

Zulphas frowned and exhaled, unable to look at her. "Azeldya, this smacks of war to me. We are supposed to have neutrality with the gods." His voice wavered with quiet anger.

Azeldya blinked in response and rounded on him. "If they come for Saiyah, then it will not be *that* promised war they speak of. It will be a war on the Albion Circle alone. Everything we worked for will be lost." Her tone was loaded with demonic energy, final and flinty.

Zulphas looked to his feet, and no one dared utter a word.

"Take what you can from the embassy, Saiyah," Azeldya instructed. "Burn it all if you have to."

With silent finality, the meeting dispersed. Saiyah tried to follow Zulphas, but he moved as if devils snapped at his heels.

THE EMBASSY WAS ENCASED in divine protection. The doors were firmly closed so even a shadow couldn't slip inside. Gabrielle was mute. Even Medea couldn't get a peep out of her.

Hex and Jack would give Saiyah sympathetic looks and offer words of comfort, but they didn't understand. She couldn't even drown her sorrows with them, not properly. She needed to stay sharp in case Silas sent *The Host* after her.

Courting danger, she headed to Hyde Park, to the place she'd often walked with Idris. The last time they'd been there together it'd been the cusp of spring. Now, the crocuses were wilted and dried from the sun. Saiyah removed her jacket and sat down against one of the trees where they'd agreed to work together. Staring up at the sky through the rustling canopy, her vision blurred with tears. She'd give anything to be criticising his dogma right now, or listening to him chide her for being difficult.

She wiped her eyes and stared at Daniel's name in her phone for a moment. No. It was too dangerous to involve him.

As she stood, something silvery glinted above her and she gasped, a smile flickering to her face. But there was no one there, just something glinting in the tree behind her. She grabbed a branch and pulled herself up with some effort, not wanting to risk using her shadows to climb. As she neared the source of the reflection, she heard something flapping around, something that wasn't an animal or leaves. There was a little silver knife wedged deeply into the trunk of the tree, guarded by branches. It held a rain-splattered plastic wallet containing a folder. Idris's energy was all over it. Holding the knife, she pulled, as if she was part of Arthurian legend. When it came loose, she lost her footing and cut her finger on the blade as she grappled with the branches. The package fell and she scrambled down the tree to retrieve it.

Frantically opening it, she recognised Idris's handwriting on the first page. The rest contained documents she'd never seen before. Idris must have been doing some research on his own before being sent away. The note read:

Dear Saiyah,

I've been ordered away under suspicious circumstances. I fear someone in the embassy has become suspicious of you and what you might be, or perhaps of our discoveries. I will be gone for four weeks definitively, after which I will try to return in whatever capacity I can. Stay away from the embassy if you can help it. Your life could be in danger. Be brave and await my return.

Yours faithfully,
Idris

Saiyah was shaky and lightheaded when she finished reading, perspiring despite the mild breeze. Goosebumps tingled her bare arms. So, he wasn't completely removed by force after all. The circumstances were frightfully like her parents' letters; it sent a chill through her. She steadied herself against the tree and pressed his handwriting against her lips, drawing comfort and resolve.

She endured almost two weeks of waiting before her true breaking point came. Silas called her to the embassy. Saiyah paid little attention when someone else entered the room, focusing on remaining calm. Then a familiar face caught her eye. It was Daniel. His face was alert and fearful, and her own poker face wavered.

"This is Daniel Cassiel," Silas said casually. "He will be staying with us for the foreseeable future. We will all treat him well while he is here. You will behave yourself while he is here, child."

Saiyah quelled her panic and took a breath. "Of course," she said, as nonchalantly as she could manage. "It is good to meet you." She strained to keep her voice even.

Daniel was not as good a liar as she was, and his face betrayed him. Silas stood before her, smirking, and as usual held out his hand. She clenched her fists, and unthinkingly glanced at Daniel, watching helplessly in the corner.

Outside the embassy, she made it halfway home before she screamed in frustration, scaring pedestrians as obscure night fluttered at her fingertips. She desperately wanted to unleash her energy upon Silas. She tapped the moon charm Daniel gave her repeatedly.

The light was on in Bezbiel's house. She collapsed on his doorstep before he answered. He scooped her up and they huddled together on his sofa, calming music playing in the background.

"Silas has Daniel! He has my godfather!" She wept. "I can't take it. I just can't do it anymore. I hate him!"

Bezbiel, alarmed at her distress, held her while she cried and stroked her head. "I'm so sorry, Saiyah," he whispered into her hair. He pulled her upright by her shoulders. "You can do this, I know you can. You have fought demon assassins *and* seduced a god. He's trying to catch you out, make you reveal something, but you can't let him. This is a different kind of fight." He offered her a wan smile and wiped her tears.

She nodded resolutely, though she couldn't stop crying.

"The coven will protect you—I will, too. We're going to get you away from here soon, I swear."

She continued, her voice wavering. "Daniel was scared, and that bastard is holding him captive there. Silas *knows* he raised me. He was blatantly taunting me."

"Gods don't play games like that," Bezbiel said, sending a chill through her.

"This one does."

Bezbiel suggested that Titania help Saiyah practice with her full shadowy force. She was by far the strongest half-demon with physical manifestations of energy, claiming to be a descendant of Fey, which came to be known as demons in the eyes of gods. Saiyah didn't mind knocking her about a bit, shadow against light. It was a test of willpower more than anything. The discord between them hadn't dissipated, but a hint of comradery amongst her coven members was forming. The whole purpose of the coven and the kinship it created collided with her. They weren't just bonded together by their lust of knowledge and freedom; it was more than that. They only really had each other.

XXVI

A Taste of the Original Apple

S AIYAH COUNTED THE DAYS until Idris's return, clinging to the idea that he would make everything go back to normal somehow. The fourth week came and there was still no sign. Saiyah's stomach began to flutter with panic. She barely slept at all. It dawned on her that he might never return, and the strict laws of the gods would keep him out of this world forever.

One afternoon she was training with Titania, aching from receiving blunt blows. It was pure luck she'd not bled and revealed the pearly sheen to her blood.

Tangible light flooded from Titania's sides. It wasn't just brightness, but heat too. There was something ethereal about it. At first, she would have likened it to sunlight, but it was more like plasma, or the trail of light on the back of a comet.

Jack knocked on the door of the near-empty and battered 'group study' room with a bewildered look on his face.

"What is it?" Titania hissed irritably.

"There is a–"

Gabrielle brushed past him, her graceful form almost three heads taller. Saiyah beamed and ran to her, but Gabrielle stopped her from embracing. She regarded her sternly, but there was concern behind it all, like a mother with an unruly child.

"Now, listen to me. I don't like the situation here at all, and I want no part of whatever you two are up to."

Titania raised an eyebrow. "So, it is true," she muttered.

Saiyah shushed her so Gabrielle could continue.

"Follow me, as a shadow. You'll meet him in the library. Briefly. Then I'll take you to Daniel. It's at *his* request that I'm here."

"Thank you. You don't know how much this means to me." Saiyah teared up.

The goddess's face softened. "Yes, well, don't thank me yet. You're far from out of the woods."

CLINGING TO THE SHADOW of Gabrielle's cloak as she sped through London, she entered the embassy and followed her towards the library. Gabrielle babbled away with the librarian, distracting him so Saiyah could drift away from them.

Silent as a shadow, she peered between pillars and rows of books for any sign of Idris or Daniel. Neither were sitting at the tables, and Saiyah began to panic. She walked between the narrow rows, looking down every aisle. A crease appeared on her brow. Towards the back, the space between shelves grew narrow and books and scrolls became smaller. The light was dimmer and richer.

She paused, facing a dead end. Dejected, Saiyah slouched against one of the pillars, set between the shelves. Her eyes welled and she took an angry breath before pushing herself upright again.

Something caught her wrist, and she turned her head to see what was obstructing her. She started to gasp when she saw a hand, and abruptly something clamped over her mouth. She was pulled backwards with godly speed to the darker side of the obstructive pillar and spun around.

Confronted with Idris's large eyes, he released her and pressed a finger to his lips. In the narrow gap, she was close enough to feel the heat of his body. Saiyah held her breath, not wanting to look away from his stern but mesmerising face. Something pressed firmly into her, and she looked down to see Idris handing her a little book, the one his niece had been reading. She took it unthinkingly, and their fingers brushed, faint with the static of energy. Idris's energy was gentle and soothing. She could've wrapped herself in it. They stared at each other fervently. He delicately squeezed her fingers.

Saiyah's head turned as Gabrielle made a fuss about something to the librarian, explaining that she had papers to sign before the end of the day.

Saiyah took one last look at Idris, but he'd already vanished.

Saiyah followed Gabrielle to her office, materialising as she shut the door quickly. Daniel's gangly figure appeared from behind it. Saiyah beamed and leapt towards him, shifting from shadow to solid form. They held each other for a long moment.

"What on earth were you thinking, getting involved in all this? Hezekiah told me everything." Daniel shook his head dismissively. "What happened to keeping your head down and having a quiet life away from the gods?"

Saiyah bit her lip apologetically. "Well, I–I may have formed an attachment to the captain," she admitted with a wince, biting her lip.

Daniel put both his hands on his head and made a sound somewhere between a sigh and a groan. Gabrielle's head lifted in astonishment. He sucked air through his teeth. "Right. Okay. *Might?* I thought he infuriated you?"

"He does," she replied, lowering her head. She folded her arms and raised her chin before continuing. "That's the least of our problems. Besides, I don't have enough emotional capacity to deal with that along with everything else. Are you alright, Daniel? Silas hasn't hurt you or anything?"

A tender look crossed his face. "I can look after myself, Saiyah," he assured her.

She wiggled her brows playfully. "I'm sure you can. But I don't have this red armband for nothing. I've battled scavengers since we last met."

"I know," Daniel said shakily. "Gabrielle here gave me a full brief. She's been an angel to me," he said, shooting her a smile.

Gabrielle beamed coyly back. They both tittered quietly at each other, forgetting their troubles momentarily. Saiyah was the first to become serious again.

"I'm certain Silas knows the secrets of all three of us. I'm going to flee to Hell with the Katomet of Dualjahit, Malik Abnawah. Somehow, I'll come and get you before we go."

Daniel was distraught, but smiled warmly. "I can't, Saiyah. I've contemplated this outcome a lot recently, and I'd feel more comfortable going to the cathedral to make my stand. My energy is stronger there." His eyes sparkled at her.

Saiyah placed a hand on his. "Whatever the truth is, you've been more than a father to me, you know," she said blunderingly, making Daniel wipe at his eyes.

He cleared his throat and collected himself, glancing at the door and windows cautiously.

"Don't rely on the Katomet for protection, I'll say that much," Gabrielle told her seriously. "You've got a few hours together here." Gabrielle turned to Daniel. "I'll return to collect you."

Once they were alone, Daniel and Saiyah chatted as if they'd never spent any time apart. She teased him about Gabrielle. He admitted he'd fallen for her during the time he'd been at the embassy.

"Daniel, do you know a story called 'The Sorcerer and the Princess?'" she asked tentatively.

"Why, yes," Daniel said, somewhat astounded. "How do you know about that?""Zillah was reading it. What happens at the end? After the Princess drinks from the cup and the Sorcerer collects her drop of blood?"

Daniel looked up as if trying to recall. "As I remember it, it's a bit like a *Snow White* kind of story. Glass coffins, frozen or preserved bodies, something like that."

When Daniel leaned forward to examine her puzzlement, Saiyah squared her shoulders and beamed, shaking off her doubts.

"And what about Idris Hezekiah?" He said sternly.

Saiyah let out a long breath and flopped backwards onto the bed. She turned to her side and faced Daniel, propping her head up. He twisted his body and leaned back.

"There is nothing to say. Not now," she said glumly, casting her eyes down. "I really liked him, Daniel. But to him I am just a mortal. Gods can't love mortals, not really, can they?" Her voice broke as she spoke.

Daniel's brows came together. "Oh, my sweet girl," he said, leaning forward to place a hand on her head. "You know, I remember when you were very young, teaching you how to read and write. It seems only moments ago to me; mortals and demons grow so fast. To think now you're fluent in at least three languages not of this world, and accomplished enough in a fair few which are. You're smart enough to know what you're getting into, and what you want in life. You've proved that in the last few years. I always knew you were stubborn, but I'll admit, I hadn't realised quite how tenacious you are."

They chuckled lowly.

"Just know that whatever happens, you can always come back to our little house in Winchester. You'll always have me, and I will always love you."

Saiyah pressed her lips together to stop them trembling and smiled. She reached out for Daniel's hand and squeezed it.

"Thank you, Daniel," she said sincerely, wiping her eyes.

After Daniel and Saiyah said her goodbyes, Saiyah rushed home and burst into her house, startling Hex and Jack. She set the book down on the dining table, glaring at them both passionately.

"What now?" Hex said with deflated annoyance, but her face quickly softened. "What's wrong?" She added, standing and shuffling her Tarot cards away.

"Daniel is... my godfather is..." she stuttered before shaking her head and pulling herself together. When she spoke again her voice was steady. "I need the aid of your brilliant manipulative powers. Well, yours and Bez's. Will you get him, Jack? Meet us in the reading room."

Jack was sceptical, but nodded. Dark feathery wings sprouted from his back before he became completely raven formed.

Hex stood slowly but resolutely, her recently dyed electric-blue eyebrows creased together. "Saiyah, not to come across wimpish, but I'm not sure I'm comfortable with exercising my ability. Bad things have hap–"

"We'll just need the threat of it," Saiyah assured her. "You don't have to do anything. I'm counting on Bez for that. You three are the only ones I really trust."

Hex nodded and gathered her things.

They walked briskly towards the main building. The boys stood together with matching expressions of sus-

5

picion. There were others in the reading room, so Saiyah tilted her head to indicate they should go into the corridor.

"What's all this about?" Bezbiel said sternly.

Saiyah explained her need to know who was trustworthy, and what she needed Bezbiel to do. A pained look crossed his face. She told them about the strange mention of 'Moon Face' in her parents' letters, the half of John Greyson's book Zulphas had, and the mysterious fire.

"Wouldn't Azeldya know if there was someone suspicious in the coven?" Hex said.

Saiyah shrugged. "She could be blind to this one. He knows more than he's letting on. I'm certain."

"But it would be a gross misuse of my power."

Saiyah shook her head, unconvinced.

"I'll do it if you won't," Hex said, though her voice was thin.

Bezbiel shifted his stance and ran a hand through his hair. "Fine." He was already walking towards Zulphas's office in the library. "But remember, this was your idea."

The four of them burst into the room, making Zulphas startle, his owl-eyes wide. Bezbiel slammed the door in an overconfident manner and advanced towards him, flagged by Saiyah and Hex. Jack hung back, his wings poking through his hoodie. Bezbiel grinned and let his forked tongue flicker a little. The whites of

358

Saiyah's eyes became black, and there was a reflected red light in Hex's.

Zulphas fumbled for words. "H-how may I help you all?"

Bezbiel held out his hand and Saiyah passed him John Greyson's book, still stained with blood.

"Sorry, old man. We need you to answer us truthfully." He slapped the book on the desk and Saiyah thought she saw a glimmer of fear from Zulphas. "How did you come by this?"

Zulphas was open-mouthed, and his gaze flickered to Saiyah briefly.

"Come on, Moon Face," Saiyah said viciously. "I know you knew Asramenia."

Zulphas's forehead creased but he regained some confidence, though it took him a moment to fathom the right words.

"I think you'd better get talking," Hex said harshly.

Zulphas seemed to collect himself and stood slowly. "There's no need for violence," he said, holding up a hand.

Saiyah stepped forward and gave an expectant wave of her hand.

Zulphas cleared his throat. "I first came across it when I was a boy. I was travelling with Asramenia, and other revolutionists. There was one among the group who possessed the book."

"John Greyson?" Saiyah asked.

He was shocked. "Yes, that was the name he went by. I saw both of them examining the book often. One day I stole into his tent and read it. I realised even at that age there was something unusual about it. When I asked my father, he became angry and wouldn't speak of it. It unsettled me, so I never forgot what I'd read. Years later, when John Greyson died, I took it from Asramenia's belongings. She was distraught, but I understood that the contents were dangerous. Only after meticulous study did I realise how perilous the rituals within were. The other half of the book was lost during a battle. I was never able to recover it." He peered at the blood-stained pages, a wave of animosity crossing his face.

Saiyah relaxed. Zulphas was speaking so calmly and eloquently that she wanted to believe him. "That's a very nice story, now would you care to explain the fire in the library after you showed me to that section? Or why in one of my mother's last letters before she died, she named 'Old Moon Face' as someone to be wary of?"

Zulphas shook his head, dumbfounded.

Bezbiel was glaring at Zulphas with a hatred she'd never seen in his face before.

"A child of the divine and eternal night," Saiyah quoted.

Zulphas looked up in alarm, his mouth opening and closing as he tried to speak.

She walked up to Zulphas, narrowing her darkened eyes. "You'd better speak quickly. Was it you who betrayed my mother?"

Bezbiel was close behind her, laying a hand on her shoulder as if to hold her back.

Zulphas stepped back. "I did not betray her, but I knew there was something wrong with her lover, the god. He was responsible for..." He gestured to Saiyah. "Asramenia was tainted with something baneful and corrupt, but nothing in that book ever held the answer, so I reported him to the embassy." He fumbled with a bundle of papers. "For my part in her death, which I painfully regret, I would like to do all I can to make it up to her."

Saiyah clenched her teeth and snarled, surprising herself. "It was you! Because of you both my parents were killed!"

Zulphas took on an austere expression, reading a rebuttal, but shadow erupted from her fingers, and she leapt towards him. Darkness cascaded from her back. Bezbiel reached for her, but his arms passed straight through.

Zulphas's form shifted rapidly. Feathers surfaced on his brow and his arms became like two great wings, stretching the span of the small room. Like a bird trapped in a net, he writhed as Saiyah clawed at him with shadowy bolts of energy, rippling blue and silver like a galaxy. Books were knocked over and glass bell jars shattered. Jack put a wing around Hex as they were knocked off their feet. Zulphas's feet were like talons, clawing at Saiyah and Bezbiel. The door rattled open under his grip and swung open, allowing his owl-like form to escape. The four half-demons ran out after him, just in time to see his dark wings stretch out as he swooped through the vast canopy of books and smashed headlong through the great window.

XXVII

Broken Promises and Broken Aches, False
Hangings and Trap-Doors

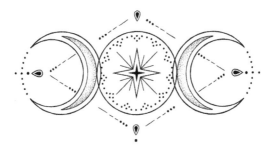

S AIYAH RETREATED TO HER room with a glass of wine,
closing her curtains. From her bag, she retrieved
Zillah's book Idris had smuggled to her. She flicked
through the pages, letting them cascade through her
fingers. Wedged in the centre was something unexpected. Wrapped in a selenite-white cloth with embroidery
which looked to be pure gold thread, was something
which felt familiarly, like paper. As she set the mysterious bundle down on her desk, a captivating resonance
of energy, the essence of heaven, emitted from them.
Saiyah placed her hand over the pile and allowed the
celestial energy, which was all at once alien and com-

fortingly familiar to her, flow over her. It wasn't like Idris at all; his energy was distinct and full of his character. This was just like the children's book, only purer. Like Zillah herself. Saiyah's eyes closed gradually and with anguish.

> "*Abashed the Devil stood,*
> *And felt how awful goodness is, and saw*
> *Virtue in her shape how lovely—saw, and pined*
> *His loss.*"

She muttered the passage from *Paradise Lost,* then with a sharp intake of breath unwrapped the bindings.

For all its outer grandeur, the paper inside was disappointingly modern. It clearly wasn't of this world; it had that trademark velvety texture of whatever the gods made their paper from. It was nearly all written in sapphire ink, swirling beautifully in their ornate language. She flicked through the mountain and released a puff of air from her chest, but as she reached for her drink, something snagged in the neatness of it all. A handful of crumpled papers written in onyx-black and occasionally a faded slate colour was set in the middle of it all. Their energy was incongruous and barely contained a hint of the same harmony–these had certainly been to Hell. She eased them out, sheets brushing against sheets, and the word 'Khabrasos' caught her eye.

It was, of course, no surprise that these documents all related to John Greyson, which was the whole point in having them. However, she'd not anticipated this new research to bring her so close to home. The text was hastily written and scratchy, much like her own writing. A smile passed her lips as she began to read.

Approaching Khabrasos is a treacherous endeavour of late. The tyrant Katomet is attempting to segregate the land in a bid to eradicate the rival Katomei. Already, masses of waste-land, both on the Hitades side and Khabrasos, have been obliterated. The chasm runs deep, and from what we can tell there is no way of safely estimating its depth. We have joined forces with the Katomei to put a stop to the damage (she is one of the revolutionists—if she can even still be called that now). The Host cannot afford for Khabrasos and its chaos door to fall into enemy hands.

The Hitades have constructed a dubious transport across the chasm: a chain boat, with the chain being fashioned by an unbreakable golden mineral and the boat of simple wood. This seems too dangerous for transporting people, but is effective for supplies.

From the encampment, Khabrasos can still be accessed across the wasteland as always. Although wasteland is a poor name for what it is, even wilderness does not do it justice. Yes, this stretch of nature may be void of all life save for birds, insects, and smaller mammals, but it is an oasis of colour before the darkness. Lush emerald greens fade to amethyst, encrusted with a blush of flowers and rosewood gorse. Like-wise, the fast-moving little birds share this empurpled shade, flitting carefree beneath skies of furious blue. The vegetation is low-lying, coarse grass up to the knee, but trees with deep wine bark start to crop up on approach. Hanging amongst their dark leaves are fruits which look like grapes but are denser, fragrant, and bitter.

Beneath the canopy of eternally mulberry autumn, the shy orchids are enveloped in velvety shadow. Priestesses of Xalvas tis Nyx once hunted here for lost souls which entered through the door deeper in their lands, ones which had made it this far to safety. That is no longer the case, though the few priestesses left can frequently be seen taking walks here.

Following one of their trails, we came to a grove of trees with a pool of rippling water. The lilac-reflecting water flowed from a small stream which became entangled with a series of rocks, acting as a dam, before overflowing in a sort of low waterfall. The break in trees gives way to their eternal night above, and where the water collects and stills at the bank, stars are reflected.

Saiyah paused, reading the description over again, for pleasure more than anything.

She retrieved the little children's book from her bag. It resonated with a very pure, ethereal energy which certainly wasn't Idris's. Opening to the bookmarked page, she realized it wasn't a bookmark at all, but a note in Idris's handwriting, hastily written.

Meet me tomorrow in the park.

She glanced around before continuing. Inside the book, she couldn't help but notice, was a beautiful illustration almost like a miniature renaissance painting. It was the same on each page, accompanied by a short story or poem. In angelic script, the title of the page was 'The Princess and the Sorcerer.' The painting depicted a woman with sparkling eyes in a silvery dress and a crown with a moon on it. She floated in the air, descending towards a man who looked remarkably like 'the magician' in Hex's tarot deck. The story was short, or perhaps it was a poem, but it didn't translate well:

'The Princess met with her love in secret, and she ran into his arms. They drank to their love from a crystal chalice, but when it touched her lips, the jagged glass cut her. No sooner did her blood spill, her love transformed into the deceitful sorcerer. The chalice had been poisoned and the Sorcerer collected one drop of her blood, placing her under his spell. The Princess fell into a deathly sleep.

Fearing she might be rescued, the Sorcerer hid the Princess where only he would ever find her. Now she sleeps for eternity, waiting to be woken from her slumber and be reunited with her love.'

It was just a story, but something about it made Saiyah's blood curl. She turned the book over and leafed through it; there was no author.

SAIYAH NEARED THE GATEWAY as Bezbiel strolled in. He ushered her to one side, between the statues.

"I've made a deal with Malik," he said quietly. "He's agreed to take us to Hell, and protect us while we're there."

"What are the terms?" she said briskly.

Bezbiel shook his head. "That's not important."

Saiyah gave him a hard look. "Bez, you have to tell me."

He chuckled. "I will tell you when we are in Hell. It's nothing involving you anyway." He was already moving away, strolling out of the garden.

Saiyah sighed in annoyance and chased after him. "I'm going to meet Hezekiah. I thought you should know, in case..."

Bezbiel frowned deeply, and looked to the side disapprovingly. "I'll send Jack to keep an eye out. I'll be in the area, just in case."

Saiyah thanked him and left, heading to Hyde Park.

Her fingers trembled and she gripped the strap of her satchel to steady them, repressing a smile as she approached the park. The sky was just beginning to lighten, and dew clung to the grass. It was quiet, aside from the occasional dog walker and early morning jogger.

Saiyah turned off the path on a familiar route towards the grove of trees. A figure stepped out wearing a grey hooded jacket and jeans, but it was undoubtedly Idris. Saiyah hesitated. A thrilling sort of anxiety crept over her, but she beamed nonetheless and quickened her pace. She was running by the time she reached him and ignoring his look of surprise, she rushed headlong into his arms. She gripped the back of his jacket as if to make sure he was real. Idris held her close, a hand placed protectively over her head, but only for a moment. Saiyah stayed very still, though her heart was racing. No doubt Idris would feel it hammering against him. She'd never been so close to him, and there was a heady strangeness to it.

"Our research—"

"Safe. I hid it all before I left," he said calmingly. "I'm sorry you've had to fend for yourself." Idris was barely whispering, but his voice was full of feeling and his hold on her tightened for a moment. "The way Silas is behaving, it's not usual."

Saiyah peeled herself away so she could look at his face. Her eyes were welling, and that troubled him.

"Can't you tell your brother? Get him to send him away?" She said as he delicately brushed away one of her tears with his thumb.

"No. There's nothing inherently wrong with what he's doing, in the gods eyes, and Ezra relies on him too much to doubt him," he explained, his face filled with kindness. "Besides, there are more pressing matters than Silas."

"The conflict in Kuruh?" Saiyah folded her arms.

He collected himself and straightened. When he spoke again his voice lacked the emotion from before. "My primary concern is the mortal world and the human reaction. The last thing we need is the panic we had to deal with years ago."

"I've seen it already. They hate us again, like they did before."

"There is an upcoming ball of Malik's. Though frivolous, it might be worth it for once. There will be influential people there..."

"The coven can make a good impression." Saiyah echoed his thoughts.

"Yes. Though it'll take time to undo the damage done by a few desperate demons. My brother wants me to lend more of my men than I'm able. Already, many have been deployed to Kuruh. Azeldya must travel to the region to urge a ceasefire, and Zulphas to the Hitades to offer aid and organise evacuation. Their trade routes through the mountains have been blocked, and they may take up arms out of spite."

"Zulphas is gone. I confronted him and he confessed to reporting my father," She explained hurriedly. "But, what about Khabrasos? Are they involved in all this?"

"All silent, as usual." Idris said slowly, casting her a suspicious glance. "I doubt they'll involve themselves."

"What are they fighting over, exactly?"

His posture stiffened. "It's difficult to say. *The Host* reported the revolutionists attacked them first, and the revolutionists claim vice versa."

"You sound like you don't believe what your superiors are telling you," Saiyah said.

He watched her steadily. "I trust they believe they are in the right. Regardless, it is all senseless violence. The area has always had conflict. It'll be over soon enough."

"And if it isn't?" Saiyah asked.

Idris grimaced. "I predict the revolutionist group will be outcast from the rest, and war waged against them. A small war, but war, nonetheless. The full force of"–he pointed upwards–"will come down against them. It'd be over quickly."

Saiyah shuddered. Idris and *The Host* were strong, but ancient supernatural entities from his homeland rendered them pale in comparison. Visions of such a battle raced through her mind, along with the descriptions in her mother's journal of Nyx looming behemoth in the sky. She shook off such thoughts.

She raised her chin, touching her pendant. "Silas noticed something was odd about my necklace, and clearly knows about Daniel."

Idris glanced around warily and drew Saiyah further into the trees. "Silas is more than aware of your mother. You'll recall at least one mention of him in our findings. Did you read the book?"

Saiyah pulled the children's book from her bag. "The story is..." She shook her head in disgust.

Idris nodded gravely. "I know. I thought it was odd."

"It could be a coincidence," Saiyah said. "But after finding John Greyson's blood..."

Idris took the book and flipped it open to the page, turned it to face her and pointed at the illustration. "Look here in the background."

Saiyah squinted. The scenery depicted a grassy plain with woodland in the distance, but there was something between that Idris pointed to. Water. No, a lake, curiously painted in shades of black and grey.

"A black lake. The Acheron," Saiyah breathed, looking from the book to Idris. "That's where Asramenia asked Tobias to meet her. Malik said they found her body in the lake."

He furrowed his snowy brows. "I know it's just a story, but there must be something in it," he mused, closing the pages. "It's likely that Silas interrogated Tobias Malkiel prior to the execution. He may know more than either of us. Did Zulphas tell you anything else?"

Saiyah passed a hand over her face and massaged her head. "He thought something was wrong about Tobias. He didn't stick around for any elaboration. But there's more to it than Zulphas's betrayal. I spoke to Malik, and he said his men found Asramenia's body while the gods were still looking for her. It wasn't them."

Idris closed his eyes with a pained expression and dipped his head.

Saiyah gave his arm a comforting squeeze. "It's alright. I know you were amongst them, but you weren't directly involved in all this." She offered a thin smile.

Idris looked at her hand studiously. The distance between them wasn't great, but as the rays of honeyed afternoon sun danced between them, it appeared as a vast gulf. He lifted his head, giving one of his intense stares as he reached into his pocket again. He slowly retrieved an envelope which he passed to Saiyah, hesitating as he handed it over. "Please don't think any less of me for keeping this from you."

Saiyah carefully took the envelope; the seal was already open, and it was dated sixteen years ago. "I wanted to tell you before, but I couldn't."

Saiyah removed the letter, worn at the edges and crumpled. It was addressed to Idris in strangely familiar handwriting. He gave her space to read it:

Sergeant Hezekiah, 5th Squadron,

I write to request a favour on behalf of 7th. Captain Josiah informed me you are due to be posted in Dualjahit to pursue defected soldiers. We've recently had cause to believe the revolutionist leader Asramenia is plotting to launch an attack against us and break alliances. She is currently dwelling deep within Xalvas tis Nyx but is likely to head North on your path if confronted.

Before you leave, would you be able to put your excellent skills to use, smoking her out of her den? She is watchful of our movements, and the element of surprise would be in our favour. Even the notion of your presence within her dominion should cajole her out, from which point my Squadron can manage her. In the event we are both posted North, it would be beneficial to support each other on our respective hunts.

Asramenia is highly likely to have a child with her and is not to be harmed due to the potential for causing political unrest in the region. If a child is discovered on her person, it is to be delivered to 7th Squadron.

I look forward to working with you,
Tobias Malkiel.

Saiyah gripped the letter so hard that it crumpled. Betrayals, betrayals all around her. Demon or god, it made no difference. There she had gotten her hopes up that her father was some kind, forward-thinking god, someone like Daniel, and that Idris really did have her best intentions at heart. It was all lies, falsehoods and deceit. It made her sick to her stomach.

Idris took a few paces back, watching her with a mixture of anguish and remorse. "I thought I was carrying out orders." He placed his hands in his pockets. "I never questioned it, even when Malkiel was arrested. I never ascribed to the rumour because of that letter. Not until now, the blood stains, and then the book..."

Saiyah took a breath and straightened up. Her arms fell limply to her sides. "All these gods and men, deceiving my mother, and you amongst them deceiving me," she whispered. "You knew all along! You chased my mother out of her home to be hunted!"

He stared at her breathlessly, and gradually nodded.

Saiyah clenched her teeth and marched up to him. "You didn't think to mention this before? Even when we spoke of it?"

"I didn't want to hurt you," he said, unable to look at her.

She understood then. The pain in her chest confirmed it. The enchantment had lifted now, and he was free to hurt her. Her face was hot, and her throat tightened.

"I apologise for concealing the truth," he said quietly.

Saiyah shook her head guiltily and bit her lip. "Bezbiel put–*I* let him put an enchantment on you. That's why you said nothing. That's why you started thinking you cared for me. For that, I'm sorry," she said, suppressing a sob.

He raised his eyebrows and tilted his head. "I had a feeling he'd tried something that night," he said indifferently before exhaling steadily. "I had my Father perform an exorcism, just to be sure."

"When?" she asked suspiciously.

"On the same night," he said, watching her with stony faced sadness.

She fumbled for words and shook the letter at him. "So why *didn't* you tell me sooner?"

Idris spoke cautiously. "Because I cared what you thought of me."

She backed away, leaving him offended. The whites of her eyes became black–she couldn't control it. "What I *thought* was that you were unlike the rest of The Host, but as it turns out you're just the same: cold-blooded and...and indifferent to us *lesser beings*!" She turned to leave, a hand flying to her face.

Idris glowered and came rushing forward at inhuman speed. He appeared before her and grasped her by her arms, shaking her gently. "Listen to me, Saiyah," he said in a gravely tone. "Don't presume to know me. I have lived over five times of your life and done things you couldn't fathom, things I struggle to associate myself with. If I were what you accuse me of, then I could have easily brought you here to turn you in, or worse, knowing what you truly are. Even your own kind would understand I was simply doing my job."

Saiyah stood open-mouthed, too startled for tears now.

He relaxed and let go, her feet firmly planted on the grass again. Idris sighed and shook his head with an ironic smile. "I forgave you for all your secrets, your vicious remarks, trickery, and enchantments. Still, I expected more from you, and you've the nerve to say I'm akin to the worst of *my* kind." He ran a hand through his hair.

Saiyah caught her breath and let her eyes come back to a normal appearance.

"We are natural enemies, you and I," he stated monotonously. "When I first met you, I saw into your heart and felt the capacity of your demonic energy. You will have the potential to take on the gods and demons. Perhaps not now, but one day. The Host will notice and be afraid."

"I'm not going to take on the gods," she said venomously.

He looked at her strangely. "I'd be a fool not to consider it."

"Are you afraid of me?" she asked in disbelief, tripping over her words.

He gave a mystifying shake of his head. "We should go our separate ways, as we always should've done. I will not tell anyone what I know, but I will no longer aid you. "Besides, I have *deceived* you, as you say, we can no longer trust one another."

Saiyah's face betrayed that her heart had just been ripped from her. "What?" She choked. "What about Silas? If you can get rid of him, what then? What will that mean for us?"

Idris blinked and dropped his hands. "Us?" he repeated, eyebrows rising. There was something about him that really did look afraid.

She moved unconsciously towards him until they were almost touching and slipped her hand into his, feeling his sweet divine energy sweep over her on the morning breeze. He looked down at their entwined hands with a pained look and tried to pull away. Saiyah held fast, and he let her.

"Saiyah, please." His hand came up to touch her face but never made contact, hovering uncertainly.

"What's the matter?" she whispered.

"I didn't think it would be this easy to fall," he whispered back.

They stayed like that for a long moment, as if they might turn to stone or twist into the likenesses of the trees around them like the gods and deities of old.

Eventually, Idris spoke. "Don't cross *The Host*. I'll not be able to help you. I wish you luck on your search for John Greyson, and your mother's killer."

Saiyah looked at him imploringly, not bothering to hide her tears now.

Idris's long lashes fluttered down as he looked over her shoulder. He took a slow, deep breath, and murmured as if ashamed, "In another life, it would be different. Perhaps if I were mortal."

Abruptly he was gone, without his usual glint of white. Saiyah's hand was startlingly empty.

XXVIII

She, Who Thicks Mans Blood With Cold

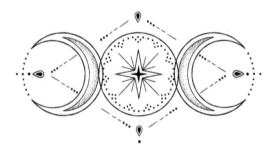

NEARING THE OLD ROADS, Saiyah was roused from her grief when she saw Bezbiel at the gate. She took a breath to steady herself, but as she approached, detected the distinct feeling of unfamiliar, low demonic energies. She touched her moon pendant. In raven form, Jack landed on her shoulder, his head tucked low to his wings.

"The wards are down," Bezbiel breathed.

Bezbiel held out his hands, making intricate gestures and chanting banishing spells in Old Demonic. Saiyah mimicked him and they shared a fretful glance. They entered the Old Roads.

Approaching the crossroads, they spotted a group of demons they didn't recognise, several of them red-eyed scavengers. Amongst them was Hex, in her pyjamas. She seemed to be distressed. Beside her, Titania shimmered like an iridescent heatwave. Saiyah had to squint to look at her.

Saiyah ran towards them, eyes fixed on the strangers. The scavengers amongst them wore mismatched armour and stood straighter when they saw her coming. Their red eyes were strangely alert and intelligent.

One demon who seemed to be the ringleader turned to Saiyah. The whites of his eyes were red, and he had short, triangular horns protruding from his dark curly hair, not unlike Hex's.

Hex cast wild looks between the two groups, her mouth agape, but it was Titania that spoke.

"They broke the wards," she snarled, a shimmering blade in her hands.

"They're not here to hurt us!" Hex defended breathlessly, standing before Saiyah and Bezbiel, as if to defend the newcomers.

"What my sister says is true," the man with the curly hair said calmly, without taking his eyes off Xaldan. "But *they* are."

A scavenger demon appeared at one end of the street, this time with the more familiar wild appearance. Saiyah summoned her shadows like a reflex and partially became one. Bezbiel reached for his malachite, crouching as he began to scratch a crude circle around him.

More red-eyed demons emerged like a pack of wolves. They were surrounded. The man who was apparently Hex's brother and his group drew weapons of bronze and obsidian blades and formed an outwards-facing circle, ready to do battle even with their own kind.

Abruptly, the surrounded group were pounded upon, and wild cries were taken up by the invaders. A scavenger lunged at Saiyah with a solid blade, knocking her off her feet with a sound of shock. She held it off as best she could and grappled with shadow and fingernails as it snarled and gnashed its teeth at her. Hex's brother bore down on it furiously, his sword tearing through flesh with a harsh ripping sound. The scavenger howled with insanity with one look from him, before abruptly shrivelling up and dying. The feral redness of Hex's brother's eyes looming overhead made Saiyah flinch.

He was gone in a blink and Hex stood protectively over her, brows furrowed and on the brink of tears as she screamed at the top of her voice, "Kill your own kind! Murder your friends! Kill your own kind!" She shouted repeatedly. A ghastly demonic energy accompanied her words.

Instantly, scavengers turned on each other. Only a few resisted Hex's enchantment. Saiyah felt the weight of her words wash over, becoming increasingly profound.

382

She straightened up, her shadows deadly around her. The whites of her eyes turned black, and a snarl curled on her lips. Impulsively, she approached Bezbiel, kneeling in his protective circle where he cast spells. She had a compulsion to separate his head from his body, to tear at his throat. The tips of her fingers became claw-like with a flash of gold, and she raged against his protective shield.

A hand landed on her shoulder. "I release you," Hex whispered close to her ear.

Saiyah's compulsion evaporated, and her vision became crisper. Hex and Bezbiel looked at her, aghast.

Titania was picking off the few unaffected with the help of the newcomers. She darted about like a comet, wielding a blade of some kind and attacking as she blinded them.

Hex let out a cry, and Saiyah turned to see one of the scavengers had pounced upon her. Its needle-like teeth were buried in her arm as she used the other one to shield her face. Saiyah rushed towards her, crying out as she saw a lump of flesh ripped from her friend. Dark red half-demon blood gushed onto the crossroads. Saiyah tripped, falling hard on the rough path and grazing her hands in the gravel. When she looked up, Jack was scratching at the eyes of the demon attacking Hex, and she winced as he plucked out an eye with his beak.

A blood-chilling roar came from nearby. It was close to the cry of an animal, but distinctly human. The form of Hex's brother rushed over Saiyah's head, trailing with shadow similar to her own, although his was fainter and tinged with red. Jack darted upwards in a scatter of feathers just in time. As he despatched his sister's attacker, the black-red substance emitted from him in a wave, knocking down everyone in sight, but particularly affecting the enemy scavengers, who screamed in the same kind of madness before succumbing to a gruesome death. Most of his men had ducked in time, but not all were spared from the furious wrath. When the cries died out, they were left in utter silence.

Under the thick, rosewood light of the Old Roads, bodies lay strewn about them in a mess of blood and ash.

WRAPPED IN A PLUM tea-gown, Saiyah paced in front of her bedroom fireplace. She was acutely aware there were strange demons downstairs, some of them scavengers. Titania and Bezbiel were keeping a watchful eye over them. Hex lay on her bed, soaking the sheets in blood while Medea did her best to heal her arm. Jack held her hand under the watchful eye of the brother, who'd introduced himself as Deimos, and she finally stirred out of her induced sleep. Saiyah came to Hex's side as soon as Medea backed away.

"What did you go and do that for?" she whispered tenderly. "You didn't need to use your abilities."

Hex made a grunting laugh. "Saved your arses, didn't I?" She croaked, making them all smile thinly.

"They'll not bother you for much longer." Deimos's deep voice sounded in crisp New Demonic. He wore tarnished bronze armour across his chest and on his legs up to the shins. Beneath was a dark tunic of some kind, flecked with a faded blue pattern, and around his neck a deep red cloak. He held a battered helmet under his arm. "Their employer hasn't been forthcoming with payment, and after this defeat I doubt they'll bother with him again."

Saiyah's eyes widened, as did those of everyone else in the room. Deimos had an aloof expression on his face.

"Who *is* their employer?" Bezbiel said, standing.

Deimos stood eerily motionless. Saiyah wished he would speak, but after witnessing his horrifying decimation of the scavengers as well as some of his own, she thought better than to push him. He smirked and then glanced down at his sister.

"I would've suggested making a deal with you, half-demons. But, as you have healed my sister, and I can tell that *you* also hail from Khabrasos,"–he fixed his eyes on Saiyah–"I will tell you."

They waited with barely contained anticipation.

"My friends tell me it is a god who employs them. *The one with the white eyes,* they say. He sees and knows all."

Saiyah's breath caught. There were plenty of gods with white eyes–it was the mark of the noble second-sphere gods. However, there was only one that she knew of who hated her.

"Silas," Saiyah said firmly, at the same time as Titania. They exchanged a knowing look.

"That means it's likely him opening the Hellgates. If we can prove he is responsible, *The Host* will surely remove him," she suggested.

"They'd do more than that," Medea offered in a delicate voice.

"Gods wouldn't hire assassins, much less let demons into this world. If they wanted a demon slayed, they would simply do it. Besides, this all started long before Silas came." Bezbiel stepped forward, cradling his chin. "He's working alone. Silas's behaviour has smacked rather ungodly already, and it's clear he has a vendetta against you."

A chill ran through Saiyah.

A curt laugh came from Deimos. His eyes were still stained red. "This person–Silas, as you name him, is not alone. He has been exploiting Khabrasos for many years alongside his ally, the current Katomet. Your assassins ride the trails left by a warlock that moves from world to world, as we did. Now Silas focuses his attention on the nation of Hitades. We won't abide it. If the Albion Circle can be rid of him, I will leave with you one of the *Eurynomos* to give a statement." He gave a slight bow.

Bezbiel explained later that *Eurynomos* was the official name for the scavengers, preferred by those in control of their own minds.

Saiyah viewed Deimos with a kind of awe. Here was a revolutionist, living and breathing before her, battle worn but resplendent. And not only that, Khabrasos was his homeland–Hex had never mentioned it! Though, they were half-siblings, so the same wasn't necessarily true of her.

"We would be more than happy to," she told him ardently.

He placed a hand across his chest and offered a half-bow. "I leave his fate, as well as my sister's, in the hands of the Albion Circle." With that, he strode out of the room.

Saiyah and Bezbiel followed him, watching from the landing as he descended the stairs.

"Do you think the warlock they spoke of could be John Greyson?" Saiyah asked in a quiet voice.

Bezbiel shrugged. "I do not know. There could be many occultists in London."

"That can travel to Hell?" She said in an accusatory tone.

Bezbiel shrugged and held his hands out in an apologetic gesture.

"The current Katomet of Khabrasos is my mother's old adversary, right?" She asked.

Bezbiel responded with a weary nod and rolled his head back. "If Silas is working with him, we're going to need to move you to safety sooner rather than later. I can't believe I'm saying this but, can Hezekiah do anything with this information?"

Saiyah drew the violet robe closer around her. "Yes. Although I don't think we're really on speaking terms."

Saiyah paused to look out the window and was shocked to see a sunlit London. She blinked in surprise, and in an instant her usual view was restored: a leafy garden under the old road's pinkish light with more blackened, red-brick houses behind it. The world faded into a rosy smudge of abyss beyond that. She rose slowly and walked over to the window, pressing her hands against the cool glass. She stared for a moment and moved away, leaving fading fingerprints.

Saiyah looked at Bezbiel, who was gazing at the window with a perplexed look that matched her own feelings. Cautiously, they descended the stairs of her house and crossed the entrance hall to the door. She opened it and looked out across the square at the other houses and library beyond, but it wasn't there. She gripped the doorframe, which was still very much there, as she stared instead at the British Museum in the distance, so like the Baraquel building, but bathed in normal light and milling with tourists. She'd not slipped through worlds. Her house was still here, but the rest had changed.

Bezbiel was staring at the museum-library with a similarly bewildered expression "That can't be good," he whispered.

"Could it be Zulphas? Or is this Hellgate?" Saiyah's voice was hollow.

Bezbiel clenched his fist open and closed around his Malachite. "Only one way to find out."

"Will the library be in real London?" Saiyah took a step in the direction of the gateway.

Bezbiel stopped her and shook his head. "I don't think so. I've a notion that it's a lot more complicated than that." He started towards the museum with a brisk stroll and indicated with his chin that she should follow.

He slowed as they reached the grounds and told her to "act natural." Saiyah didn't feel very natural as she glided down the path to the great museum steps in a flowing tea-gown. She looked straight out of another time. Bezbiel wasn't much better with his countryside gentleman style, albeit in modern attire. She would've made a now very tired old joke about him attempting to mimic *Indiana Jones*. Bezbiel Brady: Gatherer of ancient books, scrolls, and relics in Hell, and museumgoer on Earth.

There was a tremor around them that none of the mortal museumgoers seemed to notice. Bezbiel's form flickered so he was opaque for a few moments. Saiyah grabbed his arm instinctively and he responded with a concerned but bemused look.

"Let's keep close." He linked his arm through hers as if he were escorting her through a regency ball.

Saiyah barely restrained herself from rolling her eyes, but she gripped the sleeve of his pale suit jacket tightly. They proceeded carefully with synchronised steps. Inside the entranceway, the echoey noises of footsteps and people disappeared abruptly. They turned their heads about for a moment and Saiyah began to let her grip slide from Bezbiel's arm. He clasped her abruptly with his other hand and shook his head.

"Not yet. Something doesn't feel right. Can you feel it?" Silence. Saiyah frowned.

"You know I've been playing around with teleporting? Using the astral plane for short movements, quick spells? It feels like that. Astral." He tilted his nose into the air.

"I can't feel it unless I go into it."

"You may need to yet."

They continued up the stairs, a mirror world of their library which thankfully was close to the style of the museum. They tripped at inconsistencies in the steps and bumped into people as they materialised in and out of existence. Once they were on the first floor, they kept their backs to the walls and rested by a visitor information board, arms still linked.

"This isn't good," Bezbiel muttered as people bussed past them, casting them looks of unwanted intrigue, and in many cases, fear. "They know something's going on here, and they think it must be us."

"At least they're not materialising into the Old Roads."

"Don't hold your breath," he said in a low growl.

Whispers began, as if the half-demons couldn't hear them. They were familiar to Saiyah by now, but not in places like this. There was malice behind it all. They continued through the galleries at the perimeter of the building, winding their way towards where their library would be. It would be over the British Museum's atrium, where they would fall to their deaths if they took a wrong step.

The museum faded to the familiar layout of the reading room and they both breathed a little sigh of relief. It only lasted a moment. There were three young coven members there, all staring at a cabinet which stuck out like a sore thumb in the middle of the room. It was incongruous, yet solidly mundane. Beyond the glass of the case front, Saiyah could see reflections from the real world of a storage room.

Bezbiel drifted to it as if possessed, dragging a bewildered Saiyah along with him, and put his hand to it in disbelief. Inside were drawers and layers of protective paper which were presumably wrapped around items no longer on display. Labels scribbled in cold-war biro indicated the case contained bronze items c. 330-730

BC. He opened the case swiftly but carefully, opening a lower drawer which contained papers and notebooks. He lifted one and rifled through it. She had no doubt he knew what he'd find in that drawer; he'd been allowed to view certain items in this and other museums for research many times before.

"Yes, yes, yes," he muttered under his breath, drumming his finger on something.

Saiyah didn't have time to ask what he was talking about before the book was offloaded onto her. It contained a meticulous but shabby copy of a day-book from decades ago. Bezbiel was withdrawing something from one of the shelves, something small and wrapped in the uncomfortably smooth off-white paper. He checked the faded label, which was carefully sellotaped to it, before pocketing the item and putting everything else back in its rightful place.

"You didn't see anything," he told the young coven members with a wicked grin, which charmed them into compliance. They were too inexperienced to sense the flow of demonic influence over them. "You three stay here. Come on," he said to Saiyah as they proceeded to the edge of the library.

Bezbiel placed one foot out cautiously and met solid ground. Saiyah did the same. They tentatively made their way along until they could see Zulphas's office. The door was wide open, but completely empty and windswept with papers as they'd left it. Saiyah felt as if she'd swallowed a stone.

Bezbiel's face was dark as he twirled his Malachite between his fingers, and with a minute green flash he appeared metres away in Zulphas's office. Saiyah turned to shadow, lest she fall through the floor, and followed him in. Bezbiel was already examining Zulphas's workings.

"Summoning spell," he muttered, baffled.

Saiyah looked over his shoulder and ran her hand over Zulphas's notes. The papers moved at her touch, and she caught a glimpse of ancient parchment and erratic handwriting in Old Demonic. "John Greyson," she read aloud. "He has been trying to summon him."

Bezbiel stared back at her with barely contained worry.

XXIX

Our Fate Cannot Be Taken From Us

BAD NEWS SPREAD FAST amongst the coven, and none failed to notice the fabric of their little world shifting. Older demons who'd not left the safety of the Old Roads found themselves propelled into the mortal world without warning. After a rushed patch-up, some were busy creating teleportation grounds to give themselves a route of escape to Hell, in case things went bad for the coven. Creating a gate of this scale would take months, and keeping it a secret from *The Host* would be the real test. Azeldya wouldn't allow it, as they had a duty to comply with *The Host*. Yet at the same time, her protests were weak. Saiyah couldn't blame them either.

Azeldya's office's emerald-green tones appeared unsettlingly sepia in the evening light. Every surface seemed to glint with obscure embossed patterns of gold and silver, yet the effect was not overbearing. Saiyah's feet sounded unnecessarily loud on the dark marble as she made her way towards the ancient demoness. Standing beyond her desk, Azeldya wore loose, grey, desert-worthy clothing, in keeping with her usual monochrome appearance. Black armour with ornate, swirling patterns was laid out on the leather-covered desk, and she fixed her guards to her forearms. They flickered in the light from dark obsidian to barely visible glass.

She was without a doubt pleased and somewhat relieved to see Saiyah, but there was a seriousness to her that hadn't surfaced in a while.

"Are you aware of the situation?" she began, as if she already knew the answer.

"Yes," Saiyah said as she exhaled, making herself comfy on the sofa.

Azeldya's forehead creased minutely, her pretty white curls bouncing on her shoulders. "The amalgamating of our worlds." She snapped her fingers. "Zulphas and I had been looking into it. In its own way, it's like a form of Hellgate, and we suspect some manner of occult is involved. There are traces of that energy left behind, and only a small percentage of it is demonic. I've not sensed occult energy like this since Crowley."

Saiyah's jaw slacked but she gathered herself. "Could it be Greyson?"

Azeldya froze. "Do you have reason to suspect that it might be him?"

Saiyah nodded.

Azeldya frowned and spoke in a low, soft tone. "I must admit the notion that he died long ago never sat well with me." She placed her hand lightly on her desk as if to steady herself, her gaze locked in the past.

"If he lives, I intend to find out," Saiyah assured her.

Leaving Azeldya to don the rest of her armour and contemplate, Saiyah's shadow lifted her satchel onto her shoulder and she marched purposefully out of the office.

S AIYAH WAS RESTLESS, AND was as uncomfortable on the Old Roads as anywhere else now. She and Bezbiel laboriously walked the halls of the British Museum, the real one, checking for cracks in reality.

"He said yes," Bezbiel said, dumbfounded, looking at his phone. "Malik agreed to have you as his guest, though he has a few conditions. What on earth did you say to him in Prague?"

Saiyah smiled in relief and a vague expression of admiration crossed Bezbiel's face.

"What are the conditions?"

"He wants to meet with you again first, alone. At his place. Tonight."

Saiyah went pale.

"I don't like the sound of that," Bezbiel said offhandedly.

"Me neither. But I must go. Attending that ball may be my only way of letting Hezekiah know that Silas is up to something... suspicious."

Bezbiel gave her an odd look. "You'll be careful?"

" Do you think I'm in any danger?"

"It's not that. Malik can be difficult, yes, but it's not like he's going to hurt anyone. Just don't make any deals with him, okay?" He added with a weary smirk.

Saiyah swallowed and nodded. "I won't. I can do this. Now, as for the ball, what do they wear in Hell? I think I'd like to represent my people as I'll soon be going there. I want to wear something devastating."

There was a warning in his glance, but he smiled roguishly.

It was the weekend, and families dragged their rosy-cheeked children around the museum, trying desperately to get them interested in the displays with varying success. They gave wide berths to mothers with prams, not wanting to evoke the ire of a new parent faced with a demon.

"Do you have family, Bez?" Saiyah asked carefully.

"Yes," Bezbiel said blandly, extraordinarily interested in a display.

They'd found John Dee's scrying mirror, which he apparently used to communicate with angels to do his bidding. When they looked into it, the reflection showed a distorted view of a room that appeared to be in the Old Roads.

"Do you miss them?" Saiyah pushed him.

"No," he said evenly, adjusting his hair in the reflection of a glass cabinet. "I see my Mum all the time."

Saiyah grinned in surprise, and gradually coerced the information out of him. His human mother lived in South London, working as a teacher at a Catholic school. She wasn't a fan of demons, especially after her encounter with his father, and Bezbiel had a challenging relationship with her. She'd always hoped he would cast off his demonic nature somehow.

Despite his evident discomfort at his family situation, Saiyah couldn't help a pang of jealousy, though her guilt was immediate. He'd had a mother to raise him, a loving parent to guide him and watch him grow. Daniel had been a mother and father to her, of course, but she would never know if it was the same or not. What would her life have been like if her mother wasn't killed? What would've become of them both if they'd been allowed to live together in peace? Would her childhood have been spent skipping through the twilight forest of

Nyx, knowing every trail and stream, familiar with the whispers of the trees?

Her smile wavered and she forced herself back to the present.

"Why do you have a name like Bezbiel then?" Saiyah asked.

He grinned ironically, and eventually erupted into a melodic chuckle, startling other museum goers. "It's what my father named me when he claimed me," he admitted. "Not my birth name."

Relieved that the mood had lightened, she hounded him for his birth name. He refused.

"Either you tell me what your name is, or you tell me what you've promised Malik in your deal."

Bezbiel's face dropped. He shook his head.

"Bez, forget the name. In all seriousness, I appreciate what you're doing–everything you've done for me. You didn't have to. I hate to admit it, but despite everything, you're probably my best friend." She gave a bashful laugh, shaking her head. "Just tell me so I don't have to worry."Bezbiel's face changed tremendously as she spoke, from flattered, to concern, to guilt.

He rubbed his hands together thoughtfully and took a seat on one of the viewing benches. Saiyah joined him,

"I promised in exchange for safe passage and to pro-tect you, I would commit myself into his service."

Saiyah furrowed her brows. "What does that mean? You'll work for him?"

Bezbiel shook his head. "It's not quite so simple. It'll be a while before I need to keep my end of the deal."

Saiyah recoiled upon realisation. His soul. His soul after his eventual death. Her face was impossibly angry, and her eyes glowed with astonished dismay. "What the actual hell?" she said in a raised, cracking voice. She was drawing attention to herself. "How stupid can you get!"

Saiyah made swiftly for the exit while Bezbiel attempted to stop her.

"It's fine, honestly! The deal can't be broken anyway," he said as they grappled each other like children in a scuffle.

"I'm sure there is something I can do. You can't stop me from leaving, Bez!" She shouted, transforming to shadow and gliding through him with a shudder.

At Malik's London address a housekeeper answered the door and asked if she was 'Katomei Saiyah.' Reluctantly, she said yes.

Saiyah was incongruous in the atrium of the lavish Georgian home decorated with beautiful works of art, both historical and contemporary. She glimpsed at herself in a long mirror at the foot of the staircase. Her hair was windswept, and her clothes were simple: a dark roll neck and paper bag trousers with her lazy, oversized, tartan jacket. She was staring at her surroundings for a while before noticing Malik leaning in a door frame.

He grinned at her bewitchingly. "I knew you'd come and see me eventually."

Before she could speak, he backed into the room beyond, beckoning her. Saiyah followed him into a room filled with curiosities, reminding her a little of the Pitt Rivers Museum in Oxford, and it was indeed filled with curiosities. Dark framed glass cabinets lined the room, sheltering delicate objects of antiquity. Photographs from Malik's travels and objects of all cultures were proudly framed and displayed amongst hints of gilt and soft leather. He sat down on one of the sofas either side of the fireplace, offering her refreshment. Saiyah refused and sat opposite, abnormally nervous. There was a swell of demonic energy in the room which made her feel slightly lightheaded, as if she'd been drinking.

"Is there something you want to ask me about our upcoming event? Or are you here to thank me perhaps?" He said melodiously.

Saiyah swallowed. "Yes, thank you. I appreciate your help. It's something else, the deal you made–"

"You're here about your friend, Bezbiel Brady," he stated, lounging into the chair.

"I'd like to renegotiate terms," she said commandingly, though her voice was quiet.

Malik laughed sinisterly. "My dear little Katomei, I'm afraid that's impossible." He held out a hand in anticipation of her argument. "However, if *you'd* like to bargain for his soul, we could come to another arrangement, I'm sure."

Saiyah scrutinised him distrustfully and pressed her knees together. He looked her up and down with yellow and blue eyes. Something about the way they reflected in the light was ghoulish.

"I understand you spend a lot of time with the gods," he continued. "There is something I want from them." He flashed his sharp teeth at her.

"What is it?"

"I want the soul of one god. That would be more than enough in payment," he told her cheerily.

Saiyah half smiled in confusion. "Gods don't have souls."

Malik narrowed his eyes. "Maybe. Maybe not."

Saiyah gave him a puzzled look and opened her mouth. He held up a finger to indicate she shouldn't speak. He stood and walked to the back of the room, obscured by odd sculptures and furniture. Saiyah heard wood scraping against wood and he returned holding something that looked like a book. As he turned the yellowing pages, Saiyah leaned forward, her eyes growing wide. The illustrations were strikingly familiar.

"Where did you get that?" she gasped.

Malik regarded her seriously for the first time, concealing the pages. "That's none of your business. This book contains the proof that gods have something like a soul which can be obtained."

Saiyah got to her feet sharply. "That's John Greyson's book!"

His face turned wrathful. "How do you know that?" He stood and advanced towards her.

"I have the other half. My mother knew him. Once."

The demonic energy grew, and Saiyah swayed. She was truly out of her depth. Malik peered down at her and revealed one of the pages. Saiyah tentatively reached for it. They were more battered than the other half of the book.

"*Once,*" Malik scoffed.

As Saiyah examined the page, her heart rate increased. The ritual described was remarkably similar to the ones in her mother's journal, but this was more detailed, better planned, well-articulated. This was the ritual for how John Greyson stole fire from the gods. He obtained a soul.

Saiyah shook her head. "This won't work," she said, glancing warily up at him. "The other rituals, they're all nonsense, experimental and flawed."

Malik laughed wickedly and snatched the book back from her. "Correct, which is why I discarded the other half. Besides, I don't need it to work, this book is simply the proof I need that gods have a soul of kinds. I would like to collect one."

Saiyah resisted the urge to touch her moon pendant for comfort. Malik put the book down on the table between them and walked around so they were toe to toe.

"What do you say? Do you think you can manipulate one of your god friends for me?" He said with a pointed grin.

Saiyah put a hand on her face in thought. "That's the only thing you're willing to exchange?" She ventured.

Malik pondered, stroking his chin, then nodded definitively.

"Fine," Saiyah said, adopting a light tone. "However, you said yourself, that's more than enough. If I can give you the soul of a god, I want you to do something else for me."

His eyes lit up with interest and he leaned forward. "You seem to always want something from me, little Katomei, and it never seems like *I'm* getting all that much in return," he said in honeyed tones.

Saiyah flushed lilac and his grin widened.

"Very well, name your price," he said genially.

She cleared her throat. "I want you to kill Akrasiel Silas."

Malik's face dropped. Saiyah held out her hand unwaveringly.

His eyes glistened gleefully as he pondered for a moment, then chuckled. "You drive a hard bargain, little Katomei."

Malik reached out his hand, but instead of shaking it he grabbed her by the wrist and pulled her forwards, turning her palm upwards. Saiyah gasped girlishly as he allowed the golden-tipped claw of his thumb to slice across her hand. He paused, inspecting the colour of her blood with curiosity and mirth as it dripped on the carpet. Saiyah was stunned, and locked eyes with him pleadingly. A knowing smile crept upon him. Carefully, he made a similar cut on his own hand and released her, placing his hand in hers. There was a jolt of energy between their palms. The deal was done.

XXX

Hearts of the Most Reckless

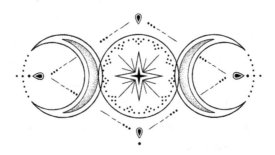

S AIYAH WORE AN ELEGANT black evening gown, low cut and backless. It was made of a flowing, ghostly material from Hell. Tiny iridescent gold and green beads draped over her back, as well as a few over her head and ears.

"What do you think?" she asked as Medea fussed with her hair, already immaculate in her red and gold dress.

Bezbiel edged further into the room and looked her over with an ironic smile. "I think if he spots you, you'll break his heart," he said in a soft voice.

Saiyah furrowed her brows at his strange comment, but grinned. "Thank you."

When she walked or twirled, vibrant, jewel toned greens and blues showed through from the underlining. She flaunted the effect in front of Bezbiel.

Malik had extended his invitation to any guests Saiyah wished to invite. It was all in aid of promoting relations with half-demons after all, and since Azeldya was at present completely absent, Jack, Hex and numerous other coven members were there. She started to suspect getting invited to these things wasn't as difficult as Medea made out.

Inside London's Natural History Museum, the skeletal form of a whale stretched from one end of the gothic ceiling to the other. The cathedral-like hall was lit up with artificial light in sea-blues and greens, ultraviolet rays projecting down on the throng of guests. Saiyah watched Hex and Jack descend the steps into the hall, their path lit with dotted yellow lights. Bezbiel followed, and Medea made her way confidently down in her candy red and gold dress. Saiyah hung back in the darkness to catch her breath before the onslaught of social interactions. She'd gotten quite good at these sorts of things recently; she'd had to, since Idris could be so serious. Instead, her mind was dark with notions of bad dreams and revenge.

At the door, she glimpsed Malik on a balcony above, surrounded by laughing people he towered above them. Saiyah showed her invite to an attendant as people glanced suspiciously at her red armband. She took a glass of something from a waiter who directed her up a flight of stairs. Malik was gone from where he'd stood before. Whispers flowed around her with disapproving eyes. She'd completely lost sight of her companions.

At the top, one pair of eyes watched her differently from the rest. A skinny young woman who wasn't much older than herself stepped artlessly forward, beaming with excitement.

"I love your dress," she said genuinely, admiring Saiyah.

Relieved, Saiyah thanked her, returning the compliment. She introduced herself as Emily. She wore an expensive green dress, and had the faintest whiff of the occult about her, though she didn't seem the type.

"I don't think I'm welcome here," Saiyah admitted coolly, taking a sip of her drink.

"Don't worry, it was the same with Lord Malik at first," Emily assured her with a laugh.

"Do you know where–?"

A portly man pulled Emily aside. "Stay away from my daughter," the man boomed, drawing attention.

Saiyah frowned helplessly, trying not to spill her drink. A crowd formed. Calmly she began to explain, but Emily's father started calling for security, and Emily quietly tried to reason with him. Saiyah cast around for Malik, edging closer to the stairs. Her placid demeanour broke as she tried to defend herself peacefully. Suddenly, the man became quiet, and a smug look appeared on his face. Emily looked towards the stairs, distressed.

Expecting security men, Saiyah was stunned to see Idris in a tailored suit, frozen in position a few steps down from her. He carried a sword with a ceremonial sash, half drawn, but let it drop back into place, speechless.

She smiled cordially but aloofly at him. "Captain Hezekiah."

He assessed the situation, looking at the man who'd shouted at Saiyah, but continued up the last few steps without speaking. Without taking his eyes off Saiyah, he stood a little distance away. He inclined his head like a small bow and took her hand, raising it to his lips. He noticed the cut with a flicker of realisation.

"Katomei," he said in greeting, his voice icy.

She took a steadying breath and blushed at the word. Idris must have been informed of Malik's plan to introduce her as such. She offered him the bare minimum of smiles in thanks.

"You look–" Idris paused, steadily looking at her from head to toe "You look beautiful," he finished haltingly.

Saiyah grinned triumphantly, but couldn't hold it. "Thank you, Captain."

Idris's intense, unblinking eyes relaxed as he turned towards Emily's father and introduced Saiyah formally. He reluctantly shook Saiyah's hand before making his excuses, trying to coax Emily away without success.

"What are you doing here?" Idris said in a low voice, not masking his irritation well.

"I have something I need to tell you," she replied smoothly, glancing warily at Emily as her attention returned to them.

Saiyah spied Malik making his way through the throng of people, wearing his usual charming grin. Idris followed her gaze and clenched his jaw, while Emily became increasingly flustered.

"I was just wondering where you'd got to, my dear," Malik said, taking Saiyah's hand and kissing it. "Hezekiah." He greeted the captain with a nod.

"Malik," Idris replied coldly, causing Malik's face to brighten with amusement.

Saiyah introduced Emily, who was standing just off to the side, and she looked as if she was going to faint.

"I didn't realise it would be you and your esteemed brother here tonight, Captain," Malik said after briefly acknowledging Emily. "I'll admit the number of gods I sense on the perimeter is unnecessarily heavy-handed. Where is that lovely secretary of yours?"

"She was called away," Idris said bluntly.

"What a shame," Malik responded patronisingly. The ensuing awkward silence didn't seem to affect him. "Diverting as this conversation has been Captain, I think we'll take our leave now, Saiyah?" He slipped his arm through hers and she smiled cordially, her eyes lingering on Idris as she walked away.

Malik led her into the next room, a large space with classical architecture and a polished floor. There was a string quartet camouflaged amongst the grand paintings, and a small orchestra had arrived to join them. Malik seemed to be well integrated in this society and chatted amiably amongst the human elite, though an undercurrent of mistrust and apprehension was apparent. Saiyah was complicit in their reactions as Malik repeatedly introduced her as the Katomei of Khabrasos. They'd no idea where or what that was, of course. He never mentioned anything regarding demons or gods, keeping his conversation rooted in the mortal world, and deftly avoided topics that brushed on the supernatural.

The room slowly became crowded, alcohol flowed, and the volume of music grew along with the chatter and merriment. Evening gowns rustled and glasses clinked. She spied Emily in her peripheral, wanting to approach but hanging back. Idris drifted between the crowds, keeping a genial smile on his face as he spoke to people, but Saiyah caught his eye more than once.

"Do you dance?" Malik asked without a hint of irony, regaining her attention.

"Not very well," she admitted coyly.

His face lit up with amusement and his pointed teeth showed. "If I promise not to sweep you off your feet, will you do me the honour?" He said courteously, holding a hand out. "That way we can talk with less chance of being interrupted."

Saiyah spied his matching cut like a line of dark ink, healing more cleanly than hers. Though apprehensive, Saiyah accepted. Medea would've wanted her to. As he pulled her towards the centre of the room, people watched them as a novelty. Saiyah held her chin high, maintaining a gracious smile.

Amongst the other dancers, Malik held her in a closed position as they began their demonic waltz. She flinched at the pressure on her injured hand, which didn't go unnoticed.

"So, why did you want to come to this party so much, little Katomei?" Malik asked her in an unexpected flourish of New Demonic.

Saiyah's brain rushed to catch up with her mouth as she tried to recall how to have a conversation in the dialect. "My business is my own."

Malik shook his head and slipped his thumb under her bandage, tearing it and letting it drop to the floor in one deft movement. He held her hand tightly, but gently, keeping it covered. "I don't know how you came to have this blood, and I don't want to know either. But rest assured I'm not going to tell anyone. You can trust me, Saiyah. At least in this matter."

There was a tingling of demonic energy on her palm and the dull aching pain alleviated. It'd healed cleanly, but wasn't completely gone.

"Thank you," she managed to articulate. Gaining confidence, she looked up at him. "Can I ask how you came by John Greyson's book?"

He paused for a moment before speaking. "When he was alive, I remember him always having it on his person. I thought little of the ramblings of a mortal. I assume you know that he became much more than that?" He waited for Saiyah to confirm before continuing. "I remember Asramenia being rather distressed that it'd disappeared, though she tried to disguise it. It was some years later that I came by it again, in the possession of Zulphas."

"He had the other half," Saiyah put in.

"Precisely. After all the fuss she'd made, I had a look at it, and quickly realised how John Greyson came to wield that kind of power. The early scribblings of his youth were useless, so I took the part of the book that mattered." Malik chuckled and unexpectedly turned her about. "I expect it took decades for the boy to realise the back of the book was missing."

Saiyah steadied her footing. "You said you wanted to 'collect' a soul. What do you want to do with it?" she asked, furrowing her brows.

Malik chuckled again. "Exactly that, to collect. What I do with it is my own business," he said, raising an eyebrow. "Come on now. Tell me what you're doing here. Do you have another burning favour to ask of me?" He asked dramatically.

Saiyah couldn't help but smile at his theatrics, and shook her head. "No, no, it's nothing to do with you."

"How refreshing!" he said brightly.

Saiyah rolled her eyes, finally in the rhythm of the dance. "It's Hezekiah. I need to pass information."

Malik's brows drew together playfully. "Are you still on the side of the revolution?" He asked. Saiyah nodded resolutely and he grinned amiably, slowing the dance. "Then what are you waiting for?" He drew her away from the dancing and bowed, planting a kiss on her hand. "Find me again afterwards."

She swiped a glass of something from a waiter as Malik retreated into the crowd, and caught a glimpse of Idris watching her again. But no sooner was she off the dancefloor then she was surrounded by people wanting to talk to her. Saiyah was regarded warily, but it seemed as if people thought it was probably alright, as the captain was right there after all. No harm would befall them. Soon there were those curious and brave enough to ask her questions.

"Do you actually come from Hell?"

"I was born there, but raised in this world."

"Someone said they heard Captain Hezekiah called you a Duchess?"

"Katomei," Saiyah corrected. "But I'm not. My mother was one, not me."

"So, you're the same as Malik?"

Saiyah took a sip of her drink to slow the questioning.

"Have you met him before? I've had the privilege to dine with the captain many times before. Isn't he wonderful? Quiet, but he's always terribly polite, and really quite sweet," someone said with a girlish giggle.

The amusement on Saiyah's face was evident. She sensed his familiar presence before she saw him and straightened up, mentally preparing herself for battle. He didn't say anything as he appeared in her peripheral, overlooking the bright colours and sounds of the party at the top of the steps and making small talk with dull aristocrats, employing every social tactic she'd taught him. She knew he could tell she was watching him, but was pretending to ignore her.

Medea came to her rescue. Saiyah was thankful to have her there, as she was unquestionably a good ally when it came to navigating this social sphere. She introduced her to guests she thought had the most influence, no doubt people she'd mingled with over the years. Many she knew already from other functions with Idris. Most spoke in a plummy accent, or near enough, and Saiyah always got the impression they were trying to catch her out while being superficially pleasant. Thankfully, her quick mind and sharp tongue got her out of being patronised instantly. Or it could have been the red armband.

"What is your opinion on all these demons coming through unannounced?" asked a man in his mid-twenties, the son or nephew of lord such-and-such politician. He had a tone which suggested he was teasing her, but not unpleasantly, just patronising. His comment was met with a few chuckles, including Saiyah's, but her face was serious with a melancholy smile.

"I think it's a tragedy," she told him softly, her voice full of empathy. "Those poor people have nowhere else to go, completely displaced from their homes, and they are met only with violence and intolerance."

The young man frowned. "I think you'll find *they're* the ones inflicting the violence."

Saiyah frowned as well. Nervous laughter.

"There is violence on both sides, I will concede. Like most things, all this comes down to lack of information and cultural differences. If the gods hadn't cut off the food supply of these people, albeit inadvertently, and there was an allied neighbouring land for them to go to, then I expect they would've gone there. Not everyone is so lucky to have friends and relatives in other regions of Hell." They flinched at that, and it gave Saiyah a sadistic glint of amusement. Emily appeared in an emerald dress, slotting quietly into the group. She raised her glass to Saiyah in greeting.

"So, it's the gods fault?" The young man asked with bravado, seemingly undeterred with her statement.

Saiyah grinned in a way which mimicked Malik's charming yet dangerous expression.

"Isn't it always? They are the ones who pull the strings, moving in mysterious ways. They have the power to put things right and re-home these *refugees*, even temporarily," she said with a tilt of the head. "Unless perhaps they're not as powerful as they'd like you to think."

She was met with blank worried faces. Through the crowd she could see Idris looking directly at her. He may not have heard what she said, but he'd seen the reactions of those around her and was giving her a warning glance.

"Well, that was rather heavy," she finished in a lightened tone.

The group let out a laugh of relief and the tension in the air lifted. Emily shot her a wide grin.

Idris drew near and members of the group started to look guilty, worried to be having such diverting conversations with a demon. He approached with a stern expression as she turned on her heel to regard him smugly, adjusting the fabric that trailed from her shoulder.

"Hezekiah–"

"Captain," he corrected unthinkingly, causing further amusement which didn't wash over him easily. "What is going on here?"

"Why, Captain, we're just discussing the nature of demons. Tell me, do you think demons are evil, influencing, deceiving, etcetera, because they have no soul, or is it something else?" She asked sweetly.

Idris folded his arms and sighed. "You are a half-demon Miss Greyson, which means you have half a soul, remember?" He said, dismissing her comments. "I hope this demon isn't bothering you all?"

He was met with a chorus of genial denial and jest, particularly from Emily. Saiyah tensed, remembering her deal with Bezbiel. She couldn't let herself reveal that accidentally tonight.

"Saiyah is fascinating company as always, Captain," Emily protested.

"As long as you're not suggesting we're in any danger from her?" The young man chimed.

Nervous laughter.

Idris regarded Saiyah, almost playfully, before he answered. His gaze softened. "No, I'd say you're not," he admitted with a slight smile.

As the group settled into more relaxed conversation, Saiyah felt a tug on her elbow and Idris moved her to one side.

"Is that the message you're going with tonight?" He asked amiably. "It's all our fault and we're the ones who should fix it?"

"When you put it like that, yes," she said lightly.

Idris made a noise halfway between a laugh and a groan.

"Am I wrong?"

"Perhaps you should focus your efforts on giving reasons why the mortals shouldn't be so outraged at their presence. Give them some understanding."

Saiyah caught a glimpse of Bezbiel chatting effortlessly to a high-status couple. Medea was by his side. The couple were laughing at whatever Bezbiel was saying, utterly charmed by him. She wondered if their reaction was natural or not. Soon found she was watching Hex and Jack as they spun each other around on the dancefloor. She smiled in spite of herself. What was more harmless than showing a pair of carefree young half-demons to the world? It would probably look inappropriately familiar for her and Idris to be doing something like that.

Then there was Ezra. Saiyah hadn't expected him to be here, and it chilled her. He oversaw Silas. Surely, he wasn't involved in whatever dealings were happening between him and the Katomet of Khabrasos? He was exclusively speaking to other gods, his own men, and members of *The Host*. No mortals, no half-demons.

Sucking in her pride, she signalled for Idris to follow her. Leaving the room and gliding down the staircase, she slipped through another door which led out into a garden courtyard. Lights illuminated a fountain with a statue at the centre. Raised beds of purple flowers framed the area. Saiyah took a moment to catch her breath, enjoying the airy night on her skin.

"This is a different side of you than I've seen," came his voice from behind. Idris walked past her, taking a seat on the edge of the trickling fountain. "Have you always been this devious or is it all an act? Perhaps it was all an act before."

She placed a hand over her heart. "I could be the sweetest, loveliest version of myself, and you would still think I'm a deceitful demon," she said sarcastically.

He looked at her disapprovingly. "What do you want, Miss Greyson?"

Saiyah hid her dismay at the way he referred to her and squared her shoulders. "I've discovered something about Silas which might help us."

Idris glanced around in alarm and shushed her; his fingertips absently rested on the olive-branch hilt of his sword.

"He's here tonight, on the perimeter, keep quiet," he warned in a whisper.

Saiyah sat with him on the edge of the fountain and lowered her voice. "He sent the scavengers. The ones who half destroyed your home and ran you through, remember?" She whispered fiercely back.

Idris raised his head, startled. "Can you prove it?"

Saiyah grinned slyly and reached inside her bra to retrieve a tightly folded piece of paper. "We have one of them in the Old Roads. He'll admit everything he's seen Silas do. He's working with the Katomet of Khabrasos."

Idris looked away but discreetly took the paper. It vanished into his pocket.

"There's more. The scavengers are getting here by hitchhiking off a Hellgate made by an occultist. A mortal occultist using demon energies. Seems like too much of a coincidence, doesn't it?"

"Don't get involved any further. Let me handle Silas."

"You said that before, but it seems I'm the only one making headway," she said icily.

Idris glared at her then got to his feet and turned. "I am sorry about what I said before," he said as he adjusted the cufflinks on his sleeves. "It wasn't my finest behaviour."

"Likewise," she retorted flatly, adjusting her shawl as she stood. "But that doesn't mean I can ever forgive you. You were right."

He nodded in acknowledgement and glanced at the door. Idris lowered his head. "You looked well, dancing with Malik."

Another triumphant smile grew on Saiyah's face. "You're not jealous are you, Captain?"

"Just be careful," he said quietly. "The cut on your hand–"

"That's none of your concern. Malik is the least of my problems," she said sharply, hiding her hand in her gauzy shawl.

Idris watched her sternly, trying to gauge any truth in her words. He gave a slight nod. "If you're in any kind of trouble, I want you to know that as your registered Captain it would be natural to come to me for help."

"Judas," Saiyah scoffed under her breath. "That's rich coming from you. I thought you didn't want us to have anything to do with each other. Or are you insinuating that I continue slipping into your house in the middle of the night like some kind of–"

He gave her a hard look and shushed her. He glanced up towards the muted night sky. "Don't say things like that here."

Idris pulled her under one of the archways, where they were obscured by shadow. He scowled at her and stiffened his jaw. "You are the *most* difficult woman I've ever had the misfortune to know," he whispered harshly, grabbing her hand and pointing at the partially healed scar. "And you've no idea what you're getting into!"

Saiyah tore her hand away. "Calm down. I know how to handle him. Regardless, he's my only way of getting to Hell safely." She tilted her head and drew her brows together, but spoke calmly. "You can't have it both ways. Either we distance ourselves and you keep your opinions on what I do to yourself, or we carry on sneaking about in the shadows like this. Which is it?"

Idris lowered his lashes and looked vaguely past her in resignation. She made to move past him, but he held his arm out to block her, drawing her slowly back to where she'd stood. His eyes were intense as they day she'd first met him, almost looking through her with their luminosity. It was a moment before she realised he was staring at her unblinking.

He exhaled unsteadily. "I'm definitely going to Hell for this," he muttered.

Idris stepped abruptly towards her. Saiyah faltered as his hands gripped her waist. She stumbled back against the stone archway as his body pressed against hers, uncertain breath caressing her cheek. Arms slid around her as his gaze flickered from her eyes to her mouth, then his lips lightly brushed against hers. Saiyah allowed her eyes to close and slid her arms around his shoulders, pressing her mouth eagerly against his.

A ripple of divine energy flowed over them, but it wasn't the comforting energy she'd come to know from Hezekiah. There was something sickening about it. Saiyah opened her eyes and gasped as she pulled away from Idris. A deathly banshee scream echoed from inside the building, coupled with sounds of distress. Saiyah knew that voice.

It was Hex that'd screamed.

XXXI

His Waxen Wings Did Mount Above Reach And, Melting, Heavens Conspired His Overthrow

P EOPLE WERE MOVING AROUND her, trains of dresses rustling in haste. She felt a cool hand on her shoulder and turned, expecting Idris, but instead the angelic face of Gabrielle smiled pityingly down at her. More demon slayers had appeared, and their very presence gave calm to the remaining guests. With minimal guidance from Gabrielle, she found herself being gently ushered back into the main ballroom.

Medea appeared at her side, pale and shaken, but more alert than Saiyah. "This is all we need," she hissed, sucking in air through her teeth. "Panicking mortals at a time like this. *The Host* will have—" She was interrupted by the tapping of a microphone that reverberated around the hall.

A sickness spilt from side to side in Saiyah's stomach. Her heart beat at a quickened pace, as if it were about to take flight, and her head was light. Jack is gone. Where are Hex and Jack? The affliction was almost too much to bear.

Someone said something into the microphone, and she heard the name *Ezra Hezekiah*. Snapping to attention, she watched as he walked to centre stage, ignoring the modern contraption of voice projection. Saiyah was sure his eye caught hers and she forced herself to breathe slowly and listen. Without turning her head, she cast her eyes about for Idris. She found him close to the stage at the perimeter of the room. Bezbiel was pushing his way through the crowd purposefully, the only movement in the room.

"Ladies and gentlemen," Ezra began, his god-voice making the crowd flinch, "I have an announcement that diverges from this evening's festivities, and one I did not expect to be making so soon."

Medea gripped Saiyah's hand. "I don't like this, I don't like this, I don't like this," she whispered repeatedly.

"None present will have failed to notice the carnage in the streets inflicted by a new scourge of demons." There was a murmur of acknowledgement, one less cordial than any of the half-demons would've liked. "Nearly two decades ago, mankind suffered a wave of demons entering this world through mortal birth, and now a scourge directly from Hell threatens you all. As your newly appointed protector, I promise that these violent legions will be put down." Each word was emphasised, and with it grew a kind of jeering encouragement in the front row. "This is your world, made for humankind, and it is not to be shared by these foul creatures. I pledge that not only will I slay them, but those who call themselves half-demon will be brought to justice for their crimes, and smited."

Cheers rose now, and Saiyah felt eyes on her. She drew closer to Medea and glanced at Idris. His eyes were fixed on his brother, a scowl of outrage on his face.

Ezra clicked his fingers and two members of *The Host* appeared on the stage in a subtle flash. Between them they held Hex, her hands behind her back and hair dishevelled. She looked as though she were trying to struggle from side to side, but she was no match for their grip. Her jaw hung slack, and her eyes were alight with rage and fear. Bezbiel called out from somewhere at the front of the crowd and a commotion began to brew.

"The audacity of these half-breeds has risen to such that even in the presence of the gods they will willingly cause distress and chaos." He turned to Hex. "This woman was found to be exercising demonic power outside of the home, against gods, no less. For this, the punishment is imprisonment or banishment. However, we will no longer be so lenient. An example must be made. This woman will be put to death."Saiyah clenched her teeth, anger filling her. Something else brewed within her, too; shadow flickered at her fingers. She exhaled deeply and prepared to make herself invisible. It wouldn't be difficult getting through and getting up onto the stage unnoticed. Prying Hex from them would be hard, but once she had her, Saiyah could conceal her and get her out of there.

Medea's hand shook as Saiyah prised hers away. She took a step forward but found that something hard blocked her by the ribs. Idris held an arm across her, suddenly right at her side. He shook his head gravely.

The commotion in the crowd grew as Bezbiel clambered toward the stage. Many hands pulled him back, others urged him on, thirsty for blood. Most of the socialites were leaving. Better not to get mixed up in all this, don't want to witness anything like death anyway, ruins the evening. It was the diehard politically minded that remained. Malik was also strategically absent.

Some words were spoken between Ezra and one of his men. Something was passed between them, godly papers to most, but that book was startlingly familiar to Saiyah. It was John Greyson's book.

Suddenly Bezbiel was on the stage too. His snake eyes were startlingly visible as they reflected in the coloured lights. Hex was dragged towards Ezra as he drew his sword. Bezbiel was just behind, held firmly by two gods.

Saiyah lurched forward again, but this time Idris held her firmly with both hands around her waist.

"Don't," he whispered harshly.

Saiyah could've growled at him. "He's going to *kill* them," she said, loud enough to draw attention. "If you're not going to do anything, then let me. You must let me go!"

A pained look crossed Idris's face. He exchanged a look with Gabrielle over Saiyah's head and reluctantly let her go. Saiyah simultaneously sprang from his arms and melted away into obscurity.

Gabrielle put an arm around Medea, who was on the verge of screaming, and they both disappeared in a rush of air. Idris dimmed his light and returned to the corridor of arches at the side of the room, one hand on the hilt of his sword.

Ezra was about to bring his sword down when something jolted him. He turned slightly to one side and half-smiled. The soldiers holding Hex and Bezbiel blinked in confusion and quickly their gazes became completely blank. Their eyes swirled with a smoky darkness, and they swayed, oblivious to their surroundings.

She'd never attempted her mother's technique for trapping souls before, the one she'd read about in her journals. She wasn't even sure if she could replicate it, or if it would work. It wasn't engulfing them in darkness and hypnosis in the elaborate web Asramenia wove, but it was good enough for now. Yet their grip didn't diminish.

Much to Saiyah's satisfaction, Ezra was turning about, examining the air as he looked for her. She stayed just out of reach from his sword as she crept around him. She axe-kicked the hands of one soldier holding Bezbiel. Bezbiel cried out as his wrist was caught also, but he was sharp enough to think to slither out of their grasp speedily. He drew his malachite from the inside of his coat pocket and scrambled to draw a quick circle around where Hex knelt. He was a clear target, and Ezra advanced.

"Brother," came a calm but commanding voice from behind. Ezra didn't halt his advance, but it was enough to make him slow. "Brother, I regret to inform you that our actions here have distressed, and are still distressing, many mortals."

His sword lowered slightly, and Saiyah creeped forward, seeing her chance. "That is a small price to–" Ezra began, then grunted in surprise as Saiyah's shadowy form kicked him in the gut.

There was a flash of green, and Bezbiel and Hex were gone. Such a quick spell couldn't get them far, though. Screams came from the back of the hall, and Saiyah saw the pair of them running up the stairs followed by a small raven. Ezra's eye was on them.

Saiyah made herself visible as immediately as her demonic energy would allow. The effect caused swirls of smoke-like darkness to emerge rapidly from her before fading away. Ezra's mouth twitched into a cruel smile and his sword lifted. She was the greater prize. Her vivid green eyes caught Idris's stricken expression as she scooped up her trailing dress and leapt deftly from the stage, forming a cloud of darkness to soften her landing. Ezra leapt eagerly after her. She fled into the depths of the museum, fading in and out of visibility to keep him on her trail, slipping away each time he nearly caught her.

The corridor became narrow, and she wasn't certain where she was going. The long, gothic windows were all sealed for security reasons, and there wasn't a single crack she could slip out of. She came to a door reading 'staff only' and slipped underneath. She found herself in a dark corridor, darker than she should have liked. Only a faint red dot of light from an alarm lit the way. She ran on through the network of corridors, darting in a direction which seemed promising. She found herself around the side of a tall filing cabinet and paused. The terrifying godly presence left her for a moment, and she caught her breath.

A deafening crash of the door being completely obliterated roused her to continue running. The alarms were set off, screeching painfully in her ears. She tripped on her dress and her hand caught something as she grappled at the wall for balance. A door handle. It was locked of course, but she slipped under it easily.

She was in a hall of low, upward facing display cabinets, all filled with bugs and butterflies, perfectly preserved and pinned. Feeling exposed, she continued. She'd been here before; she should be able to remember the directions. She'd been here with Idris not long ago, the closest thing they'd had to something like a date. Unless you counted all those rainy afternoons and misty mornings spent in cafes around London and secret dalliances to Hyde Park. Yet nothing seemed familiar in the dark, and from the unusual direction she'd come from.

The press of Ezra's intense, bone-shaking energy was at her heels. Glass cabinets and obscure shapes passed by her. All she needed was one fire exit, one window ajar and she'd be out. She was considering hiding in the corners of the ceiling like a spider, when she nearly ran headlong into an enormous taxidermy wolf, its eyes almost level with hers. She skidded to a halt and gasped audibly, then clamped a hand over her mouth quickly. She knew she should run, but for a split second she was transfixed with those cold, glass, predatory eyes. Piercing blue. She dragged herself away, ducking past a polar bear and a tiger, shaking off the unsettling visage of the wolf.

"It would be easier if you stopped running, for your sake," Ezra's voice came from behind. He was just entering the room.

Saiyah moved on. The enormous silhouette of a plastic-looking blue whale dominated the next room. Saiyah jumped over ropes and into the exhibit, passing between an elephant and something else in shadow. She came face to face with more icy blue eyes and a pair of hands caught her firmly by the arms. She gasped and began to move back but the gentle energy of the figure and his insistent shushing calmed her. It was Idris.

"I'm going to get you out of here," he said. "No time for questions."

His arms wrapped around her and she held on to him tightly, burying her head in his shoulder and clenching her eyes shut tight. There was a rush of energy, light, and air about them. Once Saiyah felt solid ground beneath her again, she opened her eyes. The night air was cool, and the sounds of London echoed in the distance. They were somewhere behind the museum at a service entrance.

"Go home. You'll be safe there," Idris instructed. His speech was rushed, and he backed away from her. He couldn't be seen to be missing for long.

"I don't think I will be." She was breathing heavily, and her voice trembled.

Idris took her hands eagerly, rubbing her palms in circular motions with his warm thumbs. "No," he admitted dejectedly, "not for much longer." He hesitated, frowning deeply and closing his eyes. "You should leave. Get to Malik, go to Dualjahit, whatever you need to do."

A moment of quiet passed between them.

"This is your brother's doing, isn't it?"

"I pray it is not," he said in a low voice.

Saiyah looked up as something suddenly caught her eye. A tall figure in white robes stood directly behind him, watching them. Untangling himself, Idris whirled about and drew his sword.

Silas regarded them both mirthfully. Idris pointed the tip of the blade at Silas's chest, his other arm protectively outstretched, blocking Saiyah. She was still gripping his shoulder, rooted to the spot.

"Hezekiah," Silas greeted him. "I'll admit I had my suspicions you were embroiled in something, but I never imagined you'd completely succumb to the demons."

Idris reverberated with indignant energy.

The door to the entranceway slammed shut of its own accord, making Saiyah jump. The sounds of the party muffled, and the hum of a ward surrounded them. They were trapped. Silas paced the courtyard, a slight swagger to his steps that was unusual from a god of his rank.

"Go back to the embassy this instant, Silas said. He seemed to enjoy every syllable he uttered. "Adriel will escort you. You're to be placed under house arrest until a trial can be arranged. Resist, and you'll be taken by force. You can leave the demoness to me." Silas peered at Saiyah expectantly, and her resolve faltered.

Idris was frozen to the spot. He turned his head slightly towards her and spoke under his breath. "When I break the wards, turn to shadow and run."

Before she could reply he pulled out his ceremonial sword, and his energy rose overwhelmingly. Saiyah retreated, shielding her eyes as his body grew brighter, and pale blue sparks of manifested energy rebounded around him.

Silas took on a similar form and they rushed at each other, clashing blue and yellow, like a terrible sunset on the sea. Saiyah gasped and tried to feel out the wards. Abruptly it went dark again. Silas stood calmly where he'd been before, and Idris was nowhere to be seen. Saiyah frantically looked around for him.

Without warning, Silas was upon her. He grabbed her by her hair. She felt a tug at the back of her neck as the chain of her pendant snapped. She slipped into shadow instantly, leaving Silas only vaguely aware of her whereabouts.

"Nephilim," he hissed.

There was a static in the air which prickled Saiyah's skin; it clearly affected Silas, too. The wards were down. Idris appeared behind Silas with his sword raised and a smear of pearly blood on his lip.

Saiyah hesitated, her eyes welling. Idris started to back away and Silas gave chase, the two of them gradually moving upwards onto the balconies, then the rooftops. Saiyah lost sight of them both. Like a ghost, she moved through the party and out onto the streets of London. Trembling, she ran with conviction, teeth clenched and fists tightened.

XXXII

Decent Like Nightfall

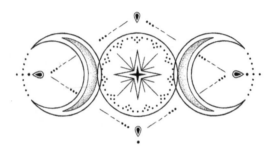

SAIYAH RUSHED BACK TO her house, full of juxtapos-
ing life and warmth. She let her shadow elongate
towards the kitchen as her feet pounded up the stairs.
The fridge opened independently of her, and her shadow transported the sealed wine bottle full of her partially congealed god's blood up towards her. Grabbing
her satchel from beside her bed and darting about the
room, she shoved the first half of John Greyson's book
into it.

She flicked through the documents Idris had given
her. There was the execution warrant for her father,
displaying beautiful calligraphy on vellum. As he'd sus-

pected, 'Akrasiel Silas' was amongst the names in purple ink who'd signed it. Even the flourish of his pen was arrogant.

There was a calamitous crash outside the house, and a sound of panic and shock came from the room above. Saiyah wiped her eyes and went upstairs to Hex's room, which overlooked the street. Jack stood in his underwear, hastily putting a hoodie on. Suits and dresses were discarded on the floor. Hex approached the window cautiously. Saiyah drifted with her. There were demon slayers near the crossroads. Coven members filed nervously out of houses but were barked at to return to their homes.

"I don't like the look of this," Hex whispered. "We have to get out of here."

Saiyah shielded her eyes as a flash illuminated the sky, coming from the Barbatos library. Screams echoed in the Old Roads and smoke started to rise from seemingly everywhere. It became a blur of silver, with one flaming figure amongst them: Azeldya.

"Yeah," Saiyah breathed as she watched in horror.

Her phone vibrated, bringing her back to reality. It was Idris. She opened the message and her face crumpled. Dark energy shuddered between her fingers. Her hands trembled uncontrollably as she tried to call him back through a blur of tears. There was no answer.

"What's wrong?" Jack whispered, his voice full of concern and he glanced between the girls.

Saiyah breathed heavily and sank down against the edge of Hex's bed, holding out her phone. Jack read the message: 'Daniel has been arrested, get out.'

Everything she'd ever feared caught up with her. Her heart rate was rapid, and a familiar knot of anxiety twisted inside her. Hex and Jack were speaking to her in strained, fearful tones, but they were muffled beneath the blood rushing in her head. Blurry flares of light exploded like sinister fireworks outside.

Saiyah had her hands clasped over her heart and was staring wildly between Hex and Jack.

"Saiyah, please! You have to get up!" Hex shouted desperately, shaking Saiyah's unresponsive body. "Can you hear us? Jack, do something!"

Jack was agape and trembling himself. "Right," he said decisively. He dashed to Hex's worktable and took something. Hex held Saiyah as she shook, her phone discarded on the floor. He grabbed Saiyah's hand and opened her fist, palm upwards. Hex grimaced as he brought down a sewing-machine needle into the centre of her palm. Saiyah let out a cry of pain, groping for the needle and pulling it out quickly.

"What the hell?" she choked through her tears.

Hex shook her again and Jack returned with a used wine glass filled with water, which he threw over her. Saiyah was alert enough to wipe her face. She gained enough control to pick up her phone, keeping one hand over her heart as if it would steady it.

"Let's get her up," Jack said, and they proceeded to lift her to sit on the bed.

"They got Daniel," she croaked.

An earth-shattering quake made Jack stumble. They flocked to the window, Saiyah practically dragging herself. Something like a meteor had crashed amongst the gods at the crossroads. A form within straightened and Azeldya emerged, emitting a light more blinding than Titania's. Lifting her shoulders, two great fiery wings unfolded, gradually followed by a further two pairs, burning white. Even from where they were, it was clear her face was one of terrible wrath as she hurled flames at the intruders. Every step made the ground tremble, and the gathered gods cautiously backed away from her. She walked leisurely forward, and those who approached were engulfed in waves of fire on either side of her.

Saiyah lost sight of her in the commotion, and suddenly the door burst open. Hot air rushed in. Instinctively, Saiyah turned to shadow, her eyes glowing from within darkened sockets. Azeldya stood with her burning wings and a flaming sword in hand, flecked with a mixture of black and silver blood. Saiyah returned to her normal form, still distraught.

Azeldya stood before her, making her squint, and stroked her face. The shock of her startling appearance gave her something to focus on.

"Don't be afraid, Saiyah," she said softly.

Saiyah tried to swallow her anxiety as she'd done many times before. Accepting her current mental state, she stood abruptly with a shudder.

"Are they here for me?" she asked.

"They are here for all of us," Azeldya said in a flinty voice. "You must all leave now. I will hold them off."

Saiyah opened her mouth to reply but, in a flash, she was gone. Stomach acid threatened to rise as her adrenaline levels climbed.

"Jack, tell Bez to go to Malik's house. Hex, meet us there and tell him I'll be there soon. Even if I don't show, you'll be safe."

"Bez went to Medea's," Hex told her. "He seemed sick or something."

Saiyah groaned. "Fine, just meet me at Malik's."

Jack's clothes disappeared around him and he flew out the window in bird form. Saiyah hastily ran downstairs, calling Medea as she ran, but there was no answer.

"I don't think I should leave you alone," Hex said, reaching out for Saiyah.

"No, Hex. Not while you're still healing up. Trust me." Then Saiyah turned to shadow and disappeared.

S AIYAH APPROACHED THE ASTRONOMY tower, rattled the door handle, and knocked. Xaldan opened it, wearing only his trousers. There were painted markings across his chest, and Saiyah sensed the remains of a ritual circle behind them.

"What?" he demanded.

"I need to talk to you, it's important," she said, pushing past him. He closed the door behind her irritably.

"Don't touch anything!" He called.

Brassy implements made from intricate parts and cogs were arranged in a maze across the tables.

Titania was standing by the window, clutching her sword as she watched the chaos below unfold.

"Silas knows everything!" She said, unable to stop herself from sobbing. Her hands trembled.

"Well, what are you doing here?" Titania said with mild alarm. "Go to Malik!"

"Weren't you just with him?" Xaldan said, putting on his shirt.

"I can't, not yet. That damn Bezbiel–"

Xaldan approached, cautiously holding his hands out. "What *about* Bezbiel?"

Saiyah ran her fingers across her scalp. "I need your help to do something, a ritual. You can't tell Bez," she said sternly, pointing a finger at him. "He's made a deal with Malik. His soul in exchange for my safe passage to Hell."

Xaldan straightened up, frowning. "That's not what he told me.""All for *you*?" Titania added with a hint of anger.

Saiyah exhaled. "I'm not going to let him go through with it, but I need your help."

"What do you need?" Xaldan said pragmatically, his dark green eyes alert.

"Go to Malik's, bring your usual ritual implements. And John Dee's obsidian mirror." She panted, already backing towards the door. "I'll meet you there."

There were three gods guarding the gateway, and she caught a glimpse of Adriel's inflexible face as she issued commands. Saiyah ducked into a side road and out of sight.

"Come on," she whispered to herself, holding one hand over her heart and the other over her stomach.

Unexpectedly, she buckled over to dispose of most of the champagne she'd drunk. Wiping her face, she pressed her back against the side of the house, gasping for breath. She beat her fist on the brick and the deep needle puncture stung, grounding her. She relaxed her body, forcing herself into a state of astral projection in her shadow form. Momentarily her body slipped away from her, and her soul floated.

In the darkened world of eventide, her mother stood before her again, on the edge of glistening water. Saiyah reached her hand out to the flickering, ghostly figure.

"Help me," she whispered in the demonic language.

A hand, cold as clay, grasped hers, and in an instant Asramenia stood wide-eyed before her. Immense pain in her chest took hold as her body, soul, and shadow was forced through worlds and into reality.

Electric lighting lit her surroundings, and though dazed, she knew she was exposed. The gods would sense the rift she'd caused in the Old Roads, perhaps even follow her through it.

Medea's house was frightfully close to the embassy, and she caught glimpses of midnight-blue uniforms at the corners of most streets as she ran stealthily to Belgravia. At Medea's beautiful townhouse, she slipped through the letterbox, causing Medea to gasp as she sat in her pyjamas in the darkened living room. Bezbiel was crouched on the floor, head between his knees, perspiring greatly. He looked up with wide, reddened eyes when he saw her and straightened.

"Why didn't you just stay with Malik?" Bezbiel scolded, staggering to his feet. "The sun will be up soon, we'll have to move quickly. I don't care what kind of counter-bargain you've made; we are going to Hell and that's the end of it."

"No! We–" Saiyah started to raise her voice but another knock at the door interrupted her.

Medea stumbled back helplessly. Saiyah stood in front of her, raising a divine shield and holding up shadowy fists. Bezbiel edged towards the door, precariously putting his eye to the peephole. Saiyah steadied herself, her body clenched in anticipation. Bezbiel stood back abruptly and opened the door. He grabbed a small, pale figure and pulled them inside, slamming the door shut behind. Jack stood with his mouth open, drenched in sweat and completely naked after travelling as a bird. Medea flung a throw from the sofa in Jack's direction, in which he wrapped himself, pulling away from Bezbiel.

"Is there any chance you were followed?" Saiyah asked austerely.

"I hope not," he replied, panting. "Azeldya has been taken."

Bezbiel swore and passed a hand over his face, striding over to the window defeatedly and slumping down. Anger flooded over Saiyah; she was about to erupt when she caught sight of Bezbiel's expression. Worried he'd seen something out the window, she crept over.

"What's wrong?" she asked.

He waved a hand dismissively and shook his head, unable to look her in the eye. His neck was unnaturally slick with sweat. Medea fetched him some water and thrust it at him unsympathetically. His hands shook as he held the glass.

"Come away from the window," Saiyah told him. "Bez, I really need you right now. You're by far the most experienced person here when it comes to defence. What can we do to make you better?"

Medea made a noise of disgust. "He's got withdrawal symptoms," she hissed. "You idiot, Bez. If you insist on getting high when the coven needs you most, you can at least bring your supply with you. You can't rely on deals with Malik. I've told you! Especially with reeka."

Saiyah scowled at both of them while Jack stood awkwardly by the door, wrapped in the blanket.

"All out," he mumbled. "Get to Malik's." Bezbiel gulped and bobbed his head rhythmically.

His shirt was drenched, and Saiyah stared in horror, but her face swiftly contorted to anger. "What?" Her voice caught. "You've made some kind of deal with Malik to get your next fix?"

"It was always part of the deal," he muttered. "Please. Medea." Bezbiel spluttered, ignoring Saiyah. "Do you have any? I'll get you more, I'll pay you back."

Medea shot daggers at him and looked as if she was about to scream, her ghostly face flushed with anger. She exhaled, fuming. "I can't believe this," she mumbled, storming upstairs and into the depths of the house.

Saiyah sat with Bezbiel, an arm around his shoulder. "You sold your soul, just for this. Is that what you're saying?" She hissed.

When Medea returned, she was holding a small mint tin, which she handed to Bezbiel. "You can bloody make it yourself. I was saving that for a special occasion!"

Saiyah caught a glimpse of the reeka as Bezbiel snatched it. It looked like a dried-up red weed. He shakily got to his feet and stumbled to the kitchen. Saiyah followed with interest, motioning for Jack to keep watch at the window.

Bezbiel proceeded to heat the reeka in a bowl over a pan on the gas hob, as if he were melting chocolate. It liquified into a viscous substance, like congealed blood. He pulled a syringe from inside of his coat and Saiyah shut her eyes, choosing to leave the room rather than watch.

Jack was making noises of distress by the window.

"They're here. Jack must've been followed," Medea said, letting out a strangled whimper.

Bezbiel came stumbling back into the room, blinking as if he'd just woken from a long sleep. He marched up to Jack and grasped him by his shoulders.

"Go now and warn Malik we're coming," he said firmly.

Jack dropped the blanket and became a raven again. Bezbiel hovered with his hand over the door handle and looked back over his shoulder. His face was full of anguish.

"I'm going to try to speak to them and cover your escape. Swap my safe passage for Medea's, or anyone else's, and go to Hell," he told them in a decidedly final note.

This time Saiyah managed to grab him and held him fast by the arm, her jaw set hard. Medea watched them both unsurely, taking deep controlled breaths.

"Oh no," Saiyah said commandingly. "You don't seem quite–"

"This is no time for sentiment," Bezbiel said assertively.

"I'd say the same to you!" She yelled impatiently. "Listen, I need to speak to Silas before we go anywhere."

Bezbiel raised his eyebrows and shook his head. "Are you *actually* insane?"

"I have a plan. Trust me," she said, making eye contact with both of them pleadingly.

Bezbiel swore under his breath and closed his eyes. "Alright, alright. Try whatever it is you want to do, but I'm still going out there first. But if they turn on me, or whatever you're up to doesn't work, can you promise you'll stick to the plan and run?" When Saiyah didn't reply he took her by both hands and softened his voice. "Swear to me?"

Saiyah's forehead creased and she glowered at him. "Fine."

Satisfied, he allowed himself to breathe as he sidled back to the door. Saiyah slipped her hand into Medea's as they watched him leave. Medea pulled her to the window where they crouched, peering through the blinds. There were a number of gods out in the street, including Adriel, all excessively kitted out in demon slaying armour. Saiyah took a moment to process what was going on while Medea fretted and murmured something about what the neighbours would think.

"Why do you not want to go with Malik?" She whispered as she watched Bezbiel through the window.

Bezbiel was approaching Adriel with caution, hands held up. They spoke for a moment, and he lowered his hands. More gods approached him and appeared to be talking in a group, but then Bezbiel began to back away. Hands flew to swords, ready to draw, and Bezbiel was leapt upon. Saiyah gasped as she watched him being swiftly gagged so he couldn't use his silver-tongue on them. Saiyah's shock was paralysing, and it took a moment for her to register Medea's hands on her shoulders, pulling her away.

Half shadow, she followed Medea through the kitchen and out of the back door.

"Wait." Saiyah stopped her before they went through the gate to the alley. "I'll go first, follow after me." The sound of the front door being kicked in interrupted them. "Meet me there when it's safe," Saiyah whispered, pushing Medea towards an old coal shed.

Adriel appeared at the door at the top of the steps. Saiyah already had her back turned and slipped through the cracks in the gate. The narrow ally hid her well as she moved swiftly onwards, pressed flat against the walls. Adriel was close behind as she ran. Swords rang out on the brick walls. They were close behind when she emerged out onto the street.

Gabrielle appeared before her, cloak rippling, making Saiyah skid to a halt. Her usually ceremonial sword was slim and delicate, but glinted nefariously at its razor edge.

"Stop!" Gabrielle called out militantly, a harsh frown on her face.

Saiyah hesitated. She certainly didn't want to fight Gabrielle, and though she wasn't a slayer, her abilities were undoubtedly superhuman. Saiyah's face was pained at the sight of the woman she'd thought of as a friend coming at her.

Gabrielle leapt right over Saiyah, landing just in front of her. The clamour of armour and footsteps behind dwindled.

"Stand down, Sergeant Adriel," Gabrielle said assertively. "You are not to arrest this half-demon, under orders from the Elders."

There was a pause before Adriel spoke. "I am under orders from Director Silas. I cannot step aside," she replied flatly, though a sadness registered in her eyes.

Slayers from behind Adriel began to edge forward. A clash of blades between Gabrielle and Adriel broke Saiyah from her astonishment.

"Go!" Gabrielle ordered in a strained voice, her footing already slipping as Adriel attacked.

Saiyah turned to shadow; it blended with her perfectly. As she fled, a low vibration of divine energy rippled
through the city.

XXXIII

Stars Move, Time Runs, the Clock Will Strike

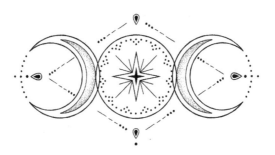

THE AREA AROUND MALIK'S house was strangely quiet, void of any divine energy. She slipped inside as a shadow. The entranceway was dark, but light flickered from the room she'd been in before. She rounded the corner to see Hex sitting stiffly on the sofa by a roaring fire. Jack crouched in front of it like an angel of death, naked, covered only by his great wings. Malik was the first to notice her as she entered, taking his fascinated eyes off Jack; he regarded her with similar interest. Like her, he was still wearing the clothes he'd worn to the party, although far less dishevelled.

"Ah, there you are," he said, pouring golden liquid from a decanter into two glasses. He pushed one towards her across the table. "A change has come over you in the last few hours, it seems."

Hex shot up and engulfed Saiyah in a hug. "I'm so glad you're okay," she whispered.

Saiyah returned the gesture but didn't take her eyes off Malik.

"It appears the time has come for me to escort you through the gates of Hell," Malik said with a smirk.

Saiyah shook her head resolutely as she approached him, taking the drink. It burnt as it hit her empty stomach, still tender from vomiting. Hex and Jack watched the exchange warily.

"I still intend to uphold our *revised* deal," she said firmly, taking another sip of the golden liquid.

Malik chuckled. "I think time is running out for you, little Katomei." He brought his hand down on the table, giving the impression of looming over her. "If you are not able to complete your end of the bargain, I will happily drag you there myself."

Saiyah held her ground and squared her shoulders. She glanced across the room to where the second half of John Greyson's book still lay on the coffee table.

Malik laughed, revealing his sharp teeth. The whites of his eyes yellowed menacingly. "Don't tell me you're going to offer me yours?"

Saiyah restrained herself from shivering and glared at him.

Xaldan and Titania entered the room, and the front door closing echoed in the depths of the house. Saiyah's relief was evident.

"Did you get it?" She asked.

Xaldan nodded. "Don't you think we'd better get on with this?"

Saiyah moved across the room to retrieve the book. "Malik, we need to cast a circle, where would be best?" She kept her tone businesslike.

Bemused, Malik strolled leisurely to the fireplace. Jack shuffled out of his path. He grasped one of the ornaments on the mantle, pressing something behind it. Saiyah half expected the back of the fireplace to fall away to reveal a secret passage. Jack stumbled as the floor beneath him moved. The rug opened in a circular pattern, and the sofas fell back to reveal a large area of stone beneath. Embedded in the stone was a circle of encrusted gems, obsidian, malachite, amethyst, and clear quartz, with a reverse pentagram inside an inner circle. It explained why she'd felt so uncomfortable sitting there with Malik before. Likewise, Jack instantly looked more like himself once he'd stood aside.

Xaldan opened a rucksack and he and Titania began to get to work in the circle. He handed John Dee's obsidian mirror to Saiyah. Malik stood back, watching with amusement.

Realisation spread on Hex's face as she read John Greyson's first book over Saiyah's shoulder. "Are we doing a summoning spell? Looks intense."

"Yes," Saiyah confirmed, locking eyes with her. "We're summoning Silas and then" –she opened the correct page of the second half of the book–"we're going to perform the soul-ripping ritual."

Everyone in the room shared a similarly shocked expression, except Malik, who's eyes gleamed impishly as he stepped back to watch.

Saiyah helped Xaldan mark out the alchemical and instructional symbols with chalk, trusting his guidance. He ushered everyone into strategic places. Each of them stood in the outer circle, parallel to the different points of the star. The mirror was laid in the centre. Saiyah passed him the chilled bottle of her syphoned gods blood, shimmering like liquid mercury.

"Are you sure this is the stuff?" He asked warily, giving it a sniff.

Saiyah nodded assuredly.

Xaldan began to chant in Old Demonic. Titania and Hex caught on quickly and joined in, followed by Jack and Saiyah. He raised his hands with palms flat as if holding a barrier. The others mimicked him, raising the energy. The crystals began to gleam.

Xaldan uncorked the bottle and poured. Once the celestial blood hit the stone, a powerful hum of divine energy joined their chorus. It trickled aimlessly at first, but gradually began to follow the chalk markings. Saiyah and the two older initiates held the energy well, but Hex and Jack struggled.

The ethereal light from the stones rose at an angle to form a cone shape. The air prickled, and the energy became audible.

"Akrasiel Silas. Lordship. God of the second sphere, I summon you!" Saiyah called out in the language of the gods, repeating it as loud as she could whilst the others continued the demonic chant.

For a split second, Silas's form flickered before her. His sword was drawn.

Jack buckled to his knees, hands raised as if he was praying, his face contorted in pain. Hex looked as if she was holding back a great weight, and even the others had sweat trickling from their brows.

"They can't hold it!" Titania called out.

Saiyah looked to Malik imploringly, but he sat on one of the sofas and reclined, sipping his drink casually.

"I'll hold it for Jack!" she shouted over the high-pitched whirling.

Blood trickled from Jack's nose. They were holding the power of gods, and he was using all his mental strength to cope with it. Saiyah's resolve wavered. Eventually, she'd be the only one able to hold it, yet couldn't do it alone. She spread her arms wide, ready to take on his burden, and called out to him to stop. Hex pleaded with him, but he ignored the dark blood dripping from his ears.

Silas appeared again, stronger this time but still ghostly. He was agitated, and there was pearly blood on his blade.

"Harmonise!" Xaldan yelled.

Saiyah relaxed her mind and the pressure of her hands, without letting the energy of the circle completely wash over her. Jack toppled backwards and she deftly caught his portion, arms spread wide. The noise lowered in tone, like the sound of a ringing wine glass, overpowering but not unpleasant.

"I'll catch you if you go," Xaldan breathed to Hex, whose injured arm was trembling.

Silas turned to Saiyah with a look of rage, assessed the situation, and then smirked patronisingly. "You will not be able to keep me here forever, even with your devil's looking glass. None of you are strong enough."

Saiyah allowed her irises to brighten, and her whites darken. "We'll not need to hold you for long," she said confidently, glancing down at the notes in front of her.

They stared at each other menacingly, testing the other's nerves. Saiyah started to chant, and the others attempted to accompany her.

Silas's form became warped, appearing in doubles. He grasped his head in pain but straightened up instantly. "Even if you are able to hold me here for more than a few moments, Daniel Cassiel will still be taken for execution. Idris Hezekiah's body will be found next to mine, and he will be taken, too. Not to mention your silver-tongued friend with all that reeka in his veins. I wonder how the mortal part of his soul will cope in Hell in that state." Her poker face wavered momentarily, and their grip on his soul slipped for a moment, spurring Silas on. "I will see to it that your she-demon leader is obliterated, and your laughable organisation raised to the ground."

Xaldan and Titania were visibly rattled.

Silas noticed them for the first time, and their apprehension pleased him. He sneered and turned his attention to Hex. "It looks as if your other silver-tongue won't last much longer."

Hex took a deep breath and gasped. The first trickle of blood came from her nose. Their hold on Silas fell away completely, and Saiyah glared at Malik again, though he showed no intention of helping.

"What do you want from me, Silas?" Saiyah spoke up, deterring Silas from distracting the others any further as they continued to chant.

He gave her a strange look. "I want you executed, as you should have been at birth."

"Fine. I'll come quietly with you then," she said. "But only in exchange for something."

"You want to bargain for the lives of your friends?" He replied patronisingly.

"No," she said simply, taking him off guard. "I want your soul."

He blinked in surprise, and even Hex seemed taken aback, despite her weariness. Silas sniggered lightly.

"Even if I were to accept, once you are executed, our deal will be void. I do not make deals with demons."

Hex dropped to her knees. Silas regarded her with a swish of his robes.

Medea entered the room and Malik stood to greet her like a true gentleman, blocking her path. Saiyah narrowed her eyes and Silas tried to follow her gaze, but they were too far out of the circle. She gritted her teeth and motioned with her chin for Medea to come over.

"Take over for Hex," she commanded.

Medea placed her hands over Hex's and took the weight of the energy, making the circle immediately stronger. Hex dropped to the floor, panting, and leant over Jack's unconscious body.

"We've all of the Albion Circle here," she lied, glancing at Malik, whose face was a mixture of annoyance and amusement. "We can do this as long as you like."

"Enough of this, Nephilim!" He exclaimed, shedding some of his calm.

Titania stumbled as if she were going to faint, and Xaldan's eyes widened. Saiyah kept her face stony. Their slight waver was enough for Silas. His image flickered and faded as he became free of the summons, and the power began to dissolve.

"Hold him!" Saiyah called desperately.

There was a rush of air in the room as Zulphas burst in, eyes glowing and great wings rising magnificently from his shoulder blades. He was wearing unusual flowing clothing in a shadowy kind of cloth. He darted towards where Jack had stood and took on his burden. A jolt of strong, steady energy joined the circle, and the strain became weightless in comparison. Saiyah felt dizzy with the amount of power he produced. Zulphas locked eyes with Saiyah and she opened her mouth to speak but Silas appeared again, enraged.

Zulphas spat out unintelligible Old Demonic words, causing Silas's speech to become tinny, and then die away. Zulphas sighed theatrically. "I think we'd all benefit from not being distracted by him. Hello, Saiyah."

Saiyah nodded to him austerely but couldn't hide her relief. "Why would you help us?" She asked in a strained voice.

"I cannot leave the coven in its hour of need. I would never betray them. Or you." He bowed his head. "It was never my intention to cause any harm to your mother, I only wanted to protect her. Now, what are we doing with *him*?"

Saiyah shook her head in disbelief, biting back accusations. Her face expressed a myriad of emotions, but she forced herself to focus. "Id–The Captain. He's bleeding out. I must help him."

"Why?" Xaldan said accusingly.

Saiyah ignored him. "Zulphas, I'm going to need you to take Silas's soul on my behalf and give it to Malik. Can you do that for me?"

Zulphas frowned and let his eyes close for a moment. "Go. I can hold him, and we will attempt the ramblings of John Greyson."

Saiyah nodded faintly in thanks. Slowly, she backed away from the circle, relinquishing her power to Zulphas, who took it on with ease. With a cursory glance at Hex to make sure she was alright as she cradled Jack's head, she made for the door. Malik stood before her, arms folded and eyes glowing with contempt.

"Let me pass," she said, pulling at his arms with little effect.

"No one but you can fulfil our bargain. It looks like you're not getting your soul. You know what that means," he told her devilishly.

"Let me through!" she called out angrily.

Slipping into her shadow form, she seeped past him with ease. Malik grasped for her without success as she slipped back out into the night.

A FTER SAIYAH LEFT, HEX was still mumbling an incantation over Jack, pressing a small piece of clear quartz to his forehead. His eyes fluttered open, and his breathing became easier.

"*Is* she a Nephilim?" Xaldan muttered with contempt.

Silas tried to answer him, but he was voiceless. Medea's already startled face changed, confirming the truth.

Malik growled like an animal, entering the room again. They all regarded him warily as he sauntered up to Medea. Suddenly he grabbed her wrist and pulled her away, throwing her backwards. He took on her role in the circle and spoke clearly in Old Demonic.

The other half-demon's faces were blank, but Zulphas's eyes widened as the light emitted became a hellish red. Medea squealed as Titania fell backwards, and after a battle with a nosebleed, Xaldan did the same.

"We need to get out of here," Hex whispered to Medea.

Zulphas' face contorted as he fought off the contaminated energy.

Malik grew in stature, his legs becoming wolf-like, his teeth and claws similarly canine.

"Now," Malik said calmly, "perhaps you and I can come to some kind of arrangement, Silas."

XXXIV

Candle, Book, and Bell

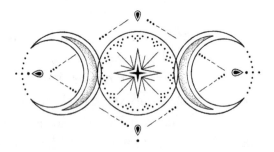

T HE CHILL OF THE first light was thick with divine energy, but the sun was not yet above the horizon. Tiny flashes of white glinted above, and Saiyah's lungs ached as she ran.

She burst into the embassy, creating a narrow line of light in the grand foyer. It was eerily empty, and she could barely see. Stepping inside, heart in her mouth, she clapped her hands in the way Idris did, conducting divine energy. The orbs above flickered weakly, casting the large space in an abnormal sepia light.

There were scorch marks on the ground so strong that the marble was cracked. Her eyes followed a path of destruction: shattered pillars and broken brickwork, smears of pearly blood. Apprehension overcame her and she gripped the door frame. The atmosphere was nauseating.

Cautiously, she made her way through the embassy the only way she knew. In the corridors leading to the residency, a disturbing smear of blood trailed to Idris's office. Saiyah's knuckles were white. She peered around the open door.

The room was empty, and a bleak morning light came through the double doors. There was a puddle of blood in the middle of the floor. Saiyah recognised Idris's faint marks of energy encircling it and allowed herself a drop of hope.

Out on the lawn, all was calm. The breeze was lazy, and birds sounded in the distance. A figure in a midnight blue cloak lay motionless under the dappled shade of the apple trees, white hair glinting. Saiyah's body tensed and trembled simultaneously. Shock blurred her vision. Too scared to breathe, her shaky legs moved as if independent from her, gaining momentum as she neared Idris. She dropped to her knees amongst the grass and premature apples, all flooded with silvery liquid. Her head swam as she tried to take in the sight. His body lacked its usual heat, and his eyes were wide open. As she steadied herself, she realised he was blinking, turning his head to her, and his hand lay over his chest, dimly glowing.

"Idris!" she spluttered, shaking his shoulders weakly.

He made a grunt of discomfort and winced.

"Sorry!" She exclaimed softly.

Saiyah placed her hands over his, adding to the healing energy. He put all his weight on one elbow, rolling to the side as his face regained its godly countenance.

"Help me up," he croaked.

Saiyah had an arm around his shoulders instantly. Instead of lifting him, she froze as an uncomfortable energy resonated behind her.

"I would not do that if I were you," a cold voice resounded.

Saiyah glowered at Silas, standing under a pretty portico of the embassy. He had smears of blood on one arm, and the smoke blade the scavengers had used was tucked into his belt. With a jolt, she noticed Bezbiel crouching beside him, gagged and bound. His eyes were hard and rebellious.

Undeterred, she kept her healing hands on Idris defiantly. "Why not?" She asked, buying time. Idris's sword lay parallel to him, obscured in the grass. The cold hilt pressed into her knee.

"Because if you step away from the captain now, I will spare your little demon friend," he told her monotonously.

Something clicked within Idris, and Saiyah was satisfied he'd be strong enough to heal himself. He was a god, after all. She lifted Idris's hands and laid them over his wounds. Through an expression of alarm, he offered a slight nod of courage. Standing, she left the bloodied sword concealed and positioned herself between him and Silas.

"I've done what you asked, now let him go." She nodded to Bezbiel.

Silas's expression was unyielding as he tossed Bezbiel casually to one side. He landed heavily on the steps, letting his shoulder take the brunt and groaning in pain.

Silas raised his sword, but Saiyah didn't flinch.

"I'm sure you know by now that I won't come quietly?" Saiyah said, stepping backwards slightly into a fighting stance.

Silas let out a strange peal of laughter. "Indeed. I think you've done enough to warrant execution on sight."

Instantly, Silas was gone from where he'd stood. Saiyah barely managed to turn herself to shadow in time before his sword crashed through her. She stumbled back, repulsed at being walked through. His surprise was moderate, and he discarded his sword, favouring the smoke blade.

Saiyah sank into the ground and retreated to the shade, appearing by Idris to collect his sword. It glimmered through the pearly blood and sang with divine energy.

Silas snarled and advanced. The smoke blade sliced violently at her chest, tearing the neckline of her dress. She tried to evade but the sting of it struck her, and she fell back. Quickly she threw up a shield, but with a wave of his hand it disassembled. Panicking, she lurched up and their blades met. Conducting demonic energy into the sword, she caused Silas's footing to falter. Angered, he lunged forward. She parried but he twisted her blade, so she was locked at the hilt.

"Give in now, and I'll make your death swift," he snarled, twisting her sword arm painfully.

Saiyah swore viciously at him. Her arm shook under the pressure. She let go and instantly tried to recover the sword. Silas grabbed her and threw her across the lawn like a doll. She shielded herself to cushion the impact but crashed into the wall of the embassy regardless. Air rushed painfully from her lungs. She smelt her own blood as she landed in the dirt, coughing. Silas loomed over her as she pushed herself up on her hands and knees, blood dripping from the back of her head. The edges of his mouth twitched at the sight of it.

Saiyah narrowed her eyes, lifting one palm for a demonic attack. He kicked her hands from beneath her, then kicked her torso to roll her onto her back. One foot pressed on her chest where he'd slashed at it, and she cried out at the pain.

Suddenly, Bezbiel leapt up onto Silas's back and wrapped his chains tightly around his neck, using his weight to pull the god backwards. Silas made an enraged noise, thrashing to release himself.

Saiyah managed to stand just as Bezbiel was tossed aside. With sheer force of will, she held her palm up and heaved out a tangible shard of night, driving it into Silas's stomach. He winced and staggered. An unworldly wound formed in his side that oozed purplish shadow. He gaped in disbelief.

Still chained at the wrists, Bezbiel pulled off his gag and ran to Saiyah, pulling her roughly towards the entranceway.

"Hezekiah will die if we leave him here!" Saiyah protested.

Bezbiel groaned.

A bright light emitted from nearby, rippling through the air towards Silas with a bluish tint and a familiar energy. Saiyah was speechless with relief. Idris swept in and reclaimed his sword from Saiyah with ease, holding it before him like a staff, eyes fixed on Silas.

Silas paced backwards, wrathful as he tried to heal his strange wound while defending himself from Idris's pulse of energy. One arm was outstretched, pushing against the azure storm of energy flowing and crackling around him. Saiyah and Bezbiel shielded their eyes as Idris's terrible but mesmerising power grew. His stance was precarious though, and pearly blood dripped as he backed towards them. He frowned in pained concentration.

"I am the only one he needs to kill in order to get away with this!" Idris shouted over the maelstrom. "Go! I will cover your retreat!"

Bezbiel tugged at Saiyah.

"We are not going to let him get away with this! Come with us!" She cried out.

"I will follow as long as I'm able," he assured her breathily, glancing back.

"We don't have time for this," Bezbiel growled.

Saiyah let herself be pulled away, running with Bezbiel through the ominous gothic corridor, trusting that Idris would follow. An earth-shattering crash shook the corridor and the tunnel of faint daylight behind them diminished. Saiyah screamed and stumbled, the cut across her chest opening more as she fell. Bezbiel lifted her as best he could in his chains and urged her on. The darkness was suddenly illuminated, and another crash shook the ground. They ran on determinedly.

Idris was close to the cave-in, glowing faintly. Running backwards, he cast another bolt towards Silas as he emerged from the rubble.

Through the entrance they'd taken, Saiyah had no idea where she was going, hoping Bezbiel knew which direction he'd come from.

"This way!" A voice called out as they took a wrong turn.

She glimpsed Idris briefly, pointing in another direction before disappearing in a rush of air.

A hiss of orange flame spiralled, threatening to singe their backs. Her bare feet slammed onto the stone floor so hard they could've bled. The hum of other-worldly energy caused an instinctual fear in her, and her anxiety threatened to outweigh her adrenaline.

Without warning they emerged into the grand foyer, skidding on the bloody ground and landing with a slap on the marble. The fire burned out over their heads as it emerged into the large space. Saiyah looked back for Idris, seeing only a faint white glow. The archway crumbled, taking down the wall above with it. Her eyes widened and she gasped as the light disappeared.

Bezbiel choked for breath as he stood. The building trembled and threatened to buckle. Saiyah focused on not crumbling herself as the pillars around them groaned ominously. She spied the archway which led to the cells and hesitated at the memories of strange wails from eldritchesqe demons. The cells. If Daniel was arrested, that's where he'd be.

A tremor from the rubble and a flash of sapphire strengthened her resolve. She pushed herself up, and with a tug at Bezbiel's sleeve, ran headlong into the dim archway. She didn't need to see Idris to picture his displeasure at her for taking that direction.

"This isn't the way out," Bezbiel hissed, attempting to pull her back to the foyer.

"I have to get Daniel," she responded with urgent bitterness.

Bezbiel glanced from her to the entrance of the cells and made a sound close to a growl, giving in to her.

The hallway was vast, undecorated, and showed signs of conflict. Ahead was a meshed barrier and door humming with wards. Bezbiel pulled his malachite out and made hasty but elaborate hand gestures, chanting something. There was an inaudible shift of energy, and they heaved open one of the great doors together.

Abruptly, they came to a steep, spiralling staircase and Saiyah nearly fell headlong. Descending with brisk, accurate footsteps they came to an area lit by fluorescent light, somewhat 1940s in appearance. There was a desk and a rack of keys. Bezbiel skidded over it and clawed at the keys, searching for one which fit his shackles.

"Your Godfather is further in. Past the first section where the wards are heavier. We'll need a key, but I don't know if it's here or not," he explained hastily. "He was in a bad way when I saw him." A clicking noise resounded in the mechanism of his shackles. He dropped them unceremoniously and took up a couple of the larger rings of keys.

Saiyah caught her breath and clutched the back of her head in healing as she staggered towards the door. She grabbed it fiercely, resisting the repulsion of the wards. Drawing on a well of anger, she used her divine energy to push it to one side. Bezbiel smiled slyly.

"Your godlike nature may come in handy," he muttered.

They rushed down a galley of crude, empty cells with that same wartime appearance and came to an incongruous gothic archway. Here the cells were densely inhabited with miserable-looking demons who glanced at them curiously. Saiyah paid no attention as they hurtled through the labyrinth of bars. Their voices raised with questions as the pair shot past.

Bezbiel slowed his pace, coming to a halt before a cell with heightened wards. Daniel slumped at the back of his dark cell, barely visible aside from his white-blonde hair.

"Daniel!" Saiyah called out, but he made no reaction.

Bezbiel got to work with the keys, his hands fumbling.

Saiyah held out her hand and tried to make a sphere of light appear. It battled with her shadowy emotions before flickering into being. Daniel's bloody and battered face illuminated, and she gasped. He was out cold, wearing pyjamas which were torn and dirtied. Swallowing a lump in her throat, she stepped back and began to examine the wards. Though she felt a strange affiliation with the divine energies, it was alien to her. She looked to Bezbiel hopefully.

"I know nothing about wards," she said in a thin voice. "I don't know where to start!"

Bezbiel was having no luck with the lock, and the bed-lam of inmates increased. "Well, you're going to have to try! These wards are to keep a lesser god in check, and I know *nothing* about that!" He said irritably.

A low rumble resonated through the air and cen-turies-old dust and grit was shaken from above. They met each other's fearful gaze and the inmates hushed for a moment before building their cacophony again.

"What would you do if you were breaking a demonic ward? What did you do before?" She asked earnestly.

Bezbiel made the same hand movements again and she tried her best to follow.

"What did you say before? In English?" She demand-ed.

"I uh, it was: *May the Gods of Acheron be favourable to me, monarchs of burning hell, I ask that you open the way to me.* Or near enough."

Saiyah didn't have time to question the meanings or origins of his words. Hastily she translated it into the god's language. She'd only seen some of the words written, and they felt ugly and unnatural in her mouth. She performed the incantation with its symbols. There was another rumble of energy in response, but this time it came from elsewhere. The bars rattled, turning white with scalding heat. Bezbiel gasped and dropped the keys, his hand singed. The incantation ended and the bars cooled. The ward was lifted, but there was a heavy presence in the air which unnerved them both. The inmates grew quiet; some chuckled darkly.

"Come on," Bezbiel said with a wary look at Saiyah. "We may be able to break this open by force now."

She laid her hand over the lock and willed divine energy into it as she raised it above her head, but a strange urge overtook her and instead the familiar, comforting sensation of shadow flowed through simultaneously. There was a purple spark and a swirl of darkness. The lock was severely damaged and warped, but showed no sign of release.

There was a hiss amongst the prisoners, and they turned to see an encroaching orange light from the deep. Then a speck of blue showed at the end of the corridor. Saiyah's face lit with astonishment as Idris rushed toward them.

"What are you doing down here?" He roared at them both, his brows furrowed in fury.

Swiftly he struck the lock and the steel sheared as if it were paper, leaving tiny blue embers in its path. Bezbiel pushed into the cell and stooped to lift Daniel.

Saiyah opened her mouth to speak but Idris held a hand up.

"Never mind. You must all leave here. Now!"

Saiyah stared at him, mesmerised. She absently reached out to touch his arm, as if to be sure he was real.

"I can draw a circle to teleport," Bezbiel put in.

"It won't work here," Idris said, glancing back over his shoulder as the howls of the inmates signalled Silas's arrival.

He clasped Saiyah's hand, his footing faltering as he decided which direction to take. He swore in English, which would have been funny if the situation weren't so serious. Exhaling with angered despair he let go of Saiyah and went to take Daniel from Bezbiel.

"Follow me. Do not fall behind," he commanded, lifting Daniel over his shoulder with ease.

They took an unorthodox route away from the exit. The cells became larger and thronged with powerful wards. Bezbiel grasped his head in pain as they ran, and Saiyah tried to ignore the inhuman wails of the inhabitants.

They emerged into a cavernous space which resembled an empty church, though where windows would have been was solid brick. The perimeter was lined with chains and holding points, while the centre of the floor was coated in layers of dried demon blood. Saiyah clutched her stomach and Bezbiel was visibly disgusted.

Idris waved a hand. Gradually the heavy stone door grated against the flagstones. The orange light brightened frighteningly in the distance. As the doors came together, it diminished the light before closing with a foreboding rumble. Sealed in their silent tomb, the darkness was complete.

Idris's body gained a faint luminance, lighting the area around them. Saiyah followed suit by letting her ball of light materialise again.

Bezbiel ran a hand over his head. "Are we safe here?" He asked.

Idris replied with a sorrowful look. "No. He won't get through easily, but we have to keep moving."

"Where does this lead?" Saiyah asked, peering at the only apparent exit.

It was a narrow passage of darkness, darker even than where they were. Idris laid Daniel down carefully. He wiped blood off from his sword with his sleeve, poking out from under his dark armour. He shook his head despondently.

"Damn it, where does it go, Idris?" Saiyah demanded.

His momentary alarm at being addressed informally amongst company only showed for a moment before his grim countenance reappeared. "It's where we take those whose crimes are not quite sinister enough for death," He explained slowly. "Those who are to be banished."

"It goes to Hell," Bezbiel whispered.

XXXV

The Other Shore; Into Eternal Darkness

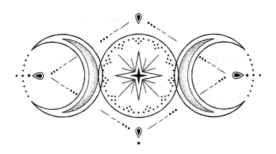

S AIYAH KNELT BY DANIEL, laying her faintly glowing hand over his battered head, but no matter what she did, he wouldn't wake.

"Help me, will you?" She said pleadingly to Idris.

He knelt beside her and let his hand hover over Daniel. "This is beyond my capabilities. Broken bones and punctures I can handle, but he'll require more delicate hands." He stood suddenly. "We'll keep him stable and get help at the encampment in Dualjahit," he said authoritatively, lifting Daniel.

Saiyah squeezed her dirty fist tight, letting Jack's pin prick distract her. The journey down to Hell would be demanding, especially without any food or supplies. Idris said they were a day away from water, so long as they weren't particular as to the quality.

"Nephilim! Defector! Traitor! You will all perish in the darkness!" an echoing voice resounded from beyond the entrance.

Saiyah shuddered at the sound of Silas's voice. She looked to Idris beseechingly. His face betrayed nothing, stony and determined.

"Quickly now," he said, making towards the darkened passage. "My wards will delay him, but we must move fast."

The three of them stood before the darkness, and Idris drew one of his daggers, drawing a circular glyph-like pattern in the air. Tiny particles floated like moondust in its wake, operating as a keyhole. Suddenly, the shimmering particles vanished in a rush of stale, sulphurous air, as if Hell itself were sentient and had awoken with a roar.

Idris glanced at the half-demons soberly. "Do exactly as I say, and we will all live," he said, glaring at Saiyah in particular. He proceeded into the dark without hesitation.

Bezbiel paused, glancing back to where they had entered in contemplation.

"Bez? Come on," Saiyah urged.

He nodded as if to assure himself and followed her into the passageway.

The darkness was infinite, and the strong sense of demonic energy was nauseating yet exhilarating. Her head was dizzy with power, and she supported herself on the slick walls of the passage to stay upright. Bezbiel's slow, controlled breathing behind her indicated he was experiencing the same problem. After a time, the passage widened and she couldn't tell how far away the other wall was, or if there even was one.

Idris's celestial glow was barely visible, diminishing gradually as it was consumed by the dark. Despite her comfort amongst shadow, not knowing what lay ahead in the unbounded abyss was gradually affecting her. This was more than the darkness of night; it was the darkness of despair and doom.

Visions of ghastly faces appeared, but before she could let out a sound of fright they vanished in a blink. She didn't dare turn to shadow for fear of being swallowed whole. Her breath was uneven as her teeth chattered. Her heart rate quickened. Knees trembled. Something reached out and grabbed her in the darkness. She let out a shriek and lost her footing. The echo of sound didn't seem to end.

Idris appeared beside her, sword drawn, with a terrifying look on his face. She looked down to see Bezbiel's hand on her arm, trying to steady her.

"Sorry, I'm sorry!" He breathed, equally shaken himself. His face was obscured in the gloom, but his terrified, serpentine eyes reflected subtly in Hezekiah's faint glow.

Idris relaxed and looked around, despite not being able to see anything. "Keep moving," he said sternly.

Saiyah stiffened her jaw and reached behind her for Bezbiel. He grabbed her and they walked arm in arm. Each step was torture, and the journey seemed never ending. The only thing keeping her going was knowing her friend was by her side, even if he was equally fearful. And Idris, whatever he was to her now, was visible ahead.

Unsure if they'd been walking for hours or minutes, blurred in the eerie silence, their footsteps were the only noise. Soon thirst set in, making her head sore. Despite her practised stints of staying awake for almost a full day, she wasn't sure if she could do so for more than two days. The dryness in her mouth was inescapable. Hunger would've come if it weren't for the dread already filling her stomach.

Idris's breath became as husky as theirs, and Saiyah let a few tears of desperation slip loose, squeezing Bezbiel's arm and comfortingly receiving one in return.

Idris stopped, and the pair nearly walked into him.

"What is it?" Saiyah whispered, her voice wan and squeaky.

"We're almost there," he said with obvious respite.

Stepping aside, he allowed them a glimpse of the light ahead, small as a needle's-eye. The relief at seeing that tiny ray warmed her heart, and they all quickened their pace. It was still a great distance, but seeing it kept Saiyah's feet moving.

It all happened instantly. The pale light grew blindingly fierce, and they emerged suddenly into bleak grey fog. Damp air descended upon them, and Saiyah stared out at a vastness of water, lapping lamentably under the horizontal mist.

Bezbiel staggered to one side and rubbed his eyes at the contrast in light while Idris lay Daniel down, a strained weight of divine energy lifting. They stood on drab stone which composed an ancient sea wall, running endlessly and parallel to a cliff edge from which they'd surfaced.

Instinctively, Saiyah moved towards the water's edge, so thirsty she could smell it. Seaweed and slick algae clung to the edges. She steadied her footing and approached with caution.

Without warning a gnarled, bony hand, riddled with erosion, reached from the water. Its muculent fingers grasped at her arm. She gasped and in an instant Idris grabbed her shoulder and pulled her back, striking the creature so she slipped easily from its grip. Saiyah was dragged away as more limbs and skeletal faces appeared, writhing and churning the water. Emaciated and haggard fingers clawed at the wall, some with flesh still clinging to them, but they lacked the strength to climb, or it was too slippery. Falling backwards with

Idris crouched beside her, she stared at him with shock and accusation, her throat too dry to speak.

"Only he can go near," Idris said breathily, pointing to Bezbiel. He loosened one of his smaller curved blades from his belt and glanced hesitantly from it to Bezbiel before handing it over. "Use the sheath to draw water. Keep hold of it for now."

Bezbiel nodded unsurely and approached the edge. The ghostly faces had lost interest and the water calmed. Idris kept close watch over him as he retrieved water. Saiyah and Bezbiel took turns drinking. It was dusty in texture and tasted stagnant, but they didn't care.

Bezbiel carefully handed the sheath full of water to Idris. "Thank you," Bezbiel whispered with a hint of reluctance.

Idris nodded in acknowledgement and sipped the cloudy water.

Behind them, abandoned and dishevelled ashen buildings filled with rubble were carved into an impossibly high cliff face. There was no sign of life, but the place had the appearance of a ghostly fishing port. It was void of any colour. Even the water below, sluggishly lapping against the rough stone, was dingy and sombre.

Idris looked around calmly. "Wait here."

Confused and fearful, Saiyah watched Idris walk briskly away down the narrow pathway. She stroked Daniel's head and cleaned the dried blood off him. Bezbiel sat heavily beside her, his usual swagger absent, no clever words or jokes. He stroked his hand; the palm was inflamed and pussy with the sheen of a burn mark.

The deep, ominous, sound of a bell tolling startled them. Saiyah sucked in her breath as she looked for the source. Idris stood a little way down the narrow path, pulling on a rope which led up to a rusted, oxidised bell. She relaxed and gave her fist a quick squeeze of assurance.

"Let me fix that," she said, gesturing to Bezbiel's hand.

He held it out wordlessly and she placed her palm over it. Silvery light emitted and he sighed with relief.

"I take it this wasn't the way you came before?" Saiyah whispered.

"No. It was nothing like this," he replied timorously. "I see now why Azeldya won't take anyone this route." He pulled out his malachite with his free hand and fiddled with it distractedly. "I'm sorry," he muttered.

Saiyah gave him a puzzled look. "What for?"

"You and him," he said frankly, pointing his chin to Idris in the distance. "I was the one who encouraged you to get close. Then I realised, well, you know."

Saiyah nodded understandingly, strangely unbashful. "It's alright," she assured him. "I've no doubt Silas would still be pursuing us even if we'd not become close."

"He's not so bad," he admitted slowly, then took a shaky breath. "I was jealous, I'll admit it. I thought that it would endanger the coven, being with him, but now..."

"But now the coven is in danger anyway, regardless of him," Saiyah finished with a sympathetic smile.

"Right."

Idris appeared nearby and regarded them both with resentful indifference as they sat hand in hand. "Are you both alright?"

Saiyah nodded soberly, followed by Bezbiel.

"What were those things?" Saiyah asked, looking at the water. "And why don't they want Bez?"

Idris looked sorrowfully at the water. "They are the souls of the damned from long ago. You and I are part of a world which they long for, whereas Mr. Brady is not."

"What was the bell for?" Bezbiel asked.

"Our mode of transport. You'll need to pay the ferryman." He looked directly at Bezbiel. "Do you have anything?"

Bezbiel thrust his hands into his pockets, pulling out a few loose coins with a satisfied nod. Idris gazed watchfully out onto the bleak horizon.

Bezbiel began to inventory his crystals, salts, and small vials of liquids, strengthening his charms and sharpening his malachite for good measure, though his fingers still trembled.

Saiyah shuffled to Daniel's head and leant down to kiss him on the forehead, smoothing his hair out of his eyes. She then leaned back against the cliff face. Taking a deep breath, her chest stung where she'd been cut, and she let out a wheeze of discomfort. Idris immediately turned to her concernedly and knelt at her side, examining the wound tentatively. Silas had cut her deep enough to scar, but hadn't penetrated her chest.

"Let me," Idris said softly as she feebly tried to bat him away in annoyance. He cleaned the wound with what was left of the water and his hands moved over her without touching, emitting his healing light.

"When we reach the encampment, they will know what you both are. It is my hope that news of Silas's apparent corruption and affiliation with the scavengers will have reached them. However, news travels slow down here. If they've heard nothing, then they will have to take my word for it." His brow creased in worry.

"And if they know what I am, what will they do?" Saiyah asked.

Idris paused to contemplate her. "I don't know," he said quietly, "but I will not let them take you."

Bezbiel piped up, his honeyed voice rough with trepidation. "If these gods choose to help us, will they be able to get us back?"

Idris turned slightly and nodded. "That is my hope."

"And if they don't?" Bezbiel muttered.

Idris glimpsed something on the horizon and looked up. "I don't know the answer yet," he said vaguely, causing Bezbiel to scowl.

Gliding on the water through the mist was a boat, and although ghostly, it gave Saiyah a serene sense of hope.

"Charon," she whispered to herself.

Idris went as close to the edge as he dared as the rough, barnacled boat came closer. The ferryman was a sinewy, bearded old man. He threw ropes out, which Idris caught, helping him moor up. Though weak in appearance, he lifted a rotting plank from the hull which supplied a precarious gangway. He had the appearance of someone who'd been strong and muscular in youth, but was ravaged by age. He wore a ragged piece of blood-red cloth, draped over the shoulder and tactfully around his waist. Goat-like horns emerged from his bone-white hair. He examined the group as they came to the edge of the gangway.

"I am Idris Hezekiah, Captain of the twenty-seventh squadron of The Host, Ambassador of the fourth embassy on Earth, and I require passage for myself and my companions."

The ferryman nodded and cast his dark, beady eyes upon Saiyah and Bezbiel, letting out a rasp of a chuckle. "You may pass, Captain of *The Host*. It has been decades since I have allowed a living soul to pass. Do you have payment, boy?"

Bezbiel stepped forward, holding out his pound coin to the outstretched, aged hand. Charon eyed it unsurely but accepted it anyway. Idris nodded for Bezbiel to alight, and he cautiously ascended the gangway and into the damp hull of the boat. Idris followed, carrying Daniel, but Charon pointed a bony finger at Saiyah, almost making her lose her balance.

"I know of you, daughter of Prometheus and Nyx," he croaked irritably.

Saiyah froze in apprehension at the name. Prometheus—it was what John Greyson had referred to himself as, according to Daniel.

Idris stood quickly, swaying the boat. Gasping, the waters beneath her rippled and the faces of the damned appeared. She stared at Charon's sunken face imploringly.

"Let her pass!" Idris boomed, allowing a wave of energy to enter his voice.

Charon waved a hand and Saiyah continued, steadied by Idris. He half put an arm around her, but she gave a look to assure him she was fine.

Inside the boat was draped with a thin, gauzy muslin-like material, rotting and frayed. They retrieved the gangway hastily, and with a flick of his bony wrist, Charon brought in the mooring ropes. He plummeted his oar into the lively water, and they cast off. "It is lucky you've been invited here, girl," Charon mumbled.

"Invited? By who?" Saiyah asked, fearful of the ancient deity.

"I know not," he said indifferently, rowing on into the mist.

Bezbiel held a hand to his temple. "In the cells," he murmured, "when you tried to free Daniel. You used my words in the god's language and there was a strange energy. Someone wants you here."

Saiyah shivered involuntarily, but she had little time to dwell on it as the haunting bell tolled. The ferryman mumbled in displeasure and the three of them became alert. Idris raised himself and looked back to the shore, but quickly ducked down again. "He is here."

Saiyah tensed and took a few deep breaths, unable to look back out of fear. The bell continued to ring, faintly but urgently.

Idris crouched beside her, addressing both of them. "Whatever you're feeling isn't real, remember that. This route to Hell is designed to cause despair and break a *mortal* soul. Therefore, you both will be able to resist... somewhat." His voice took on a note of compassion. "Get some sleep if you need it. I'll keep watch."

Bezbiel was dubious, but huddled in some of the gauzy material, drawing his knees up. Saiyah settled close to Daniel with her arm over him and her head on his shoulder. Staring up at the bleak sky obscured by stale mist, she allowed the rhythmic rocking of the boat to take her.

XXXVI

With a Red Light of Triumph in His Eyes,
and With a Smile that Judas in Hell Might
be Proud of

A JOLTING MOTION WOKE Saiyah. Idris's concerned face was above her and a gentle energy blanketed her.

Saiyah pulled his cloak around her, and Idris glanced over to where Bezbiel was huddled, still sleeping. He shifted closer to her until they sat side by side and put an arm around her, stroking her shoulder. Saiyah let her head fall onto him. There she dozed for a while until Idris shifted and raised his head.

Land was visible through the mist in the distance, and with it an impending sense of dread.

"Thank you. For coming to my rescue before," Idris said hoarsely.

Saiyah grimaced. "Don't be ridiculous. I'm not so selfish that I'd just let you die."

He bowed his head. "Even so," he said sincerely, taking her cold, bloody hand in his warm, dusty one.

The rhythm of the boat quickened as they entered shallower water. Bezbiel mumbled groggily and shuffled in his nook of the bow.

The boat slowed and Charon set his oar against the current. A grating sound came from the hull as they banked on sand. Bezbiel stood and swore resignedly under his breath as he looked ahead. Saiyah hopped out of the boat onto the pale sand and groaned at the sight materialising through the humidity.

It was Malik, both menacing and grandiose, with a full entourage. Standing at twice the height of his human form, he was golden and muscled with a jackal headed crown of black and gold. Though bare-chested, he wore exquisite garments of ivory, lapis, and crimson, woven with gold thread. He smiled with pointed teeth and devilish charm. He was surrounded by jackal-headed attendants with spears, and draped with snake-eyed demons in revealing clothing. He sat on a golden throne against the backdrop of a vast desert in hellish iron-red.

"Hello, little Katomei!" He called brightly, standing from his throne. "Welcome to Dualjahit." He gave an elaborate bow.

Saiyah couldn't help smiling ironically as he approached. "What are you doing here, Malik?"

Idris joined her with an assertive, divine voice. "We have no time to be detained, Katomet Abnawah, let us pass."

Malik smiled unnervingly, and held out his hands as if offering something. "By all means, Angel. But first allow me to speak. I wish to protect and accompany the Nephilim and half-demon to their destination."

Saiyah folded her arms warily. "How kind of you," she said bluntly, "but if we accept, you'll take Bez's soul. I'm not an idiot."

At the mention of soul-taking, Idris gently gripped the olive-leaf hilt of his sword.

"Come now. Surely, you're eager to see my famous kingdom? It is, after all, the final resting place of your mother. You don't want to visit the beautiful tomb I had constructed for her?" Malik's words were heart-wrenchingly appealing.

"Don't listen to him," Idris muttered to Saiyah. "His kingdom is nothing but sand and mud-brick walls."

Before Saiyah could assure Idris that she was wise to Malik's tricks, Bezbiel called out.

"We don't need your help now," he said roughly.

Malik turned his predatory eyes to him. "I am by far the most reasonable Katomet to serve under. Besides, your soul will arrive here regardless. I see more than one wrongdoing weighs heavy on your heart."

Bezbiel made an involuntary hissing sound with his forked tongue, appearing more demonesqe than ever in this land.

"It's still no. Now let us pass." Saiyah gritted her teeth and adopted a steely tone.

The wolf-headed attendants moved their spears in alert readiness.

"Very well. However, one last thing before you go," Malik said, testing their patience. "I have a gift for the half-demon, Bezbiel."

Unhurriedly, he returned to his throne and the cloud of people moved to reveal two large, gilded chests. They opened to reveal they were brimming with crimson strands of reeka. Bunches of it fell to the sand. Bezbiel's eyes widened, and he took an unconscious step forward. Saiyah held out an arm to block him. He looked at her desperately.

"I am willing to alter my deal and take you all above instead. All you need to do is take it," he told him genially with a pointed grin.

Bezbiel made to move forward again, and Saiyah gripped his arm tightly.

"No, Bez," she said firmly.

He tried to twist away. "I have to!" He yelled hysterically.

Idris detained him from behind whilst Saiyah grasped his arms and held them together. She brought his hands to his chest whilst he pleaded wildly.

"Stop it! It's not worth your soul!" She tried to reason.

"You don't understand!" He snarled back. "You don't know what it's like!"

Malik grinned at the chaos unfolding and let out a peal of laughter as if he were at one of his dinner parties. "Testing mortals is so entertaining, is it not?" He mused to his entourage. They rippled with agreement. Then Malik became despondent and rolled his eyes, glancing at the trees.

Bezbiel broke free from their tussle and pulled out the knife Idris gave him. He held it warily and Saiyah retreated. Desperation reflected in his eyes.

"Bez, you're right, I don't know. The coven will help you; we will help you overcome this together. But right now, you *have* to leave it!" She pleaded, dirty palms outstretched.

From the trees came a blinding flash, emphasising the relative dinginess of the shore. Standing between Malik's entourage and them was a god. He wore a uniform similar to Idris's, but in jungle green and with heavier, battle worn armour and a helmet. His sword was drawn.

"What's going on here, Malik?" The newcomer asked casually but confidently. He looked from the jackal lord to the three of them, singling Saiyah out instantly.

Idris stepped forward, still with one hand on Bezbiel's shoulder. "The Katomet intends to take the mortal part of this half-demon's soul."

The god marched over to Malik's demons, undaunted. The chests were hastily closed but hadn't gone unnoticed as he retrieved some of the fallen reeka and examined it.

"Reeka. A lifetime's supply of it, too. That, along with taking a soul before it's time, would go against the agreements of our truce, don't you think?"

Malik sneered at the god and made a sign for his men to stand down. He turned to Saiyah, bowing magnanimously. "A pleasure as always, little Katomei. Our revised deal still stands, and I hope to see it fulfilled." He winked at her, and he and his party vanished as if they were a mirage all along.

Bezbiel dropped to his knees in relief.

The god examined the area to be certain they were gone before approaching the trio. His sword was drawn, pointed at the ground, and his eyes were fixed on Saiyah.

"Captain Hezekiah," he greeted in the gods' language, pointing the tip of his sword directly at Saiyah's neck so swiftly there was no chance to evade.

She stood with her breath held and Idris half drew his own sword.

"What brings you here in such unusual circumstances?"

"Stand down, Sergeant. She's with me," he said with warning in his voice.

The Sergeant frowned at Idris questioningly. Eventually, the sword withdrew from her neck, then slowly the blade lowered. Saiyah let her breath out and he looked her up and down.

"I never imagined a Nephilim to appear so ordinary," he said distantly, then turned to Idris. "Do you have papers to prove what you say is true?"

"No. But I will shortly," he said briskly. "By all means, apprehend us and take us to the main encampment, I'm sure news on the matter will come upon request."

He regarded them all vigilantly, narrowing his eyes, but smiled slyly. "I could almost have assumed you were defected," he said amusedly.

"Please, Sergeant." Saiyah spoke in the gods tongue, surprising him. "This man needs healing." She indicated Daniel.

The Sergeant regarded the lesser god and knelt beside him. He placed a hand over his head and made a decisive nod. "I will take him. My outpost is not far, and we have a healer. Follow the path and I'll send a few scouts to aid you presently." He pointed eastwards along the coast, lifting Daniel as if he weighed nothing.

"Thank you, Ezekiel," Idris exhaled.

They disappeared in a flash, and the three stood alone in the surf.

Bezbiel was collecting his wits while Idris was tearing purposefully at his already damaged cloak, still wrapped around Saiyah. She made no move to stop him, the heat already slowing her mind. The air was so warm she was short of breath without even moving. Idris wrapped some of the cloth about his head, conjuring makeshift protection from the hellish sun which threatened to peel the flesh of their skin. He helped Saiyah with hers. He offered Bezbiel what was left of the ruined cloak.

Onwards they moved in the harsh terrain. Though the light wasn't blinding, it was the opposite to their previous journey in the dark. The light reminded Saiyah of the Old Roads, but instead of the filtered, rosy, pink it was harsh red, as if there were a tin roof over them rather than a sky.

"Where are we, exactly?" She asked, following Idris single file through the narrow path where the water dampened the scorching sand.

"The south bank of Dualjahit." He pointed behind them. "If we followed the coast this way, we'd reach the mountains of Kurch."

"Then onto Hitades and around again to Khabrasos," Saiyah added in a low voice. She didn't need to see Idris's nod; she'd memorised the map.

"You're not serious about going to Khabrasos?" Bezbiel asked with a nudge. "It's far too dangerous."

She looked across the giant river, presumably Styx, which they'd come across. She should be able to see Khabrasos from there, but there was only the smudge of dusk on the horizon. Its stormy inkiness appeared welcoming in comparison.

"What about the Acheron? That can't be far, can it?"

Bezbiel relaxed. "No, but still far enough." Bezbiel glanced behind as if he was expecting Silas to rise from the water. "You two go. I'll meet you in Dualjahit, I know the way."

Saiyah frowned. "We're not going to Dualjahit. Not after what just happened."

"We'll go to the northern encampment," Idris said with a note of finality.

"You'd be safer amongst demons than gods," Bezbiel mumbled.

After a moment lasting long enough to prove he'd ignored Bezbiel's comment, Idris turned back and said, "We should go to the black lake, I must agree. Perhaps we can discover something about the circumstances of your mother's death if you use the astral plane."

Saiyah nodded gravely and stumbled in the slopes of sand, colliding with Bezbiel at her side.

"I need to tell you something," he said in a low voice as he steadied her.

She eyed him acrimoniously. Idris approached and Bezbiel shrank away before he had a chance to speak.

"If we go, we'll have to be quick. I don't want the scouts to accuse us of running away," Idris said.

Saiyah nodded and went to him, taking up a familiar position in his arms previously used for running her in and out of the embassy at lightning speed. He held her awkwardly and averted his eyes.

"Ready?"

"Ready."

IN ASTRAL SLEEP, GREEN eyes whispered to Saiyah.

"Mum?" She called out, her voice detached from herself. "Did you invite me here, Mum?" Her voice was strained with shadow.

The green eyes grew clearer and dainty brows accompanied them. Pale faces with black lips and skin of lavender and periwinkle stood around Asramenia. The darkness became crisper, and particles of dusky mauve floated in the gloaming.

"Who killed you?" Saiyah asked, taking shaky steps. "Was it Tobias? Was it John Greyson?"

Asramenia flickered and her face appeared abruptly before her. Saiyah flinched. A darkness grew from Asramenia, its appearance familiar but greater than her own shadowy ability. This was a deep, enveloping night which spread like wings. It swarmed, and her vision darkened.

Blinking at the strangeness of it all, the darkness lifted as quickly as it'd come, and she opened her eyes to a strange but familiar landscape. She'd been standing here with Idris only moments ago. The heat was intolerable, the sun an unearthly red orb blending with the sky. Sand surrounded her, flecked with gold, but ahead were smudges of green with the promise of shade. Saiyah stood from where she'd fallen. Sand cascaded from the folds of her dress. She stumbled over dry tufts of grass to the greenery and spotted her mother standing in the shade of a small tree with vivid red fruit emerging from crimson blossoms. The dark lake behind her glistened sinisterly.

Asramenia was no longer a pale flicker, but a solid form infused with life. She wore grey hooded desert garb, and on her back was a quiver of arrows and an indigo cloak. She held a bow and was turning around, as if expecting to be ambushed.

Saiyah approached. "Mum?" She said tentatively, gaining no response. "Asramenia?" She tried again.

Asramenia's face changed to a mixture of surprise and relief. "Tobias!" She called in a girlish voice. A figure in silvery armour and light leather came rushing past her. A red cloth wrapped around his head to protect him from the sun. He drew it away from his mouth as he approached. The faded russet of his cloak fell in a familiar way–the cloak of a demon slayer, despite the colour.

"Where is little Saiyah?" He asked with a note of alarm.

"Safe, my love," Asramenia said briskly, drawing away. "But we have more pressing matters to discuss."

"Zulphas?" Tobias said with a frown. "Surely his actions cannot be more important than our–?"

"It's you, Tobias," she said as sternly as her gentle voice could manage. "John," she added, stroking his face wistfully.

Saiyah's jaw dropped.

"I know the truth. I've heard the whispers from your followers." She placed her fingertips over his lips. Tobias's golden brows drew together and Asramenia continued with incredibly slow words. "You still mean to proceed with your revenge, don't you?"

Tobias, or John, stopped her with a shushing sound. "Yes." His voice was clear and earnest. "Don't oppose me, Mina. Something great could be born from this, a better world for all of us–for our daughter!" He spoke with her pleadingly, taking her hands in his.

"And what of everything I have worked for?" Asramenia hung her head with a sorrowful nod.

He lowered her hood and drew her close, whispering into her ear. Saiyah stepped closer but missed what he said.

"I can't allow you to do this, my love," Asramenia whispered back. She stroked his face. "You will always have my heart."

Saiyah's father held her ever tighter, eyes clenched tight. Swiftly, Asramenia reached behind to grab an arrow, but he held her wrist above her head, stopping her. They stared at each other, paralyzed.

John's eyes were glassy. "Don't," he said hoarsely.

Shadow swirled at Asramenia's fingertips. In a nimble motion, John drew a slim blade from his belt.

Saiyah called out.

There was a swift puncturing sound as the dagger pierced her mother's heart and air escaped her body. Asramenia gazed at him in shock as her knees buckled and he lowered her gently. They knelt facing each other. Malice shone through her bewilderment, releasing choked breaths, clasping the hilt of the dagger.

"I can still heal you." His voice tremble., "I'm not asking you to join me, just don't stop me," he spluttered, tears running down his face.

Asramenia's delicate features contorted to wrath. "Enjoy your mortality," she spat vehemently.

Strenuously, she pulled the dagger out and made a swipe at the soft flesh of his throat. John jumped back in a celestial motion and clasped a hand to his neck where a shallow cut dripped pearlescent red, healing it instantly. Inky blood poured from Asramenia. She dropped the dagger and fell forward, motionless. Saiyah watched in horror as her father caught her in his arms. He turned her over with shaky hands and placed a kiss on her dark lips, his head lingering on hers. He lifted her like a doll and walked through the flora to the shores of dark Acheron. Wading in, he stopped and held her for a moment, half lowered into the water. The gentle waves drew her away.

Saiyah clenched her fists, realising her sword was still in her hand. As John Greyson trudged out, stony faced, she screeched and ran forward to strike him. The blade flowed through ineffectually, but he stopped and looked at his chest. Gasping, Saiyah stepped back. He looked directly into her eyes, and she was certain she'd seen his pale blue eyes before. She stumbled, readying her sword again as he advanced, but he stepped directly through her, oblivious.

E MERGING FROM ASTRAL SLEEP, Saiyah quickly wiped her tears and sat up. Idris peered down at her in concern.

"Charon was right. John Greyson is my father, and Tobias is John Greyson." She looked at Idris, her eyes wide. "I saw it, I saw him kill my mother."

XXXVII

Hateful as the Gates of Hades

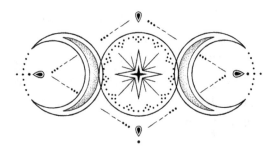

RETURNING TO THE EDGE of the shore they'd arrived on, Saiyah and Idris found Bezbiel where they'd left him. He sat leisurely in the sand, though the heat was palpable, his knees were drawn up and he was surrounded by a multitude of footprints where he'd evidently been pacing. He held his malachite in his hands.

"What on earth have you been doing?" Saiyah asked as she approached, an unnecessary hint of anger in her voice. Saiyah stopped abruptly; there was a tingle of occult energy in the air.

Bezbiel jumped upon hearing her voice and stood. "I uh, well I just..."

A few paces back, Idris's eyes narrowed, and he surveyed the area filled with the lingering energy. He opened his mouth to say something to Bezbiel, but spun about suddenly, looking out over the vast river. Saiyah saw it reflecting oddly in his eyes first, then saw for herself the glow of smokeless fire reflected on the water back near where they'd first landed.

"Silas," Bezbiel breathed.

Idris rushed to Saiyah's side, splashing in the sludge momentarily where skeletal souls started to reach. He drew his sword as well as one of his smaller blades, which he handed to Saiyah, pressing it to her as if its closeness would save her. "Run. The scouts will find you."

Uncertainly, Saiyah glanced at Bezbiel, who brandished his borrowed weapon and clutched his malachite in his free hand.

Before either of them could move, Silas came to fruition in a fiery inferno. As he slowed it whirled around him, and Saiyah felt the hairs on her arm singe. Idris held his arms out and the inferno was quelled with a wave of cooling light. Silas's back was ablaze as if he were the devil himself. The ground beneath him hissed as it dried.

Saiyah's resolve wavered as he advanced. She weighed her options—the desert on one side of her, the river of corpses on the other, and this vengeful god before her.

Bezbiel tugged on her arm. "Let's go," he said in a pleading tone.

Silas turned his attention to Bezbiel, and he performed a chilling grin. "Leaving already? Surely you wish to stay to witness this pair receive the retribution you called for?"

Saiyah's forehead sunk into a deep frown. Her green eyes, rimmed with red from heat and sand, peered at Bezbiel. He looked from her to Silas, open mouthed. Idris didn't move, but Saiyah sensed a subtle change in his energy. He was furious.

"Wouldn't you prefer to stand behind me?" Silas spoke to Bezbiel again, gesturing.

Bezbiel's face contorted with anger. His eyes appeared more serpentine than ever. With a cry he darted forward. Silas raised his blade, but Bezbiel ducked, grabbing a fistful of the dry sand and throwing it in his face. The blast of fire avoided him narrowly and he was thrown into the sand.

Idris swept in and stalled his next lunge, saving Bezbiel from Silas's blade and allowing him to slither away.

Idris had the same look in his eyes he had when battling demons. He didn't hold back. A pulse of energy emerged from him, knocking Saiyah back. Static filled the air. The water stirred. An intense glow around him, the like of which called to mind heavenly voices and pearly gates, caused them both to squint. But when Idris moved, the effect was altogether more terrifying.

His attack was ruthless, easily matching Silas. As Saiyah struggled to her feet, she recognised his calculated, precise swordsmanship, but this burst of power was causing him to slip.

Something closed around Saiyah's ankle. A goulash face in the water, green with age, stared at her out of blank eyeholes. In her shock, she didn't make a sound as she was pulled abruptly down the slope of the sand. She wrestled onto her front, clawing for anything to grab onto as the noise of the waves lapped against her ears. Greyish water filled her mouth so she could only splutter as she was pulled under. Through the watery sludge, blasts of silent fire and Idris's pale static energy danced harmoniously, filling the sky.

Grappling with slimy bones, she lifted her head just enough above water to make a gasp of a scream. A figure was instantly at her side, pulling her out of the water with one arm and hacking at the souls with a sword. They squealed like pigs being slaughtered and receded. Relief flooded her at the realisation that the scouts had arrived.

Saiyah pushed her robed saviour away and used her shadow to retrieve her borrowed sword. In a fiery flash, Silas's face was inches from hers. She threw up a shield at the last moment. She cast about for the soldier, or soldiers, but could see no one. Panicked, she lunged at Silas, but he avoided her rushed attack. Idris came between them, grabbed a fistful of Silas's robes, and threw him off balance. Saiyah kicked him in the chest, and he stumbled into the sludge.

Skeletal hands clawed at him. Idris took her arm, trying to pull her away though she wanted nothing more than to put an end to Silas. The whites of her eyes were black as night.

Silas didn't stay down for long, though. No sooner had they scrambled back than he emerged from the water, souls on fire, and sped towards them.

Idris swung close to Saiyah, making her dodge. She thrust her sword at Silas. It was a difficult angle, but he'd not expected it. With her arm fully extended, the tip of her blade just barely touched his torso. Snarling, she willed demonic energy through the sword. With a sound like thunder, shadow energy jolted through him and he cried out.

Idris shot a bolt of blue, crackling with blood-curdling energy in the humidity. Sand scattered on the wind. The desert groaned in displeasure, unsettlingly close to a human voice. When the small sandstorm settled Silas was clutching his chest, pulling himself up after being thrown onto his back. With a deft movement, Idris kicked his sword into the water.

"Stay down," he barked, holding the older god at sword point.

Silas's face was cast down and he breathed heavily. Where his torn robes caught in the wind, Saiyah could see black scorch marks from her shadow bolt.

"I am not your enemy, boy," Silas said, graceful in defeat as he sat calmly in the sand.

Unblinking, Idris glanced over his shoulder where there was another sandstorm approaching–the local squadron approaching at speed.

"You'll be taken into custody and tried for your crimes," Idris responded flintily.

Silas nodded, head bowed. He turned his attention to Saiyah. "Your existence is a danger to us all."

Saiyah narrowed her eyes at him. Suddenly there was a flash of white, bright as magnesium, which caused her to blink. Idris made a low grunt as if something had knocked the wind from his lungs. It was over in a moment. When she could see again, she just had enough time to see Idris falling into the water as if he'd been pushed. She reached out for him, and a sharp pain radiated through her sternum.

Saiyah was dimly aware of her name being called, but everything was muffled to her. She looked down at herself to see Idris's sword embedded in her. Blood bloomed slowly about the area. Memories of her mother's demise merged with her reality. In the distance, she thought she saw the figure of John Greyson in double, flickering like a motionless mirage beneath the desert sun.

Anger fuelled her resolve and she reached for the blade in her chest, her whole body trembling as she glared at Silas, who looked back at her with murder-ous triumph. Instinctively, she became shadow, freeing herself from of the blade. It dropped to the ground. Vertigo set in and blood spilled from her translucent form. She staggered backwards and her knees buckled, becoming solid again at the jolt from meeting the ground. Oblivious, she was dragged to the water's edge where the sound of frantic water grew louder.

Without warning, Saiyah's view of the world fell sideways. Bezbiel entered her line of sight, buzzing with demonic energy and flanked with serpentine minions. Perhaps it was shock, but he was more reptile himself than ever. Oversized snakes flew, seemingly towards her. Silas entered her vision, swinging his sword as he advanced to Bezbiel, decapitating the first venomous assault. Still more snakes came. The vigorous movements of their spines as they coiled and sprung forward caused Saiyah to flinch. Their jaws dislocated and fangs sank into Silas's body, arms, legs, and neck. Relentless.

Muffled to Saiyah, Silas cried in agony, and Bezbiel staggered forward to loom over him, his forked tongue flickering. Silas was so bitten and coiled around that his arms were held stiffly in place.

Divine light and a whirl of sand rushed around them. Snakes hissed in unison and turned to intricate sculptures of sand before crumbling away. Hands seized her roughly. She was dragged rudely away from the water's edge. Painfully blinded by celestial light and grit in the air, her limp body was forced to a kneeling position, her hands detained boorishly behind her back. The cold touch of steel at the back of her neck made her shiver as she coughed dust and blood.

Something hit Saiyah like a punch, making everything startlingly clear. The pain in her chest numbed and her breathing eased.

"It is tragic to see members of The Host like this," said a lilting voice.

Saiyah didn't dare move her head, but she raised her eyes. The Sergeant from before stood ahead, leaning on his sword with an overconfident grin on his face. But the person who'd spoken was an amazon of a woman, blonde hair piled in braids and a helmet under her arm. She wore the same uniform as the dozen other gods surrounding them, but she had a white sash at her waist: she was their captain. She looked down at Silas and Idris, who were also held at sword point, kneeling a little distance away.

Idris was motionless, his breathing controlled. Silas glowered at the new captain, embers emerging from the ground around him. Soldiers ran to help detain him and Idris was dragged roughly to the side.

"Unhand me! I demand that you release me!" he spewed, cinders erupting from his breath. "I'll see that you and your infantry spend the rest of your days in the pit for this! I am of the Lordships!" He was like a spoiled child, and it was almost humorous.

The captain spoke calmly but ominously. "Be still, Akrasiel Silas, or it'll be you who ends up in the pits."

He writhed uncontrollably, screeching in rage. The captain made a disgusted face ,and in one deft movement, stepped forward and hit him with the hilt of her sword without even drawing it. A wave of overwhelming and breath-taking energy swept over them all, and Saiyah felt like she'd been slapped in the face. Silas went limp in unconsciousness.

The captain stood over Idris, and she spoke to him in a calmer voice which Saiyah couldn't hear. He replied in his usual hushed tones, his head still pointed down submissively. Involuntary tears clouded Saiyah's vision and she glanced to her side, gritting her teeth at Bezbiel the deceiver. Close by him was a circle drawn in the sand, still emitting demonic energy.

At length, Idris was allowed to stand. He rubbed the back of his neck where the blade pricked him, and his weapons were returned. The captain stood over Saiyah and Bezbiel. Idris watched intensely, void of any emotion.

The captain's fierce eyes regarded Saiyah's limp form. "Let them up too, but hold them. If their story is true, we'll know soon enough." She turned back to her men. "Take them all to the central encampment."

As she was brought to stand, Saiyah felt lightheaded and weak. The faceless soldiers supported her as she faltered. Air rushed around her as she was carried away.

The central encampment must've been far from where they were; she'd never travelled with Idris at such speed for so long.

"The central encampment?" Idris turned to Sergeant Ezekiel as the soldiers started to disappear, his expression grim.

"Daniel spun me a strange tale in his delirium. I thought it sensible to take it to the top." He held his arm out to Idris and they grasped each other by the elbow as a form of greeting. "It's good to see you. Though you've looked better." He looked over Idris's dusty, bloody, and swamp-covered attire.

He gave his friend a curt nod before following the direction Saiyah had been taken.

S AIYAH APPEARED OUTSIDE THE encampment and steadied herself against the soldier holding her. She could walk on her own, but still had her arms held behind her back. Ahead, the camp looked like a shining beacon in the hellscape. Rows of sharpened timber defences surrounded it, strewn with bodies of tangled animalistic demons, charred and burned with divine power. She was sure she was only being brought this way to scare her.

Inside the encampment, silvery banners hung proudly above large, established tents. Sweet smelling vapours filled the air as soldiers cleaned their dirty uniforms. A faded black was the colour in this region. Everyone was busy with activity, with gods sharpening weapons and scrubbing armour and boots.

Without protest, she allowed herself to be half-carried, half-marched to a healer's tent. From there her vision darkened, and she entered a tranquil, dreamless sleep.

XXXVIII

Sinners and Sufferers

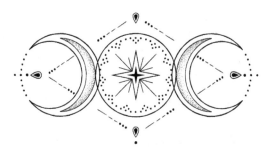

S AIYAH WOKE AS IF surfacing from underwater. It was the sound of increscent tapping that first reached through the darkness, like the dripping of water. It wasn't water, though, She was in a place that was cool, dry, dim and buzzing with holy wards designed to detain demons. She struggled to sit up, making the dried grass around her scratch against the stone beneath. The tapping stopped.

"Ah, you're awake," came a familiar voice.

Saiyah turned her head sluggishly and her demonic vision kicked in. Through thick bars she could see a face in a neighbouring cell illuminated faintly from snake-eyes within.

"Where are we?" She asked, unable to stop her speech slurring.

"The cells below the encampment," Bezbiel replied bitterly.

Saiyah rubbed the side of her head, then suddenly her hand flew to her chest as recollections of what happened returned to her. There was dried blood on her dress, but in the centre of her chest was only a rippling bruise. "How long have we been here?"

Bezbiel flashed his teeth in a grin. "Less than an hour, I'd say."

The tapping began again as Bezbiel threw a stone against one wall of his cell and retrieved it as it bounced back.

The cells were lit by a flickering of pale fire somewhere further down the corridor on the other side of the bars. Most likely at the entrance, where a light breeze just about reached them. It was all earthy tones and stone, and the scent of strong vegetation from outside masked the damp within.

Saiyah pressed the base of her hand to her temple, trying to make sense of everything. She'd been stabbed by Silas, that much she remembered. She and Idris had fought with him... had there been snakes? That was surely Bezbiel.

"Bezbiel," she said coldly.

The tapping stopped. "Ah." Bezbiel looked at Saiyah cautiously.

"Is it true? Was alerting Silas your doing?"

He got to his feet and turned to face her, approaching their communal bars as if she might bite him. "Please, listen to me, Saiyah."

"I don't believe this," she said under her breath.

"It's hardly important now," he said in what was meant to be a soothing manner.

"You really are a selfish, jealous little snake." She pulled herself up to face him square on. She could feel her vision changing as the whites of her eyes darkened.

He raised his arms defensively. "You're right, I was selfish, I was jealous. If it helps, I was on reeka at the time—no, that doesn't help. I never meant to put you in danger. I was just trying to get at *him*." He softened his voice to a whisper. "I want to say I did it for you, to ease his suspicions. That's how I justified it at the time. But I'll admit now I understand how foolish it was."

Saiyah narrowed her eyes at him.

"I wanted to undo what I did right away, but of course there was no way, and Adriel had already processed the report. I did *everything* I could to stop them from discovering you," he said desperately.

"That's why you tried to sell your soul," she stated in a low voice.

"Could you forgive me?" He asked hopefully.

Saiyah swore and looked away. "You can't be serious."

515

Bezbiel closed the remaining distance between him and the bars. His hands met them with a thud, and he curled his fists around them. "I am deadly serious. Saiyah, I am a demon, I have done far worse than that. Things you have yet to discover."

"Nothing half so treacherous, I'd wager."

He blinked hard and his jaw slacked, his resolve leaving his face.

"What else have you done?" She whispered, edging closer to him.

Bezbiel shook his head and pushed the bars away. He rubbed the back of his neck and paced his cell. "You'll find out soon enough, no doubt."

Bile rose in her throat. "If it's any danger to me, the coven, or anyone I love, you'd better say."

He looked at her with wide-eyed despair. "I would never hurt the coven, or you. Not knowingly."

"Knowingly?" She exclaimed, scoffing. "I don't forgive you, Bez. I don't trust you—I'm not even sure I like you."

He took a deep breath. "I understand. Just promise me, do not go to Khabrasos, please. Don't seek out anything to do with your mother or John Greyson. It's too dangerous." Just then a clang resounded from further in the cells, followed by the sound of armour clinking. From around the corner appeared Ezekiel, flanked by two angelic soldiers. He paused in front of Saiyah's cell, looking at her curiously. After a moment he shot an irritated glance at one of the soldiers.

"Come on then, we haven't got all day," he said, waving his hand.

The soldier stepped forward quickly with a rattling of keys and unlocked Saiyah's cell. She stepped out and followed them to the exit. She glanced at Bezbiel, though she actively fought not to, so glared at him instead as he was left behind.

CAPTAIN JOSIAH'S WAR TENT was adorned with heavenly silks and demonic furs. The surfaces were splayed with maps and scrolls with small, ornately carved counters for strategy. Upon seeing the magnificent woman in shining armour, Saiyah couldn't help but think, *you would make a worthy enemy*. She shook her head, as if her thoughts might be heard.

Standing at either side of Josiah were Idris and Ezra respectively, as well as other reasonably high-ranking military gods in robes of green, red, black, and beige, depending on which part of Hell they were stationed in. Saiyah gulped but was nowhere near as nervous as she would once have been.

Josiah looked her directly in the eye, unblinking but with a faint smile. "It has been many centuries since a demigod has walked among us. Tell me, Hezekiah–*Idris* Hezekiah," she clarified without looking at him. "Why did you not inform anyone of this discovery?"

Idris took a slight step forward. "I was not aware, until recent events." He settled a glance at Saiyah.

Pride blossomed in her chest. He'd become such a subtle liar. Lying by bending the truth, and how attractive he was whilst doing it.

Josiah acknowledged this without a word.

"Captain, this is not simply a combination of god and mortal, like in the tales of old." It was Ezra who spoke this time, his voice dominating the room. "This is an abomination, and should not be allowed to live!"

There was a murmur of agreement, and this time Josiah's eyes flickered to Ezra.

"Perhaps. But this is not for us to decide," she said vaguely, walking towards Saiyah with her hands laced together behind her back. "Saiyah *Greyson*." She let the name linger. "Tell me, what do you intend to do with the divine powers you possess?"

"Do?" Saiyah spluttered. "I don't intend to do anything. I'd rather not have them at all, they've caused me nothing but trouble."

It was not a lie, and Josiah smiled briefly.

"You'd rather be rid of them?"

"Yes."

This caused further murmuring in the gods language. They couldn't understand why she wouldn't want that power.

"Why did you join the Albion Circle?" The golden captain asked.

Saiyah frowned minutely. "For the pursuit of knowledge, to learn demonic languages, and to control my powers."

Josiah didn't say anything, just watched her. The silence in the room irritated Saiyah. She was waiting for more.

"And because of my mother. I thought if I joined the Albion Circle, I would be able to find out how she died," she admitted in a low voice.

Josiah raised an eyebrow. "And did you?"

Saiyah nodded.

Josiah glanced at Ezra. "Well then. It seems you have achieved your goal with little damage of your own doing. My recommendation to the second sphere will be that you continue living under the supervision of the Albion Circle, and the watchful eye of your nearest embassy, as long as you swear to abstain from use of your godly gifts as long as you may live."

Idris's expression didn't change, but Saiyah saw a flicker of relief. Conversely, Ezra looked as if he was about to fly into a rage.

"It is the second sphere who will make the final decision," he warned.

Saiyah blanched at the idea of Ezra and his peers judging her fate.

"What if they do not agree?" She asked.

"You will be executed," he said smugly.

"And what if they do agree, but I make a mistake?" She directed the question at Josiah.

The captain shrugged. "That decision will lie with the Hezekiahs, but execution is not to be ruled out."

Saiyah remained motionless to prevent herself from swaying with shock and dehydration.

"You will remain here until a decision is made. Your mentor, Azeldya, will be notified."

Saiyah tilted her head to the side, looking from Ezra to Tova Josiah. "Azeldya was captured by demon slayers of *The Host*. Ezra Hezekiah is capturing and killing demons and half-demons all over London, he–"

Ezra cleared his throat and held up a hand to silence her. "No one shall be killed. It is simply a matter of order and discipline."

Saiyah took a step forward, her voice coming out in a high pitch. "That's not what you said at–"

"That's enough." Josiah cut in; her tone was one of boredom. "It would appear Akrasiel Silas had incorrect information to offer regarding the situation? The number of wanted demons entering the mortal world was not as great as he'd imagined?"

"Indeed not," Ezra responded flatly, looking to the floor.

"What Captain Josiah means to say," came the jovial voice of Ezekiel to her side, "is that Lord Ezra made a grave error in judgement by trusting Akrasiel Silas. It would appear he had his own dealings with demons and the like, would it not?" He nodded towards Idris.

"Indeed, that appears to be the case. Perhaps he even knew of Miss Greyson's state before any of us."

"Only his interrogation will prove that. And support your case." Josiah nodded to Saiyah. "In the meantime, you may remain within the camp outside of the cells. You are not permitted to leave or use any demonic energies whilst you are with us, is that clear?"

With little choice, Saiyah nodded. Josiah waved her hand dismissively and Ezekiel tugged her away.

T HERE WAS NO FOOD in the camp since the gods didn't eat, but some unusual looking dishes were supplied from a nearby demon settlement. She hardly cared, she was so hungry.

Greased with days of grime, blood, and dust, she didn't care one bit about the female gods required to guard her while bathing. Dark fabric sheets separated them from the rest of the camp. Just to be clean and smelling of sweet herbs was bliss. She detangled her hair and tied it in a low bun. She was given plain robes, tied at the waist with a corded belt.

Refreshed, she marched in the direction of Idris's tent. The only midnight-blue uniform drying by a fire outside was a clear indicator of which was his. She strolled in confidently, and for a moment, it appeared empty. There was a rough bed in the corner with battered armour leaning against it. Wearing simple black robes like herself, Idris lay upon it, motionless. Saiyah stepped closer, certain he was resting his eyes, but deep, slow breathing indicated otherwise.

There was a rustle of fabric as someone entered the tent. Ezekiel grinned boyishly at her and tilted his head in a motion to leave. Flustered at being caught staring, she followed wordlessly.

"I thought gods didn't sleep?" She said once they were outside.

"We don't need to, but we can," he said with a shrug. "Best you don't mention it to anyone." His eyes darted to the entrance of the tent.

Saiyah liked him instantly. He was politely curious about her, 'The Nephilim,' and she answered all of his questions discreetly. Eventually Saiyah plucked up the courage to ask a question of her own.

"Why is Bezbiel still being held in the cells?"

Ezekiel's grin fell away and he folded his arms. "It's a mystery that only Idris can answer. Either he'd be too much trouble let loose, or he's under suspicion for something. I don't know."

He left Saiyah wondering while he continued with his own questions.

She spent her time beside Daniel as he slept and recovered with the healers, and though she spotted Idris, he never approached, always in the company of Captain Josiah.

It was curious, being in Hell. Here in the camp all felt so calm and organised. Her senses were heightened to the energy which fizzled around her, no longer disconcerting or unbearable, but like a comforting warning of when a god was too close. Because of this, when Azeldya stepped foot in camp, Saiyah was the first to know, not least because of the commotion caused at the main gate.

Indigo light entered through a triangular entranceway of her tent. It was red in colour, contrasting greatly with the storm light outside and the dark earth at their feet. Saiyah abandoned her uncomfortable camp bed and ran barefoot in the dust down the main path of the camp. There were soldiers busy as always, barely paying her a second glance as she glided, ghostlike, in her borrowed robes.

Azeldya was there, fresh as a daisy in her white trench coat, black suit-dress, and perfect ringlets framing her horns. Saiyah ran straight into her arms, taking the ancient demoness by surprise. Instantly she found herself holding back tears.

"Oh, my dear girl," Azeldya said, stroking her cheek.

"Tobias is Greyson, and Greyson is Tobias," she spluttered. "He killed my mother, and I think he might still be alive."

Azeldya controlled her anger in the presence of the bewildered gods witnessing the spectacle. She pressed her eyes closed and forced a smile. "Then you have done it. You've fulfilled everything your mother asked of you in her letter. Rest now, you can leave the rest to me and Zulphas."

"Zulphas?" Saiyah asked in alarm.

"Do not worry. He and I have spoken at length. Though he was indeed hiding things from both of us regarding your mother, he is not the traitor here. It seems he was framed."

Saiyah gritted her teeth.

"Bezbiel."

Azeldya only offered her a pained expression. They walked together to greet Captain Josiah, then to Saiyah's tent where Azeldya prepared food and supplies for the journey back.

"This could be a little optimistic," Saiyah commented.

Azeldya pressed a finger to her lips and handed her something from her coat pocket.

"If that is true, your escape is not over yet."

Saiyah examined the paper. It was a freshly torn piece of a map, showing only the central encampment where they now were, a great chasm, and then Khabrasos. There was a small area circled in red biro not far from Xalvas tix Nyx.

"This is your haven, should you need it," Azeldya explained.

Saiyah nodded and hid the map amongst her robes.

"What about Bezbiel? He told me he'd done worse he couldn't speak of, and not to go to Khabrasos."

"I'll deal with him. Though I do wonder..." Azeldya stood straight and placed a hand to her chin.

"What?"

"Medea reported that Xaldan went missing from Malik's house shortly after Zulphas arrived. He took a bottle of pure god's blood. I would wager they each knew something about each other.

"There was no one he trusted more than Xaldan," Saiyah muttered. "If I am permitted to leave, what will happen to Silas?" She whispered, glancing over to the cells.

Azeldya scowled. "He is too well connected to be executed, or reprimanded too harshly."

"Surely, they'll not let him get away with all this?"

Azeldya shook her head. "I expect he will be comfortably imprisoned for life." She replied let slip a note of irritation. As if sensing it, they both glanced out of the tent entrance to see Idris walking in the direction of the rear gate. "If there's anything you want to do, you'd better do it now," she said with a mischievous twinkle in her eye before turning away.

XXXIX

Into this Wild Abyss

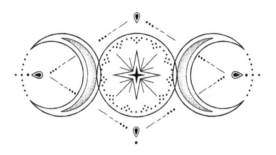

T HE REAR GATE OF the encampment was at the north-
ernmost point, where the row of spiked defences
obscured the dark landscape beyond. As Saiyah stepped
delicately through the small doorway, she was watched
closely by soldiers on the ramparts. Abruptly, a huge
chasm of darkness came into view, seemingly dropping
to nowhere. Everything was eerily still. Looking into the
void, she saw obscure clouds of darkness drifting in the
black, and when she squinted there were vague shapes
amongst them. Something rippled like leaves of a forest
in the breeze, and she tentatively took a step out of the
camp. Slowly, she advanced until she was close to the

edge of the chasm; it was a sheer drop. Saiyah gazed across the abyss. Beyond was an unmistakable land with violet swells of colour. A little further along from where she stood was a rusted chain with glints of gold tethered to a great iron ring. The chain seemed to run parallel across the chasm, but disappeared into the inky mist.

"Don't get too close," came Idris's voice as he joined her on the edge.

Saiyah stared longingly at her distant homeland. The compulsion to go to it filled her, a torrent of emotion greater than anything she'd ever experienced. It was a melancholy yearning, a hunger, greater even than her hunger for knowledge. Or Idris.

"Is it possible to cross?" She whispered.

"The region is unstable. You'll find none willing to take you. Besides, you'd never be permitted."

Saiyah sucked in her breath. Despite his words, she felt she could easily defy Idris, so great was her ire towards him. What he meant was, *he* wasn't willing to take her. He'd not attempted to speak to her once in days, not even glanced at her as he passed. Khabrasos was *right there*. She was like Tantalus.

"I'm guessing you haven't been there since you drove my mother to her death?" She said sharply.

Idris exhaled irritably. "If I had known she was in-nocent, or that it was Tobias–Greyson–behind the or-der, I wouldn't have considered doing it." He chose every word meticulously. "I only tracked her footsteps and lingering energy. Once she was on this side of the chasm—before there was a chasm—I abandoned the task. But I am sorry for my part in it," he finished with his voice low. "I wish I had known her."

Saiyah's brows were furrowed, and she looked up at him. He glanced warily from her back to the ramparts, as if worried they'd be spotted acting so familiarly. He took a breath and faced his body towards the darkness again.

"Daniel is awake," Idris said a little more brightly, "and the second sphere has made a decision on you."

She turned to him suddenly, unable to contain her apprehension.

"Your life is safe, as are your secrets, regarding John Greyson anyway. You are permitted to return to the mortal world."

Saiyah's heart fluttered, and she managed a thin smile. This should be what she wanted.

"There will of course be many restrictions placed upon you." He turned, expecting her to follow.

Saiyah stayed put, gazing once again at the dark jewel of Khabrasos. She could feel the crumpled map in her pocket.

"I forgive you for what you did," she said monotonously. "You thought you were doing the right thing, as always. Are you doing the right thing now, I wonder, in keeping me in the mortal world? Treating me as if I'm a bomb that could detonate at any moment?"

Idris started to step towards her, but stopped, glancing back at the camp. "Saiyah, much is beyond my control." He shook his head helplessly.

Saiyah couldn't look at him. "So how minutely do I need to step out of line before you dispose of me?" She said nefariously.

Disgusted, Idris took a step towards her, but halted himself. "Don't do anything rash," he warned. "I can guess what you want, but there are proper ways to go about this. We can discuss it when we're back."

"If I leave now, would you stop me?" She asked with a laugh.

"You're not yourself," he growled.

"I am more myself than I have ever been. Come with me." She gestured to Khabrasos.

Idris blinked in bewilderment and his jaw slacked. She spied that look of wistful longing she'd seen on him once before.

"You should not even joke about such things."

"I am deadly serious. Come with me. We could be free of all this bureaucratic zeal and find John Greyson together! *We* could be together."

Idris did not answer. Suddenly the distance between them felt greater than the chasm below. The breeze rustled through their hair.

"You're asking me to choose a side," he stated. "If I stop you, I betray your trust forever. If I let you go, I betray my people and risk losing you. Forever."

This time it was Saiyah who stepped closer. "Then come with me."

"Then stay with me!" He exclaimed. "We will never be here again. Never as we are now. I was wrong. You are more than a mere flicker of a mortal life, you are the brightest star I've ever witnessed. In an immortal life there are periods of darkness, and then there is light. You are one of those lights."

"Yes, well. Even stars have to burn out eventually," she said in a low voice.

Saiyah wanted nothing more than to run into his arms, but she held her ground. His vivid blue eyes threatened to drown her. She forced herself to look away.

"I don't want to be parted for the precious decades you have left. Please don't do this."

"I thought you said you could never love me?"

Idris opened his mouth, but someone called out to Saiyah from the camp. There was a flicker of white at the gates. Her face lit up momentarily at the sight of Daniel walking out towards them but faltered as she turned back to Idris.

"I want nothing more than to stay with you," she said in a hushed tone, "but I will not be a prisoner. I will not be watched my whole life and live in fear of falling out of favour. It's like the poet said, *better to reign in Hell than serve in Heaven*."

Idris's face darkened.

Unable to look upon him any longer, Saiyah ran headlong into her Godfather's arms. He swung her around, laughing and weeping with happiness.

"After all this time, we don't need to keep you a secret any longer," he said, brimming with naive joy. "Let's go home."

Saiyah nodded a moment too late, but threw her arms around him nonetheless. As they made their way up the path, she glanced back at Idris and her homeland, both diminishing from view, and gripped Daniel's hand all the tighter.

S AIYAH COLLECTED THE BAG of supplies Azeldya had made up for her, ready for the journey home. She stood by the door of Saiyah's tent like a centurion.

"You'll have to make sure there is a significant distraction if you're to do this. Do you want my help?" The demoness asked.

Saiyah shook her head. "I've had enough help from others. But thank you. For everything."

"Likewise. You know where to find me if ever you do need anything from another again." Azeldya smiled minutely.

It dawned upon Saiyah then that out of everyone, Azeldya was the one she should've trusted the most. She gave her a discrete squeeze of the hand as she passed by.

"Good luck," she whispered.

None of the soldiers paid much attention as Saiyah strolled through the camp. She was a regular sight by now. She scratched her palms. As she walked around the cell block, she turned to shadow. The light grew dimmer in the prison entrance. Two guards sat inside, chatting away in the gods' language. Saiyah pressed herself against the wall.

At the bottom of the staircase, it was silent as a crypt. She glimpsed other inmates through the grated doors. One woman was chained and covered in bite marks where she'd tried to chew herself to freedom, the cuffs miraculously untarnished. The bars grew thicker, and her view of the captives distorted. Some cried out in wild rage, barely resembling anything humanoid, spewing dark, demonic curses. Saiyah consoled herself that these were the kind of demons that would harm humans without a second thought. She passed Bezbiel pacing in his cell and muttering to himself. She hoped he'd stay quiet through this, or better yet not notice a thing.

She came to the cells reserved for powerful, animalistic demons. The hum of wards rang in her ears. Sat on a stool in the centre of one such cell was Silas, staring straight out at her unblinkingly. She let herself become visible and he blinked at her apparition.

"What do you want?" He said with an air of impatience.

"To make a deal with you."

Silas gave one of his strange smiles. "Why would you want to do that? Do you fear me still?" He got to his feet in some form of weak intimidation.

"I imagined you'd rather make a deal with me than spend the rest of your infinitely long life locked up by an institution of your own making?"

Silas laughed then sighed, like a parent humouring a child. "Speak, Nephilim," he said, inching towards the door.

"Rather than face a humiliating trial, questioned by the Hezekiahs and all your peers, I can offer you a swift end, as well as an afterlife in Hell."

Silas sneered grimly. "You do not have the power to do this," he said darkly.

"I do. In exchange for your soul, you would dwell in its owner's dominion."

He looked down with cynical amusement. "You have no dominion," he said bitterly, turning away.

"No. But I assure you, your essence will live on regardless." She purposely used a tone that hinted at indifference and disinterest.

"Do you know why I tried to have you killed?" He asked lightly.

Saiyah only glared at him.

"It was because of your father."

"You always knew I was a Nephilim," she half questioned.

"I did. But not for that reason. Your being a Nephilim has nothing to do with it. John Greyson was always the enemy."

Saiyah frowned and shook her head. "Perhaps you should have been hunting him instead."

Silas chuckled, his mannerisms somewhat more casual than usual. More unhinged. "I have tried many times since I learned of his plans. I have sent gods, demons, scavengers, and even the soul-ripper Molek after him." Saiyah shivered at the name. "He is always protected, slippery as an eel. That is why it had to be you after your mother died."

She took a step closer, realisation blossoming on her face. "You knew everything, didn't you?"

"And it would seem you also know, in some way."

Saiyah steadied herself. "Tell me. You have nothing else to lose, so tell me."

Silas smiled cruelly. "You were a tool in your father's plan. Your mother and her ambition was too great for him. I suggested he have a child and dispose of the Priestess. A child to carry the demonic bloodline he was tied to. Only to do this, Greyson would have to become mortal, temporarily, and relinquish his stolen godly and demonic powers. This gave me a chance to dispose of him. But I failed."

"He became a god again," Saiyah said.

Silas shook his head. "No. He simply retained a touch of the demonic as well as the occult. When he killed the Priestess, he was weakened, and you were his link to his former power."

"So, when I found my divine energy, you tried to have me killed in order to destroy him."

"Precisely." He drummed his fingers on the bars, staring at her blankly. "But do not mistake me, I am on your side. We both want the same thing. Let us alter the deal you suggest. I will agree to your terms in exchange for the death of John Greyson. He cannot be allowed to live and enact his plans."

A sly smile crept onto Saiyah's face. "I will accept these terms. But first, why did you try so hard to prevent Idris and I from being together?"

The white-eyed god beamed widely. "It is against our laws, after all. That, and the fact that I could not permit the Greyson line to continue while its source was still living."

She cleared her throat, almost feeling remorse for what she was about to do. She forced herself to remember Daniel's helpless face as Silas's prisoner, and the evening where she'd been chased by Silas and Ezra through the museum.

"Akrasiel Silas, I offer you a swift death, a place in Hell, and the death of John Greyson in exchange for your soul. Do you accept?" Saiyah held out her hand as far as she dared. Her fingertips hovered through the bars, tensing to stop her hand from shaking.

Silas's face curled into a cruel grin as he gradually reached out and met her hand with a tight grip. "I accept," he said with a firm shake. Saiyah meant to release herself, but he pulled her forward so her face was close to his as he leaned down. "It is a pity I wasn't able to contribute to your execution in the same way as your mother's." He snarled. "Then again, you are as stubborn as she. Perhaps you would've refused to die also. Though I think not."

Saiyah tugged her hand away with a grimace, unable to hide her shock. Staggering backwards, she turned to shadow to prevent him from seeing her disgusted expression. She was a split second too late.

The cells tremored, and confused sounds came from above. She heard her name being called by Bezbiel and could just about make out one of his eyes peering at her from the difficult angle behind. Saiyah shrank back against the wall as a spiral of fire appeared in the cell beside Silas, defying all wards. Even he was aghast.

Malik appeared in his full glory, flanked with two reptilian demons– Saiyah couldn't decide if they were more animalistic or humanoid. His sickly yellow-blue eyes were wild, and his pointed teeth were larger and more menacing than ever. Gold flashed at his clawed fingertips and Saiyah scrunched her eyes as he reached out to Silas. The god cried out grotesquely, and as his screams quelled, she risked a glance. Pearly blood splattered the cell as Silas's chest was torn. She flinched, but strangely, the unearthly colour of the blood made it easier for her to stomach.

Malik glanced over his shoulder and his eyes locked with Saiyah's momentarily. She shuddered inwardly before he turned his predatory gaze back to the twitching god, and he and his demonic assistants pounced upon the body.

Sounds of commotion came from above. No doubt Malik's great demonic presence hadn't gone unnoticed. She turned and caught sight of Bezbiel at the edge of his cell. His arm was outstretched, and his face was contorted in pain as he persevered through the wards. He was holding something out to her. Without thinking, she took the little bronze object from his hand. It was the amulet which he'd stolen from the British Museum, now with a leather cord attached to it for wearing. Bezbiel retrieved his arm and gave her a knowing glance as she melted into the shadows.

XL

I Sang of Chaos and Eternal Night

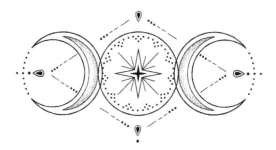

B ATHED IN SHADOW, SAIYAH stood at the edge of the void. She couldn't linger. If she was going to do this, she'd have to make a decision quickly. This was her choice. She tightened her grip on her backpack and let herself slip away into the shadows of the craggy earth. She slithered towards the golden chain which connected the two lands and wrapped herself around it as she glided through the loops and locks of the links.

The abyss looked from below like Erebus himself, threatening to engulf her. But in this diminished form, she was confident of her hold on the thin chord which held her life in its metallic hands. When she was halfway across, the emptiness of the below seemed to emit the prolonged echo of a voice, as if it were alive. The voice soon gave way to the rustling of trees, the cawing of night birds, and the creaking of boughs.

Saiyah came into her land as a shadow, pulling herself upright to a humanoid form. She could feel the gentle long grass through her feet and legs, brushing on her shins. It was enough to make her weep. She thought of John Greyson's description of Khabrasos. There was still a memory of that meadow amongst the twilight foliage before the forest engulfed it.

A mist of darkness loitered between the daunting trees, but to Saiyah the cover was comforting. Consulting the map Azeldya had given her, she glided over the maze of roots, some of which looped over her head in great arches. She made for what looked like a clearing, but was pleased to discover that it was a path. She let herself become solid, and the world around her sharpened. The air was damp, rich with the scent of bark. The path was a litter of detrition, lined with pale mauve fungi which were startling against the wine dark trees. She could barely see the upper canopy, it was so high, but low hanging and fallen branches betrayed leaves of deep green and mulberry. Besides the deep rustle of leaves, it was eerily quiet. As she stepped carefully along the path, her own footsteps were the only noise, occasionally punctuated by the call of an owl. A far cry from the chaos of soldiers and steel she'd left behind.

Every living thing in the Xalvas was silent as a whisper. Once as she rounded the corner of a tree, she startled a fox with a midnight black coat the size of a large dog, sending it scampering into the trees. A number of times, she felt something feathery brush past her face, which she first thought were bats, but turned out to be giant moths. They left trails of powdery grey dust in their wake, and their wings reflected the barest hints of moonlight.

She was getting close to the place Azeldya had circled, but the path wasn't coming to an end or obvious destination. It continued on for far too long, winding in strange directions. Circling and spiralling. She stopped her search for a moment, convinced she was at the same cluster of mushrooms as she'd been earlier. Saiyah stepped off the path and seated herself in the roots of a great tree.

"In a dark wood where the straight way was lost," she huffed.

Saiyah opened her backpack and examined the contents: enough food for three, maybe four days if she were careful, a blanket, and some coins of a currency she vaguely remembered reading about. At the bottom of it all was her mother's journal. Azeldya must've taken it from her room, but she wasn't sure why she needed it. She took the familiar leather-bound book in her hands and opened it, letting it naturally fall open to whatever page it wished. But the page it opened on wasn't by chance; there was something lodged within the pages. It was a key. Saiyah picked it up. It was small, light, and made with interwoven wires of silver and gold. There was a small green gemstone, not at the base where one might expect, but right at the end in the complicated weavings of the fork. Though it was light in her hand, it was weighty with demonic energy. Energy that belonged to her mother.

Saiyah stood, the key in one hand and the crumpled map in the other. Naturally, why else would she be given a secret key than to find a secret location? Walking back to the place which seemed most likely on the map, she set about searching for a keyhole in a tree or a secret door in the path. But there was nothing. Despite that, the key tugged subtly in her hand like a magnet. She stepped off the path and was quickly clambering over the oversized roots, amongst moss so dark it was almost black, and bluebells that appeared neon in the darkness.

It pulled her towards an unremarkable opening between two ivy-covered trees. Saiyah stopped walking. All was quiet except the energy resonating through her. As with the Osiris box, she turned to shadow, taking the key with her. It slipped into an invisible hole, as if she'd been close already, but gravity pulled it closer. She smiled and turned the key, and felt a click. Nothing changed, but as Saiyah stepped forward, she felt a barrier. It was like moving from London to the Old Roads.

She was somewhere else, somewhere others couldn't find, and there was a path ahead.

Lanterns hung on decoratively carved posts to the side of the path filled with an unfamiliar bluish light. It would've been barely visible under normal circumstances, but in this perpetual dusk they glimmered like night insects. She wondered if they had been burning here for decades, waiting for her mother's return, or if the opening of the gateway had triggered them.

Following the path, which became clearer and more purposeful with each step, a low structure was visible amongst the trees. Stone pillars supported a balcony, and beyond, wooden beams with a purple hue framed a small but grand dwelling. Above the doorway and engraved in stone was the name *Melanthios*. Her mother's family name.

Saiyah walked as if in a dream up the stone steps onto the half-moon veranda. There was a small pool filled with not water but silvery light, the purpose of which was alien to her. Within the house it was partly open to the elements, only decorative wooden panels up to her waist separating inside from out. The ground floor was largely bare, with some low furniture with sumptuous cushions and upholstery of crimson and violet. There was a singular stone wall at the back, just behind a long table. As Saiyah got closer, she saw it supported a fireplace which was crackling with blue-green flames. Her entrance must have activated it somehow. Shelves lined the walls, filled with dust-covered jars of pickled items, plants, and powders, of which she wasn't sure what was food and what was for craft. The table was still littered with half-chopped plant life, some of which had heavily decayed, and others crumbled to dust. There were measuring cups, bowls, pestle and mortars, and knives simply abandoned. It was as if she'd intended to come back to the task later, but never did.

In one corner there was a spiral staircase which partially went outside of the building. Saiyah followed it. As soon as she got to the top, scattered leaves drifted playfully about her ankles. A narrow landing encompassed the perimeter of the house, but the centre was empty space, looking down on the living space below. She passed a few small, vacant rooms, but she could already see where her mother's bedroom was. Only lilac and indigo gossamer separated it from the rest of the house, and the fabric danced in the light breeze. The floorboards creaked welcomingly as she entered. The room merged effortlessly with the balcony, looking out over a small glade a short way off where there was an inky pool filled with borrowed starlight. There was a table and two chairs right on the edge. Saiyah noted there were two glass goblets, one empty and one with a dark crust remaining from an evaporated liquid.

To one side was a bed which looked like it had formed directly from the branches of trees. It was unmade, and the pale silk still held its lustre. Saiyah's heart tightened.

She was compelled to walk to the unmade side of the bed and sit where her mother had slept. She stopped suddenly, noticing what was on the other side of the bed. A small crib.

She sat on the bed, landing wearily, and placing a hand on the edge of the crib just as her mother might have done. There was a moth-eaten blanket inside, hand-embroidered with cornflowers and nightshade. Saiyah touched it, the wool soft with age. She could imagine her mother sitting where she was now, holding her as a child, perhaps singing, or playing. This could have been her home. Tears threatened to spill, and Saiyah leaned back.

Something cold and hard touched her hand and she jumped up. Looking to the bed, she saw she had uncovered something at the edge of one of the pillows. She lifted it to find an ornate dagger.

Asramenia really had been afraid. Perhaps with so many people around her turning against her, this was her safe haven. The sanctuary that Idris Hezekiah had driven her from. Saiyah gritted her teeth.

Saiyah wiped her eyes and lifted the dagger, clutching it to her chest.

"This will be my home," Saiyah whispered, as if swearing it on her new weapon.

She would not be driven from here as her mother was. She would clean the house of all its dust and decay, keep the fire lit, and bathe in the nearby pools. She would live off the land and continue her studies–if she were able too. It would be a relief from the chaos of the coven. She'd never need to question again who around her could be trusted. Perhaps she could even visit Xalvas tis Nyx and see the temple her mother was once High Priestess of. Maybe there were still some remaining priestesses.

Saiyah stood purposefully and went to a chest at one corner of the room next to a mirror. Inside she found bundles of clothing, mostly regal gowns and jewellery wrapped in silks. She discovered a plain black tunic-style dress which came to her knees, a sturdy pair of boots, and a decorated but practical belt. She secured the dagger to her new belt and tied her hair into its usual low bun.

Hesitantly, she retrieved the amulet Bezbiel had given her. On one side was a multi-winged fiery figure, with an inscription in Greek: *Lord, do not give strength to my enemies, for your right hand always protects me. Turn evils unto their heads, Lord our God; do not give them power.* And on the other: *Sisinnius tramples you down, filthy one. You no longer have strength. Solomon's seal has rendered you impotent. Michael, Gabriel, Uriel, Raphael tie you down, Alimerbimach.* It was just a bit of superstitious protection, not made for the likes of demons or gods. He'd charged it with some kind of energy, but she only really felt a great nothingness exuding from it. She tied the leather around her neck and tucked the amulet under the neckline of her dress. Checking herself quickly in the mirror, she resembled a dark form of Artemis, but without the bow. She nodded in approval and walked to the balcony, ready to begin her tidying.

Her steps faltered as she spotted a movement in the distance. Surely her eyes were deceiving her. It was a ripple on the water. There were birds chirping here, she had heard them before, so there were surely fish in that water, and other fauna. But all the sounds of nature had fallen silent. The water rippled again, and she saw it, the reflection of a man in pale robes. She followed the image upwards towards its owner. Her fists tightened. His appearance was unmistakable. It was John Greyson.

XLI

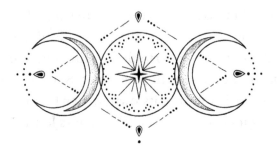

TORN BETWEEN WEEPING AND rage, Saiyah approached the water's edge. The glade was vibrant
with more varied shades of purple and green, dotted
with small white flowers. The earth turned to stone
near the water's edge, creating miniature rock pools and
caves. She had been here before, in her dreams and
in astral sleep. There were no nymphs on this plane
though, nor any spectre of her mother. It was just her
and the man called John Greyson, who was her father.

He stood opposite her at the other side of the watery
battlefield, on a cluster of rocks jutting out into the pool.
He wore simple cream robes which thinned and frayed

at the edges. A worn-out red cloth was tied about his middle, holding a battered sword and dagger. His fair hair was long and drawn back into a long ponytail, just as it had been in Prague. He had aged since she'd seen him in her vision, no longer a young man but on the cusp of middle age. Yet his eyes were still alive with the indifferent coldness of a wolf.

He looked down towards her and smiled, and there was genuine warmth in it. "I am so glad you were finally able to get here," he said, with a slight crack in his voice.

Saiyah was taken aback, but she kept her composure.

"It was you who invited me," she stated indifferently. "Why?"

His expression was one of near embarrassment. He made a move to withdraw something from his robes and Saiyah flinched. John Greyson slowed his movements to show her he meant no harm, then continued to remove something made of glass from his cloak.

Saiyah squinted at it from across the water. It was a bottle. A glass wine bottle full of silvery liquid. Her very own syphoned god's blood. Her eyes widened.

"I had hoped to obtain a sample of your blood, with your permission of course, but this could do far better. It was wasted on your summoning ritual, you know."

"Where did you get that?" Saiyah demanded in an insipid voice. "Zulphas? Bezbiel?"

John Greyson smiled good-naturedly and shook his head. "No. It was another one of your friends who gifted this to me. Zulphas is a fool and Bezbiel, though diligent, has been somewhat capricious of late. The boy was tasked with bringing you here, but no matter, you've found your own way, my daughter."

Saiyah's face slipped. "I am not–!" She choked. "You killed my mother!" She screamed at him, a tear running from each eye.

His face crumbled and he hung his head. "Yes," he said, barely audible. "It is my one regret. And an action I wish to rectify, if you will let me?" He held the bottle as if he was going to hand it to her.

Saiyah was dumbfounded. Her brows furrowed and she forced herself to breathe steadily.

John Greyson shook his head and took a step forward, directly into the water. As he did so, it lightened around him to amethyst, and Saiyah knew instinctively that this was the true colour of the water. He continued to walk through the water, his face darkly serious. He held out a hand, seemingly towards her, and the water cleared. Saiyah took a step back, ready to turn to shadow. But it wasn't directed at her. Something was rising from the centre of the pool, and John Greyson slowed.

Saiyah knew what she was looking at before the sight came to fruition. Perhaps she sensed something of the familiar, or it was a demonic instinct. Either way, it sickened her. Her throat was dry, and her mind in shock.

Surrounded by jewelled ripples was the body of her mother, encased and preserved in some kind of crystal. Her form was blurred, but Saiyah could see her raven-blue hair flowing around a dark dress adorned with glimmers of gold and ruby.

"You're going to resurrect her?"

John Greyson nodded. "Yes. I would like your blessing, and help, but I shall carry out the ritual regardless." He held out a hand, outstretched towards her.

Saiyah took a breath and felt tightness in her chest. It was like the opposite of being frozen in place, where her mind might not let her move, now it was not letting her stay. She took a faltering step into the shallows. Then another. She was like a woman possessed. Soon she was close to the body of her mother, floating like a water flower before her. It was just like the story about the princess. Except there was no evil sorcerer or princely rescuer. They were one in the same.

She looked to her father and saw he was watching her expectantly, his face filled with emotion.

"Why did you kill her?" She asked softly.

He looked down and into his hands. "I do not know. It seemed important at the time. She was a powerful woman, and will be again, but she opposed my plans to make this realm a better place for its inhabitants. Your mother was ambitious, but only saw as far as Khabrasos. The rest of Hell and those who suffered, demon or mortal soul, didn't matter to her."

"That doesn't seem a good enough reason to murder someone," Saiyah spat. "Nothing does."

"No. No it doesn't," he replied vaguely. "I am sorry. Truly, I am. But despite what you may think of me or my foolish actions, will you help me bring your mother back to us both?"

Saiyah looked upon her mother, frozen in time. She wanted nothing more than to hold her mother in her arms like she should have done all her life. She should have been taught their native language by her, taught about her demonic power by her. In another life where John Greyson hadn't betrayed them, perhaps he would have been a good and loving father.

A gasp of a sob ripped through Saiyah's body. How could she kill John Greyson like this? It wasn't even close to how she'd imagined this moment. She was too weak.

Her father took a careful step to one side, beginning to walk around the body of his former love. "I can understand what you might think of me, what I did, and I hope to repair that thought one day by proving myself as a father. There are only two regrets I hold in this world. One is betraying your mother, and the other is leaving you in the care of another."

He neared the distance between them, and Saiyah stepped back quickly. The water suddenly felt as thick as sand to her. He held out his hands in a peaceful gesture.

"I thought the life I led was no life for a child. Indeed, it may not have been, but I should have been a father to you. I know that now."

He was barely a foot away from her now. Saiyah went to move backwards again and stumbled on the slippery rocks below. In a quick movement, her father caught her and brought her upright. She realised then she was gripping his arm for support.

"I am sorry," he said again, stroking her face with his free hand, wiping her tears. He handed the bottle of blood to her, but did not let go of it. "I am sorry."

His proximity forced Saiyah to gain alertness. She wiped her remaining tears away on her arm. No more crying.

"If this works, what will you do if she decides she can't forgive you? If we can't forgive you?" She said in a stronger voice.

"Admittedly, it is my hope that she will not remember what happened. As for you, my daughter, I can only beg your forgiveness for the rest of my life. And with your mother alive, I will have eternity to right my wrongs."

Saiyah looked up into his face, noticing some similarities between herself and him. They had the same eye shape, the same hairline. She was so nearly taken in. She placed a hand on the bottle of blood.

"You'll become immortal again. To be with her."

John Greyson nodded patiently.

"And what if this does not work? Will you...will you still stay with me and be my father?"

His face erupted into a grin, causing fine lines around his eyes. She would look like that one day, too.

"Of course! Of course, my daughter, my Saiyah." He stood close to her then and kissed the top of her head.

Saiyah scrunched her eyes closed and tightened her grip on the bottle. No crying.

"Whatever happens, we will unite all nations of Hell as a family. And we will be at the forefront of the holy war between Hell and Heaven. There will be freedom for all demons, all your people, and an end to suffering for the souls here. A glorious kingdom of Hell. You want that too, do you not?"

Saiyah nodded. She stepped back and smiled at him weakly, letting her hand slide away from the bottle. Her father returned the look, stroking her face one last time. He withdrew the bottle and began to turn.

Saiyah touched the amulet, gripping it in one hand for courage. In a swift movement, she withdrew her mother's dagger and brought it down instantly. There was a sharp sound. John Greyson froze, faltering only slightly in the water. He turned awkwardly, his movements restrained by some unnatural force, to look back at his daughter, tears filling his eyes.

There was a shattering sound as Saiyah twisted the knife in the crystal cocoon, corrupting it with a divine energy. Tiny cracks formed throughout her mother's body. Her father's face betrayed his broken heart. She'd hurt him in the only way that mattered. He tried to step towards her, but it was as if a force was keeping him from getting too close.

"I do want those things you speak of," she said in a low voice, "but not at the expense of war. Not at the expense of those who are still living. There are other ways," she whispered, looking at her mother's body.

The divine energy did its work, and the crystal coffin shattered with a light tingling sound. John Greyson dropped to his knees, his arms around his former love as he tried to hold together what remained of her. It was useless. Asramenia crumbled into silt-fine pieces, slipping through his fingers and into the bed of the water.

John Greyson stared at Saiyah, agape. She took a breath and advanced, still holding the knife. She started to lift it, but hesitated. Destroying any hope of her mother was one thing, but how could she simply kill her father in the same breath?

Now it was John Greyson's turn to look enraged. He bared his teeth in a way not unlike Saiyah and scrambled to his feet. Without a word he began to emit a shadow-like energy, a bastardised version of her mother's power, heavily mixed with the occult. It was like watching him be swallowed into a black hole. There was a lingering trail of a Hellgate, and Saiyah considered jumping in after him, following him to fulfil her side of the deal. But standing in the shimmering remains of her mother, she simply fell to her knees.

"No crying," she whispered to herself.

All energy, demonic, divine, and occult evaporated. She was left only with herself and the sound of the breeze through the canopy.

MOMENTS PASSED, PERHAPS HOURS. Saiyah vaguely recalled scrambling to the water's edge where she sat in wet shoes, staring at her mother's blade. It was a short while later that she thought she could hear her name being called. It was coming from the entrance-way, beyond the invisible barrier. She pulled herself to her feet and wearily began to walk towards it.

As she approached, she could clearly see Bezbiel. He called her name again, and she realised then he could not see her. She looked to her mother's house for a long moment before turning back with a sigh. Of course, he knew exactly where she would be. The traitor.

She placed her hand on the invisible barrier and it disappeared. Bezbiel barely had a moment to express his surprise before Saiyah's palm landed across his face and he stumbled back.

"I definitely deserved that," Bezbiel muttered, nursing the side of his face.

"How could you!" Saiyah screamed at him.

"I'm sorry! I tried to explain before. I didn't know I was doing any harm helping him, I didn't know that he had anything untoward planned. *'Protect my daughter,'* he said, *'reunite us when the time is right.'* I wasn't thinking of the consequences. You know me. He offered me knowledge, Saiyah, rare, powerful knowledge. *You know* what it's like to want that."

"I would never betray anyone for it. I would gain it through my own merit," she said in a tight voice.

"Yes, well, neither would I. But I didn't know you then like I do now."

Saiyah scoffed at him. "Spare me." Then her tone softened. "Why didn't you just tell me once you realised?"

Bezbiel held his hands out, palms skyward. "I didn't know how. I was conflicted, and afraid of hurting you. I tried to warn you, and make you distance yourself from me. Then suddenly it was too late."

"It was all you. The fire in the library, visiting the alchemists' tunnels... giving my blood to him–that's why you really wanted it."

Bezbiel frowned. "I never gave him any. You didn't give me it, remember?"

Saiyah caught her next scolding word and examined him for the truth. "Well, he has it! He has that pure blood from my botched ritual!"

Bezbiel's face was chillingly still. "Xaldan. He was the one who told me about the job. Who else could it be?"

Saiyah rubbed her head. She'd been so naïve. Bezbiel reached out for her, but she flinched away.

"Can you forgive me?" He asked.

Saiyah raised her chin. "If you think that's possible then you're a bigger fool than I. Wait there," she said, disappearing back through the barrier.

She marched back to the house and to her mother's room—her room now—to where she'd left her backpack. Moving aside the dusty glasses at the table, she retrieved her mother's journal and tore a few spare pages from the back. She began to write. Her words were careful and heartfelt, though they would never be enough. She spent what felt like hours on them.

When she returned to the entrance, Bezbiel was still there. He sat cross-legged in the fallen leaves, staring into the distance forlornly. Besides him was Zulphas, standing with arms outstretched and muttering something whilst exuding demonic energy. When she appeared, he stopped and Bezbiel stood.

"I've strengthened the wards here. Hopefully it should keep any unwelcome gods out," Zulphas said sheepishly, taking a step back.

"Or Occultists?" She asked.

"You didn't kill him?" Bezbiel said, his serpentine eyes wide.

Saiyah hung her head. "I couldn't."

Zulphas chewed his lips. "Then yes, this will keep him out as long as you maintain the wards." Zulphas paused. "The bottle of god's blood. Was it yours?"

Saiyah nodded.

"I had feared that. He must be found before he is able to use it, although it may already be too late. I will inform the gods, which should distract them from the pair of you for a while."

Saiyah grimaced. "I'll never be free of them. They'll drag me back to the mortal world where they can follow my every movement."

Zulphas allowed a small grin. "Oh, I wouldn't be so sure. John will be their main concern now, and you are...well connected with the gods. I'm sure they'll allow you some time here. I'll see what I can do, on behalf of the Albion Circle."

Saiyah almost chuckled. Seeing the tall, owl-like man with a twinkle of mischief in his eye was the most character she'd ever seen in him. "Thank you, Zulphas." He nodded and unfurled his humongous dark wings. "Please understand, I never meant to put your mother in any danger. I was trying to help her."

Saiyah held up a hand before he could continue. "It's alright. You were just one of many caught up in the schemes of others." She held out one of the letters she'd written. "Will you give this to Hezekiah when you see him?"

"Give it to him yourself," Bezbiel interjected. "He's looking for you, along with others. They think you'd have gone to the temple. He'll be back this way."

Both Zulphas and Bezbiel smiled at her in a knowing way which made her feel exposed. Zulphas gave a final nod, then beat his wings. He left them in the wake of a whirlwind of leaves as he disappeared into the mist of trees.

Saiyah and Bezbiel looked at each other awkwardly.

"What will you do now?" Saiyah asked, hiding any interest in her voice.

He shrugged. "Lie low. Perhaps go to Dualjahit, see my father, and do what I can to find John Greyson."

Saiyah gave a look of approval, then sternly held out the two other letters. "This is for Hex, Jack, and Medea. The other is for Daniel. Do not read either, but do tell Daniel I am sorry."

Bezbiel took the letters stoically, bowing his head.

Saiyah removed the amulet from around her neck. "Thanks for this. I think it might've helped, but you need to return it." She almost smiled at his exasperated expression. "Think of this task as one of many on your road to forgiveness."

Bezbiel suppressed a grin. "I shall. Goodbye Saiyah, and good luck." He held out a hand for her, and she contemplated for a while whether to shake it or not.

"Likewise," she said, finally clasping hands with him.

She watched him retreat down the path before stepping back into her sanctuary.

F ROM THE BALCONY, SHE was able to partially watch the entranceway. She'd taken a glass from the kitchen and cleaned it in the stream which led to the rock pools. It sat full of the indigo-tinted water on the little table beside the letter addressed to Idris. She contemplated what she had written. Was it right for her to tell him those things? Should she even need to explain herself in any way? They'd been back and forth so many times over the same problems and opinions, did it really need to be said again in a different way? They were hereditary enemies, more so now than ever. He'd said so himself when they'd last spoken. Perhaps there was nothing more to really say. Still, it was better her thoughts would be laid to rest with him.

She allowed herself to let go of thoughts of Idris, fears of *The Host*, suspicions of the Albion Circle, and allowed the tranquillity of the house to fill her. It was so peaceful. The soothing whisper of the wind and the chimes of the night birds calmed her. Still, she couldn't quite let go of Daniel. Guilt lay there. Then there was Hex and Jack, even Medea, and though she hated to admit it, Bezbiel. She would miss their camaraderie. She didn't want it to be so, but she sensed her time in the mortal realm wasn't quite over, not completely. Perhaps it never would be. She was part of that world, also.

It was moonset when the pool of water at the entranceway below began to glow even more brightly, giving off a sound like a faintly ringing bell. Saiyah smiled, realising now what it was. She descended the balcony like a shadow in order to move faster and headed down the path towards the gateway. She slowed when she saw him, standing where the others had stood, no doubt sensing their presence.

Idris radiated what was left of the hellish moonlight, his vivid eyes alert with intelligence and sadness.

On the other side of the invisible barrier, Saiyah was close enough to touch him. She raised her hand to open the way, but slowly let her arm fall back to her side. He wouldn't understand, not in the way she wanted him to.

Saiyah remained, watching his graceful movements for a while as he examined the area. Eventually he raised his head, satisfied there was nothing more for him to find here. Then, on an impulse, she threw the letter through the gateway. Idris halted and turned towards it, carefully picking it up. He opened it briefly and gave a slight smile. It was the first time she'd seen him appear so relaxed, apparently unwatched. He folded the letter away.

"Goodbye," she whispered, unheard.

Almost as if he'd heard her, he glanced around watchfully. Something in his words chilled her, but he spoke genially.

"I hope to meet you on the battlefield, Saiyah, daughter of Asramenia."

As if spirited away by the forest breeze, Idris vanished.

Saiyah didn't linger. It was best not to. Her task was more than complete. She'd found her mother's murderer, acquired knowledge unknown to mortals, and discovered her own power. It was time for her to begin a journal of her own.

THE END

I N A WORLD FILLED with endless possibilities, a young
girl named Kathryn discovered her love for story-
telling. Growing up in Southampton, she would scrib-
ble down stories with her Mum, dreaming of one day
sharing her tales with the world. In the years to come,
her passion for writing only intensified, and she spent

countless hours honing her craft. After graduating from the university of Southampton and moving across the country she tried her hand at writing again, filling the void between boring office jobs. She poured her heart and soul into crafting stories filled with magic, adventure, and unforgettable characters. Eventually she went on to work in museums and libraries, sharing her love of history and art with children and teens. Kathryn is passionate about providing access to literature for all and encouraging reading for fun. But even as she pursued her professional career, her love for writing never wavered. In fact, it only grew stronger. In 2022, Kathryn's dream of becoming a published author finally came true with the signing of her debut novel, The Shadow of the Scholar. The book captivated readers with its vivid world-building, intricate plot, and relatable characters. It quickly became a hit in the Young Adult Fantasy genre, garnering critical acclaim and a loyal fanbase. Today, Kathryn lives in Cheshire with her husband and continues to write stories that capture the hearts and imaginations of readers around the world.